Waldemere

A Jack Sullivan Mystery

By

William G. Krejci

Copyright © 2012 by William G. Krejci

Author photograph by Rebecca E. Haaga
Front cover photograph by William G. Krejci

All rights reserved.

The characters and events depicted in this story are fictitious. Any similarities to persons living or dead is coincidental and should not be inferred.

Author's Note:

Although this story takes place in the greater Cleveland area, I have used fictional street names and communities in scenes where violent crimes have occurred. Furthermore, while there already is a notably famous haunted house located on Franklin Boulevard, and Waldemere very much resembles that structure, the similarities end there.

For Carl and Dora,
You were right. It does make for a good story.

Chapter 1

The Cleveland City Court House on the northwest corner of Public Square was filled to capacity. Curiosity seekers had come from as far away as Cincinnati and Buffalo to witness the events that had unfolded in recent days. It was not a trial that they had come to attend, but rather a hearing to see if there was enough evidence to proceed with a criminal trial. The courtroom would have been packed regardless of whomever it was that stood accused of these crimes, but the fact that it was now one of Cleveland's most well respected financiers, an unusually larger amount of people were in attendance.

Northern Ohio had been pressed under the thumb of a stifling heat wave for the past week and a half and this humid Monday morning was no exception. Men dressed in black suits sat tightly packed together in the courtroom, fanning themselves to stave off the heat as best they could. Many of them were eyeing the defendant jealously; not for the position he was in, but rather for the tall pitcher of water that sat upon the desk before him. Every few minutes, the defendant would take a refreshing sip from a glass, set it down and say something to his lawyer. No one could make out what he was saying. Not because his words were inaudible, but more for the fact that hardly a soul in that courtroom could understand a word of German.

After a few minutes, the bailiff announced the judge and all stood as a short man in a long black robe entered the room.

"With the exception of the accused, you may all be seated," instructed the judge. Every man in the courtroom gladly took his seat. The judge reviewed a small stack of papers that sat upon his desk. After a moment of this, he looked up and addressed the tall man that now stood before him.

"Heinrich Engelhardt. You stand accused on three counts of the heinous crime of murder in the first degree, to which you have entered a plea of innocent. I wish now to review each count on a case-by-case basis." Mr. Engelhardt nodded in agreement. "On count number one of murder in the first degree, you stand accused of the brutal murder of one Miss Anna Stadler, age twenty, who has not been seen for nearly four years now. Miss

Stadler is the daughter of your cousin, Mr. Simeon Stadler of Wisconsin, and it is understood that she came to live with you and your family in the autumn of 1878?"

"That is correct, Your Honor," Mr. Engelhardt replied with a thick Bavarian accent.

"Furthermore, it is your claim that Miss Stadler was last seen by you in the company of an unknown man at the Reservoir Park on Franklin Street on the evening of August the 25th 1879. This man you describe as being short in stature and as having red hair?"

"Also correct, Your Honor."

"Yes," the judge considered. "Likely an Irishman and therefore likely a scallywag and a rogue: someone not to be trusted. It is your belief that she left Cleveland with this man that very night?"

"It is."

"Very well," the judge replied. He paused for a moment and consulted the papers laid before him. "On the second charge of murder in the first degree," he continued, "you stand accused of killing one Miss Harriett Fischer, age seventeen, a servant in your house."

"A cook, Your Honor."

"A cook then," the judge said, slightly annoyed at being corrected. "It is your testimony that Miss Fischer left your house on the night of March the 2nd 1881 and that the following morning there were a number of items missing from your residence at 225 Franklin Street?"

"Yes, Your Honor, a set of silver candlesticks, some silver flatware and some of my wife's jewelry. The jewelry had slowly been disappearing over the last few weeks prior to Miss Fischer leaving us. My wife and I were going to dismiss her, but we believe that she got wise to our suspicions."

"And took what she could and left in the night?"

"A burglary, I believe, Your Honor."

"It would seem so." Again, the judge glanced down at the papers. "And so we now come to charge number three of murder in the first degree. Heinrich Engelhardt, you stand accused in the slaying death of one Miss Katherine Fitzgerald, age sixteen, also a servant in your house. Was she also a cook?"

"No, Your Honor. She was a chambermaid."

"I see. And it is your sworn testimony that your family last saw Miss Fitzgerald on the afternoon of October the 3rd 1882. You claim that she had been suffering from a bout of melancholy as of late and that she may have decided to end her life. This testimony is reinforced by Doctor E. L. Matthews of Pearl Street, whom it was that attended to her shortly before her disappearance. Doctor Matthews states that he had prescribed calomel to treat her condition. And it is further recorded that a corpse, fitting a close description of Miss Fitzgerald, was discovered one week following her disappearance along the rocks at Whiskey Island."

"It is my belief, Your Honor, that she may have jumped from the Detroit Street Viaduct."

"That is a possibility," the judge concluded. He looked down again at the papers on his desk and began to scribble a few notes upon them. After a few moments of relative silence in the courtroom, the judge looked up and addressed the accused once more.

"Heinrich Engelhardt. After reviewing these cases before me, it is of my firmest opinion that your cousin's daughter, Miss Anna Stadler, did depart Cleveland on the night of August the 25th 1879 with an Irishman: a member of an untrustworthy race. No corpse has been located for her to even suggest the slightest hint of foul play on your part.

"It is also of my firmest opinion that Miss Harriett Fischer did, on the night of March the 2nd 1881, burglarize your house and defile the sanctity of your family's trust. Again, it is noted that there is no corpse to denote a murder, or any other proof for that matter, to compel anyone to believe that you had any hand in her disappearance.

"In regards to the case of Miss Katherine Fitzgerald, a corpse was discovered following her disappearance that, according to the coroner, showed no signs of outside involvement in her death. The presence of water in the lungs of this corpse suggested that she had succumbed to drowning.

"I am therefore compelled by reason, Mr. Engelhardt, to find you innocent of all three charges laid before you on this day, Monday, the Thirtieth Day of July, in the Year of Our Lord Anno

Domini One Thousand Eight Hundred and Eighty Three. You are hereby cleared of all charges and claims made against you concerning this matter."

And with those words, the gavel fell. The courtroom immediately broke out into mumbled discussions about what had just transpired. The judge spoke up again.

"If I may continue," he announced in a raised voice. The crowd quieted down at once. "I would like to take this opportunity to extend the sincerest of apologies to you, Mr. Engelhardt, on behalf of the City of Cleveland. It is truly a sad state of affairs when a man of such prominence as you is brought forward on despicably false charges such as this. You sir, are one of Cleveland's favorite sons. I cite the jealousy and envy of your neighbors, who have not succeeded in this world to the degree in which you have flourished. May it be long remembered what has transpired here this day and I furthermore hope not to see another case such as this, brought before me, where there is no proof whatsoever, to imply that one of such good standing be faced with such an embarrassment and besmirching of a good name. This hearing is now concluded."

At this, the judge arose from his seat, collected the papers from his desk and retired to his chambers. Heinrich Engelhardt's attorney stood up and firmly shook his client's hand. Everyone who was close enough to hear them stood in bewilderment at what the two men were saying to one another. They were speaking in German again.

Chapter 2

Jack Sullivan sat in his black 2002 Mazda Protegé 5 on Franklin Boulevard, eyeing the massive sandstone house with curiosity. It was four stories high, ornamented with balconies, Flemish gables, dormers, gingerbread, stone cherubs and a main turret that seemed to reach to the heavens. A three-foot high wrought iron fence surrounded the property and two stone pillars that distinctly bore the name "Waldemere" flanked the main gate. Further down the driveway, Jack could see a porte-cochere protruding from the side of the building. In the back sat a two-story carriage house.

Many times Jack had driven down Franklin on his way to the county archives office and many times he had passed this house. He was aware of the legends and was vaguely familiar with the brief histories that had accompanied them. Being a historian, he was always intrigued by the structure, which seemed to come right out of an Edgar Allen Poe story. Furthermore, he had been drawn to the fantastic tales that had been spun about this house since he was a boy. Jack always loved a good ghost story and his father was always a fine one for telling them. A beautiful house with an incredible legend to accompany it: that was Waldemere.

In his hand, Jack held a printout of an email that he had received earlier that morning, inviting him to come to the house to meet with its new owner. Jack looked down and reread its content.

Dear Mr. Sullivan,

To you I send greetings on this beautiful Sunday morning. Please allow me to introduce myself. My name is Henry Engelhardt and I am the new owner of the house famously known as Waldemere. I was referred to you by Miss Maxine Rybarczyk, a colleague of yours, whom it was that sold me this house. I desire to know more about my recent acquisition and Miss

Rybarczyk highly recommends you as the person best suited to aid me in this endeavor.

I request that we meet here at Waldemere this afternoon at 5:00 to discuss the matter further, should you be interested and available to take on this case. I look forward to meeting you in person.

Sincerely,
Henry Frederick Engelhardt

At first, Jack thought that the email was a hoax. The last time he had checked, Waldemere was in the possession of a man that lived in Kentucky, who hardly ever came up to Cleveland. With the exception of a caretaker that lived in the carriage house in the back, the house was largely unoccupied. Most Clevelanders believed it to be abandoned. Furthermore, Jack would have thought that Maxine would, at some point, have mentioned this transfer in ownership to him.

After Jack had finished listening to Gerry Quinn's Irish Program on the radio, a Sunday morning ritual of his, he got on the phone with Maxine and asked her about this curious email that he had just received.

"Well, I'm glad that he finally took the time to contact you," Maxine had said. Jack could tell that she was smiling on the other end.

"So, this is no joke?" Jack asked.

"Of course not," she'd replied. "I know this is right up your alley, but am a bit surprised that it took him this long to contact you. I sold him that house nearly a month ago."

"So, why didn't you mention any of this to me?"

"Mr. Engelhardt had requested anonymity in his purchase. In fact, the house isn't even in his name, but rather in the name of his corporation. Jack, you should really meet with him. I think you're going to be quite fascinated by what he has to say and the offer he's willing to make to you."

Jack glanced over at the house once again. Its sandstone edifice seemed to be staring back at him. He looked over at the gate, which seemed to be padlocked. Realizing that there was nothing else for it, Jack mustered up his courage and stepped out of the car, putting his foot down in a puddle of slush four inches deep. He immediately withdrew his foot from the puddle and shook it vigorously. It was a good thing, he thought, that he was wearing a sturdy pair of boots and that he'd been lucky to avoid getting a soaker. Still, the bottom few inches of his jeans were quite wet. This was a fine way to make an impression, he thought. He continued to climb out of the car, avoiding the puddle as best he could.

He crossed the street and approached the front gate at the end of the driveway. As he drew nearer, he could see that the front walk had not yet been shoveled. Greater Cleveland had been the victim of a late winter snowstorm the previous evening and had picked up close to a foot of snow: not unheard of for early to mid March, but annoying to say the least. It's usually by this time of year that people begin to seriously consider moving away to warmer climates. Were it not for the fact that April and May were so pleasant, Cleveland might have been abandoned shortly after being settled.

Jack checked the gate once again. Sure enough, it was padlocked. There was no phone number listed on the email that he had received that morning and, therefore, no way to call Mr. Engelhardt to let him know that he had arrived. Perhaps, he thought, he should have replied to the email to confirm that he would be there. Just then, he was struck with an idea. He pulled his cell phone from his pocket and scrolled through his list of recent calls until he came to Maxine's number. He was about to press *send* when he saw the front door slowly inch open.

Crossing the threshold was a tall man, with wispy silver hair, somewhere in his late seventies. As the man donned a heavy black overcoat, he waved his hand to acknowledge Jack standing at the front gate.

"Just one second," the man announced as he descended the front steps and reached into his pocket. A moment later, he withdrew a large key ring with a number of old-fashioned keys on it. He approached the gate and began to fumble around with the ring. "Let's see, it's one of these," he said as he began to try a couple of keys in the padlock. The third one did the trick. He removed the lock and opened the gate.

"Mr. Engelhardt?"

"Henry, please. And you must be Jack."

"I am," Jack replied with a smile, extending his hand. Mr. Engelhardt gladly shook it. Jack was fond of informality and could tell that he liked Henry Engelhardt right away.

"Your friend Maxine speaks very highly of you, Jack."

"Does she?"

"Absolutely. She tells me that you know just about everything there is to know about Cleveland history and its more famous structures."

"Well, I'm certain that there's always more to learn."

"Which is why I've invited you here today. But we can discuss that inside. Please, come in out of the cold."

"Thank you."

Jack stepped through the gate and followed Henry Engelhardt to the massive oaken front doors where they entered. As Mr. Engelhardt closed the door behind them, Jack was suddenly awestruck by the incredible grandeur of the interior of the house. The floor of the foyer was decorated with an intricate mosaic tile design and finely crafted woodwork and moldings surrounded them. Mr. Engelhardt enjoyed seeing Jack's reaction.

"Welcome to Waldemere," he said with a smile on his face.

"Thank you," Jack replied.

A moment later, Mr. Engelhardt noticed that the bottom of Jack's left leg was quite wet.

"What happened to your pants, Jack?"

"Oh, I stepped in a chuckhole getting out of the car."

"I'm sorry, but you stepped in a what?"

"A chuckhole. You know, a pothole?"

"Oh. I've never heard it called that before."

Jack considered this for a moment.

"Hmm. You must not be from Cleveland then."

"That's correct. I'm from Boston."

"We call potholes in Cleveland 'chuckholes'."

"And why is that?"

"One of our past mayors, Charles Otis, had reallocated

funding from the road maintenance budget some years ago. Soon after, the roads began to deteriorate. Ever since then, potholes in Cleveland have been referred to as chuckholes. I think the term goes back to before Mayor Otis' time, but that's how it came to prominence around here."

"I see." Mr. Engelhardt gave Jack a good look from head to toe. "Well, we can't have you walking around like that all day." He walked over to a long, gold braided cord that hung from the wall near the foyer and gave it a yank. At once, a bell sounded and Mr. Engelhardt returned. "Please, follow me."

Jack did as he was instructed and followed Mr. Engelhardt up a short run of stairs and into the main hall. A moment later, a very lovely young woman in her mid-twenties with dark red hair approached them.

"Ya rang for me, Mr. Engelhardt?" she asked with a distinctive Cockney accent.

"I did, Emily. Mr. Sullivan here has stepped into a *chuckhole* and requires a fresh pair of pants and socks. I figure that we're about the same size," he said, turning back toward Jack.

"Oh, I don't wish to be a burden."

"Nonsense, Jack. Go with Emily here and she'll get you fixed up right away."

Jack realized that there was no way out of it. He followed the young woman up the main staircase and to a large door.

"This is a spare bedroom," Emily informed him. "Actually, almost all o' them are spares, but I'm sure that Mr. Engelhardt will want to give ya a tour 'imself. Now go on in and I'll be back in a moment with a change o' trousers for ya." She smiled at Jack, turned and walked away: her dark red ponytail bouncing behind her.

Jack entered the room, which was incredibly large. He couldn't quite believe that this was a spare bedroom and began to wonder what the master bedroom must look like. He walked over to a marble fireplace and examined its finely engraved details. He was so impressed at the amount of work that must have gone into it. Turning his attention across the room, he caught sight of a window frame. This too was quite ornamental.

A moment later, there was a knock at the door.

"Yes?"

"Are ya decent Mr. Sullivan?" Emily asked.

"I am."

The door opened and Emily entered carrying in one arm a bathrobe, a pair of dark brown slacks and a pair of black socks; all neatly folded. In her other hand, she held a pair of slippers.

"'Ere ya go," she said as she handed him the change of clothes. "Now put these on and I'll wait outside for ya."

"Thank you," Jack said as she left the room and closed the door. After a couple of minutes, he emerged from the spare bedroom.

"Well there ya are then," Emily said with a smile on her face. "Much better. Mr. Engelhardt is waitin' downstairs. I'll take ya to 'im and come back for your trousers after. Should 'ave em' ready for ya by the time you're ready to leave."

"Thank you, but you don't have to…"

"Now it's no trouble whatsoever, if that's what you're thinkin'."

Jack shrugged his shoulders and followed her back down the stairs. Emily escorted him across the main hall and over to a large set of pocket doors. She opened them and gestured for Jack to enter. Inside, Mr. Engelhardt had been sitting on an antique armchair in front of a warm fire that was burning in the grate of the fireplace.

"Ah, Jack. That looks much better," Mr. Engelhardt said as he rose to meet his guest.

"Thank you again, Mr. Engel… Henry," Jack caught himself.

"Will there be anythin' else, Mr. Engelhardt?" Emily asked.

"No, thank you Emily," Mr. Engelhardt replied. "I'll call you if there is though."

"Thank you," she said as she turned and left the room, closing the large pocket doors behind her.

"Well, Jack." Mr. Engelhardt said as he motioned to another antique armchair that sat opposite the one he had been sitting in. "Won't you please have a seat and join me by the fire?"

"Thank you," Jack replied as he sat.

"Can I offer you a drink? Something to help chase away the chill?"

"Do you happen to have any Jameson's?"

"I'm afraid I don't have any Irish whiskey, but I do have a pretty good single malt scotch."

Mr. Engelhardt held up a small bottle of Dalwhinnie.

"Scotch will do just fine," Jack replied. Mr. Engelhardt poured two large tumblers of scotch, re-corked the bottle and offered a glass to Jack, which he gladly accepted.

"To your health then, sir," Mr. Engelhardt proposed as he raised his glass. Jack raised his and nodded his head slightly. Both took a sip and set their glasses down on a small round table situated between the two chairs. Mr. Engelhardt took a seat in the chair opposite Jack.

"Well then," he began. "Down to business, Jack. First off, how familiar are you with the story of Waldemere?"

"I'm afraid to say that I'm not that familiar with it at all. Everything that I know about it has come from stories that my father used to tell me as a boy."

"And what did he tell you?"

"Well, It's supposed to be haunted."

Mr. Engelhardt lightly chuckled at this.

"What else did he tell you?"

"Not much else," Jack continued. "I guess there's a story about a past owner having killed his servants here. My father told me that they're the ones that haunt the place. He also said that most people who buy the house don't usually stick around for very long and that the house changes ownership every few years because no one can tolerate the disturbances."

Mr. Engelhardt nodded for a moment, then spoke up.

"Well," he said as he raised his glass of scotch, "let me tell you a story then." He took a sip from his glass and set it back down on the table. "This story starts back in the mid-eighteen hundreds with the arrival of an immigrant family from Germany. They came to these shores seeking a new life in the New World and found prosperity within just a few short years: the youngest son in particular. Oh, his name was Heinrich, by the way. So this Heinrich eventually became quite rich in the banking trade, married and had three children. Somewhere during the 1870's, he had amassed such a fortune that he could afford to build a grand house for his family: this house.

"By the 1890's his children were married and he and his wife no longer had any need for a house of this size. They sold the home and moved out to the country where they spent their later years in relative peace and quiet."

"What became of Heinrich's children?" Jack asked, quite intrigued by the story.

"Well, there were two sons and a daughter. The daughter married a man from Cleveland, but she and her husband would have no children. The younger of the two sons would die during the early 1890's."

"And the other son?"

"Conrad. He married a young socialite from the east coast. They would ultimately move there and have two children: a son named Frederick and a daughter named Sophia. Sophia would die young, but Frederick would become quite financially successful, marry and have a son of his own."

"I see."

"Oh, incidentally, Heinrich's last name was Engelhardt."

Jack turned his head from the fire and shot Mr. Engelhardt a curious glance.

"So Heinrich Engelhardt was…"

"My great grandfather."

Jack was quite amazed by all that had just been related to him. He took a sip from his glass of scotch and set it back on the small table.

"Conrad was your grandfather and Frederick was your father then."

"Never heard that story before, have you?"

"No," Jack said with intrigue. "That one's new to me. So now you've come home; so to speak?"

"In a sense, yes."

"So how can I be of service to you?"

"Well, Jack. I'd like to point out the story that you had just related to me… about the house… the one that your father had told you."

"Yes?"

"I first found out about *that* version of the story a few years ago, while I was doing some genealogical research on my father's family. As it turns out, this house has been mentioned in quite a few books, mostly to do with mid-west haunted houses. These stories paint my great grandfather as a murderous tyrant; something that he most certainly was not. What I'd like you to do is to find out the truth: the truth about this house's history and about the kind and gentle man that Heinrich Engelhardt really was. As I understand it, if anyone can set the record straight, it's you."

Jack stood up and carefully considered this offer for a few moments before giving his reply.

"My rate is two hundred dollars per diem, plus expenses."

"I'll double your rate if you forgo the expenses," Mr. Engelhardt offered. "I'm sure they won't amount to much anyway."

Jack thought again and began to nod.

"Very well. You have yourself a historical researcher."

Mr. Engelhardt took Jack's right hand and shook it vigorously.

"Thank you so much, Jack. I'm sure that whatever you find will be extremely valuable to me."

Jack finished off his scotch and set the empty glass on the table.

"It should take me about a week to find out all that you're asking for."

"A week sounds good." Mr. Engelhardt likewise emptied his glass. "Well then, I guess I had better show you the rest of the place."

Chapter 3

Jack followed Henry Engelhardt out through the pocket doors and back into the main hall.

"I guess we'll start here on this level and work our way up," Mr. Engelhardt suggested. "There are four levels to this house. The one we're currently on is actually the second floor. There's an English style basement below us that once housed the servants' living quarters. We can end the tour down there."

"After you then," replied Jack.

The two men strolled over to another set of pocket doors, which Mr. Engelhardt slid open.

"This is the main dining room. There's another one on the level below us that was used by the servants. It's the same size as this, but not nearly as elegant."

Jack examined the details of this room quite closely. The first thing that jumped out at him was the fireplace. It was identical to the one in the room they had just been talking in, but was of a different color of marble.

"Hey," Jack began, "that's the same…"

"Fireplace?" Mr. Engelhardt replied. "Close. There are slight variations. Aside from the color of the marble, it's about two inches taller and about a half a foot wider than the one in the parlor."

Jack nodded in agreement, though he never would have been able to tell this without measuring the two. He next turned his attention to the colorful leaded-glass chandelier that hung over the large dining room table. Upon closer inspection, he could see copper tubing running down the center of it from the ceiling.

"Is this chandelier original to the house?" he asked.

"It is. Made by Tiffany and Company of New York." Mr. Engelhardt replied.

"This house was once lit with natural gas," Jack noted.

"It was? How can you tell?"

"Well, look here. This tubing that comes down from the ceiling is actually a gas line. I'm also noticing these wall sconces throughout the house. They too have tubing running to them. I'm guessing that at some point the house was converted over to electric light and that the wires were simply run through the existing gas lines."

"That's brilliant, Jack. You've already started your work."

Jack smiled at this.

"Come on then," Mr. Engelhardt continued. "There's still so much more to see."

They continued on into the back of the house where Jack was shown two bedrooms that sat across the hall from each other. Between them was a dumbwaiter service.

"There are seven bedrooms in this house; only two of which are currently in use. Mine is up on the third floor and Emily's is downstairs on the first. These, I'm guessing, were once occupied by my grandfather and his brother."

Again, Jack was struck by the detail of the rooms. Each contained its own fireplace and had magnificently detailed woodwork throughout.

"By chance," Jack began, "you wouldn't happen to know the name of the architect, would you?"

"It was a firm called Surrey and Middleton. Their names are on the cornerstone. I don't know much about them, but I'm sure that you can find that out for me."

"Certainly."

Jack followed Mr. Engelhardt up the broad back stairwell and onto the third floor. Again, there were two bedrooms in place directly over the two that they had just viewed. One of these, Jack had changed in roughly a half an hour earlier. Again, the dumbwaiter service was situated between them.

"These are two more bedrooms. The left hand one, I believe, was occupied by my grandfather's sister and the one on the right, occupied by my great grandmother."

"Not your great grandfather as well?"

"No, Jack. Back in those days a husband and a wife didn't share a bedroom; not in more affluent houses at least. My grandfather's room, or *rooms* actually, were here across the hall."

Jack turned to see a large, ornamentally carved wooden door. Mr. Engelhardt opened it for him and the two entered. The first room they came into was directly above the dining room and was about the same size. It contained an equally ornamental fireplace, many wonderfully detailed built-in cabinets and a black walnut four-poster bed.

"This is the master bedroom," Mr. Engelhardt informed him. "My great grandfather Heinrich had occupied this room, but now it's where I sleep."

"Magnificent," was all that Jack could say.

They crossed the bedroom where Mr. Engelhardt opened another set of pocket doors and walked into the next room, which was directly above the parlor.

"This was my great grandfather's sitting room. I guess that if he and his wife wanted to slip away from the children for a time, this is where they'd have gone." Mr. Engelhardt chuckled slightly at this. "Oh, do you happen to have any children, Jack?"

"No. In fact, I've never been married. Do you?"

"Yes. I have a son and a daughter and five grandchildren now."

"And Mrs. Engelhardt?"

"Deceased."

"Oh, I'm sorry. I..."

"No. Don't be, Jack. My wife Claire passed away nearly fifteen years ago. The cancer took her rather quickly and she didn't suffer for very long. Still, I'm sure that she would have loved to have known our grandchildren, but I'm certain that she can see how well they're growing up."

There was an awkward silence between them for a moment or two before Mr. Engelhardt finally spoke up again.

"Well then. Let's continue on. Shall we?"

They returned to the back stairwell where Mr. Engelhardt led Jack up to the fourth floor. The stairs immediately led into a large room that occupied nearly the entire level. The walls here were slightly tapered inward and Jack at once noticed that there were no fireplaces in this room and only two large windows at the south end. The wall here at the south end of the room was, also, something of a sight to behold. With the exception of the windows and a doorway on the left that led into the turret room, the entire wall was covered, floor to ceiling, with dark hand-carved woodwork. Furthermore, it was ornamented with a wide variety of figures that included flowers, musical instruments, birds and beasts, a set of crossed rifles and swords and a couple of people's faces that bore frightful expressions. In the center of it all was a large clock face that measured about eight feet across. Jack could hear a distinctive mechanical noise of clicks, ticks and tocks coming from behind this wall. In many ways, it reminded Jack of an old Bavarian cuckoo clock, only that it was enormous.

"Really something, isn't it?"

"I'll say," Jack replied, still awestruck by the amount of detail and craftsmanship that must have gone into it.

"It was in pretty bad shape when I moved in. Took me a few weeks just to get it going again."

"What is this room?"

"This," Mr. Engelhardt announced with pride, "is the ballroom. You can just imagine the parties that my great grandfather used to host up here."

Jack walked away from Mr. Engelhardt and strolled into the middle of the room. He was so taken back by the sheer size of this space. Again, there were Tiffany chandeliers hanging down from the ceiling and the floor was decorated with finely crafted wooden inlays. Across the room and along the western wall was a long mahogany bar with an ornate liquor shelf and mirror behind it. Carved into a heavy oaken beam above the bar was an inscription. Jack attempted to read this, but found that he couldn't. The phrase was written in German.

"What does that say?" he asked Mr. Engelhardt.

"I don't know. I don't speak German but I think that it's a poem. I've been meaning to have it translated, but haven't gotten around to it yet. Perhaps you could?"

"Absolutely."

Mr. Engelhardt smiled warmly at Jack.

"Unfortunately, none of the lights in the ballroom work. I keep changing the bulbs, but they all seem to blow out within a week's time. Must be something wrong with the wiring. Just another thing that I keep meaning to get to, but never do. Oh, there's another bedroom here in the back and a bathroom that comes off of that."

He led Jack back towards the stairs and opened a door near the landing. Jack entered and was immediately drawn to the commanding view from the back windows. From here, he could see the entire Cleveland lakefront. To his left sat Edgewater Park and to his right was the Flats District. Immediately below him, he could see Wendy Park, Whiskey Island and the Sunset Grille: a place that he would spend his Sunday afternoons with his friends during the summer months. Currently, the bar was closed and the parking lot full of boats on their trailers and racks. Out in the distance sat the Five Mile Crib. The ice on Lake Erie was slowly breaking up and in two months time, the waters would be dotted with a multitude of pleasure craft, freighters and fishing boats.

Turning his attention from the vista out the window, Jack looked over the details of this bedroom. There was a fireplace on the eastern wall and a four-poster bed across from it. In the northeast corner of the room sat a beautiful built-in oak desk. Also, the dumbwaiter service reached its highest level along the southern wall. This room didn't have a chandelier like the ones in the ballroom, but rather was illuminated by a series of wall sconces that were shaded by Tiffany glass.

"Waldemere literally means *Woodlands by the Sea*," Mr. Engelhardt informed him. "Quite appropriate for a Cleveland residence; this being The Forest City and all. As I understand it, the view from this room is what inspired the name. Originally, that was all that could be seen from this window: woods stretching all the way down to the lake. Furthermore, this house shares a name with a mansion built in the 1860's by P. T. Barnum. As I understand it, my great grandfather had met Mr. Barnum on more than one occasion. It took me some time to find that out."

"I see." Jack's mind wandered for a moment as he thought briefly on an item in his private collection of curiosities that had once belonged to P. T. Barnum.

"Well, There's still one more floor to show you and it's something of a hike. Fortunately, it's all downhill."

Jack followed Mr. Engelhardt back down the stairs, six

flights of them, until they were on the lowest level of the house. Here, the stairs let out into a short hallway identical to the ones on the two floors immediately above it. To their left sat a dining room, looking much as Mr. Engelhardt had described it: the same size as the main dining room, but not nearly as elegant. To their right was another room, but the door was closed.

"That's Emily's room," Mr. Engelhardt told Jack. "Actually, I rarely come down here. Over here's the laundry and utility room," he motioned to another room just past Emily's, "and at the end of the corridor to the left is the kitchen. Through here is the servant's dining room, but we never use it. There's no reason to, really. Emily and I usually take our meals upstairs together."

Jack really liked the informality and generally relaxed attitude that Henry Engelhardt carried. Still, he was a little curious about why he had insisted that Jack refer to him as Henry while Emily called him Mr. Engelhardt. Perhaps, he thought, Henry Engelhardt was a bit chauvinistic or was insistent on servants remembering their place in a house. Whatever the case was, Jack thought better than to bring up this difference in how he was addressed. It would serve no purpose to do so.

Mr. Engelhardt led Jack across the dining room and over to another set of pocket doors. He opened them revealing a room, the same size as the parlor upstairs, but again, not nearly as elegant. Emily was seated in a chair across the room watching the television. At once, she stood up and addressed her employer.

"Mr. Engelhardt. Is there anythin' that I can do for you?"

"Yes Emily. Mr. Sullivan and I are just concluding our affairs and I was wondering if his clothes were ready."

"They are, indeed," she replied with a smile. "I'll bring them up at once."

"Thank you, Emily."

With that, Emily turned off the television and left the room. Jack and Mr. Engelhardt slowly made their way towards the back stairwell and ascended the steps until they were on the second level once more.

"Well, Jack. If you'll go upstairs, you'll find that your clothes are dry and waiting for you. I'll be down here when you're done changing."

"Thank you, Henry."

Jack turned and continued up the stairs to the next floor where Emily was waiting for him beside a bedroom door: the one that Mr. Engelhardt had indicated as having once been occupied by his great grandmother.

"Roight through 'ere, Mr. Sullivan," she said as she motioned him into the spare bedroom.

"Please, call me Jack."

"It's better that I don't, sir. I could get me a demerit for that."

"Well then. When you're boss isn't around, call me Jack. I insist."

"Very well then, *Jack*." She had almost whispered his name as she said it. Jack entered the spare bedroom and closed the door behind him. As he changed back into his clothes, he thought about what Emily had just said about getting a demerit. Perhaps Henry Engelhardt didn't have as much of a relaxed attitude as he had first thought.

When Jack had finished changing, he left the room and walked down the front stairs to the second floor where he found Mr. Engelhardt waiting for him in the parlor.

"Is everything to your satisfaction, Jack?"

"It is. Thank you again."

They walked out of the parlor together and back into the main hall.

"Before you leave, I must ask you. Is there anything that you'll be needing from me before you started?"

"Now that you mention it, there is. You had said that you'd done some genealogical work on your father's family. Reading over your notes would be a tremendous help."

"Done. Is there anything else?"

"There is. Maxine had mentioned that you had requested anonymity when you had purchased this house. Am I permitted to talk about this case or would you prefer continued anonymity?"

"No, Jack. Feel free to tell who you like. That was just until the sale was final. Besides, it's about time I started to get to know some of my neighbors."

"Good. Now, there was one more thing, but I've been a little hesitant to ask it."

"And what is that?"

"Well, it's a bit foolish, I suppose, but my father would kill me if I didn't ask."

"You want to know if the house really is haunted, don't you?"

Jack smiled and slightly nodded his head.

"I'll tell you what, Jack. I've just had a wonderful idea." Mr. Engelhardt walked over and pulled on the gold braided cord that hung from the wall near the main front stairwell. Again, the bell sounded. "I'll give you the opportunity to find that out for yourself. You said that it should take you about a week to complete this task. Why don't you stay with us here at Waldemere while you do your research?"

"Oh," Jack began. "I wouldn't dream of imposing…"

"Not at all, Jack. You'd be here as our guest and we'd be glad for the company. Perhaps you can show me around Cleveland some and better acclimate me with the city."

Footsteps echoed up the corridor and Jack looked over to see Emily approaching.

"Did ya ring for me, Mr. Engelhardt?"

"I did, Emily. Please prepare the guest bedroom on the fourth floor for Mr. Sullivan here. He'll be staying with us for the next week or so."

Emily smiled at Jack and her freckled face seemed to shine at this news.

"I'll get meself started on it at once."

With that, Emily left them and headed towards the back stairwell.

"I noticed that you seemed to like the view from that room. Should we expect you back in a couple of hours then?"

"Um… tonight may be a little too soon for me. I'll need to get together some clothes and other necessities for the stay. I'll also need my notebooks, laptop and research guides and will have to find someone to take care of my cats while I'm away. Tomorrow might be better, really."

"Tomorrow it is then. Can I look for you in the morning, say somewhere around ten?"

"Ten works for me."

"We'll see you in the morning then, Jack. I'll set out everything that you need. Oh, wait a moment." Mr. Engelhardt reached into his back pocket and withdrew his wallet. For a moment, Jack thought that he was going to receive an advance on his fee, something that he didn't need, but saw that Mr. Engelhardt was pulling out a business card. "This has my phone number on it. Give me a call when you get here in the morning and we'll let you in the gate. You can park your car around back."

"Thank you, I will."

"You have a good evening, now."

"And you, Henry. Thank you. And please tell Emily that I said thank you for taking care of my clothes."

"I will."

With that, Henry Engelhardt opened the front door and let Jack out. As he descended the front steps of Waldemere and trudged his way through the deep snow to his car, Jack thought more about the case he had just taken on. It wasn't his first time researching a house with a storied past or one that had been rumored to be haunted, but it was, by far, the most elegant.

Chapter 4

Jack made his way west on the Shoreway, back towards Lakewood, but decided that he would stop off at McNamara's Public House on the corner of Lake Avenue and West 87th Street for a pint of Guinness. It was nearly seven-thirty in the evening and the sun was just now starting to set. It being the first day of daylight savings time was a good sign, Jack thought. Spring would be right around the corner and along with it, the warmer weather. He didn't think that he could deal with another snowstorm like the one Cleveland had just gone through the day before. A little over a month earlier, the groundhog had seen his shadow and therefore had forecast a longer winter season. Jack felt like making groundhog stew for dinner that evening. Still, the winter, he knew, wouldn't last forever. It was six more days until the buzzards made their annual return to Hinckley and eight more until Saint Patrick's Day, always one of his favorite holidays. Playing in an Irish band pretty much ensured that he would be quite busy that day; something he hadn't thought about when taking this case for Henry Engelhardt. He could only hope that he'd be finished with his research by then.

He found a parking spot on the street directly in front of McNamara's, stepped out of his Mazda, hit the lock button on his key fob, and strolled into the pub. Compared to the mid-twenty degree temperatures outside, the place was quite warm, even though Gary, the bar's proprietor, kept the thermostat set at a chilly sixty-six. The place was all decked out in much more green than it normally was. With Saint Pat's just around the corner, they were expecting a large crowd to pass through the bar and wanted to greet their guests in fine Irish fashion.

Jack pulled up a stool near the end of the bar and was greeted at once by his long-time friend and bartender, Positive Bill.

"Guinness, Jack?"

"You bet."

Bill poured three-quarters of a glass of the thick and creamy stout and left it to settle under the tap. He walked back over to Jack and shook his hand.

"So where have you been hiding? I'd have expected you in a lot earlier than this. You're not one of those people that gets all thrown out of whack by the time change, are you?"

"Actually, I am," Jack explained, "but I had an appointment earlier this evening that I had to keep."

"New case?"

"Bingo. And you wouldn't believe me if I told you what it was."

"Hey Jack," called a voice from the other end of the bar. Jack looked over to see his friends Jerry, Brion and Ed congregated together over a few bottles of beer. It was Jerry that had spoken up.

"What's going on, guys?" Jack asked.

"Not too much," continued Jerry. "Did you just say that you've taken a new case?"

"I did."

"And he says that we won't believe what it is," added Bill.

"After that one that you had back in the fall," broke in Ed, "we'd believe just about anything that you said."

The previous October, Jack had taken on a case that involved a missing girl. He'd ultimately led federal investigators to the house where she was being held and to her kidnapper; a man named Bob Woodring. Nearly a week had passed before his name was released to the media as being the one who had helped to solve the case. As to the details, like who it was that had hired him in the first place, he'd withheld that information: and for a very good reason. As it turned out, his client, a young woman named Shelby Tomlinson, was also a victim of Bob Woodring's and had been murdered by him nearly fifteen years earlier. If he'd gone around telling people that the ghost of a dead girl had hired him, people might look at him funny. It was best to keep that part to himself, he thought.

"Are you able to talk about this one?" Jerry asked.

"I am. It's Waldemere."

"Awe, you're kidding!" Bill exclaimed as he started to laugh. Jerry and Ed were both awestruck at the very thought of it. Brion, on the other hand, was quite confused.

"I don't get it," he said at last. "What's Waldemere?"

The others turned to Brion with a look of surprise. Positive Bill shook his head in disbelief as he handed Jack his Guinness.

"What's Waldemere?" Ed couldn't believe what he was hearing either. "It's only the most haunted house in Ohio. I can't believe that you've never heard of it. You know, creepy old mansion on Franklin?"

"Old man Engelhardt murdered three of his servants there," added Jerry. "Supposedly, he drove one of his children to suicide. Furthermore, they say that everyone who buys the house only stays for a short time and that they're either driven away by the ghosts or driven to madness."

"I've heard some of this too," said Jack as he raised his glass to take a hearty pull.

"So how did all of this come about?" Bill asked.

"Well," Jack began as he set his glass back down, "I was contacted by the new owner this morning and he wants me to find out as much as I can for him on his recent purchase."

"Yeah, before the ghosts drive him off. So who's the new owner?" asked Ed as he took a swig from his bottle.

"Henry Engelhardt."

Ed nearly spit out his beer, but gulped it down and looked over at Jack with a mixed expression of both shock and disbelief.

"You've got to be kidding me."

"No, I'm serious. Why?"

"Is he related to old man Engelhardt?"

"Yeah, Henry's his great grandson."

"Jack," Ed started, now with a look of great concern on his face. "How much do you know about the Engelhardt family?"

"Not too much, really. Just the generic legend that my father told me and what Henry Engelhardt had to say this afternoon."

"And what did he say?"

"That his great grandfather really wasn't the monster that everyone has made him out to be in recent years; that his grandfather moved to Boston and raised a family there and that his great aunt never had any children of her own. He said that these stories about murder and mayhem are absolutely preposterous. That's one of the reasons that he's hired me: to ultimately find the truth about his great grandfather and, God willing, clear his good name."

"Jack, most of that's not true." Jerry, Brion and Positive Bill hung onto every word that Ed spoke. "Heinrich Engelhardt was only cleared of those murders because there wasn't enough evidence to convict him. He really was something of a monster, at least when it came down to business and finance. His daughter *did* have children and his son didn't *move* to Boston, he was driven out of town."

"And you know this how?" Jack was rather intrigued by this new information.

"My family has had dealings with the Engelhardts in the past."

"Hmm." Jack sat pensively for a moment.

"It wasn't pretty either," Ed continued. "My great grandfather used to own a store at the top of the Angle along West 25th Street. He had once borrowed a sum of money through Mr. Engelhardt's bank to make a fairly sizable purchase of wholesale merchandise. He was originally given two months to pay the amount back, but after three weeks, Mr. Engelhardt demanded the first half of the payment. He threatened foreclosure on the store, which would have ruined him."

"What did your great grandfather do?"

"What could he do? He didn't have a lot of money and he was Irish; not very well looked upon back then: even in Cleveland. He borrowed the money from a few neighbors and made the payment. Many years later, he sold the store and went into banking himself. It was his hope that no one else would ever get stuck in an unfair lending situation like he had. In truth, he probably should have borrowed the money from his neighbors in the first place. That community always looked out for its own, but you wouldn't know much about that; seeing as your family was lace curtain and from Willeyville."

"Just couldn't help yourself, could you?" Jack said indignantly as he set down his glass.

"I'm just saying."

The oldest rivalry among the Irish in Cleveland had nothing to do with being from the east side or the west side, but rather went back to the few little clusters of Irish communities that had sprung up along the west bank of the Cuyahoga River during the mid-eighteen hundreds. Those who hailed from the Angle and Irishtown Bend were referred to as "shanty" or "pig in the parlor" Irish, while the more well-to-do families settled above the Flats, attended church at Saint Patrick's and were called "lace curtain" Irish, due to the fact that they could afford amenities such as that. It was an old rivalry, one that was nearly forgotten, but Ed liked to bring it up from time to time, more as a joke than anything else, and to get Jack's dander up.

"So does the job pay well at least?" Jerry asked, hoping to change the subject from neighborhood rivalries; something that he, being first generation Irish, didn't want to get in the middle of.

"Four hundred dollars a day."

"You're joking!"

"No, I'm serious. What's more, I've been invited to stay there for the next week while I do my research."

Ed had further misgivings.

"I'd be careful, Jack," he replied at this. "And I wouldn't trust this guy as far as I could throw him."

"Well, I met him earlier and he seems fairly decent enough."

"I'm sure he is, but just exercise a little caution, if you please."

"Duly noted. Which reminds me. Brion, being an attorney, have you ever had to look up old court records?"

Brion's ears perked up at this.

"Depends. How old are you talking about?"

"Eighteen hundreds."

"Well, nothing that old, but I'm sure they'd be pretty easy to find. Just go down to the Justice Center on Lakeside. Criminal court records are housed up on the second floor. If they're not there, then they'd be down in the basement of the old courthouse, across the street."

"I don't have to be an attorney or anything like that to get in there and view them, do I?" Jack asked as he made a short memo of this on his cell phone.

"Not at all. You just go through security and they'll point

you in the right direction. Do you think there might be something on this Engelhardt guy?"

"Well, as Ed has just pointed out, he was cleared of charges, therefore, there must be some sort of a case file."

"I don't know. They didn't have courtroom stenographers like they do today."

"Well, it's still worth a check, I'd think. Thanks."

"No problem. If you have any other questions about it later, feel free to call me."

"Will do."

Jack saved his memo and noticed the time on the display of his phone. It was well past eight and he still had a lot of packing to do before tomorrow morning. He hadn't mentioned it to Mr. Engelhardt, but part of the reason that he wouldn't have been able to spend that night at Waldemere was because most of his laundry needed to be washed.

He quickly killed off his Guinness, paid his tab, and said goodbye to the boys. It was going to be a busy night.

Jack arrived back at his place on Hathaway Avenue in Lakewood sometime after eight-thirty. He walked up the two flights of stairs and into his apartment where Fionn, his ever-faithful little yellow cat, greeted him.

"So how did it go at Waldemere?"

Jack nearly jumped out of his skin. Across the living room and sitting on the couch was Shelby Tomlinson, her disembodied spirit anyway. Aislinn, Jack's other cat, was curled up and sleeping beside her. Jack caught his breath and regained his composure.

"I really wish you wouldn't do that to me," he told her.

"Well what do you want me to do, rattle around some chains or something when you're coming up the stairs?"

"Don't be facetious. You know what I mean."

"Jack, I'm a ghost and I'm afraid you're stuck with me."

Shelby had been doing quite well as of late in coming to terms with her condition. For the first couple of months, she had been quite depressed about it; especially around Christmas, but as the winter wore on, she began to amuse herself by pulling pranks on Jack, which perked her up some. On one occasion, she had hidden in his bedroom and waited for him to stagger in during the middle of the night, as he often did. Making his way to his bed, still in a half-slumber, she yanked the blankets from the mattress and threw them over herself, scaring Jack half to death. On another occasion, she had accompanied him downtown to the Main Branch of the Cleveland Public Library. As he browsed through the history department, she began to follow him, pulling books from the shelf and dropping them on the floor; making it appear as though he was the one that was doing it. This was all fun and games for her until she encountered another ghost that accosted her. Neither she nor Jack thought that something like that was even possible. Afterwards, Shelby had let up on the practical jokes a little and had taken to making fun of herself and her condition. It seemed more and more like she was finally accepting the situation that she was in.

"To answer your question," Jack continued, "It went quite well." A thought then dawned on him. "Wait a minute. How did you know where I was? I haven't talked to you today."

"Oh. I read your emails."

"I really wish you'd stop doing that."

"Why? Is there something that you don't want me to see?"

"No, but they're private and they're my business."

"I'm sorry, Jack. I can't help myself. I get really bored hanging around here all day."

"You didn't answer any of them, did you?"

"Of course not. I haven't done that since December."

"Yeah, and that was really funny too: inviting all of my friends over for a last minute holiday party when I was sick."

"Well, what can I say? You looked like you needed a pick-me-up and I like your friends."

"And I'm sure that they'd like you too: if only they could see you."

"Bad cheek, Jack."

"Sorry. Couldn't help it. Still, I don't think they believed me when I told them that my email account got hacked. They probably thought that I sent out that email while I was heavily medicated or drunk."

"Why don't you just tell them about me?"

"Are you kidding? I can see how that would go down. 'Hey guys, I'm being haunted by the spirit of a girl that was brutally murdered fifteen years ago. What's more, I'm romantically involved with her.' They'd have me locked up in a heartbeat."

Jack took off his patchwork wool cap and leather jacket and hung them on the newel post. He was completely beside himself.

"Awe, you're so cute when you're flummoxed," Shelby said as she walked over to him and placed a hand on his cheek. She was about to kiss him when he stopped her.

"If you're going to do that, I'd better sit down."

"Good thinking."

Jack walked over to the couch and plopped down beside Aislinn, startling her out of her catnap. She jumped up at once and bolted into the kitchen. Shelby followed Jack over and took up the spot beside him. The reason that Jack had wanted to sit down was because every time that he and Shelby had physical contact with one another, it caused a slight dizzying sensation in Jack; not a nauseous feeling that one gets after drinking too much, but more of a sleepy, daydream-like feeling: very pleasant and very serene. The fact that she was a ghost didn't matter that much. He could physically touch her as much as he could anyone else. His cousin Trish, a noted medium, had no explanation as to why this was. Jack didn't really care about the reasons why. Neither did Shelby. They were content with the fact that they were tangible to one another.

"You know," began Shelby as she started to run her hands through Jack's hair, "Trish would back you up; if you told your friends about me, I mean."

"They'd probably lock her up as well."

"Really? Don't you think any of your friends would believe you?"

"Of course I do. I just don't think that it's the right time for me to tell them about you."

"Well, what are you waiting for?"

"The right opportunity, I guess."

"And when is that going to be?"

"I don't know. When I'm sure that they're not going to freak out and run off."

"Why do you think they would do that?"

"Because that's what I, or any other sane person for that matter, would probably do. The only reason that I didn't run off when I found out that you were a ghost was because I had already known you for about a week and knew you to be good-natured. That and it looked like you needed me."

"What else?" Shelby asked with a smile as she scooted over and sat on Jack's lap. He could feel his whole body begin to tingle.

"Okay, there's also the way I feel about you."

"I knew it, Jack. You love me!"

Shelby threw her arms around him and planted a big kiss on his lips. Jack's vision blurred some and he started to feel slightly intoxicated. After a moment, he came to and saw Shelby sitting a couple of feet away.

"What the…"

"Sorry about that," she apologized. "I got a little carried away."

"No. That's okay."

"So what happened at Waldemere?"

Jack related to her all the events that had transpired throughout the meeting, told her about the tour and of the invite to stay there for the next week. Shelby looked a little troubled at this later news.

"So are you going to take him up on his offer?" she asked.

"Sure. I'll only be over in Ohio City and can stop by during the day if you're worried about us not seeing each other."

"It's not that, Jack."

"Then what?"

"It's supposed to be a haunted house."

"Or so I'm told."

"Remember the library, Jack? Remember what happened when I was messing around with the books?"

"Well, I promise not to mess with his books."

"That's not what I mean." She was growing anxious.

"Then I promise not to fall in love with another ghost."

"I'm serious, Jack!" Shelby's bright blue eyes flashed green for a moment and she shoved him roughly in the shoulders. Jack found himself overcome for a fleeting moment by a sensation of fear. Realizing the affect that she'd just had on him, Shelby recoiled with embarrassment. "I'm sorry, Jack. Got a little carried away again, I guess."

"No. It's okay. Look. I promise that I'll be careful. I don't even think the house is really haunted. I mean I would have seen something while I was there. Right?"

"I guess so."

"So don't worry about it. I'll be fine.

"Okay."

Although Shelby claimed to be fine with all of this, Jack could tell that she still had misgivings.

Shelby kept him company while he set himself to the task of doing laundry, packing his clothes and necessities, gathering his notebooks and research guides, and packing up his laptop. He made arrangements with Corley, his downstairs neighbor, to take care of the cats while he was away; should he not be able to come by the house for a couple of days. The next thing Jack knew, it was after eleven and he was getting tired. Suddenly, he remembered that there was one other thing that he wanted to pack. He walked over to his bookshelf and browsed the many volumes until he came to one book entitled *Ghost Stories of Northern Ohio*. He pulled it from the shelf and tossed it into his suitcase.

"What's that?" Shelby asked.

"It's a book that an acquaintance of mine wrote about local ghosts."

"Ooh. Am I in there?"

Jack cracked a smile at this.

"You wish."

"Waldemere is though, isn't it?"

"Yep. I'd been meaning to read this for a while now, but have never really had the time to. I figure that it'll give me a chance to familiarize myself with some of the basic legends behind the house. It's always a good starting point when trying to debunk an urban legend."

"Jack, you look tired. Perhaps you should get to bed."

"Good idea. Will you be around in the morning before I go?"

"Are you kidding me? I'm staying by your side all night."

Jack moved his suitcase from the bed to the floor. He changed into his sweatpants, turned out the light, and crawled under the blankets. Shelby settled in next to him and gave him a gentle kiss on the forehead. In no time at all, Jack was fast asleep.

"Goodnight, my love," she whispered into his dreams.

Chapter 5

Monday morning came on cold and cloudy but it was still dark when Jack had woken up. There were a few of things that he wanted to do before leaving the house that day. As he rolled over in bed under the half-light of the dawn, he saw that Shelby was still there, lying beside him. She slowly opened her big blue eyes and smiled.

"How'd you sleep?" she asked.

"Like a baby."

"You crapped yourself and woke up screaming every two hours?"

Jack chuckled as he rubbed his eyes.

"You know? I never really thought about it like that. How did *you* sleep?"

"Like the dead."

"Very funny."

Jack sat up and stretched, feeling every vertebrae pop. As he lowered his arms, he noticed Shelby's hand slowly caressing his back ever so gently.

"What time do you have to leave?" she asked.

"Quarter to ten at the latest, but I might stop off and pick up a coffee on the way."

"You do know that it might be easier, and cheaper, if you'd just buy a coffee maker, don't you?"

"Actually, I think I have one somewhere packed away, but have never used it."

"Why not?"

"Well, it only makes full pots and there's no way that I'll ever drink that much in one go."

Shelby saw the logic in this.

"So what have you got to do before you leave?"

"Really, just wash up and check my email. Might try to catch some of the news."

"Can we just lay here for a bit?" Shelby asked as she lightly brushed her fingers across Jack's forehead. He looked over at the clock and saw that it was just after seven-thirty. He looked back at her and smiled.

"Of course," he said as he stretched back down.

Shelby placed her hands on Jack's shoulders and pulled herself in closer to him, resting her head on his chest and listening to his heartbeat. He wrapped his arms around her and slowly began to feel more relaxed than he had felt in a long time.

The next thing that Jack knew, it was a quarter to nine and Shelby was shaking him.

"Jack, get up. Come on. We've overslept."

Jack quickly sat up and looked over at the clock.

"Damn it!" He jumped out of bed and started for the bathroom but immediately realized that he was nude. "Whoa! Where the hell are my pants?"

He slowly turned and looked at Shelby, who was sitting up on the bed giggling.

"Just couldn't help myself," she explained through a broad grin.

Jack noticed his sweatpants lying at the foot of the bed. He retrieved these, threw them on in haste and continued into the bathroom.

After shaving and taking a shower, Jack realized that he didn't have much time for anything else. He opted to watch the morning news rather than check his email. Besides, his laptop was already packed up and he didn't feel like digging it out. He could always check it later.

It turned out to be a slow news day: not very interesting, but a good thing nonetheless. Jack was tired of hearing bad news and lately the media was full of it. He finished dressing and carried his suitcase into the front room. It was just after nine-thirty and he needed to leave.

"Shelby?" he called as he started to put on his distressed leather jacket.

"I'm here." She replied from right behind him. Again, Jack nearly jumped out of his skin.

"God! Don't do that."

Shelby shoved him up against the wall, wrapped her right leg around the back of his thighs, firmly grabbed the collar of his jacket, and began to kiss him passionately. For a moment, Jack thought he was going to fall down the stairs to his left, but Shelby withdrew herself before he lost consciousness.

"That's just to make sure that you don't forget about me."

She turned with a smile and casually strolled into the kitchen. Jack picked up his suitcase and ducked his head around the corner. He loved to watch her walk away, but she was already gone. With that, he descended the stairs, walked out the front door, threw his suitcase on the passenger seat of his car, and drove off.

He pulled up at the front gate of Waldemere just before ten o'clock and remembering Mr. Engelhardt's instructions from the previous evening, withdrew the business card and his cell phone. He punched in the numbers and hit the *send* button. A familiar Cockney accent answered the phone.

"Good mornin'. Engelhardt residence."

"Good morning, Emily. It's Jack."

"Ah, Mr. Sullivan. I'm afraid that Mr. Engelhardt is currently on the phone with 'is son. 'Ave ya arrived?"

"I have."

"Lovely. I'll be out in a jiff to let ya in."

Jack hung up the phone and a moment later saw the front door open. Emily bounded down the front steps with the large key ring in her right hand. She raced over to the gate, unlocked it and pulled it open. As Jack drove in, she waved to him and motioned to the side entrance. He nodded and continued into the back, where he found a parking spot beside a red Lexus roadster. He stepped out of the car with his suitcase in hand and leisurely strolled back up the driveway to the side door where Emily was waiting for him.

"Did ya 'ave a good evenin', Mr. Sullivan?"

"I did, thank you. And it's Jack." Emily shifted uneasily at him saying this. "How was your evening?"

"It was good." She looked about her once to make sure that no one else was around. "Thanks for askin', Jack," she said in a whisper. "Well," she continued at full volume, "ya best come in out of the cold."

Emily opened the side door under the porte-cochere and escorted him in. As Jack crossed the threshold, he distinctly caught the aroma of freshly cooked bacon and coffee brewing. He hadn't stopped for a cup of coffee on his way over as he had hoped to.

"'Ave ya 'ad breakfast yet?" Emily asked as she closed the door behind them.

"No. I'm afraid I overslept a little this morning and didn't have time."

"Well, we'll get ya settled in and I'll put somethin' on for ya."

"Thanks."

Emily guided Jack over to the dumbwaiter service, took his suitcase from him and placed it on the platform.

"This'll make it a little easier on us," she said as she pushed a button. "Come on, then." The dumbwaiter made a low humming noise as the platform ascended.

They climbed the back stairs until they were up on the fourth floor and in the grand ballroom with the giant clock on the southern wall. Jack stopped again to admire the masterpiece.

"I swear, that really is something," he said after a few moments.

"I know," Emily replied. "Some o' those faces give me the willies though."

"Yeah, I can see that."

Jack continued to watch the giant clock for a few moments longer while Emily unlocked the back guest bedroom.

"Your room, Mr. Sullivan," she announced. Jack gave her a wry look as he entered. "Someone moight be listening, Jack," she softly continued as she walked over to the dumbwaiter. The low humming noise stopped and Jack's suitcase appeared. "'Ere ya go."

She handed Jack the suitcase, and pushed a button beside the dumbwaiter, sending the platform back downstairs. Jack set his suitcase down on the four-poster bed and turned his attention for a moment to the window that overlooked the Lake Erie shoreline. Clouds of iron and charcoal rolled in from the north.

"That's quite a view."

"It is," Emily agreed. "'Ere now, I want to show ya somethin'. Ya can place your clothes in this dresser over 'ere and when you're done, ya can put your suitcase down 'ere."

She strolled over to the northwest corner of the room, rolled back an area rug and revealed a trapdoor cleverly concealed in the floor. She lifted the latch revealing a space beneath. Jack walked over and looked inside. It was dark but he could tell that the space was about four feet high and continued on underneath the room.

"Now that's incredible," he said at last.

"Not really," Emily explained. "It's just a trunk space."

"I'm sorry, a what?"

"A trunk space. This was also a guest bedroom when the 'ouse was first built. Whenever a visitor would come to stay, their steamer trunk would be loaded onto the dumbwaiter and brought up 'ere, just as yours was. After the contents o' the trunk were placed into the dresser and closet, the trunk would then be stored down 'ere so that it didn't clutter up the room."

"That makes sense."

Emily closed the trapdoor and walked back across the room to a door that was slightly narrower than the one leading back into the ballroom.

"The loo is through 'ere and you'll 'ave your own washbasin and bathtub."

"Can I ask you something, Emily?"

"Of course ya can."

"I don't want to seem blunt, but Mr. Engelhardt seems to be quite easy going and laid back; to a degree."

"'Ow do ya mean?"

"Well, he insists upon me calling him Henry, yet you refer to him as Mr. Engelhardt and keep calling me Mr. Sullivan. Why is that?"

"Ya 'ave never worked in the service industry before, 'ave ya Mr. Sullivan?"

"Well, no. I haven't."

"There's a code o' propriety and decorum that must be upheld and maintained. It's in me contract that I do so."

"But he'd mentioned that you have your meals together. Doesn't that seem a bit informal?"

"We are friends and it's only the two o' us in this 'ouse. There's no reason that we shouldn't be social at mealtimes."

"I'm sorry if I was out of line. I was just curious."

"Not at all, Mr. Sullivan. Now, can I ask *ya* somethin'?"

"Certainly."

"'Ow do ya take your eggs?"

"Oh." Jack chuckled a little. "Over medium. Thanks."

"Coffee, tea or juice? I'm guessin' that you're a coffee man."

"Coffee would be great."

"Breakfast will be ready in about ten minutes then."

With that, Emily left Jack to unpack his suitcase. Once she had gone, he walked back over to the trapdoor and opened it up again. Without giving it a second thought, he jumped down inside and investigated the trunk space. He was right in guessing that it went back quite a distance. Still, it was too dark for him to see anything in there and decided that he would check it out later, after he'd gotten the flashlight from his car.

Jack arrived in the main dining room and found a setting laid out for him. A hot and aromatic mug of coffee had been poured and set just to the right. There was a low humming noise coming from out in the corridor, obviously the dumbwaiter, and he could hear footsteps coming up the stairs. A moment later, the humming sound stopped and Emily appeared with a silver tray in her hand.

"'Ere ya go," she said as she set it down in front of him. "Are ya all settled in then?"

"I am. Thank you."

"Mr. Engelhardt is just concludin' 'is telephone call and will join ya in just a few minutes."

Before Jack could thank her again, she quickly turned and left the room.

The meal was absolutely delicious; by far one of the best breakfasts that Jack had enjoyed in quite some time. The bacon was thick and peppery, the sausage thoroughly cooked and seasoned with just the right amount of sage. The whole grain toast wasn't too light or too dark and the eggs were perfect: solid whites with runny yokes. Jack cleaned his plate in a little less than ten minutes. As he sat and finished his coffee, Mr. Engelhardt entered the room with a manila folder in his hands. Jack stood up to greet him.

"Good morning, Jack. How do you find your room?"

"The room is perfect, Henry. Thank you."

The two shook hands.

"Please, Jack. Sit down and finish your coffee." Jack sat back down and Mr. Engelhardt took a seat at the head of the table to his left. "Here," he continued as he set down the folder beside Jack. "I've brought you the papers that you requested in regards to the genealogical research that I'd done on my father's family. Hopefully, it'll be a good starting point for you."

"Thanks," Jack said as he slid the folder closer and opened it to the first document, which was a printout from the 1880 U.S. Census.

"So what are your plans for the day?"

"Well," Jack began, "I figured that I'd start by reading up on these legends that have been told about the house and your family. It's a good idea to know first off what exactly it is that I'm going to be debunking. After that, I thought that I'd read over your research and make comparisons to the legends. Then I thought that I'd stroll over to the Cuyahoga County Archives up the street and see what they have on the house."

"That's the brick building on the south side of Franklin, right?"

"Yeah, that's it."

"They have information like that over there?"

"And then some. There's likely to be some information on your great grandfather and his family as well."

"Really?"

Jack nodded.

"This evening, if you don't mind, I thought I'd do a little exploring of the house on my own. Of course, I'll stay out of your bedroom, sitting room and Emily's bedroom."

"Oh, I don't mind you roaming the house. Whatever it takes."

"Wonderful. I have a feeling that most of the day is going to be spent here at Waldemere, but aside from the archives office, I might hit up this coffee shop I know and use their wireless internet service."

"Oh, there's no need to go through all of that for internet service, Jack. We have WiFi here at the house."

46

"Oh," Jack said slightly astonished. "That's wonderful."

Just then, Emily entered the room.

"Are ya finished with your tray then, Mr. Sullivan?"

Jack looked up and smiled.

"I am, Emily. Thank you."

She took the tray and hurried out of the room.

"Well Jack, I'll leave you to it then," Mr. Engelhardt said as he stood up from the table. "It sounds like you're going to have a busy day ahead of you."

"I'm looking forward to it."

"Great. I have a number of calls to make and will be in and out of the house throughout the day. Good luck."

Jack stood up and drank the last of his coffee.

"Oh, um, what should I do with this?" He motioned to his empty mug.

"Don't worry about that. Emily will clear it for you. Have a good day, Jack."

Mr. Engelhardt walked out of the room. Jack could hear him going up the stairs, likely heading back to his living quarters on the third floor. He looked down at the manila folder again and quickly leafed through a few of the pages it contained. There were a number of handwritten notes, printouts and pages that had been photocopied. He closed the folder, picked it up and made his way upstairs, back to his bedroom on the fourth floor.

Chapter 6

Jack sat at the built-in desk in the fourth floor bedroom with his copy of *Ghost Stories of Northern Ohio* opened in front of him. Beside that, he had his notebook opened to a blank page of lined paper and a black pen ready to take notes. He flipped ahead in the book to a chapter entitled *Nightmare at Waldemere* and began to read.

> *It stands as a monument to the success of one man and one man only. Others have tried to make it their own, but each new ownership soon ends in failure, abandonment or madness. It is a house that refuses to be possessed by anyone but its original master; a man named Heinrich Engelhardt.*
>
> *The house to which I refer is Waldemere: a dark sandstone mansion on Franklin Boulevard in Cleveland's Ohio City neighborhood. It's a house that has a sordid past that includes homicide, insanity, suicide and rage. The story goes something like this:*
>
> *In the late 1860's a German immigrant named Heinrich Engelhardt erected a house on Franklin Boulevard for his wife Sophia and family. Mr. Engelhardt had amassed a large fortune in the banking industry and spared no expense in the building of this grand mansion. Originally, it was believed that he had built this house to show his wife how much he loved her, but there were whispers that he had other reasons for building the home.*
>
> *Neighbors often speculated that there was a darker side to the kind and outgoing face that Mr. Engelhardt wore in public. It was rumored that he would often beat his wife and children with no just cause and that the house was actually built as a place where he could keep them*

imprisoned. Though outwardly he seemed a very friendly man, he would never invite guests over for parties or social gatherings of any kind. Stories circulated that one of his sons, a boy named Ludwig, would not be seen for years on end. This, Mr. Engelhardt explained away by telling neighbors that the child was often sick.

Then came the first of the murders.

During the summer of 1879, one of Mr. Engelhardt's nieces came to stay with the family. Her time with them was short lived. Within a month, the girl had mysteriously vanished, never to be seen or heard from again. Mr. Engelhardt would claim that she had run off with a stranger, but it was understood among the neighbors that she had actually fallen victim to his rage.

Two years later brought the next murder. That came with the sudden disappearance of a servant in the home named Henrietta. Again, there were whispers among the neighbors. This time, the allegations were that she was in fact Mr. Engelhardt's mistress. The family would claim that Henrietta had actually robbed the house and slipped off into the night, but could it have been another case of Mr. Engelhardt's rage? Or is it possible that Mrs. Engelhardt found out about the affair and disposed of the harlot? The truth was never learned.

The following year, there was yet another mysterious disappearance. That occurred when another of the Engelhardt's servants vanished. Another mistress perhaps?

The fair citizens of Cleveland had enough. Heinrich Engelhardt was finally brought up on charges of murder in the disappearances of these three young ladies. But back in those days, the city court system was as corrupt as ever. In the end, Mr. Engelhardt was cleared on all three counts. It was rumored that he had actually paid off the judge.

Over the next ten years, things at Waldemere had grown relatively quiet. Perhaps Mr. Engelhardt had realized how close he had come to being found out for his wicked deeds. Whatever the case was, there were still whispers of strange doings at the Engelhardt house. Then, on the evening of September 28th, 1892, Heinrich Engelhardt's son, Ludwig, committed suicide by throwing himself from the window of a fourth floor bedroom; possibly driven mad by his overbearing father.

Jack jumped up from his seat at the desk and looked about the room that he was in. It was clear to him that this was the only bedroom on the fourth floor and therefore had to be the room from which Ludwig Engelhardt had decided to end his life. He walked over to the window and looked outside. It was nearly a sixty-foot drop to the yard below. A jump like that could easily have killed someone. Just then, he had a thought.

He flipped the latch on the window and raised the sash. As it turned out, the window would only go up about a foot: not really enough space for a person to pass through. Then another thought came to him. The book never actually said that Ludwig opened the window and jumped; only that he threw himself from a window. Jack inspected the glass and rapped on the wooden framework. It would actually have been quite easy for Ludwig to throw himself through the window, if he had enough of a running start that is.

Jack realized that he was getting ahead of himself. This was just a story that he was reading and until he could research the facts and prove these stories, that's all that it would remain. He returned to the desk and continued to read.

Curiously, no suicide note was ever found. It was speculated among the neighbors of Franklin Boulevard that Heinrich Engelhardt had finally had enough of his son and that he had actually thrown him through the window.

Jack smiled at this last statement and gave himself something of a congratulatory pat on the back for having figured out already that no one could have fit through the window. Maybe there was some truth to this story after all. It would require further research.

Ludwig Engelhardt was 31 at the time of his death. His remains were interred at Monroe Street Cemetery, where a large monument was soon set. Oddly enough, it was rumored that Mr. Engelhardt had built Waldemere with a family burial vault in a sub-basement beneath the house, though no such vault or sub-basement has ever been located.

Mr. Engelhardt's two surviving children, Conrad and Tillie would go on to marry into society. Conrad would have a son, but Tillie would bear no children of her own.

Somewhere around 1900, with his children married and living in their own homes, Heinrich Engelhardt sold Waldemere and moved out to the country, where he and his wife would live out their few remaining years in reclusive isolation. They both would die in 1906 within two months of each other and are buried beside their son Ludwig at Monroe Street Cemetery.

A few years after the passing of his parents, Conrad Engelhardt was involved in a shady business deal and under a banner of shame, was driven out of Cleveland. It was rumored that he relocated to the east coast and was living under an assumed name.

The next owner of Waldemere was a doctor named James Grady. Dr. Grady would own the house until around 1930, at which time he sold it to a family named Frohlich. The

Frohlich's would remain at Waldemere through the late 1950's. It was then that it was sold to Mr. Thomas Young and his wife, Mary.

The Youngs were an all-American family with three small children and a dog. Mr. Young worked as an engineer with an aircraft design firm and his bride was a happy homemaker. When they first saw that the house was for sale, they were ecstatic over the idea of making it their own. They immediately fell in love with the beautiful woodwork and large rooms, the fourth floor ballroom in particular. This room featured a rather ornate bar and a giant clock that took up an entire wall. Shortly after moving in however, they realized that they had just purchased a nightmare.

The children soon began to talk about a man that they called Mr. Nobody that would come and visit them in their upstairs bedrooms at night. Mr. and Mrs. Young thought at first that this was just an imaginary friend, but soon realized that there was more to it. After just a few months of seeing this man, the children began to grow more and more terrified. On one occasion, all three children came running downstairs shortly after they had gone to bed, and were covered head to toe in scratches. These they claimed to have gotten from Mr. Nobody.

Mrs. Young was also beginning to experience some strange events. On one occasion, she thought that there was an intruder in the house. She could hear someone yelling in an upstairs room, but the words that were being shouted definitely weren't in English. When her husband went to investigate, he found the rest of the house empty.

Every so often, the children would come downstairs in the morning with new scratches on them. Neighbors were beginning to suspect child abuse. Eventually, Mr. and Mrs. Young moved the children's bedrooms down onto the second floor.

As the children got older, the Youngs realized that they weren't saying "Mr. Nobody" but were actually saying "Mr. No Body". This terrified Mrs. Young to no end. The disturbances continued and the Youngs found it harder and harder to live in the house.

At the end of their time spent residing there, Mrs. Young was driven to the brink of madness. She had claimed that the giant clock up on the fourth floor was ticking louder and louder each night and was doing so deliberately to torture her. Eventually, she'd had enough. One afternoon, while her husband was at work and the children at school, she went up to the fourth floor ballroom with a hammer, found the access way into the clock and began to smash its inner workings to pieces. It hasn't worked since. When Mr. Young returned home from work and discovered what she had done, he called an ambulance to take here to Tourney Tech, a mental hospital just outside of Cleveland. He too had had enough. He took the children and left the house. Refusing to make payments on the property, the bank eventually took it over and put it back on the market.

It was sold shortly after, but the new owner didn't stay for more than a couple of years: nor has anyone else since. All claim that when they buy it, things will be different, but things never are. All are driven away by the disturbances.

Currently, Waldemere is owned by a man from Lexington, Kentucky named Jasper Burton. Mr. Burton absolutely refuses to live in the house and with the exception of a caretaker that occupies the carriage house in the back, the home is unoccupied. When asked why he even bought the house in the first place, Mr. Burton told me that he's a collector of great oddities and that a haunted house is his crowning jewel.

Waldemere sits silent and still, looking down on Franklin Boulevard at the people who pass by and stare up at it its terrifying edifice. Perhaps it's patiently waiting for its next owner or its next victim: probably one in the same.

Jack set the book on the desk and reviewed the notes that he had written down while he was reading.

- Built late 1860's?
- Spousal / child abuse
- No social gatherings
- Ludwig (chronic illness)?
- summer 1879 - niece missing
- 1881 Henrietta - servant - mistress? robbed house
- 1882 - another servant *check court records
- Sept. 28, 1892 Ludwig Engelhardt - suicide Monroe Street Cem.
- Conrad - married - son - left after 1905 (06) East Coast (Boston)
- Conrad - Name change?
- Tillie - married - no children *double check
- House sold 1900 - moved to where?
- Heinrich / wife - Monroe Cem.
- Next Owners interesting, but not relevant to this research.

Most of what was written in this book was absolutely useless, as it was primarily idle speculation. Still, if one could get past all of the dramatic effect, it could possibly be used as a starting point. As it was, this was all that Jack had to go on. It was much more than his father had ever told him about the place and would have to do for now. Jack thought for a moment about contacting the author to see if he might have some solid records that he had based these stories on, but figured that he probably didn't. Otherwise, he'd have given specific dates as opposed to using generalities such as *somewhere around 1900*. He decided that he would next consult Henry Engelhardt's genealogical file.

He opened the folder, leafed through the pages and began to sort them into piles by classification. One stack contained U.S. Census records. Another, he set aside for marriage records. The next contained family pedigrees and a fourth was reserved for miscellaneous records such as newspaper clippings, ships manifests and passport applications. All in all, there really wasn't that much there. Nevertheless, Jack began to make notes. He figured it best that he start at the beginning.

From what he was able to piece together, Heinrich Conrad Engelhardt was born on October 7th, 1828 in the City of Nuremberg, Kingdom of Bavaria, Germany to parents Johann Heinrich Ludwig Engelhardt and Marie Anna Stadler. In August of 1841, Heinrich had come to the United States with his parents and two brothers Jacob and Friedrich. Originally, they had settled in New York, but within five years had relocated to Cleveland.

By 1850, Heinrich's parents were living on a farm in Newburg, just south of Cleveland, while the three Engelhardt brothers were living in Cleveland proper, trying to make a name for themselves. Heinrich was employed as a cabinetmaker, while his brothers were working as day laborers. Within four years, Heinrich had met and married a German-born woman named Sophia Lutz, a daughter of Joseph and Magdalena Lutz. They would have five children: Conrad Friedrich, who was born on March 12th 1857, Matilda Sophia (Tillie), born on November 20th 1859 and Ludwig Jacob, born the 10th of June 1861. Two other children, Heinrich Johann and Maria Regina, would die in infancy; Heinrich in 1856 from diphtheria and Maria in 1863 from something simply listed as fits. Jack wondered why Henry Engelhardt hadn't mentioned these other two children when he had told him the family story the day before. Maybe he just didn't think it to be of any relevance.

As Jack read on through the stacks of documents, he learned that Heinrich Engelhardt had taken a number of trips back to Germany throughout his life. On most occasions, he had brought his whole family with him. This hardly sounded like the act of a tyrannical patriarch.

Further reading revealed that Heinrich's son Conrad Engelhardt had married a woman named Catherine Walters of Massachusetts. His daughter Tillie, meanwhile, had married a local man named Charles Bell. These documents did show that by 1910, Conrad and Catherine were living in Boston. There was no mention of Tillie after her marriage to Mr. Bell, just a note that said "no issue" meaning no children. Jack would have some searching to do.

Aside from all of this, there was nothing in these documents about Waldemere or murder charges of any kind. It did go on to say that Heinrich and Sophia Engelhardt both died in 1906: Heinrich on June 3rd and Sophia on August 19th. It also said that they were interred at Monroe Street Cemetery and that both were living in Dover Township at the time of their passing. That made things a little hard for Jack. Dover Township was now the cities of Westlake and Bay Village. The question was, which one?

Just then, Jack noticed something missing from the notes he had just made from Henry Engelhardt's papers; that being the fact that Ludwig was absent from the 1880 census. He pulled that page out again and gave it a second look. Sure enough, Ludwig's name was not among the rest of his family and at once, Jack knew why. The list was continued onto the next page. He searched the stack but was unable to locate it. He'd have to go online and find it himself.

He pulled out his laptop, booted it up and in no time had managed to connect to the internet. He brought up the 1880 U.S. Census and did a search on Engelhardt in Cleveland. There they were. He pulled up the original image and clicked on an icon that brought him to the next page. Ludwig Engelhardt's name was at the top of the list, followed by quite a few others that lived in the house but weren't related: servants.

The first set of names that appeared below Ludwig's was

Herman and Viola Schilling: a husband and wife. Herman was listed as the coachman and Viola as the head servant. Jack figured that they likely occupied the carriage house in the back. Next was a sixteen-year-old German girl named Harriett Fischer, who was the cook. Jack wondered if this might actually be the Henrietta that was mentioned in the book. The last person named as living in the house was a fourteen-year-old Irish girl named Katherine Fitzgerald. She was listed as a chambermaid. These girls, he surmised, must have occupied the bedroom on the lowest level of the house that was now occupied by Emily. Jack made quick note of this census page and knew that he now had more to go on. Perhaps, he thought, it was time to hit up the county archives and see what they had on the house itself.

Chapter 7

Even though it was quite cold outside and there was still a considerable amount of snow on the ground, Jack felt like walking the two blocks down Franklin to the Cuyahoga County Archives Office. The fresh air and brisk walk, he figured, would do him some good. What he was after more than anything else was a building date for Waldemere. The county tax records were the best place to find this.

Jack walked through the front entrance, signed himself in, and walked directly into the back. He'd been here countless times and knew his way around the files as well as any of the archivists. He entered the poorly lit room on his right and immediately set himself to the task of locating the tax books for Cleveland-West starting with 1860. After a quick search, he found no listing for anyone with the last name Engelhardt. He kept searching through the books for the following years. It wasn't until 1866 that he finally found a listing for that name, but that was for Heinrich's brother Friedrich. Jack figured it likely that Heinrich and his wife were probably renting a house throughout this era, or possibly living with a family member. This would be found in the Cleveland City Directories; a number of which were kept in a cabinet in the front room.

He placed the tax book back on the shelf and returned to the front of the building. Entering the room that housed the books on local history and biography, Jack strolled over to a glass-fronted cabinet, slid it open, and withdrew the directory for 1854. He located the Engelhardt brothers in no time at all and learned that they were living together in a house on Kentucky Street, now West 38th, right around the corner from the archives office and Waldemere.

Jack continued to look them up for the years that followed. By 1856, Heinrich Engelhardt was listed as living at 276 Clinton Street, just a block north of Franklin. It also said that he was employed by a company called Darrow and Associates. Here on Clinton Street he would remain for the next twenty years. In 1877, his new address was listed as 225 Franklin Street. That had to be it. That had to be when they moved into Waldemere. Something about all of this threw Jack for a loop. He didn't think it likely that Heinrich Engelhardt, or anyone else for that matter, would rent a house for twenty years. There had to be more to it. Just then, he was struck by an idea. He returned to an earlier directory and looked up the surname Lutz: his wife's maiden name. At first, he saw no listing for George, but soon found an entry for Magdalena that was followed by a set of parentheses containing the words *widow George*. Her address was 276 Clinton Street. That solved it. Heinrich and his wife were living with his mother-in-law for those twenty years or so.

Jack walked into the back room again and picked up the county tax records book for 1870. He looked up Engelhardt, but still found no entry for Heinrich. It wasn't until 1874 that he found an entry for him with a property listed on Franklin. That must have been when he had purchased the land, which was valued at $600. By 1876, the property value had skyrocketed to $22,000. This was an unbelievable amount for a house during that period. Jack made a note of this, closed the book, and returned it to the shelf. As he turned to leave, he found himself suddenly facing a man with long graying, scraggly hair and a salt and pepper goatee, dressed in eccentric Nineteenth Century attire. The brown duster that he was wearing ended just short of his boots.

"You still haven't stopped by my shop yet, Jack. Some people might consider that rude, you know."

At first, Jack was alarmed at the sudden appearance of the odd stranger, but within a second or two, realized that he was no stranger at all.

"Orin Drury?"

"Well, at least you remembered my name. It's good to see you again." Orin extended his right hand to Jack, who gladly accepted it and shook it. "How've you been these last few months?"

"I can't complain," Jack replied. "I mean, I can but who'd care to listen to that?"

Orin Drury chuckled lightly at this.

"So I see that you're working on another case. Let me take a guess. It's Waldemere. Isn't it?"

"Yeah. But how did you…"

"I am all knowing and all seeing!"

Jack was quite thrown by this comment.

"I'm kidding, Jack. I saw your car parked in front of there yesterday evening when I was driving by."

"Oh."

"Now, I know that Jasper Burton wouldn't come up here for any reason, especially at this time of year. So I'm guessing that there's a new owner involved."

"There is. His name's Henry Engelhardt."

Orin Drury paused for a moment and didn't say anything, only looked at the floor. Finally he glanced up at the ceiling and spoke.

"Now that is interesting."

"What?"

"That after all these years, the Engelhardt's have finally come back to Cleveland. I'll have to amend my documents on Waldemere."

"Can you tell me anything about them?"

"What, my documents or the Engelhardts?"

Jack threw Orin a smug look.

"The Engelhardts."

"No, I'm afraid that I can't."

"But you seem to know who they are."

"Knowing who they are and being able to tell you about them are two very different things, Jack. No. I'm sorry to say, that you're going to have to find this out on your own. You seem to be starting in the right place though. Just remember what I told you before. There are *other* archives in this city. Feel free to stop by anytime."

"Thanks, Orin. I'll make it a point to."

"Now if you'll excuse me, I have a tax record to look up. Good day to you, Jack."

"And to you."

Jack walked out of the county archives building that afternoon with a few questions answered, but was slightly perplexed as to why Orin Drury was unwilling to fill him in on what he knew about the Engelhardt family: especially since he obviously knew a thing or two about them. He'd just have to make it a point to stop by Orin's shop and push the envelope a little further with him. He seemed to be keeping something from him and now Jack was extremely curious to know what that was.

It was just after three in the afternoon when Jack returned to Waldemere. As he strolled up the driveway, he could distinctly hear music coming from down on the servants' level. It took him a minute to place the band but soon realized that it was the Sex Pistols. Emily, he guessed, must have been a punker in a former life.

Remembering that he would need his flashlight if he were going to explore the house, Jack walked into the back yard and retrieved the small LED flashlight from the glove box of his car. He walked back up the driveway, approached the side door, and rang the bell. The music instantly stopped and a moment later, he heard Emily running up the stairs. She answered the door, somewhat out of breath, but trying to look as refined as ever.

"'Ello Mr. Sullivan," she warmly greeted. "Did ya 'ave a good afternoon?"

"I did. Sounds like you're having one right now."

Emily suddenly looked flushed.

"Ya won't tell Mr. Engelhardt about that. Will ya?"

"You're secret's safe with me."

She smiled at this, and then suddenly remembered that she was keeping Jack waiting out in the cold.

"I'm sorry, Mr. Sullivan. Please, come in."

Jack entered the house with Emily closing the door behind him.

"So you're into the Sex Pistols then?"

Emily looked a little embarrassed.

"I am," she whispered. "Always 'ave been. Are ya into them?"

"Yeah, but I haven't heard them in some time. I'm guessing that Mr. Engelhardt isn't here."

"Oh, goodness no. 'E had a meetin' downtown and shouldn't be back until close to dinnertime, which is at six prompt. Ya will be joinin' us, won't ya?"

"Sure. What are we having?"

"Well, today is Monday, so it's goin' to be brazed lamb,

stuffed grape leaves, olive salad and herrin' bisque."

"Sounds wonderful. Well, I better let you get back to your music."

"Oh, not at all, Mr. Sullivan. I…"

"Look," Jack interrupted. "Your boss isn't around. Can I get you to slip out of character for just a few minutes at least?"

Emily gave him a puzzled look. Then, out of nowhere, she let out a hearty laugh.

"Okay, Jack." She finally said, speaking his name at full volume for the first time since their meeting. "Would ya loike a beer?"

"I'd love a beer. Thanks."

Emily led Jack downstairs onto the servant's level, where she proceeded to the kitchen. A moment later, she returned with a can of Boddington's Ale and a glass.

"'Ere ya go, then."

"Thanks." Jack accepted the beer and poured it into the glass.

"Come on in and 'ave a seat," she insisted. By the time they had reached her sitting room, the ale had settled and Jack took a swig. Emily offered him a chair, which he gladly sat down in.

"So where are you from?" he asked as he set his glass down on a coffee table.

"East End o' London, originally. Came to the states 'bout foive years back and lived in Boston since."

"And that's when you started working for Mr. Engelhardt?"

"Not roight away. 'Ad me a job in a pub, I did. Sadly, the pub closed a couple o' years ago and that's when I found the advertisement for a 'ouse servant listed in the papers. I applied and was 'ired within the week."

"So how do you find Cleveland?"

"On a map."

Jack laughed at this, even though it was an old joke.

"Um, I mean…"

"No. Cleveland's pretty noice. The people 'ere seem easy enough to get on with. But is it always this cold?"

"Not at all. You should see it in the summer. It breaks a

hundred degrees every now and again."

"Yuck." Emily stuck the tip of her tongue out the left side of her mouth, seemingly disgusted at the idea of a temperature that hot.

"Ah, it's not so bad. Usually by the afternoon, a lake breeze kicks in and cools everything off. Plus, we've got this wonderful lake right here."

"People actually swim in that?"

"Oh yeah. All the time."

"But I thought it was polluted."

"It was, a long time ago, but it's gotten much better in recent years."

"Didn't the river catch fire?"

"Which time?"

"Ya mean it's burned more than once?"

"Sure. It's burned about four or five times, but it's not the only river in the U.S. to have caught fire. It's just the one that got the most attention."

"Really?"

Jack nodded and took a sip of his beer.

"So you're into punk music?" he asked as he set his beer back down.

"Absolutely. More than just the Sex Pistols."

"Oh?"

"Sure. Mojo Nixon, The Clash, Bad Brains, Butthole Surfers, Alice Donut, Dead Kennedys… the list goes on and on."

"Then I know the perfect bar for you to check out. It's called the Spitfire Saloon on West 117th and Franklin. I've got a feeling you'd really like the jukebox up there."

"Punk music?"

"Oh, yeah. Live bands too. I'll take you up there some time."

"Well," Emily noted, "It'll 'ave to be after noine at noight. That's when Mr. Engelhardt retires for the evenin'. Speakin' of, 'e should be 'ome shortly. I best be gettin' the dinner started. We don't dress up for dinner or anythin' loike that. It's pretty casual."

"Yeah, I wanted to do a little exploring of the house while it was still light."

"I'll let ya get started then, Jack."

"Thanks again for the beer. It was great having a chance to talk".

"Likewoise."

Jack finished his beer in two large gulps and handed the empty glass to Emily. He headed back upstairs to the fourth floor bedroom, where he hung up his coat and set his notebook down on the built-in desk. He really wanted to spend some time exploring the house, but couldn't decide where to start. Remembering that he had grabbed the flashlight from his car, he chose to begin with the trunk space.

He crossed the room, rolled back the area rug and lifted the trapdoor hatch. Clicking on the flashlight, he stuck his head in for a moment and got his first real look. The space went back quite a ways. At first, it looked to be empty, but as his eyes adjusted to the dim light, he caught sight of something sitting in the back. He dropped down into the trunk space and, hunched over, began to make his way down the passage.

At the end of the passage, Jack came into something of a room with a four-foot high ceiling. Straight ahead of him, he could see the object that had attracted his attention. Upon closer inspection, he discovered it to be an old steamer trunk; which made perfect sense, considering that he was now crouched down in a trunk space. At first, he thought to leave it alone, seeing as it wasn't his, but after noticing that it was covered with a thick layer of dust, he realized that it had been sitting undisturbed for many years now. It obviously didn't belong to Emily or Mr. Engelhardt, so he saw no harm in opening it and browsing its contents.

He threw the side latches open, but when he went to pop the middle latch, it wouldn't budge. He shined the flashlight closer and could now see a keyhole in the center. The trunk was locked. For a moment, he considered finding something to break the lock open with, but thought better of it. Jack definitely wasn't one for damaging an antique such as this. Granted, steamer trunks were a dime a dozen, but still, he couldn't bring himself to do it. The trunk's contents would have to remain a mystery.

Making his way back up the passage, Jack noticed

something that he'd overlooked when he'd first entered. Carved onto the wall was the name *Tom Jenkins*, followed by a date of *17th October 1876*. Jack had an idea that this Mr. Jenkins might have been one of the builders. Perhaps this was the date that the house was completed.

He climbed back out of the trunk space, closed the hatch and replaced the area rug. He walked over to his notebook, flipped it open and wrote down what he had just read on the wall. Having finished that, he considered his next area of exploration. Hearing the feint ticking beyond the bedroom door, he decided to investigate the clock.

Jack stood before the massive timepiece on the southern wall of the ballroom and stared at it with awe. He began to notice a few features that he had overlooked when he'd first viewed it. For example: near the bottom of the clock face were two hornets with inlaid maple and walnut to give the effect of stripes. In the upper corners of the facade were engraved trees on a wind-swept landscape. Beneath each tree sat a tombstone, which struck Jack as quite odd. As for the faces that bore the frightful expressions, these were of a man and a woman. The man was placed to the left and the woman to the right. In the center, close to the floor and just below the crossed rifles, was the image of a heart. Jack thought it curious that so much detail had gone into the woodwork, yet the entire time that he had been there; he had yet to hear this clock chime. Perhaps, he thought, that feature was still not working.

As he walked closer, he noticed that the windows on each side of the clock face were actually set about three feet deep. This made absolute sense to him at once. There would need to be a space behind this wall to house the clock's inner workings. Mr. Engelhardt had mentioned that he'd recently repaired the clock; therefore, Jack figured that there must be some way to access this space. He ran his right hand along the intricate hand carved woodwork hoping to locate a door or an access way of some sort, but could find none. Mary Young, one of the past owners of Waldemere, had managed to find this entrance when she had destroyed the mechanical work inside. It couldn't be that hard to find.

Then Jack had an idea. He walked over to his left and

entered the turret room. There, immediately to his right, he located a dark wooden panel that obviously had a thin gap around it. This had to be the door. Seeing that there was no handle or doorknob, Jack pushed on the panel, but it wouldn't budge. Perhaps like the steamer trunk in the trunk space, this too was locked. Still, he could find no keyhole.

Just as he was giving up, he noticed a strange feature here in the turret room that he hadn't noticed at first. Coming down from the center of the conical ceiling above his head was a chain that seemed to have no earthly business being there. He considered it for a moment and decided that it really couldn't do any harm to give it a try. With that, he reached up and gave the chain a firm yank. There was a clicking sound and the access panel slowly swung open. He turned on his flashlight and entered.

Jack was instantly greeted by the smell of dust and ancient wood. Gazing around at the narrow space he was now in, he immediately noticed the gears, pendulum and master spring that drove the clock. Aside from this, there were other features that didn't seem to belong. Coming off of the backside of the facade were a number of rods and posts. These were connected to a series of pulleys and counterweights. At the end of these were more rods. Some went up into the ceiling and others dropped into a shaft that went down to the lower floors. Jack shined the flashlight down this shaft, hoping to see the bottom, but he could not.

Jack's father had been, for many years, a pipe organ builder. On numerous occasions, Jack would help his father in the evenings and on weekends with tunings and repairs. Much of what Jack was seeing now reminded him of a tracker style pipe organ: many rods and posts, all mechanical action, but the function they served was a mystery to him. Perhaps, he thought, this was a method for winding the clock from a room on a lower level. He'd have to look into this and made a mental note that he would do so at a later time.

Just then, Jack heard a bell toll and for a moment, thought that he had finally heard the clock chime. Within a moment though, he realized that this wasn't the case. He had heard that same bell a couple of times already. It was tied into the gold-braided cord that hung in the main hall. Henry Engelhardt must have returned home and was calling for Emily. Jack crawled out of the mechanical space and closed the panel behind him. Maybe he would investigate this clock's inner workings further. It definitely was intriguing to him. Perhaps, he thought, his father would have a better idea of what purpose the added mechanics served.

    Jack made his way downstairs and learned that dinner would be ready in about a half an hour. Realizing that he was quite filthy, He returned to the fourth floor where he took a shower, changed and made himself look presentable.

    The meal was outstanding: especially the herring bisque, which he'd never had before. He told Mr. Engelhardt about all that he had learned that day at the archives, particularly about when the house was built. As to the discovery of the steamer trunk and what he'd seen inside the clock, he kept that to himself for the time being.

    After supper, Jack returned to the fourth floor bedroom and reread his notes from that day. There was now quite a bit for him to go on, but still, much more of the house needed to be explored. What he had seen behind the clock truly perplexed him. He decided to give his father a call and explain what he had found. First off, his father was quite impressed that he was researching Waldemere and furthermore, that he was staying there. He'd always wanted to see for himself what it looked like on the inside, but never had the opportunity to do so. After Jack had described it to him, it made him want to see it even more. When Jack had explained the odd features inside of the clock, his father was no wiser. He suggested that Jack take a few pictures and email them to him. Perhaps from these, he'd have a better idea of what they were for. Jack agreed to do so and after talking for a few minutes with his mother, he said goodnight to them both. He hung up the phone feeling quite drained. It had been a busy day and he was certain that Tuesday would be just as full.

    Jack changed into his sweatpants, tossed on a tee shirt, turned out the light and crawled into bed. He drifted off to sleep with the steady ticking of the clock in the ballroom echoing in his ears.

Chapter 8

Jack awoke the following morning and strolled over to the windows. He was pleased to see that the clouds were finally starting to break up over the lake. Even though he'd peered out these windows many times now, he still found the view from the fourth floor bedroom to be quite overwhelming. As he placed his right hand on a pane of glass, he had a sudden chill accompanied by the mental image of Ludwig Engelhardt flying through the window and falling to his death some sixty feet below: a shower of razor sharp glass raining down on him. He withdrew his hand from the window and was filled with a slight touch of remorse. Ludwig Engelhardt was only 31 when he'd died: just one year younger than Jack was now. He was beginning to feel as though the real story behind the Engelhardt family was one of a man surrounded by sorrow as opposed to one of a murderous tyrant. It was time to find the truth.

Jack laid out his clothes, shaved and took a shower. After dressing, he took a seat at the built-in desk across the room, pulled out his notebook and began to write down his next plan of attack.

He'd start by running past his house to check on things there. Plus, there were a couple of items that he needed to pick up. Afterwards, he'd be off to the Cuyahoga County Justice Center to see if there were, in fact, any court records on Heinrich Engelhardt regarding a murder charge. If time permitted, he'd drop in at McNamara's for a pint of Guinness. As he jotted this last part down, there was a sudden knock at the door.

"Hello," he called out. The door slowly crept open an inch and stopped.

"Mr. Sullivan? It's Emily. Breakfast will be ready in foive minutes."

"Thank you, Emily. I'll be down in a moment."

"Roight."

Emily closed the door behind her and returned back downstairs. Jack grabbed his notebook, picked up his jacket and cap and proceeded to follow.

By ten that morning, Jack was heading west on the Shoreway towards Lakewood. He'd finished a hot breakfast of waffles, sausage and oatmeal just twenty minutes earlier and although he'd have loved to stay around Waldemere for some time talking with Henry Engelhardt and Emily, he knew that he had much work to do that day.

He arrived at his place on Hathaway Avenue by a quarter past ten. To his astonishment, the driveway was completely devoid of vehicles. Corley, his downstairs neighbor, usually slept until close to twelve. Even at that, it was a rare sight to see her car not in the driveway. Also missing from the drive was the black Oldsmobile Bravada that was driven by her father, George, their landlord, who lived on the second floor of the house. From April through December, George would be out sailing on a freighter on the Great Lakes. His truck would normally be parked either at the office in Avon Lake or at some stone dock in northern Michigan. Seeing how it was mid-March, he should have been at home as well. He too was a late sleeper; a trait he had passed on to his daughter.

Seeing that the driveway was clear, Jack pulled in but left enough room behind his car should one of them return. He ascended the front stairs and entered his apartment where Shelby suddenly attacked him. She threw him against the wall and began to smother him passionately with kisses. Jack felt numb from head to toe. Seeing that he was about to fall over, she pulled away and let him regain his composure.

"Glad to see that you didn't forget about me," she remarked as he walked over to the couch and sat down. He looked at her with a curious smile.

"Like that's easy to do."

"So how was Waldemere?"

"Interesting," Jack said as he took off his jacket and set it on the ottoman beside the couch.

"Interesting how?"

"Well, I found a few things in the house that merit further looking into."

"Such as?"

"Such as a clock, the size of which I've never seen before. It's about forty feet wide and fifteen feet high. I found an access panel that took me behind the front and into the inner workings. I could see right off the bat the essential gears that drove the clock, but there were other mechanics that I couldn't figure out."

"So, you have no idea what they do?"

"None. That's one of the other reasons I stopped back here. I need to get my camera, take some pictures later, and send them to my dad. With luck, he'll have an idea what these other parts are for."

"I'd like to see this too. Make sure you save those pictures."

"Will do. Oh, I also found an old steamer trunk in a storage space beneath the room that I'm staying in."

"Really? What's inside?"

"I haven't the slightest idea. It's locked."

"Too bad. I'll bet there are some pretty interesting items in there."

"You know, I also read up on some of the legends about that house. The bedroom that I'm staying in was also the scene of a pretty horrific suicide."

Shelby got quiet at the mention of this. After a moment, she spoke up: her words barely audible.

"Whose suicide?"

"A man named Ludwig Engelhardt. He was Henry's grandfather's younger brother."

"I don't like it, Jack. Is there any way that you can request another room?"

"I suppose I could, but it's a nice room with an incredible view of the lake."

"The lake? Really?"

"Well, not only that, but nothing's happened since I've been there. I'm beginning to think that these stories about a haunting are all blarney; which is just as well."

"Still, I'd be cautious about staying in that room; regardless of whether it's haunted or not. I read that book that you wrote on Maul Manor. Even in that, you talk about impressions left behind on a site that can affect the psyche."

"I think it's pretty safe to say that I'm not going to get depressed and kill myself. Maul Manor was a different story anyway. It was only influencing those who already had a tendency towards mental disorder. Trust me. I'll be fine."

"If you say so."

The matter wasn't settled, but Shelby saw no point in continuing this discussion. Jack's mind was made up and there was no changing it.

He got up from the couch, walked over to his desk and began to root around through the clutter that took up most of his work area. At last, he located his camera and tucked it into the inside pocket of his distressed leather jacket. Next, he turned to his bookshelf and began to browse the many volumes until he came to one entitled *Tracker Organs: Manufacturing, Maintenance and Repair*. The book had once belonged to his father and had been passed on to him in hopes that one day he'd follow in his father's footsteps. Granted, there wasn't a lot of money in pipe organ building, but then, Jack's father didn't seem to think there was much in historical research either.

"What's that?" Shelby asked as he set the book down on the desk.

"One of my dad's books. I'm hoping there might be something in here that explains the added features on that clock."

He'd opened the book and had begun to flip through its pages, but decided that there would be plenty of time to study it later. He closed it and put his jacket back on.

"You're not staying?"

"Can't. I have way too much research to do."

"Not even for little while?" There was something seductive in Shelby's voice that made Jack want to spend the rest of the afternoon with her. The way that she was looking at him made him want to toss the book on the floor, scoop her up and make passionate love to her. For a moment, he almost gave in, but checked himself.

"I really can't, but wish I could."

Shelby began to pout. Just then, Jack had an idea.

"Hold on. Would you be interested in coming with me?"

Shelby perked up at this and her frown turned to a smile in an instant.

"Do you really mean it?"

"Of course I do," Jack said cheerfully. He then turned

very serious. "Just remember the rules. If you talk to me, I probably won't reply. It'll look like I'm talking to myself. If you absolutely need to talk to me, you know the drill."

"I remember."

"If we're in a social situation with other people, don't touch me. The last thing I need is to fall into a daze in front of everyone."

"Got it. No touching. Check."

"And very importantly, no high jinks or shenanigans."

"Now what on Earth do you mean?"

"You know exactly what I mean. No moving things around, no opening and closing doors and absolutely no throwing things."

Shelby sighed.

"Fine. You might as well take all the fun out of being a ghost."

"I'm serious. If we're going to spend days together like this, I'm going to need your full cooperation. Maybe in the future, I'll be able to tell someone about you, but until then, we have to act normal. Got it?"

"Alright, alright. I got it. So where are we going?"

"First stop is the county justice center. I have some court records to locate."

"Bo-ring."

"Hey, do you want to come with me or not?"

"Okay. Court records. Fun. Where to after that?"

"Well, if you can manage not to be too disruptive, we can stop at McNamara's."

"Do you really mean it?"

Jack had often talked about McNamara's Pub, but had never actually taken Shelby there; mostly out of fear that she'd slip into her usual playful self and create a scene. They'd been together for close to five months now, and he figured that it was about time for her to see where he hung out.

"I mean it. And yes, some of my friends will be up there. Just please promise me that you won't act up."

"I promise," Shelby answered with a grin. Just then, Jack's phone rang. It was Corley, his downstairs neighbor.

"Hey Jack. Are you leaving anytime soon?"

"On my way out right now."

"Okay, cause, dad and I were at breakfast and just got back. You might want to pull out so you don't get blocked in."

"I'm coming down." Jack hung up the phone and turned to Shelby. "Well, shall we?"

Jack and Shelby found a parking spot right on Lakeside Avenue in downtown, which was lucky, especially at that time of day. They couldn't spend too much time there though, as they had parked at a one-hour parking meter. Jack was glad that he always kept an ample supply of quarters in the center console of his car. If this took longer than anticipated, he'd have to make multiple trips back to the meter.

They arrived at the justice center where, at the security checkpoint, Jack was forced to set everything on his person, including his jacket, belt, suspenders and shoes, into a plastic bin. He then stepped through a metal detector and was found to be clean. Shelby, though she didn't need to go through this screening process, chose to pass through the metal detector as well. Alarms sounded and lights began to flash erratically, which really had the security guards baffled, as no one to their knowledge was walking through. Shelby stifled a laugh as she joined Jack at his side.

"Who knew I had such a magnetic personality?" she said. Jack glanced over at her with a disapproving look. He never really cared for puns.

They passed through the glass doors on the second floor and entered the Clerk of Courts office. It was here that Brion had told Jack that court records were kept. Jack approached the counter and after a moment, was greeted by a receptionist.

"Can I help you, sir?"

"Yes," Jack began. "I'm looking for records involving a court case that may have occurred some time ago."

"Request forms are located in that stack over there," the receptionist said as she pointed to a table with multiple stacks of papers on it. "Fill it out and bring it back up after you have done so."

"Thank you."

Jack walked over to the table, found the request form for

court transcripts and sat down in a chair that was located along the wall. He filled out the form with as much information as he could come up with, which really wasn't that much. He couldn't give an exact date for when the case would have occurred, only a year of 1883. Furthermore, the only name he could put down was Heinrich Engelhardt. He also added that it was a murder charge. After reviewing all that he had written, Jack brought the form back up to the receptionist and handed it to her.

"This will take some time. Please have a seat and I'll let you know when I've located your request."

Jack nodded, turned and began to make his way back to the row of chairs along the wall, but was stopped before he could reach them.

"I'm sorry, sir?" the receptionist called out to him, "but we don't keep court records this far back."

"Oh," Jack said as he walked back over to her.

"Yes, you see? This court record that you're requesting is from 1883. We only keep records from 1912 to the present at this facility. You'll need to go to the Cuyahoga County Court House across the street. Go down into the basement and find room 37. That's the Common Pleas Court Microfilm Room. They should be able to help you over there."

Jack took back the form, thanked her and left. He and Shelby stopped at the car to feed the meter, then crossed the street and entered the old courthouse on Lakeside. Again, Jack had to pass through security and again, Shelby amused herself by setting off the metal detectors.

"Do you really need to do that?" he mumbled out of the corner of his mouth as they walked down the broad marble steps that led into the basement.

"I can't help it," Shelby replied. "It makes me feel kind of funny."

"That's because you're drawing off the energy being put out by the metal detector. Sort of like when you mess with my television or the lights in my place. Trish explained all of this. Remember?"

"Yeah. But it's not doing any harm."

Jack knew that she was right. Besides, it was fun to watch the security guards scratch their heads over why their equipment was being set off for no reason.

"Let's just keep it to a minimum. Okay?"

"Fine."

"Here we are," Jack quietly said, "Room 37."

They entered and Jack approached the receptionist and explained what he was looking for.

"Criminal court records," the receptionist told him, "are arranged by year. You can find them in this drawer and view them on that machine over there." She pointed him in the direction of a microfilm viewer across the room. "If you need to make copies, do so. They'll come out on a printer behind the counter. Copies are ten cents and you can pay for them when you pick them up."

The receptionist returned to the counter and left Jack to the task of finding the court records for Heinrich Engelhardt. Nearly half an hour had passed before Jack finally came across a page stamped *July 30, 1883*. Below this was scribbled out the words: *Inquiry, Heinrich Engelhardt*. He'd found it. Without reading any of the contents, he tapped the print button on the front of the microfilm viewer and could hear the page being printed out across the room behind the counter. He scrolled to the next page and again hit print. He repeated this fifteen more times before he finally came to a page marked *July 30, 1883, Criminal Hearing: Philip Doris*: a different court case.

Jack rewound the microfilm, tucked it back into its box and returned it to the counter to be filed by the receptionist. He paid for the seventeen pages, thanked the receptionist, and left the courthouse. As he and Shelby approached his car, he could see a meter attendant making his way up Lakeside Avenue towards them. Jack checked the meter, which only had two minutes left, and got in. He started the car and drove away, thankful that he'd managed to avoid yet another parking ticket.

"So are we really going to McNamara's?" Shelby asked as they got onto the westbound entrance ramp of the Shoreway.

"Absolutely. Besides, I could really use a drink."

"Oh, come on. I wasn't that bad."

"No. You were fine. And yes, that was pretty funny about the metal detector."

"I wonder if they're going to call a repairman. Oh, let's go back. That was so much fun."

"Another time, perhaps."

Shelby rested her head on Jack's shoulder and closed her eyes. It tingled a little, but wasn't nearly enough to cause him any great distraction. In no time at all, they had reached the western end of the Shoreway and turned left onto Lake Avenue. They passed under the railroad trestle where Jack pulled the car over to the side of the road.

As they walked into McNamara's, they were greeted by a surprisingly large crowd for two in the afternoon. Shelby looked about herself with a slight touch of awe. After a moment, she turned to Jack and smiled.

"It's just as you described it."

Jack returned the smile and gave her a slight nod. He immediately took a seat somewhere around the middle of the melee and hung his jacket over the back of the stool. Positive Bill was off that day and it was Megan who came up and asked him what he wanted.

"Guinness, of course," Jack replied.

Megan, a pretty girl in her early twenties, set herself to the task of pouring the draught. Shelby eyed Jack with contempt.

"Just don't let me catch you gawking at her," she jealously told him. Jack shot her a quick look out of the corner of his eyes.

"Jack. It's a little early to see you up here," Jerry said as he strolled over. "You must have gotten the memo."

"Afraid I missed it. What's going on?"

"Oh. A bunch of us decided to take a half a day and get together for an early happy hour."

"Really? What's the occasion?"

"No occasion. Just a congregation of friends."

"Well, that's reason enough I guess. I had some work to do downtown and thought I'd pop in for a couple."

"How are things coming along at Waldemere?"

"Not bad. I just pulled some court records and plan to look over them later."

Brion overheard this and walked over to Jack and Jerry.

"So you had no trouble finding them?" Brion asked.

"None, but they weren't at the Justice Center."

"Old courthouse?"

"Yep. Found them in no time."

"I'm surprised that there was anything at all on a case that old."

"Well, the documents seem to be entirely hand-written. It'll give me a chance to brush up on my Nineteenth Century script reading skills."

"This is what you talk about up here?" Shelby asked, seemingly bored out of her head. Again, Jack simply glanced over at her.

"So the ghosts of Waldemere haven't gotten you yet?" Ed called out from two stools over. "How are they treating you up there?"

"Pretty well, I have to say."

"Well, if this Engelhardt guy gives you any grief, just let me know. We'll bring the smack-down on him, Angle style."

Jack shook his head and chuckled. Again, it was Ed with the Angle talk.

"What's he mean by that?" asked Shelby. Jack ignored her. Answers would have to wait until they were alone.

"I'll keep that in mind," Jack replied to Ed's comment. Just then, the door opened and a cold breeze crossed the barroom. For a moment, Jack thought that Shelby had opened the door; something he had asked her not to do. In turning, he found her still at his side.

"What?" she exclaimed.

Jack glanced over to the door and saw a small group of people enter. Among them, he recognized Timothy Moon, an editor from The Ohio City Argus. The Argus, a weekly paper, had taken its name from a periodical that had been published in Ohio City during the 1830's, while Ohio City was still a separate entity from the City of Cleveland. Jack and Mr. Moon had met on numerous occasions, but moved in different social circles. They were friendly with one another, but neither ever went out of their way to carry on anything even closely resembling a lengthy conversation. Thus it was that Jack was quite surprised to see him now at McNamara's. He was even more surprised when Mr. Moon approached him.

"Mr. Sullivan," he warmly greeted. "Fancy running into you up here."

"I'm here quite often," Jack replied. "But you?"

"First time. My sister's idea." He motioned to a woman that was among the small group he had entered with.

There was something quite smug about the way that Timothy Moon carried himself. It was almost as if he believed that the entire world only existed for his uses and amusements.

"Well, I highly recommend the Guinness. It's a fresh keg nearly every other day."

As Jack said this, Megan finished filling his glass and brought it over to him.

"I'll have a Smithwick's, if you please," Mr. Moon told the bartender. Megan promptly pulled out a glass and poured him a beer. "Guinness is a little too heavy for my liking." Megan set the glass in front of Mr. Moon who raised it to Jack. "To you, Mr. Sullivan."

"Sláinte," Jack replied as he likewise raised his glass, reciting the traditional Irish toast. Both took a drink and set their beers of choice back down on the bar.

"So," Timothy Moon continued, "I hear that you're currently researching Waldemere. Is that true?"

"I wonder where you heard that from." Jack said as he glanced down the bar. Jerry, Brion and Ed had returned to the conversation they'd been having before Jack had arrived.

"Oh, this city tends to talk and I definitely have ears for the listening."

"I see."

"So, is it true then?"

Seeing no harm in telling him, Jack explained the case.

"It's true. I've been hired by the house's new owner to research the property and to help clear his great grandfather's name."

"Clear his great grandfather's… you can't mean. Is it an Engelhardt that has bought the house?"

"It is. His name's Henry and he's the great grandson of Heinrich Engelhardt."

"Now that's a story."

"I guess so."

"And do you have any intentions of publishing your findings?"

Jack looked perplexed at this comment.

"How do you mean?"

"Well, like those other books that you've written."

"I really don't think that there's enough for an entire book about Waldemere. Besides, it's already been written about in other books."

"But not the true story. As near as I know, no one's ever had a chance to talk with a descendant of Heinrich Engelhardt. You're in a rare position, Mr. Sullivan, from where I'm sitting."

"I guess I've never thought about it like that."

"And you say that there isn't enough for a whole book on the subject, but maybe there's enough for an article."

Jack could finally see where Timothy Moon was going.

"This would be something that the Argus would be interested in printing?"

"Absolutely. We can't pay you anything for it, of course, seeing as it's a free paper, but still, it'll give you something to add to your résumé."

Just then, Shelby was filled with misgivings on the idea and tapped Jack's shoulder to get his attention. He ignored her at first, thinking that she was just goofing around with him.

"Jack, ring-ring. You need to use your phone," she said at last. That was their signal. If she really needed to talk to him, he would pretend to make a telephone call. This way, it wouldn't look like he was talking to himself. He nodded slowly, letting her know that he'd heard her and knew what she meant.

"Well, I'll have to run it by Mr. Engelhardt and see what he says about all of this. After all, he may request anonymity when it comes to this matter."

"I can't see why he would," Mr. Moon continued. "After all, what better way to publicly clear his great grandfather's name than to have your findings published in a local paper for everyone to read."

"Still, I'll have to check with him first."

"Ring-ring, Jack!" Shelby announced again.

"Actually, if you'll excuse me for a moment, I have to make a phone call."

"You take your time, Mr. Sullivan. I'll be right here."

Jack got up from his stool, donned his jacket and stepped out the back door and onto the patio. He pulled out his phone, pretended to dial a number and held it to his head.

"Okay, so what's going on?" he said, not looking directly at Shelby.

"I don't trust this guy," she explained.

"Why not?"

"I don't know. There's just something a little off about him."

"I've met him before. From what I know, he's perfectly trustworthy."

"I don't know, Jack. He seems like he's got some ulterior motive for wanting to publish your findings."

"What, like he's going to take credit for it or something?"

"Maybe. But don't you find it just a little odd that he happens in here at the same time that you do, a place that he's never been before, and suddenly he wants to publish your findings. I remember you telling me how hard it is to get your work published and now, all of a sudden, the opportunity falls into your lap by coincidence. It just doesn't feel right."

"I call it a lucky break. He's never asked me to submit anything to The Argus before. If I can get my name out there more often, maybe it'll open up some new windows of opportunity."

"Would you look at me and stop staring off into space?"

Jack looked directly into her big blue eyes.

"Better?"

"Yes. Thank you. All I'm saying is that maybe I'd talk to others that have submitted works to him before committing to it."

"I already have and there's never been a complaint about his presentation of their works before. He doesn't do any unnecessary editing and has always given the writer full credit."

Shelby could see again that there was no winning this argument. Jack's mind was set and if Henry Engelhardt was willing to go along with it, he'd publish his findings with The Argus.

"Are we done?" he asked at last.

"Yeah, I guess."

Jack pretended to hang up the phone and stepped back inside. Timothy Moon was still sitting at the bar where Jack had left him.

"Well, I wasn't able to get hold of Mr. Engelhardt," Jack began, "but will likely run into him later on this evening."

"Wonderful," Mr. Moon declared as he handed Jack a business card. "Please do give me a call once you've spoken with him and tell me your answer."

Jack took the card from him and smiled as he placed it in his wallet. Shelby, on the other hand, seemed quite agitated by all of this. Jack glanced at her and, seeing her eyes flash green for a moment, could tell at once what she was up to. Unfortunately, there was no stopping her. She took a large swing at Timothy Moon and knocked his Smithwick's from his hand. The glass went flying across the room and smashed into about a dozen pieces.

"My word!" Mr. Moon announced. "I'm sorry. I don't know what just happened there."

Jack turned to Shelby and gave her a look of disdain.

"I'll be at home, Jack. Maybe I'll see you the next time you decide to drop by and grace me with your presence."

Without having to open the door, she stormed out of the bar and headed west down Lake Avenue. Before she had passed the last window, she'd vanished.

Feeling bad for what had just happened, Jack ordered up another Smithwick's for Timothy Moon. He also ordered a second Guinness for himself. As he slowly sipped it, he thought about what Shelby had said to him. It did seem odd that Timothy Moon would happen into McNamara's by chance and offer to publish his findings. Perhaps it was just fate. Still, Jack wasn't one to pass up an opportunity like this. Regardless, he felt bad for snubbing Shelby like that. Maybe if he had talked with her further on the matter, she'd have been set more at ease with the idea. He definitely owed her an apology, at the very least.

After finishing his Guinness and saying goodbye, Jack hopped into his car and made his way back towards Waldemere. He still had much to research.

Chapter 9

Jack returned to Waldemere that afternoon with a lot on his mind. As he strode up the driveway, he wondered what he should research next. Moreover, he wondered how best to approach Henry Engelhardt on the prospect of having his findings published in the local paper. This, he decided, he would bring up at dinner. The worst he could say was no.

He neared the side door and, realizing that there was no music coming from downstairs, suspected that Emily might not be there to let him in. A moment later, he heard a crash from down in what he assumed to be the kitchen. This was followed by the sound of a young woman cursing with a thick Cockney accent. Knowing that it was going to be one more hassle for her, Jack rang the bell anyway. Instantly, the cursing ceased and light footsteps could be heard running up the stairs to the side door. Emily opened it and looked more flushed than she had the previous afternoon when he'd caught her in the middle of cutting loose to the Sex Pistols.

"Mr. Sullivan. Excuse me."

"Are you alright, Emily?"

"A bit o' a mishap in the kitchen. Nothin' ya should worry about though. Please, come in."

Jack entered and stomped his shoes. Most of the snow they had received from the storm that previous Saturday evening had melted. Still, there was a significant amount of it lying about in isolated pockets throughout the city. Jack had managed to step into a slushy drift while exiting his car.

"Is there anything that I can help you with?" he asked as she closed the door behind him.

"Oh no Mr. Sulli... Jack. Sorry. No, I'm perfectly alright. Just dropped a stack o' pots is all. Can I bring ya anythin'?"

"No thank you, Emily. I'm going to go up and do a little research."

"Very well. Dinner is at six as always. We're 'avin' pot roast with turnips, cabbage and russets and a noice ale and cheese soup to boot."

"Sounds wonderful. I'll be down in time."

Jack excused himself and made his way upstairs to the fourth floor bedroom. He set his notebook and his father's pipe organ repair book down on the desk, took off his jacket and hung it on a hook in the closet. He walked back over to the desk and opened his notebook. Here he reviewed what he had achieved thus far that day. The first note he came to was about stopping by his house. He instantly thought of Shelby and how upset she must be with him. Perhaps he'd go back to the house that evening to talk things out with her. After all, she had just been looking out for his well-being.

After a moment, Jack remembered why he had stopped by his house in the first place. It was to pick up his camera. He pulled out his flashlight, got up, walked back over to the closet and withdrew the digital camera from the inside pocket of his jacket. There were photos that needed to be taken.

Jack found himself standing in the ballroom once again. The beautiful sunshine that had graced Cleveland earlier that day had faded and was now replaced by a gray and overcast sky. He would need to use the flash if he was going to get any decent pictures. He stood before the massive oaken clock and began to take snapshots of every feature that the clock bore on its façade. As he got closer, he realized that one of the hand-carved hornets was slightly askew. He ran his finger along it and it turned ever so slightly. Trying to nudge it back into its original position, the figure twisted and suddenly clicked. Thinking that he may have broken a priceless item, he quickly turned it back into the position that he had first found it in. After resetting it successfully, he resigned himself not to touch any of the carvings from here on, should something like that happen again.

He next proceeded into the fourth floor turret room, located the chain that hung from the ceiling and gave it a slight yank. Instantly, the access panel swung open and Jack entered the mechanical space.

He was greeted again by the familiar musty smell and clicking of the gears. It was very tight in this space, but he managed to squeeze past most of the mechanisms. He began to take pictures of everything that he could see, starting with the parts that obviously drove the clock and eventually moving on to those parts that mystified him. As he was concluding his photo session with the clock, there was a sudden whirring sound that made him jump. He hadn't heard this sound before and was worried that it had something to do with the figure he had disturbed on the front of the clock. The sound lasted for fifteen seconds and as abruptly as it had started, it stopped.

Jack had had enough. He exited the machine space and closed the access panel behind him. As he reentered the ballroom, he took another glance at the clock and snapped one more photo. After he had done so, he looked down at the image he had just taken on the digital display and realized what may have caused the sound. It was now four o'clock. Perhaps, he surmised, the clock was trying to chime.

Jack was sitting back in the bedroom with his laptop open on the desk in front of him. He had ejected the memory card from his camera and had inserted into the slot on the side of the computer. He uploaded the images, labeled them and pasted them into an email, which he sent to his father. After checking a few other emails that he had received over the past couple of days, he looked up at the clock on the fireplace mantle in his room and saw that it was close to six in the evening. He logged off and shut down the laptop; stowing it neatly in his satchel.

He arrived in the dining room with just a couple of minutes to spare. Mr. Engelhardt stood up as Jack entered the room.

"Good evening, Jack. How was your day?"

"Not bad, Henry. Yours?"

"Productive. Any new developments in your research?"

"Not yet. Today was mostly footwork with a lot of running around. Still, I'm hoping to hear back on a few things. I also managed to locate some records earlier, but haven't had a chance to read them yet."

Just then, Emily entered the room pushing a cart that contained two large silver serving bowls. Jack could instantly detect the aroma of pot roast seasoned to perfection. Emily set the bowls on the table, moved the cart to the side and took a seat with Jack and Mr. Engelhardt. They helped themselves to portions of soup and pot roast and began to eat. The conversation was light and free flowing. As dinner unwound and Emily cleared their plates, Jack brought up his chance meeting with Timothy Moon.

"So I happened to run into an acquaintance of mine earlier this afternoon while I was about. He's an editor for a local paper called The Ohio City Argus. Are you familiar with it?"

"I can't say that I am," Mr. Engelhardt replied.

"It's a local weekly paper that highlights stories from around the neighborhood."

"I see."

"Well, apparently the editor had caught wind of my research here at Waldemere and has suggested that I publish my findings in an article for his paper." Mr. Engelhardt gave Jack a look of apprehension. "When I had explained what my research entailed, he suggested that this would be a good way to publicly clear your great grandfather's name."

Henry Engelhardt slowly began to nod, as though he could see it all before him.

"That's not a bad idea, Jack. Besides, I had mentioned that I should get to know some of the neighbors if I'm going to live here. What better way to meet them? You go ahead and publish your findings in this paper. I look forward to reading your article."

Emily returned to the dining room with a large bowl of chocolate mousse and three small dessert dishes. She scooped out the mousse and passed it around. As she did, Mr. Engelhardt told her about the article that Jack was going to write for the Argus. She didn't reply to this, only gave Jack a confident smile.

Seven thirty found Jack upstairs once again in the failing light of the fourth floor bedroom. He clicked on one of the Tiffany glass wall sconces by the bedroom door and walked over to the desk. He booted up his laptop and signed on again. There was a reply from his father. Jack opened the email and read its content.

Jack,
Looked at the pictures that you sent me. WOW! WHAT A HOUSE!!! I can't get over some of the jobs that you manage to pick up. OK. As far as the pictures go, they do look a lot like something in a tracker organ. If you remember, the rods inside that look like this are the ones that are connected to the draw knobs. This is what turns the stops on and off to give the organ its different sounds. If these were for the keyboard, they would be a set of levers, and not rods. I'm guessing that these rods are connected to something like draw knobs. You say that they simply run into the backside of the facade, but I think that there's a lot more to it than that. Look again at the front of that clock and see if you can find anything that looks like a draw knob. As far as what this might actually do, I'm afraid that I'm no wiser than you are.
Good luck and let me know what you find.
Mom wants to know if you'll be up anytime soon. The weather should be breaking in a couple of weeks and we're going to need some help cleaning up the yard after the disastrous winter we've had. There are sticks and branches down all over that need to be picked up. Give a call and let us know when you get a chance.
Dad

Jack reread the email his father had sent him. When he reached the part about looking again at the front of the clock and searching for a draw knob, Jack instantly remembered the hand-carved hornet that he had seen turned slightly askew earlier that evening. That must have been one of them.

He jumped up from the desk, picked up his flashlight and walked out of the bedroom and into the ballroom. Across the floor, in the gathering darkness, he could just make out a few images on the clock. He turned on his flashlight and slowly approached. In the bottom left-hand corner of the clock face, he located the hornet that he'd noticed was turned earlier. He carefully ran his finger along the piece once again. After a moment, he mustered up the courage, grabbed it firmly, turned it to the right and gave it a tug. Instantly there was a winding sound followed by a sudden thump.

Nothing else happened.

Jack stepped over and tried the other hornet. Again, there were the same sounds and again, nothing happened. Maybe, he thought, it wasn't just the hornets. He shined the light about the woodwork until he came to one of the two birds. At once he realized that it was a crow. Jack tried to turn the figure, but it wouldn't move. He tried to wiggle the head, but again nothing budged. He tried pulling, but it was firmly locked in place. Finally, he gave it a shove and it slowly sank beneath the surface of the rest of the façade. There were three large ticks followed by a thud, but as was the case with the hornets, nothing else happened. He tried the other crow and it did the same but nothing else.

He took a few paces back and shined the light about the rest of the clock. All of the other carved items, to the best of his knowledge, hadn't changed in any way. Then, there was a large click as the minute hand advanced and both hornets and the crows reset themselves into their original positions.

His father was right. There were in fact draw knobs on the front of this clock. They had been cleverly disguised as ornamental figures. Although Jack had managed to locate them, he still had no idea what they did.

He returned to his room, opened his notebook and jotted all of this down. No one would put these features on there if they didn't serve some purpose. He liked a good mystery, but this one really had him stumped.

Jack turned back to his laptop and decided to take his research in another direction. There was still the mystery regarding Tillie Engelhardt. Henry hadn't mentioned anything in his research regarding her after her marriage to Charles Bell, only a footnote that said "no issue." *Ghost Stories of Northern Ohio* had also claimed that she had no children of her own. Already, Jack had found holes in that story. Perhaps this was another.

He signed onto a genealogy research site and began to run random searches for Tillie and Charles Bell. His first attempt yielded results at once. The 1900 U.S. Census came up and listed them as living on Lake Avenue in Lakewood. Jack brought up the actual document and read its content.

Tillie Bell was listed as a white female, born in November of 1859 and was now forty years of age. She had been married for the past nine years, was a mother of three children, only one of which was still alive. Jack looked at the name listed below hers. It belonged to her four-year-old son James, who had been born in October of 1896.

Jack checked the 1910 U.S. Census and found Tillie and James Bell but noticed that Charles was not listed. Furthermore, Tillie was indicated as being a widow. Jack quickly brought up the Cleveland Necrology File: a list of everyone who had died in the greater Cleveland area between 1850 and 1975. He typed in Charles Bell's name and came up with many results. After scrolling through a couple of pages, he finally located Tillie's husband.

From what he could see, Charles Bell had passed away in the summer of 1906 at the age of fifty-one. It struck Jack as odd that this was the same time that both of Tillie's parents had died; likely a sorrowful and troubling time for her, he thought. The necrology file listed Charles as the husband of Tellie, an obvious misprint, and as the father of James. Burial was at Calvary Cemetery. From this, Jack knew right away that Charles Bell was Roman Catholic.

He continued to read the rest of the 1910 Census and learned that Tillie and James were now living back in Cleveland in an apartment building on the west side. Where in 1900, Tillie was listed simply as keeping house, a term used to describe a homemaker; she was now employed as a secretary at an oven making facility. The untimely death of her husband had apparently compelled her to enter the work force. James was listed as being fourteen and attending school.

Jack continued to follow the Bells through the next two censuses. In 1920, they were living in a house on Poe Avenue and by 1930, Tillie was listed as living with a friend named Frances Mackenzie on West 44th Street. James was living two doors away with his wife and two-year-old daughter, Belinda. Jack thought himself fortunate that they had given their daughter such an uncommon name. She would be easier to trace.

Next, Jack consulted the Cuyahoga County Marriage Index. Here he entered Belinda Bell's name and discovered that she had married a man named Richard Hyde. First, Jack ran a search for Richard Hyde living in the Cleveland area, but found no listing. Realizing that he may be deceased, Jack next ran a search on Belinda Hyde and came up with a person fitting that name living on Normandy Avenue in Bay Village. It had to be her. By his best guess, she would be somewhere close to eighty.

All in all, the book was wrong. So were Henry Engelhardt's notes for that matter. A visit to Belinda Bell-Hyde was definitely in order. Perhaps Henry might even be interested in meeting her. Still, Jack thought, he'd sit quietly on this information until after he'd met with her. It certainly would make for one hell of a surprise.

Jack looked over at the clock on the wall in his room. It was nearly eleven. Somehow, he'd lost track of time while looking up the information on Tillie's descendants; a common problem he'd had many times in the past. Furthermore, it was now too late for him to drive to Lakewood and apologize to Shelby for earlier. It'd be well after twelve by the time he'd have gotten back and he didn't want to wake Emily that late to let him in. It would have to wait until the morning.

Just then, he remembered the pages he'd printed out at the courthouse in regards to Heinrich Engelhardt's murder charge. He pulled these pages out from the back of his notebook and set them on the bed. He changed, brushed his teeth, swished for about a minute with some mouthwash and climbed into bed. He picked up the pages, started with the one marked *July 30, 1883, Inquiry, Heinrich Engelhardt* and began to read its content.

Being sworn before the constable named James Hopewell of the City of Cleveland, Cuyahoga County, State of Ohio comes the testimony of one Miss Bertha Johnston of same in regards to allegations against one Mr. Heinrich Engelhardt of same. These allegations were laid down on Thursday, the 19th day of July 1883.

Allegations are for the case of the murders of three young women of this city whose names are to follow.

It is sworn by Miss Bertha Johnston that on an evening in late August of 1879, Mr. Engelhardt's cousin's daughter, a woman so named Anna Stadler, was killed within the walls of Mr. Engelhardt's home on Franklin Street and that the deed was so cleverly covered up that never was there a question regarding the girl's disappearance.

It is further sworn that in early March of 1881, a servant in the home named Harriett Fischer, age seventeen years, was brutalized and slain by Mr. Engelhardt. When confronted by Miss Johnston on this matter, said Engelhardt explained that the girl had departed their home in the night, taking with her a number of items of valuable consideration. Regardless of his claim, Miss Harriett Fischer has not been seen in this city since the evening in question.

Jack remembered reading the name Henrietta in the book on Northern Ohio ghosts. He also remembered seeing a cook named Harriett Fischer living with the Engelhardts at the time of the 1880 Census. This had to be the same girl. He read on.

Miss Johnston attempted to make contact with the family of Miss Fischer, though was unsuccessful in doing so.

Miss Johnston further states that she had approached authorities at this point but was turned away, for the person whom she was accusing was of such high standings and moral character in the community.

Next we come to the case of one Miss Katherine Fitzgerald, sixteen, servant in the Engelhardt home. It is claimed again by Miss Bertha Johnston that Heinrich Engelhardt did, on the afternoon of October the 3rd 1882, brutally murder the girl...

There came a sudden banging sound from Jack's bedroom door. At first, he thought that Emily was knocking, but almost at once realized that the sound wasn't coming from his door, but just beyond. He sat the pages down and looked attentively towards the door. There was dead silence. Jack caught his breath and tried to calm himself down. The noise had startled him and he now realized that he was actually shaking. This was absolutely ridiculous to him. More than likely, Emily had dropped another stack of pots in the kitchen and the sound was reverberating up the dumbwaiter shaft. Jack picked up the court records and continued to read.

It is claimed again by Miss Johnston that Heinrich Engelhardt did, on the afternoon of October the 3rd 1882, brutally murder the girl at his home on Franklin Street. Miss Bertha Johnston successfully contacted Miss Fitzgerald's father in Ireland and it is, also, at his urging that this inquiry into the disappearances of these girls is being made.

Sworn before me on this, the twentieth day of July, 1883 by the said Miss Bertha Johnston and Constable James Hopewell, both of Cleveland.

Rt. Hon. Harrison Vincent King
Judge, Cleveland City Court

Here follows the testimony of Mr. Heinrich Engelhardt in regards to the disappearances of Miss Anna Stadler, Miss Harriett Fischer, and...

Again, there was another loud bang and Jack, so startled at the noise, nearly threw the court pages across the room. There had to be an explanation for all of this. He climbed out of the bed, donned his plaid terrycloth robe and opened the door.

Nothing.

The ballroom was extremely cold, dark and empty and the house completely still. The only sound he could hear was coming from the large clock across the ballroom floor. It ticked in the same way that it always had. Jack actually found the sound quite tranquil and easy to fall asleep to. He turned back into the bedroom and closed the door behind him. While he was crossing the room back towards his four-poster bed, he thought he heard someone talking out in the ballroom. He quickly marched over to the desk, picked up his small LED flashlight, returned to the bedroom door and flung it open.

Again nothing.

As he turned to reenter his bedroom, he heard the talking once more, somewhere across the room, in the darkness. Although the voice was more like a whisper, he could definitely tell that it belonged to a female. Perhaps Emily, he thought, may have strayed up there and was talking on a cell phone. This made no sense to him. Why would she come up there? Maybe her reception was bad on the first floor. Whatever the case, she was standing somewhere over by the massive clock across the room.

"Emily?" he called out.

There was no reply, only continued incoherent whispers.

Jack clicked on his flashlight and shined it in her direction. To his astonishment, the room was completely empty. Still, he could hear her voice. He slowly approached the clock. With each step, the voice got clearer and clearer. It wasn't until he was about twenty feet away from the clock that he realized the voice wasn't that of a Cockney girl from the East End of London. It was Irish, definitely Irish. Even at that, he couldn't make out everything that she was saying. Occasionally he would catch a word like "trouble" or "danger" but it wasn't until he heard the word "thevshi" that he found himself sincerely frightened. He knew very well what that word meant. It was the Irish word for ghost.

Still standing about twenty feet from the clock, he gave it another solid look with his flashlight. Still, he could see no one there. Just then, a thought occurred to him. Perhaps this person was inside the clock. He was about to make his way over to the turret room and gain entry to the mechanical space when he suddenly noticed that the facade was starting to move. The hand-carved figures began to twist and turn and dance about in all directions: slowly at first, then faster and faster. He also noticed that the ticking of the clock was getting louder, so to the point that it was starting to pound in his head. He heard the girl with the Irish accent repeat those terrifying words again.

"Thevshi… thevshi… thevshi!"

Jack was about to turn and run, but before he could, he heard the sound of heavy footsteps come charging at him from out of the clock and although he had his flashlight pointed in the direction from which these footsteps were racing at him, he could see no one approaching.

Ten feet away.

Five feet away.

And just like that, he was picked up and thrown backwards, clear across the ballroom floor. Jack skidded to a halt up against the far northern wall just outside of his bedroom. Though his whole body was racked with pain, he quickly scrambled to his feet and ran into the bedroom, slamming the door behind him. He threw the bolt, firmly locking the door.

Jack was truly scared out of his wits. He rounded the room and turned on every light that he could find. Within a minute, the bulbs in these had all blown out: all except for the Tiffany shaded sconce on the wall by the door. Across the room, Jack heard a snap and a creaking sound. To his horror, he watched as the window sash slowly opened about a foot, all on its own accord. A cold March wind blew into the chamber. Mustering up all that was left in his spirit, Jack ran across the room, slammed the window shut, locked it, and jumped into the bed. He lay there under the blankets with only the one light near the door to illuminate the room. For nearly two hours he holed up under the covers in terror, waiting for something else to happen, but nothing did. Eventually, he managed to fall asleep from sheer exhaustion.

That was it. He was done with this case.

Chapter 10

By nine o'clock on Wednesday morning, Jack Sullivan's bags were packed and he was ready to leave Waldemere for good. He had dressed as quickly as possible and was loading his suitcase into the dumbwaiter when Emily came knocking at the bedroom door.

"Mr. Sullivan?" she inquired.

"Yes, Emily. You can come in."

The door opened and Emily entered.

"I wanted to let ya know that breakfast will be on the table in…" Emily turned and noticed that Jack's bags were packed and the suitcase sitting in the dumbwaiter. "Are ya leavin' us, Mr. Sullivan?"

"I am."

"And is Mr. Engelhardt aware of this?"

"Not yet, but I'll be sure to tell him once I come down."

Emily was quiet for a moment, then spoke up.

"'As somethin' happened?"

"Yes. Something has."

"Did ya…" She chose her words very carefully. "Did ya *see* somethin'? Somethin' not normal?"

Jack looked at her as though he could tell that she was wise to the events that had transpired the night before.

"Why do you ask? Have you seen something?"

"I have," she whispered. Jack knew right away that her whisper was not the same one that he had heard the night before.

"And what have you seen?"

Emily's eyes darted around the room as though she were worried that someone might be listening.

"I don't come up 'ere if I can 'elp it. Not at noight, at least. I've 'eard people that aren't there and 'ave seen things that shouldn't be. That clock across the ballroom; I've seen it do things: unnatural things."

"Oh?"

"I've seen it move. Sometoimes when I come up 'ere, I get scratches on me arms, I do. Sometimes at noight, I 'ear the most 'orrible sounds comin' from these rooms. I wish that Mr.

Engelhardt would've put ya in a different room other than this one. I tried to talk him out o' it, but 'e insisted."

"Yeah. I think I may have brought that on myself."

"'Ow do ya mean?"

"Well, that first day that I was here, I asked him if the house was really haunted."

"And that's when 'e invited ya to stay the week, isn't it?"

Jack nodded.

"But I think I have my answer now and can leave."

"Please don't leave, Jack. Not until ya 'ave spoken with Mr. Engelhardt, at least."

"Is he up?"

"Yes, 'e's down in the dinin' room readin' the paper. Come on. I'll take ya to 'im."

Jack picked up his jacket and cap and followed Emily down the stairs and to the second floor where he found Henry Engelhardt sitting at the long dining room table, with a few newspapers in front of him.

"Ah, good morning Jack. Can I offer you a paper? Let's see. I have The Wall Street Journal, The Boston Globe, The Plain Dealer and look; I even picked up a copy of The Ohio City Argus. You're right. This is a pretty good paper."

"No, thank you."

"Suit yourself. So, how did you sleep?"

Jack looked at Mr. Engelhardt with a hint of surprise. There was no way that he could have possibly slept through the banging that was coming from just one floor above him.

"Um…"

"Ah," Mr. Engelhardt said at seeing Jack's expression. "So you finally got to meet our resident ghost?"

"I'd probably say that it was a little more than a friendly meeting."

"Didn't scare you too much, I hope."

"Mr. Sullivan's bags are packed, Mr. Engelhardt," Emily chimed in.

Mr. Engelhardt gave Jack a hurt look.

"Please say that isn't so, Jack."

"I'm afraid it is."

"Well, you had asked if the house was really haunted and

that wasn't something that I could simply say yes or no to. You had to find that out for yourself. I apologize if the disturbance was too disruptive, but I will say this. They're not a common occurrence. You're actually very lucky. As I understand it, many people have come to this house in the past hoping to have an experience such as that, but leave here disappointed."

"I wouldn't go as far as to say that I'm lucky."

Henry Engelhardt could see that he was losing this discussion.

"Is there anything that I can do, Jack, to keep you here?"

Jack thought about it for a moment. He had come to this house to do research and thus far, he'd made some real progress. He had asked if the house was really haunted and was pretty sure that he now had the answer to that. It was true that he could continue the research without staying there, but there were still so many mysteries about the house that needed to be solved. Having access to things like the clock, on a twenty-four hour basis, would certainly be beneficial. He milled it over in his head for another minute and ultimately came to the conclusion that it would be a shame to end his research here; especially with the prospect of having his work published in The Argus. Just then, another idea came to him. There might be a way for him to stay there without getting the full effects of the haunting. He'd have to confer with his friend Amy on this. At last, Jack spoke up.

"You say that the disturbances on the fourth floor aren't a common occurrence?"

"That's right," Mr. Engelhardt assured him.

"Then I think I may have a solution. I'll stay on, but if this doesn't work, I'm afraid to say that I'll have to drop this case."

"Jack, thanks for giving it another shot. And if there's anything that we can do to better accommodate you, please don't hesitate to let us know."

"Thank you, Henry. I'll bear that in mind."

Emily lightly touched Jack's shoulder.

"Can we get ya unpacked then?"

"Sure."

Jack followed Emily back upstairs to the fourth floor

bedroom. They entered and began to put Jack's clothes back in the dresser.

"I'm glad that ya 'ave changed your moind on this, Jack. I enjoy our little chats and would 'ate to see ya leave us so soon."

Jack was glad that she was becoming more comfortable around him and was finally using his given name more often.

As Jack drove west on the Shoreway towards Lakewood, he remembered that he still hadn't called back Timothy Moon to tell him that he was given the all clear by Mr. Engelhardt to go ahead and write the article. He pulled out his cell phone and the business card from his wallet and proceeded to dial Mr. Moon's number.

"Tim Moon," greeted a voice at the other end.

"Good morning, Mr. Moon. It's Jack Sullivan."

"Oh. Good morning. Do you have good news?"

"I do," Jack said as he reached the end of the Shoreway and proceeded down Clifton.

"That's great. How long do you think it'll take for you to write an article for me?"

"That depends. How long do you want it?"

"A couple thousand words ought to do the trick."

"Well, I should be done with my research by Sunday and could probably have an article ready for you that evening."

"Wunderbar!" Timothy Moon exclaimed, using the German phrase for wonderful, thinking it to be en vogue. "The paper goes to press on Monday and is released every Tuesday morning. Do you have any pictures to accompany this?"

"Not yet, but I may be able to come up with something over the next couple of days."

"Sounds great. Good luck, Mr. Sullivan. You can email your article to the web address on my business card. I look forward to reading it."

Timothy Moon promptly hung up and Jack put his phone back into his pocket.

Ten minutes later, he arrived at his place on Hathaway Avenue. Both George and Corley's vehicles were parked in the driveway and there was no room for him to pull in behind them.

He found a parking spot on the street about five doors down and walked back to the house.

"Shelby?" he called out as he entered his apartment.

"I'm in here," she replied from the back room. Jack joined her.

"Are you okay?"

"Oh, you mean from yesterday? Yeah, I'm fine."

"Look, Shelby, I'm really sorry about what happened at McNamara's. I know you were just looking out for me, but you know how I am. Once I get my mind set on something, there's very little chance of changing it."

"Stubbornness is not an admirable trait, you know."

"I know. I promise that I'll work on my compromising skills in the future." Jack suddenly noticed that she hadn't so much as looked at him the entire time, but rather was staring intently at the door to his spare room. "Um, what are you doing?"

"You know? I've been in every room in this apartment except for this one. I tried to go in, but for the strangest reason, I can't."

"And there's a very good reason for that," Jack replied with something of an all-knowing smile.

"I'm thinking that it has something to do with this lock."

She pointed at an iron padlock that held the door firmly secure.

"You'd be right. From what I was told when I purchased it, nothing otherworldly can pass beyond its seal."

"Looks pretty old."

"It is, early Seventeenth Century. As the story goes, this was the same padlock that was used to imprison Báthory Erzsébet."

"Who's that?" Shelby asked, finally turning to him.

"Also known as The Blood Countess, Elizabeth Báthory. She was a woman who used to round up young girls caught on the roads late at night, bring them back to her castle, and slaughter them."

"That's horrible!"

"That's not the worst of it," Jack continued. "Legends claim that she would drain their blood into a large tub or basin and soak in it. This, she believed, would keep her young and beautiful. Eventually she was arrested and locked in a tower at Csejte, Slovakia."

"And this is the same lock that was used to keep her in that tower?"

Shelby reached for the lock, touched it and pulled her hand away rather quickly, as though it had burned her.

"So I've been told. Are you okay?"

"Fine" Shelby said smartly. "Why do you keep it here?"

"Well, as the rest of the story goes, the people in the castle continued to hear the Blood Countess' screams for close to four years after her imprisonment began. It was quite hard for anyone to believe that she was actually still alive, seeing as she wasn't being given any food or water. Eventually, the tower was opened and her skeleton was discovered lying on the floor across the room. According to a physician, she had been dead for nearly all of those four years. The screams were something of a mystery that was never fully explained. A theory was put forth that the lock had managed to not only imprison her body, but her soul as well."

"Jack, did you buy this lock to keep me out of this room?"

"No. Actually, I've owned it for a few years now. The truth is, I'm trying to keep a few things in."

Shelby gave Jack a look of alarm.

"Such as what?"

"Such as... none of your business. We'll talk about it another time. Come on. Let's go into the living room."

Shelby followed Jack, but gave the lock on the spare room door another glace.

"So how did it go at Waldemere last night?" she asked.

"Well, I managed to figure out a few thing."

"Like?"

"Like that clock that I was telling you about. Apparently, some of those figures on the front are actually draw knobs that perform some function, but I still don't know what that is. Also, I've managed to locate a descendant of Tillie Engelhardt, Henry's grandfather's sister."

"Really?"

"Yep. What's more, she only lives over in Bay Village. I'm going to try to stop by there this afternoon."

Shelby gave Jack a solid look and could tell that he was keeping something from her.

"What else happened?"

"Nothing."

"Jack, you're a terrible liar."

Jack was reluctant to share his story about the disturbance he witnessed, but knew that she'd get it out of him somehow.

"Okay. I had an encounter late last night in the ballroom."

"What sort of encounter?"

"The kind where you hear voices of people that can't be seen and things move around on their own."

"Jack, I knew that something like this was going to happen. I warned you about it. But would you listen to me? No. You wouldn't."

"Look. It's okay. I've got an idea about how to prevent it from happening again. If it doesn't work, I'll drop the case."

"I wish you'd drop it right now."

"Well I seriously considered doing just that this very morning. I'm only giving it one more chance."

"Again Jack, stubbornness."

"I know, but something tells me that I need to see this through."

"Fine." Shelby got quiet for a moment before speaking up again. "So are you staying for a while?"

"I'm afraid that I can't. I have to try and meet with Tillie Engelhardt's granddaughter this afternoon, but before I do, I wanted to stop by Amy's shop."

"Amy's? You really are going to drastic measures."

"If anyone can help, she can." Jack looked over at the clock and saw that it was nearly noon. "I'd better get going. I probably won't be able to stop by later, but hope to sometime in the next day or two."

"Come here, you," Shelby demanded with outstretched arms. Jack walked over and embraced her warmly. His whole body went numb and it felt as though he were wrapped in a giant blanket of love. He regained consciousness a couple of minutes later, lying on his back, stretched out across the floor.

"I have to go," he said through a huge smile.

"Take care then, Jack"

He picked himself off the floor, put his jacket back on and descended the stairs. Shelby watched as his car drove past and out of sight. Her thoughts were always with him.

Jack pulled up outside of his friend Amy's apothecary and occult bookstore on Madison Avenue in Lakewood called *The Slithy Toves*. The name had been taken from a passage in Lewis Carroll's poem *Jabberwocky*. Amy was a huge fan of Carroll.

As far as Amy herself went, she was one of Jack's oldest friends and really something of a curious individual. When she was seven year old, Amy had asked her parents for a Voltron action figure. Instead, she had received a Barbie doll, and continued to receive more and more of them over the course of the next few years. Eventually, it got to the point where Amy and her sister Erin would end up playing a game they liked to call "Murder Barbie". In this, Barbie would always end up dead, in one fashion or another. Once in a while she would be poisoned. Occasionally, she would leap to her own death from the balcony of the Barbie Dream Home... or was she pushed? A few times, she'd been crushed by the elevator, and once she was even found beheaded: the head gruesomely discovered resting on the front seat of her sports car; the torso never fully recovered. Nine out of ten times, Skipper was the culprit, but occasionally Ken took the spotlight. That was Amy: truly as unique as they came.

As Jack opened the door, he was greeted by the deep ringing of an old Tibetan bell that hung in the doorway, which was struck anytime someone would enter the shop. The noise often made Jack want to deeply chant the word "Om" over and over again. This was the effect that Amy was going for. The main front room was two stories high with a walkway circling the second story. Along the walls up there, Jack could see endless rows of bookshelves. In the center of the ceiling above was a large oval skylight that let the early afternoon sun pour in. The walls, where not hidden by shelves, were crimson and burgundy with a ragged finish. The shop itself had an ancient feel and was ornamented with wrought iron candle holders.

Lingering in the air was the scent of sage, old paper and the music of a band called Corvus Corax: Common Crow in English. This band used medieval period instruments and heavy male chants. On shelves across the room were many colorful hinged-lid jars of jade, brown and indigo blue that contained powders and roots. Hanging upside down from the ceiling above the counter was a wide variety of herbs set to dry.

As Jack closed the door behind him, he looked down to his right and saw a few stacks of books that had yet to be filed away. Occupying a couple of these stacks were Amy's cats, Galileo and Bijou. She'd had Galileo, a large orange cat, for many years now. She'd only acquired Bijou within the last few years. Bijou, slender, brown and striped, used to live with Jack at his home in Avon Lake. When it came time to move, he could only bring two of his cats with him and settled on Fionn and Aislinn; neither of which could ever get along with Bijou. Amy was more than happy to bring this striped cat into her home.

It was no secret among any that knew her, Amy was a practicing witch, or a Wiccan, as she preferred. Her coven met here weekly and again for sacred observances. These, as Jack found out over time, were based upon a solar calendar. Equinoxes and solstices were the lesser Sabbaths with holidays such as Imbolg, Bealtaine, Lughnasadh and Samhain as the primaries. He had already familiarized himself with Samhain. Halloween, its Christian replacement, was another one of his favorite holidays.

"Jack!" exclaimed a young woman with short brown hair as she stepped out from a back room. "It's so good to see you."

"Hello, Amy," Jack greeted with a smile. "How've you been?"

"Good. Business is a little slow right now, but things will pick up once the Equinox arrives. What brings you by?"

"This is going to sound a little weird, but I was wondering if you had a remedy for keeping evil spirits at bay."

Amy gave Jack a good look up and down. He had never asked for anything like this before.

"And why do you think you would need this? I'm sorry.

I get asked that question a lot more often than you may think, but it's rarely *evil* spirits."

"Point taken. I just wanted to be on the safe side, I guess."

"Can you tell me what's up?"

Jack thought about it and saw no harm in telling her.

"Sure. It's Waldemere."

"Oh, Jerry told me about that. Heard it pays pretty well, too."

"I'm not complaining."

"Hmm. Not about that, at least." Amy thought for a moment. "Before I get myself involved, what has your cousin Trish said?"

"To be honest, I haven't told her about any of this yet."

Amy shook her head.

"What have you gotten yourself into?"

"Well, I had something of an encounter there last night and I can tell you this much, it sure as hell wasn't Casper the Friendly Ghost."

"I see."

"I thought about trying holy water on the place, but…"

"Oh yeah," Amy interrupted. "That's a great idea, if you want to piss everyone off. That'd be like throwing rocks at a hornet's nest."

"Okay. So, what do I do?"

"There are three ways to protect, but it's all a matter of strategy and which one will work best for the situation at hand. There's warding the person. It's for keeping oneself safe and intact."

Jack looked at her somewhat confused.

"Um… it's like covering yourself in a blanket of energy," she continued. Jack had an idea of what this might feel like, having spent so much time with Shelby, of whom Amy was still unaware.

"I think I follow," he told her.

"Good. The second method is blocking what's coming at you and the third is establishing a net of energy to hold and support oneself. This is not as a negation; mind you, but more as an affirmation of the existing positive. Now that I think about it,

Waldemere might not be the best environment for this. It doesn't seem like it'd make for a good anchor."

"What about sage?"

"Sage is a safe bet," she said as she began to shake her head, "but it's general and it seems like your needs are more specific. That and it might smell up the place too much and it seems like you don't want to attract too much attention."

"You're right on that."

"You also don't want to shut down all perception."

"How so?"

"Well, we don't want you walking around blindly; oblivious to all that is really there."

Jack chuckled at this.

"I don't think that you're going to have to worry about something like that happening. I mean, this was pretty hard to miss."

"Obviously, you're not sleeping very well," Amy continued as she noticed the bags under Jack's eyes. "I'm not willing to help you sleep either, because it's probably healthy that you don't."

"Why would you say that?"

"Because your body is trying to tell you that something is wrong: that you're being interfered with by outside forces. No. It seems to me that more than anything else you'll be looking to protect yourself from physical harm. You're also trying to find out as much as you can about that house. It's likely going to be impossible to separate that from the paranormal aspect. Here's a theory. I like to keep things simple. Having said that, I think it'll work. You can pick it up in forty-eight hours."

"Can you do it in twenty-four?"

"It won't be as effective, but I can swing it. Are you going back there tonight?"

"Yeah, I kind of have to."

"In that case, let me give you a stopgap measure."

"Sounds great. What is it?"

"Just something to hold you over for the time being. I need a few minutes to prepare. Please, help yourself to some coffee or nettle tea."

Amy disappeared through the curtain behind the counter.

Jack walked over to a small wooden table in the corner of the shop. He looked down and saw what appeared to be a prickly clipping from a dark green bush. The taste, he was certain, would be very akin to musty spinach and grass clippings. Needless to say, he opted for the coffee.

After about five minutes, Amy returned from behind the curtain. She walked across the shop to the front door where she threw the lock and flipped the open sign to closed. She walked back over to him and asked one more question before proceeding.

"Do you trust me?"

"Of course I do."

"Good. This'll last about twelve hours or so. I hope that helps. Anything more than that is going to be a bonus. I haven't had that much time to build the intention."

She took Jack's hand and led him into the back room. The cats watched as they vanished behind the curtain.

Chapter 11

Jack drove west on Lake Road through Rocky River feeling more relaxed than he had in a long time, aside from the moments that he would spend with Shelby that is. He looked down at his arms and pulled up his sleeves. There, as bold as day, upon his wrists, were two large black "X" marks. There was another on the back of his neck as well. Jack thought that she would have used an essential oil or ashes of some sort to make these marks, but was quite surprised to see her wielding a black Sharpie marker. There was no doubt. These marks wouldn't be going away any time soon. He was only glad that he was wearing a long-sleeved turtleneck sweater to hide it.

In no time at all, Jack entered Bay Village and soon was driving south on Dover Center Road. After a few blocks, he turned left onto Normandy and stopped outside of Belinda Hyde's house. He stepped from his car and approached the front door. The flowerbed was ornamented with garden gnomes, birdbaths and a large chrome globe on a concrete pedestal. Jack often referred to these as Parma Balls, seeing as they were so popular, along with plastic flamingos, in that suburb of Cleveland. He walked up the front steps and rang the doorbell.

After a moment, he could hear someone approaching. The door was opened by a woman of about eighty years of age.

"Can I help you?" she asked.

"Good afternoon, Mrs. Hyde. How are you doing today?"

"I'm good."

"My name is Jack Sulli…"

"If you're selling something," she broke in, "I'm afraid that I'm not interested."

"I'm not a salesman or a solicitor, Mrs. Hyde."

"No? What are you then?"

"I'm a historian."

Belinda Hyde gave Jack a funny look. She hadn't heard that one before.

"A historian?"

"That's right."

"I don't follow." Mrs. Hyde looked quite confused.

"Well," Jack began. "I'm currently researching a house in Cleveland that was originally owned by your great grandfather…"

"Oh, Waldemere," she said excitedly. "That's such a beautiful house. It's a shame about all of the stories that people are spreading about it. Can you actually believe that some people think that it's haunted?"

Jack held his tongue on that one. He'd successfully managed to pique her interests and didn't want to drive her away by telling her about what had happened to him the night before.

"Well, that's why I located you."

"I'm surprised that you did. According to what's been written, I don't even exist."

"Yeah. I saw that, but had to do my own research to find out if that was true."

"Well. I certainly am not a figment of your imagination." She looked Jack over for a moment and made up her mind on him. "Why don't you come on in, then? We can talk about this further. Just kick off your shoes here by the door."

Jack obliged and followed her in. She offered him a seat on the couch, which he gladly accepted.

"So how can I help you with your research on Waldemere?" she asked.

"Maybe we can start with your great grandfather Heinrich Engelhardt. What can you tell me about him?"

"Only what was imparted to me by my grandmother. My father didn't know him all that well, as Heinrich had died when he was only about nine or ten."

Jack pulled out his notebook and pen, ready to take notes.

"And what did your grandmother have to say about him?"

"Only that he was a sweet man. That and that he was quite handsome. She used to say that my father inherited his grandfather's good looks."

"Did she ever mention the murder charges that he faced?"

"Not once. I found out about all of that later on. A slanderous slap in the face to our family, if you ask me."

"What about your great grandmother Sophia?"

"A kind woman with a heart of gold. Great grandpa

loved her so much. After all, Waldemere was built for her."

"I've read that," Jack said as he flipped the page and continued to write. "I also read a story about your grandmother's brother Ludwig…"

"An absolute tragedy. Ludwig had been sick for most of his life. The doctors never really knew what was wrong with him. From what I was told, he was given to seizures and would be in bed for months on end. I guess when it came down to it, he just couldn't live with his condition anymore."

"And you think that's why he took his life?"

"I can't think of any other reason."

"Hmm." Jack thought about it for a moment as he wrote. He was still somewhat affected by the thought of someone as close in age to him ending his life in such a violent manner.

"Would you like to see a picture of Ludwig?" Belinda Hyde offered.

Jack looked up at her and nodded. It hadn't crossed his mind that she might have pictures of this family.

"That'd be wonderful," he replied.

"Good then. You wait here and I'll be back in a moment."

Mrs. Hyde stood up and walked out of the room. Jack could hear her shuffling around a few items in a bedroom closet around the corner. After a minute, she returned with an old leather photo album in her hands. She set it on the coffee table in front of him and opened it.

"My word," Jack said breathlessly. Before him sat a large collection of sepia-toned photographs taken during the mid to late Nineteenth Century.

"Most of the people in these are from the Engelhardt family, but there are a few Bells in her as well. Like this one." She pointed to an oval portrait of a handsome mustached man. "This is my grandfather, Charles Bell. And here," she pointed to one of a young boy, "is my father James."

"These are incredible."

"Yes. They really are something. Let me see." Mrs. Hyde carefully turned the pages until she came to an older set of photographs. "Here they are: the Engelhardts."

Jack looked down and saw, on faded photos, images of a

family lost to the sands of time. He'd come across old pictures like these on other research projects and they always seemed to be looking at him and telling him the same thing over and over again: "Tell our story." It was this that drove him to be a thorough historian. He wanted more than anything to honor the memories of these people by telling their life stories to the best of his abilities. He couldn't let them down.

"Who are they?" he asked at last.

"Well, this one," she said as she pointed to a portrait of a man in his early twenties, "is Ludwig Engelhardt." The young man had sharp facial features, dark brown hair that was slicked back, and carried himself with an air of aristocracy. Just then, Jack remembered that he happened to have his digital camera on him. He pulled it out from the inner pocket of his leather jacket.

"Would you mind if I..." he began.

"Oh, you go right ahead."

Jack turned on his camera, set up the shot and snapped the picture. He looked down at the digital display and saw that it came out perfectly. He made a note in his notebook that the first image was that of Ludwig Engelhardt.

"And who is this?" he asked as he pointed to a girl in her mid-teens.

"Oh, that's my grandmother Tillie." Jack took another snapshot and again scribbled something into his notebook. "Her real name was Matilda, but most people have forgotten that. It even says 'Matilda S. Bell' on her headstone. I wonder why people don't take the time to look up the facts anymore."

"That's what I keep asking myself."

"Oh and here," Mrs. Hyde continued, "are my great grandparents: Heinrich and Sophia Engelhardt."

Jack looked down at a delicate woman in her fifties seated beside a stern-looking man with wavy gray hair and thick, burly sideburns. There was no doubt. This man was about as German as they came. Jack took a few pictures of this photograph and added more notes.

"I have a few more pictures of them," Mrs. Hyde continued. She turned the page and pointed to more photographs of Mr. and Mrs. Engelhardt in their earlier years. Jack continued to take pictures. There were a few more of Tillie and Ludwig as well. Near the back of the book, she turned to one of a grand sandstone mansion with a large turret on the right hand side: Waldemere in its heyday. Jack had no doubt, but wanted to be sure.

"Is this…"

"Waldemere?" Mrs. Hyde answered. "It is."

Jack looked over the faded image. Most everything was the same, with the exception of a few small items. To begin with, the house was much lighter in color. Jack knew at once why this was. Over the course of the last one hundred years or so, the stone would have been covered by soot from the steel mills a few miles away. Most of the older homes in Cleveland were like this. Another thing that jumped out at him was the fact that there was a large finial perched high atop the turret. This was no longer present. He couldn't help but wonder who would have removed it.

Standing in front of the mansion were many people, far more than were actually in the family. Heinrich and Sophia Engelhardt were seated in chairs at the center of the group. A young woman, obviously Tillie, was standing beside her father. On the side where Mrs. Engelhardt sat, stood two young men: Ludwig and Henry's grandfather, Conrad. Standing behind them, dressed to perfection, was a young woman with a confident look, nearly twenty years of age. There were two other girls standing to the side, dressed in black and white uniforms and on the other side stood an older couple; dressed more plainly that the others were.

"Who are they?" Jack asked.

"Well, that's the Engelhardts in the middle there: my grandmother with her parents and her brothers. Behind her brothers is a cousin. The rest are servants, I suppose."

Jack took a picture of this photo and added to his notes. As he did so, he took another look at the photograph. Scribbled in the bottom left-hand corner were the words *Waldemere, spring 1879*. He made note of this as well.

As Belinda Hyde closed the book, Jack was suddenly struck with an odd realization.

"Aside from the picture of Waldemere," he began, "I've noticed that you have no photos of Conrad Engelhardt."

"Conrad," Mrs. Hyde scoffed. "It's just as well that I don't. Most likely, my grandmother threw them away."

"I'm sorry. Might I ask why?"

"Oh, don't apologize. There's nothing to be sorry for, unless you were that low-life of an uncle.

"What happened?"

"Well," said Mrs. Hyde as she carried the book into the other room. "My grandfather died back in 1906, just around the same time that my great grandparents did. Unfortunately, my grandfather had died rather suddenly and he didn't leave a will." Having put the photo album back, Mrs. Hyde returned to the living room and sat down on the couch beside Jack. "Everything that my grandparents owned ended up going into probate. You'll never guess who was there to contest the rightful ownership of their property."

"Conrad Engelhardt?"

"That's right."

"Why would he do something like that to his own sister?"

"It was no secret that they didn't really care for each other all that much. I think most of it had to do with her marrying a Catholic. You see, my grandfather and great uncle Conrad were business partners in a clothing-manufacturing firm. Apparently he had no problem running a company with a Catholic, but when it came down to matters of the family, well, that was another story. After my grandfather died, Conrad had claimed that all of our assets were actually property of their company and seeing how his business partner was deceased; all of that property was to be returned to the sole surviving partner: him. My grandmother, meanwhile, had to find work and raise her child as a single mother. That was a pretty hard thing to do back then."

"That's horrible."

"Well, Conrad got his in the end, I guess. He got caught skimming off the top and went down when he was investigated for tax fraud. The case never went to trial, but he could never show his pompous face in Cleveland again."

"Well, I guess that answers my next question."

"Which was what?"

"Actually, I'm working for Conrad's grandson; a man

named Henry Engelhardt. I was wondering if you'd like to meet him."

"No. It's probably best that I don't. I wouldn't have anything nice to say about his grandfather."

"That's understandable. Well, I'd better be going. I've taken up enough of your time. Thank you again, Mrs. Hyde."

As Jack stood up, his jacket slid off of his lap and onto the floor. He reached down to pick it up and for a moment, one of the black marks that Amy had placed on his wrists was revealed. Mrs. Hyde caught sight of this.

"So, it is haunted," she said as he straightened up.

"I'm sorry?"

"Waldemere. It's haunted. You're staying there, aren't you?"

"I am. But how did you…"

"The mark on your wrist. I'm guessing that there's one on the other as well."

Jack smiled slightly and nodded.

"There is, but I'm very confused as to how you would know what that mark means."

"What's the matter? An eighty-year-old woman can't practice Wicca?"

"So you're…" Jack was beside himself.

"Did you have that done at the Slithy Toves or at Skyclad?"

"The Toves."

"Amy's a dear. You be certain to give her my love when next you see her. Promise?"

"I promise," Jack laughed. He put his shoes back on and opened the door to leave.

"And Mr. Sullivan…"

"Yes?"

"Please be careful. If Waldemere is haunted, it's certainly not to be trifled with."

Chapter 12

As Jack drove back to Waldemere late that afternoon, he was quite astounded as to how small a world it actually was. Here, he had stopped by his friend Amy's shop earlier that day while on his way to a meeting, and as it turned out, the person he was going to meet knew who Amy was. What's more, she was Wiccan: quite possibly a member of Amy's coven. Jack loved irony.

Jack arrived at Waldemere at a quarter to six just in time for dinner. After Emily had let him in through the side door, he went upstairs and washed up. Looking down at the black marks on his wrists, he thought it best to continue to wear the long-sleeved turtleneck sweater. The last thing he wanted was questions regarding their purpose.

The dinner was exceptionally delicious and had been comprised of roast pork loin, sage dressing, mashed potatoes and gravy. Emily had also prepared a wonderful bread pudding for dessert. Jack racked his brain on how best to bring up Belinda Hyde. She had absolutely no interest in meeting Henry Engelhardt. In the end, Jack decided that he would just put it out there.

"Well, Henry. I met a cousin of yours this afternoon."

Mr. Engelhardt was about to take a bite of the pudding, but instead placed his spoon down. Jack had his full attention.

"I'm sorry. You met my *what*?"

"Your cousin. Her name is Belinda and she lives in Bay Village."

"How exactly is she related?"

"She's Tillie's granddaughter."

"But how can that be? Tillie didn't have any children."

"On the contrary. She had a son named James."

"You're kidding me, right?"

"Honest."

"I wonder why my father would've told me that we didn't have any family."

"Well, he may have had a good reason for saying that."

"How so?"

"Henry, I could to tell you this, but it won't be easy to listen to. Sometimes when I do research, I stumble upon family secrets and sometimes they're best left that way." Henry Engelhardt nodded. "Do you still want to hear it?"

"I have the fortitude and I think I can take it."

"Very well. To begin with, she's not very interested in meeting you. It's nothing that you did, but it has to do with your grandfather. Now, as it was explained to me, when Tillie's husband passed away, your grandfather Conrad contested all of their property in probate court. He claimed that it all belonged to their company and therefore was actually his. The courts saw it that way too, apparently. You're grandfather ended up with everything and Tillie and her son inherited nothing."

Mr. Engelhardt's heart sank.

"This is all making perfect sense to me now."

"What do you mean?"

"When my grandfather was on his deathbed, he was making his peace with the world. One of the last things that he talked about was how he had wronged his sister. He'd asked my father to set things right, but as we later learned, Tillie was already deceased. We had no idea that she had a son. Had we known that, we'd have contacted him long ago."

"The past can be a painful place to visit."

"I need to contact her, Jack."

"Well, I'd probably give it some time. Like I said, she didn't particularly care to meet you. Perhaps you can send her a letter and explain everything. Put the ball into her court, so to speak. When she's ready to talk, I'm fairly certain that she will."

"I hope so."

"In the meantime and on a lighter note," Jack said as he stood up, "she did have some wonderful photographs of your family and even one of this house."

"You don't say."

"Even better, I've got copies of them. They're on my camera upstairs. I'll be back in a couple of minutes."

Jack raced upstairs, retrieved his digital camera from the inside pocket of his leather jacket and returned to the dining room. He showed Mr. Engelhardt all of the photos that Belinda Hyde had in her album. When they came to the one of

Waldemere, he was especially moved. There, before him, was the entire family. He made it a point to tell Jack that he'd want an enlarged print of this so that he could hang it on the wall in the parlor. Jack agreed. That would be the perfect place for it.

After dinner, Jack returned to the bedroom on the fourth floor. The light of the day was failing again and Jack was getting a little antsy over the prospect of spending another night up there. With luck, Amy's spell would hold up.

He sat at the desk and reviewed his notes. He'd already solved the mystery regarding when the house was built. The book on ghosts of Northern Ohio had claimed that it was erected in the late 1860's. Jack had already found this to be false. It was actually built in 1876. As far as Ludwig Engelhardt went, Belinda Hyde had backed up the story that he'd suffered from a chronic illness. Most likely, this was what had led to his suicide.

What's more, Jack now had the names of the three girls that Heinrich Engelhardt was accused of murdering. As he thought about this, Jack remembered the photograph of Waldemere in Mrs. Hyde's collection. He pulled out his camera again and scrolled through the images until he came to the one of the mansion. He looked down at his notes and reread the entry that said *Waldemere, spring 1879*. Mrs. Hyde had told him that the girl behind Conrad and Ludwig Engelhardt was a cousin. This had to be Anna Stadler, the first of the girls to go missing. He then looked over at the two young girls dressed in black and white. She'd said that they were servants. Harriett Fischer and Katherine Fitzgerald were the names that appeared in the court records as victims two and three as well as on the 1880 U.S. Census. This had to be them. As to the elderly couple on the far right, that must have been Mr. and Mrs. Schilling, whose names also appeared in the 1880 Census.

This picture was quite a find. Not only did it show the Engelhardt family together, but also it showed Waldemere and the three girls that Heinrich Engelhardt would later be accused of killing. The answers were slowly starting to come together. Still, Jack knew that he was quite a distance from completing his research. He thought hard for a moment about anything else that he may have overlooked. If one should slowly lose their direction, he believed it best to start again at the beginning. He did just that.

Jack went back to the day he first arrived at Waldemere. He took himself back through everything that Henry Engelhardt had told him about the family and the legends. Nothing jumped out at him. He moved on to the tour of the house. Thinking back on the second and third floors yielded nothing. He then came back to the fourth floor. What a clock! Henry Engelhardt had just managed to get it working again. And what did that say above the bar? I don't know, Jack thought. I don't speak German. Jack suddenly remembered.

He picked up his notebook, pen and flashlight and cautiously walked out of the bedroom and into the ballroom. As it had been the night before, the room was cold, dark and empty. Jack half-expected to hear footsteps charging at him, but none came. He clicked on his flashlight and shined it upon the beam above the bar. The phrase was definitely in German. He opened his notebook and wrote down the phrase, every word and every letter, so that there would be no mistakes in the translation.

After double and triple checking his work, he returned to the bedroom and booted up his laptop. He signed on in no time at all, quite surprised at how fast the wireless connection was in the house, and went to an online translator website. He carefully typed in the phrase as it appeared above the bar in the ballroom. After selecting German to English, he tapped the enter key. The phrase it returned was quite odd.

A good man's sacred stone left four him to die...
Four and twenty blackbirds baked in a pie...

This made no sense at all. The passage *four and twenty blackbirds baked in a pie* came from the Old English rhyme *Sing a Song of Sixpence*. That simply meant twenty-four blackbirds baked in a pie. This sounded absolutely disgusting. Jack didn't even want to imagine what blackbird pie would taste like. As for the first passage *a good man's sacred stone left four him to die*, his guess was as good as any. The only thing that really struck him as odd about this line was the use of the word *four* instead of *for*, which would have made more sense. There was no point in pondering it. After all, it was just a ridiculous poem. He could only hope that it held some higher meaning in German.

After writing down the translation, Jack closed his notebook and pulled out the pages regarding Heinrich Engelhardt's murder charges that he'd printed out at the courthouse the day before. For a moment, Jack thought that reading these might not be a good idea, not here and at this hour at least. After all, it was at night while reading these very pages that he'd witnessed the disturbance the night before. Perhaps, he thought, reading these papers might have set something off. Realizing that this was a ridiculous line of thought, he opened the pages to where he'd left off and began to read.

Here follows the testimony of Mr. Heinrich Engelhardt in regards to the disappearances of Miss Anna Stadler, Miss Harriett Fischer, and Miss Katherine Fitzgerald.

Jack attempted to read the following pages, but found that he couldn't. At first, he thought that the handwriting was simply of a poor quality, but after stumbling over a few words, he realized why it didn't make any sense. It was written in German. He flipped ahead a few more pages until he came to something that was written in English and began to read.

Translation of Heinrich Engelhardt's hand-written and sworn testimony provided by Wilhelm Klein, Counsel for the Accused. In his own hand.

Concerning the matter of Miss Anna Stadler, daughter of my cousin Simeon Stadler of Milwaukee, Wisconsin. It is my sworn testimony that she came to live with my family and I at our home on Franklin Street in Cleveland in November of 1878.

I last saw her at Reservoir Park on Franklin Street, not two blocks from my home on the evening of August the 25th 1879. She was in the company of a man that I had never laid eyes upon before. He was a short man with bright red hair. I thought to approach her and ask her why she was in the company of such a man with no escort, but seeing as there were many people in the park that evening, I believed that no immediate harm would come to her. I decided it best to approach her later that night when she would return from her little gallivant about the park.

As it so happened, I returned home and waited up for her. Eventually, I grew weary of waiting and decided that I would confront her in the morning. To the best of our knowledge, she returned during the night, collected her most valued possessions, and ran off with this stranger.

There were a number of items missing from her room in the morning, mostly jewelry. I composed a letter to my cousin in Milwaukee, explained the situation, and inquired as to whether or not he had heard from her as of yet. He hadn't.

As for Harriett Fischer, a servant in my house, my family and I had last seen her at our house on March the 2nd 1881. A few weeks prior to her disappearance, my wife informed me that a necklace was missing from her jewelry box. I suggested that it might have been mislaid, but two days after that, a set of earrings were missing. I helped her look, but was unsuccessful in locating the missing items.

For the next two weeks, small items would turn up missing. It was then that I had decided that I would confront the servant girls. My wife and I believe that Harriett Fischer knew that we suspected her and, in the night, robbed our house of a few more items of value and departed. I notified the authorities on this matter and was told that they would keep a wary eye out for her. We never heard anything after that.

On the matter of dear Miss Katherine Fitzgerald, the poor child had been ill in the head for quite some time. I called upon Doctor Matthews, our family physician, and he attended to her. It was his belief that she was suffering from melancholy; therefore, he gave us a tonic to be administered to her twice daily. This went on for a week's time and the girl's condition did not improve.

My wife and I last saw Miss Fitzgerald on the afternoon of October the 3rd 1882. She seemed in good spirits and was happily cleaning one of the bedrooms. My wife believed that she still looked a little peaked and suggested that she lie down, but the girl refused.

I went to see how she was coming on at four that afternoon, but could not locate her.

Doctor Matthews explained to us later that someone who has decided to end their life usually seems cheerful right before committing the final deed. This, we assumed, was the case with her.

I do hereby submit this to be my absolute sworn testimony, and that all statements herein are true to the best of my knowledge.

Set by my hand on this day, Friday, the 27th day of July 1883.

H. C. H. Engelhardt

It is further recorded that this testimony, translated by Mr. Wilhelm Klein is true and without alteration.

Wilhelm Klein, Esq.

Testimony of Doctor E. L. Matthews
465 Pearl Street
Cleveland, O.

I do swear that on the morning of September the 25th 1882, I was summoned to the Engelhardt home, so called Waldemere, on Franklin Street in Cleveland, Ohio and I did attend to a girl in their home by the name of Katherine Bridget Fitzgerald, age sixteen, a servant.

I further swear that after a thorough examination of the girl, I did diagnose her as suffering from melancholy. Thus it was that I prescribed to her calomel, a derivative of quicksilver, to be taken by mouth twice a day.

Report of Doctor Tobias Grimm
Deputy Medical Examiner
Coroner's Office, Cleveland, O.
October the 12th 1882

Report of findings. Female. Dead approximately one week. Age is late teens. Location of find is rocks, Whisky Island. Deceased is approximately Five feet, three inches tall. Red hair. Fair complexion. No indication of previous physical trauma prior to death. Presence of water in the lungs, esophageal passages and mouth. Cause of death: Drowning.

Accused: Heinrich C. Engelhardt
Charge: Murder of Anna Stadler,
first degree
Verdict: Innocent
Charge: Murder of Harriett Fischer,
first degree
Verdict: Innocent
Charge: Murder of Katherine
Fitzgerald, first degree
Verdict: Innocent

Accused is so cleared of all charges and accusations against him on this matter.

Monday, July the 30th 1883.

    So there it was. Everything was spelled out in black and white. The testimonies of the accused and the witnesses all seemed to match up. There was just one more thing for Jack to find. Now that he had a date for when all of this occurred, he would finally be able to locate a newspaper article that told the rest of the story.

    Realizing that it was getting quite late, Jack decided that he would get ready for bed. With some luck, it'd be a pleasant night without interruption. He walked into the bathroom and brushed his teeth. Afterwards, he changed into his sweatpants and threw on a fresh tee shirt. As he removed his socks, he looked down at his bare feet. Two black "X" marks were staring back up at him. He didn't remember ever removing his socks or shoes while at Amy's shop.

Chapter 13

The lake was swallowing the ship whole. Slowly, it sank below the surface of the icy November waters. Jack was running aft through the rain with two other men that he didn't immediately recognize. He kept turning back to see if his friend Connor had made it out of the forward cabins. He couldn't see him anywhere. The water was rushing towards him faster than he could run. The life rafts were already in the water, but were drifting away. He had no chance of reaching them.

Jack sat bolt upright in the bed. He had no idea what time it was, only that it was too dark to see the clock on the fireplace mantle across the room. The nightmare had woken him from what otherwise would have been a pleasant night's sleep. It had been a few months since he'd had these dreams. They were mostly night terrors about the freighter that he used to work on going down in a storm. On more than one occasion, he'd considered seeking professional help, but never got around to doing so.

He reached over to the small table beside the four-poster bed and felt around for his cell phone. After finally locating it, he picked it up and pressed a button on the side. As his eyes adjusted, he could see that it was four-twenty in the morning. Just then, he heard a soft whirring noise coming from the giant clock out in the ballroom. It lasted for about fifteen seconds and stopped.

"Awe, to hell with you," he told the clock. It was late and he didn't care to worry himself with thoughts of ghosts and disturbances. All that he wanted was to get back to sleep and have a little peace. He rolled over, pulled the covers over his head and closed his eyes. Just like that, he was out again.

When Jack next awoke, it was well after nine in the morning. He'd overslept. As he rolled out of bed, there was a sudden knock at the door.

"Mr. Sullivan? It's Emily. Are ya awake?"
The door crept open a couple of inches.

"It's okay, Emily. You can come in."

She opened the door the rest of the way and entered. There was a severe look on her face.

"We're sorry about last noight. Please promise ya'll give it just one more go."

Jack was very confused.

"What are you talking about?"

"The disturbances. Last noight."

"What disturbances? I didn't hear anything."

Now it was Emily's turn to be confused.

"'Ow do ya mean, ya didn't 'ear anythin'? The poundin' comin' from up 'ere was 'orrendous. Ya must 'ave 'eard somethin'."

"Honestly, not a sound."

"Oh. Well." Emily was at a loss for words. "Breakfast will be ready in a few minutes," she said at last. With that, she closed the door and left Jack to wash up and dress himself.

After a quick breakfast and a fast perusal of the Plain Dealer, Jack left Waldemere, got into his car and headed east on Franklin Boulevard. He turned right on West 25th Street, drove a few blocks more and pulled to the side of the road, where he parked the car and got out, being certain to bring his notebook with him.

The sign above the door read *Carter's Closet: Antiques, Vintage and So Much More.* Jack had meant to stop by Orin Drury's shop for some time now, but never really had an opportunity, or a reason, to do so. The building was three stories high, constructed of terracotta brick, now blackened by the ancient soot from the steel mills, and had tall windows that reached from floor to ceiling. Over a hundred years ago, this building had housed the offices of the Rauch and Lang Carriage Company. There were still faded remnants painted on the side of the structure that advertised carriage, buggy and wagon repairs. Jack pulled open the heavy wooden door and entered.

He was immediately standing in a room with many shelves lining the walls. Placed upon these were a wide array of small antique items, vintage books and knickknacks. Towards the back of the shop, he could see larger pieces of Victorian-era furniture. One wall was completely taken up by a collection of mirrors. He could hear what sounded like hammered dulcimer music coming from a CD player and the aroma of pipe tobacco was heavy in the air.

Jack strolled over to one of the shelves and took a closer look at an item that had jumped out at him from the start: an old green navigation light from a ship.

"You break it, you buy it," someone called from the back. Jack looked over, but the phantom voice seemed to come from out of thin air. He headed towards the back of the shop in hopes of finding its source, but found no one behind the counter. Just then, he saw a puff of smoke come up from the floor, followed by the sound of approaching footsteps. Jack peered over the counter and noticed at once a set of stairs leading into the basement. The shop's proprietor was coming up these stairs with heavy feet. A moment later, Orin Drury came into full view, dressed in his familiar Nineteenth Century attire, which included a black and silver waistcoat and starched-collared shirt. A pocket watch was tucked into his upper left breast pocket and he had a pipe hanging from his mouth, which resembled something that Basil Rathbone might have smoked in an old Sherlock Holmes movie. In his arms, he carried a large box of antique books.

Without even giving Jack a glance, he set the box on the counter, pulled a handkerchief from his back pocket and blotted the sweat from his brow.

"Only five more to go," he declared as he set his pipe down in an old glass and bronze ashtray on the counter. He tucked the handkerchief back into his pocket, let out a sigh and finally looked up at his guest. "My God, Jack! I'm sorry. I didn't know that it was you standing there. I'm glad you finally made it down."

"It's good to see you, Orin," Jack replied as he extended his right hand. Orin held his up, indicating that his palms were quite dirty.

"I'm a mess, Jack."

Jack chuckled.

"I don't care."

Orin shrugged, smiled, and shook Jack's hand in greeting.

"Welcome to Carter's Closet," he said at last.

"Yeah, I was meaning to ask you about the name. Why didn't you call it Orin's Closet or Drury's Closet?"

"Well, Lorenzo Carter was the first permanent settler here in Cleveland and I guess that I was just going for a name that conjured thoughts of the city while it was still in its infancy. I mean, the name just kind of shouts *antique*."

"Yeah, I can see that," Jack nodded.

"Also, some of the items that I have here go back to Cleveland in its birthing."

"Really?" Jack was intrigued by this claim.

"Of course. Sure, some these things in here go back many centuries before that, but it's the local interest items that are my specialty."

"Such as what?"

"I thought you'd never ask. Follow me."

Orin lead Jack through a doorway just past the counter and into another room roughly the same size of the one they had just been standing in. They walked around a corner and stopped at an old iron cannon that measured nearly twelve feet long.

"It's a cannon," Jack pointed out.

"Thank you, Captain Obvious."

"Okay, it's a really big cannon."

"It's more than that," Orin informed him with a smile. "This is the cannon that used to sit on the northeast quadrant of Public Square."

"I didn't know that there was one."

"There was. Go ahead and read the inscription."

Jack crouched down and read the plaque that was mounted to the side of the wooden base.

Thirty-six pounder
surrendered by
Captain Robert Barclay to Commodore Perry
in the
Battle of Lake Erie
September 1813

"You've got to be kidding me!" Jack cried out.

"Was a real bitch trying to get it in here, too. I had to reinforce the floors like you wouldn't believe."

"How in the hell did you manage to acquire this?"

"Picked it up at an auction."

"An auction? This thing ought to be in a museum."

"It was. Who do you think auctioned it off?"

Jack gave Orin a hurt look.

"Now that's a shame that a museum would be forced to sell off something like this."

"Not from where I'm standing," Orin laughed. "I'll tell you this. Both the museum and I made off pretty well in the deal. They got a small fortune and I got to be the owner of a true piece of Ohio history. Everybody goes home happy in the end."

Jack shrugged his shoulders.

"I guess so. Have you ever thought of putting it on public display?"

"The thought's crossed my mind more than once. Only a couple of problems with that, though."

"Like?"

"Like I'm a little worried that it might get defaced, damaged or stolen. An even bigger problem would be trying to get it back out of the shop. It took me nearly a full day just to get it in."

"Is it for sale?"

"Jack, everything in here is for sale. Well, almost everything."

"Okay. So what *isn't* for sale?"

"Everything in the basement."

"And what's in the basement?"

"I swear. Your timing of these questions is impeccable. You seem to ask them just when I'm ready to tell you about them." Jack stifled a laugh at this comment. He could tell that Orin was toying with him. "Follow me."

Orin lead Jack back into the main room, behind the counter and down the set of stairs into the basement. Here, Jack found himself in a room with terracotta brick walls. The floors were also made of brick, but were set about in a herringbone pattern. The ceiling was simply the exposed heavy wooden joists and beams that supported the floor above. He was surrounded by an uncountable number of books, filing cabinets and shelves with cardboard boxes placed on them. The air was cool and desiccated.

"Here in the basement sits the archives," Orin continued. "It's a vast collection of everything related to Cleveland and the surrounding area. The Western Reserve Historical Society has been after me for years to get their hands on some of this stuff."

"And you're not selling."

"I can't sell it. It's not mine."

"But I thought…"

"A collection such as this doesn't belong to one person alone. There are many people who contribute to and support this archive: old and well established families for the most part."

"Like the Drury's?"

"At one time, yes. But that family is pretty scattered at this point. Most of the old money has been spread out and spent. Any of us that are left have built our own fortunes and have become successful by our own means. What I'm talking about here is an archive that has been added to, well maintained and properly amended over the years. Oh sure, the families that support this archive make their regular annual donations to the WRHS and the Cuyahoga County Archives, but this is the one that gets their undivided attention. Few people know that it even exists. And we'd like to keep it that way, if you catch my drift."

"Got it. Mum's the word," Jack assured him.

"Thank you. It's greatly appreciated."

"So how does one end up becoming the caretaker of such an archive?"

"That's a long story, and a fascinating one, but I'll save it for another time. I wanted to ask you how things are going with your research on Waldemere."

"Pretty good, actually. I think I'm finally starting to make some real headway."

"Really? What have you learned so far?"

"Well, last night I read the notes from Heinrich Engelhardt's trial…"

"Inquiry, Jack."

"Sorry?"

"It wasn't a trial. It was an inquiry. They were gathering

testimonials and statements and they held a hearing to see if there was enough evidence of wrongdoing to go ahead with a criminal trial."

"Obviously, there wasn't."

"The judge didn't seem to think so."

"What are your thoughts?"

"Honestly, my thoughts don't really matter. I'm just the guy who keeps the documents on an inquiry such as that."

"You mean to tell me that you have the court records here?"

"A copy of them. You had to go to the old courthouse, didn't you?"

"I did."

"You see? You'd have saved yourself a lot of time if you would have just come here first."

"So, what else have you got on the Engelhardts?"

"Probably everything, but you're asking the wrong question. These archives aren't arranged like that. Say you wanted to know something like when a certain house on Clinton Avenue was built. I'd direct you over to the file marked *Houses, Cleveland, Clinton*. Now a house with as much prominence as Waldemere gets its own file. You'll probably find things such as building records, purchasing orders for materials, labor receipts and things like that. The file won't just say that the house was built in 1876. You would need to come to that conclusion based off of what you would find in that file."

"And the Engelhardts?"

"Well, what specifically would you like to know about them?"

"Oh, I don't know. Whatever there is to know."

"Wrong, wrong. Again, you're asking the wrong questions. Let's say you want to know what Heinrich Engelhard died from. Follow me."

Orin led Jack over to a row of books on an old cherry bookshelf. He pulled down a large tome and opened it.

"This is the index book for the Cuyahoga County Death Certificates for the years 1900 through 1906," Orin continued.

"But I thought they only started issuing death certificates in December of 1908."

"Obviously, people were dying before then. Actually, they were issuing death certificates as early as 1841, but the county didn't see any reason to hang on to them, so they ended up here. Now, the entries are listed alphabetically, so we have to go to 'E' and begin looking there." He flipped ahead in the book a number of pages and stopped. "Here he is: Engelhardt, Hermanus Conrad Heinrich."

"Hermanus?"

"Apparently. What?"

"I… I just never came across that one."

"That's the beauty of a death certificate. It tells us so much more. Anyway, this tells us that his death certificate is located in Book 66, Page 572."

Orin put the book back on the shelf and started to walk over to another long row of large, leather-bound books.

"Oh, by the way," he added, "I'd appreciate it if you didn't re-file any of the books. When you're done using them, just set them on that table over there." He pointed to an old wooden table with a brass Oriental Express style lamp sitting upon it.

When he reached the next bookshelf, he scanned the titles and pulled down a book labeled *Cuyahoga County Death Certificates: Volume 66*. He opened it and turned to page 572.

"Oh, there it is," Jack said as he saw Heinrich Engelhardt's name at the top of a form. Though some of the script was almost illegible, he continued to read over the rest of the document to himself.

Name: Engelhardt Hermanus Conrad Heinrich
Date of Birth: October 7th 1828
Place of Birth: Nuremberg, Bavaria
Father's name: Johann H. L. Engelhardt

Mother's name: *Maria A. Stadler*
Date of Death: *June 3, 1906*
Place of Death: *Lake Road at Canterbury Road (Engelwood) Dover, O.*
Cause of Death: *Angina Pectoris*
Length of illness: *2 days*
Undertaker: *F. A. Burmeister*
Interment: *Monroe St. Cemetery, Cleveland, O.*

"So what did that just tell you, Jack," Orin asked with a slight smile on his face.

"A lot, actually. Some of this I already knew, but things like the location of his home in Dover Township, I was completely in the dark on. The fact that it was on Lake Road tells me that it's in the part that's now Bay Village. And this part here, I think that says *Engelwood*. I'm guessing that's the name of his estate."

"You'd be right."

"Gives me something else to look up."

"I'll save you the trouble by telling you that Engelwood was demolished many years ago."

"Now why would someone go and do something like that?"

"Modern progress," Orin scoffed. "The house that sits there now looks just like the rest. I swear, no one builds with style anymore."

"I agree."

"So tell me, is there anything *specifically* that you want to know about the Engelhardt family?"

"God, I could rack my brain for hours and come up with a million questions." Just then, Jack remembered the odd poem that he'd translated the night before. "Oh, I do have this," he said as he opened his notebook to the page that contained the passage. "I translated it from an inscription that was above the bar in the ballroom. It's a German poem, I think. I was hoping that maybe you might have an idea what it means."

Orin read the passage aloud.

"A good man's sacred stone left four him to die… Four and twenty blackbirds baked in a pie…"

"So, what do you think?"

"It's gibberish."

"Damn. I was hoping that it actually meant something."

"Maybe it does, Jack. I don't know. I'm an archivist, not an expert on German literature."

"Or maybe old Heinrich Engelhardt was just some rich guy who'd gone around the bend."

"Well, I don't think he was crazy."

"How did he ever manage to amass such a fortune, anyway?"

"Now *that's* a great question. He made most of his money in banking. Some people claim that his lending practices were somewhat unfair, and maybe they were right. Somehow he managed to get richer and richer while the rest of the community lay stagnant or in some cases suffered."

"What did he do before banking? I saw in an early city directory that it had him listed as being employed by a company called Darrow and Associates."

"Oh, originally he was a joiner."

"A what?"

"It's an old term for a cabinetmaker."

"Really? That's a hell of a jump to go from working for a company that built cabinets to running a bank."

"Well he didn't just do it overnight. I'm sure that he started making investments early on that ended up paying off later. And Darrow and Associates didn't build cabinets."

"But I thought you said he was a cabinetmaker."

"That was his title when he started with that company, but he moved up the ladder as he better learned the trade."

"So if they didn't make cabinets, what did they make?"

"Darrow and Associates? They built clocks."

Chapter 14

By lunchtime, Jack was heading west into Lakewood. He'd had an interesting time at Orin Drury's shop and definitely looked forward to going back again sometime soon. Orin had mentioned the archives that he was caretaker of, but until now, Jack had no idea what that archive entailed. As the full worth of what was in front of him was realized, Jack's eyes had lit up like a kid in a candy store. The possibilities were endless.

He pulled up outside of The Slithy Toves on Madison Avenue and stepped out of his car into the pouring rain. It was just a passing shower and didn't look to last very long. On the plus side of things, it would melt off whatever snow was still left over from the storm the previous Saturday night. This was a good sign. Maybe spring was finally on its way.

Jack walked into Amy's shop and saw her standing behind the counter talking with a couple of very good-looking women. Both were wearing their hair pulled back in braids. One was a redhead and the other a blonde. The redhead was wearing a dark green sweater and a long tie-dyed skirt. The blonde had on a jacket and blue jeans. Amy looked up and smiled as she caught sight of Jack.

"I'll be with you in a moment," she called in a very professional-sounding voice. Jack nodded and decided to busy himself by looking around at some of the items that occupied the shelves. One jar in particular immediately caught his attention. In it, he thought he could see what appeared to be a dead baby alligator: withered and dry. Scanning the rest of the nearby jars, he noticed that some contained what looked like dead spiders, crow's feet, possibly a couple of rat skulls and one that seemed to simply contain a few short sticks.

After a couple of minutes, he noticed that Amy was finishing up her conversation. Eventually, the two women turned and made for the door. As they crossed the room, the redhead shot Jack a wink and a smile. He felt himself slightly blush. After they had exited the shop, Amy called out to him.

"I'd have thought that you would've been here sooner than this."

"Oh, I had to make a stop earlier this morning a little closer to Waldemere."

"Anywhere interesting?"

"Yeah, my friend's antiques store."

"Friend, huh?" Jack could see the gears turning in Amy's head.

"His name's Orin Drury. Nice guy, but he's a little eccentric."

"Is he cute?"

"You're asking the wrong person," Jack replied with a chuckle.

"Single?"

"Don't know. I didn't ask."

"So what was his store like?"

"Oh God. You wouldn't believe some of the things he has in there."

"Like what?"

"Believe it or not, but he has a cannon from the Battle of Lake Erie."

"You're kidding!"

"No, really. It's on the first floor in the side room. You've got to see this thing. It's huge."

Amy thought about it for a moment.

"So he's an eccentric, possibly cute, possibly single, guy with a huge gun? Sign me up."

"Okay, okay," Jack laughed. "Cool it with the hormones. I'm sure you'll run into him at some point."

"You'd better introduce me."

"Promise. So, have you finished what you were working on for me?"

"I have. Oh, how'd it go last night?"

"Pretty good. I guess there were disturbances in the house, but I slept right through them. The only time I woke up was when I was having a bad dream."

"Bad dream, huh? Well, it was only a stopgap measure to temporarily protect you from outside interference. Can't really do anything about the dreams. Not right now, at least."

"No, that's fine. I've had them before and am kind of used to them at this point."

Just then, Amy's phone began to ring. Jack wasn't the least bit surprised to hear that her ring tone was Carmina Burana by Carl Orff.

"Hey, Jack. I need to take this."

"No worries."

Amy answered the phone and began to talk cheerfully with the person on the other end. Jack, meanwhile, walked over to a bookshelf and read some of the titles. In no time at all, he realized that he was in the Feminist Studies section. He located a book entitled *Woman Complete*, pulled it from the shelf and opened it. Much to his astonishment, it contained many pictures of women in nude poses and performing everyday tasks in the buff. Again, Jack began to blush, but found it hard to put the book down.

"No way. You're kidding me!" Amy exclaimed into the phone from across the room. Jack looked over and saw that she was staring at him with a big smile. "No, he's here right now." Just then, she noticed the book that Jack was holding in his hand. Her smile instantly turned to a funny scowl. Realizing that he'd been busted, Jack quickly fumbled around with the book, trying to put it back on the shelf where he found it. "I'll be sure to tell him," Amy continued. "No, you too. I'll talk to you soon. Blessed be."

She hung up the phone, walked out from behind the counter and over to Jack. Seeing that he'd misfiled the book, she pulled it off the shelf and moved it back to its proper place.

"Getting a little curious about the opposite sex?" she asked with a crooked smile.

"Oh, I was... um... I was just looking..."

"Looking? Learn anything new?"

"Can we change the subject?"

"Of course we can. How's this one? Why didn't you tell me that you were going to Belinda Hyde's house yesterday? I would have come with you."

"I didn't know that you knew each other. Had I known, I certainly would have asked you to join me. Was that her on the phone?"

"Yeah. She was telling me about this perfect little gentleman that she met yesterday afternoon."

"You're funny."

"You see, Jack. We are everywhere," Amy announced with a wispy voice. "We own the schools. We pass laws in congress. We know what's in the secret sauce. And we're pretty damn good-looking, too. I saw you checking out Clara Bloodstone when she left."

"The redhead?"

"Mm hmm."

"Yeah, she wasn't that hard on the eyes."

"I'd be careful with her," Amy warned.

"How so?"

"She could cast a spell that would make your willie shrink to about an inch long. Not that she ever would. I'm just saying that she could if she really wanted to."

"Thanks. I'll keep that in mind."

"So, anyway," Amy said as she turned back towards the counter, "let me show you what I have."

She continued on behind the curtain and a moment later returned holding what looked to be a small box that an engagement ring might come in.

"What is it?" asked Jack.

"Open it up and find out."

Jack opened the lid. There, before him, was a small dark crystal.

"I don't get it."

"Well, Jack, it's called a recorder crystal. I imprinted some of your essence onto it and what it'll do is acts as a decoy."

"A decoy?"

"Yeah. You see, all of the energy that would normally be directed at you will now be directed at this. The disturbances and paranormal events will still occur, I can't do anything about that, but at least they won't be happening to you. Not directly, at least."

"I think I get it. I put this down somewhere and when the shit starts to hit the fan again, it'll be this little crystal thingy that gets thrown across the room and not me."

Amy was sullenly quiet for a moment before speaking up.

"You didn't tell me that you got thrown across a room."

"Oh, I'm sorry. I didn't think it was important."

"It sounds like you're meddling with something that should be left alone. Is there any way that I can talk you into quitting this case?"

"No chance."

She could see that Jack was resigned.

"Very well. All I can tell you is to be on your guard. Be strong and be true to your convictions."

"Thanks for the advice, and the recorder crystal." Jack closed the box and put it in an outside pocket of his leather jacket. "How much do I owe you?"

"Jack, something like this isn't bought and sold. It's given. But I'll tell you what. Next time we're at McNamara's you can buy me a drink. Deal?"

"Deal." Jack gave her a big hug and thought how lucky he was to be blessed with such incredible friends.

"You take care now, Jack, and keep yourself protected."

"Will do." He was about to leave, when another thought came to him. "Oh, there's just one other thing that I wanted to ask you about."

"And what's that?"

"How would someone go about fortifying themselves from being overcome while having physical contact with a spirit?"

Amy's jaw dropped and she blinked repeatedly. She had never been asked that before. She stood in silence before blurting out "What?"

"Just a question."

"Okay. No. That's not just a question. This I've got to hear about."

Jack considered it for a moment, but based on Amy's reaction of shock and incredulity, he decided that this probably wasn't the best time to inform her that he'd been romantically involved for the past five months with the ghost of a girl named Shelby Tomlinson, who died more than fifteen years ago.

"This one, I think, I'm going to keep to myself for the time being," he told her at last.

"Can you give me the basics of what's happening?"

Jack thought how best to word it without giving anything away.

"Well. Let's say, hypothetically, that there's a spirit that touches you and every time it does, you feel… well… woozy, I guess."

Amy gave him a good once over.

"Woozy?"

"I don't know. Maybe numb and tingly is better."

"Is it a good feeling or a bad feeling?"

"Oh, it's absolutely the best." As Jack said this, he began to worry that he may have just said too much.

"Well, it sounds like you're pretty lucky then. If it were a bad feeling, I'd say that something was trying to drain your energy. But since it's a good feeling, I'd say that something is pumping you full of energy. If it's absolutely the best, why would you want it to stop?"

"Um… it can become something of a distraction."

"Okay. I can see that you're not entirely ready to talk about this yet. When you are, I'll be here to listen. In the meantime, I would suggest standing on copper; barefoot preferably."

"Copper?"

"Yeah. It acts as a grounding agent."

"Kind of like in electricity?"

"Exactly. It'll pass a lot of the energy into the ground and you won't become so overwhelmed. You'll still know it's happening and will be able to feel it, but it won't be as strong. Personally, I wouldn't mind a little excess positive energy every now and again."

"So what do I do if I'm not standing on copper when it happens? Should I carry some around with me wherever I go?"

Amy gave him a stern look and spoke slowly.

"Try putting it in your shoes."

"Oh. Good idea."

Jack smiled, thanked her again for all of her help and left The Slithy Toves. Amy watched him intently as he got into his car and drove away. There was more to that story and he was definitely hiding something.

Chapter 15

When Jack had returned to Waldemere that afternoon, Emily had greeted him at the side to let him in and had informed him that she would be leaving the house shortly. It was Thursday and therefore, grocery shopping day. She asked him if he wouldn't mind being alone in the house for a little while. Jack lightheartedly assured her that he'd be able to manage on his own until she returned.

As he climbed the stairs up to the fourth floor, he thought about what Orin Drury had told him that afternoon. Heinrich Engelhardt had started out by working for a clockmaker. Jack instantly thought of the giant clock in the ballroom. He wondered if Heinrich Engelhardt had personally built this. It seemed likely. Maybe he hadn't carved every detailed figure on the front, or maybe he had, but he certainly must have been the one who designed and assembled the inner workings. Jack had never seen the likes of it before and he seriously doubted that he ever would again. It truly was a one of a kind masterpiece.

He now stood in front of the clock, thoroughly examining every detail as he had already done many times before. The fact that the wooden figures were actually draw knobs of some sort baffled him to no end. He still had no idea where to begin. After a moment, he heard a car backing out of the driveway. He walked into the turret room and, looking down at the street below, saw Emily pulling away. The house was entirely his. Dinner would be at six, as it always was, therefore Emily would be back around five-thirty at the latest. He looked at the time on the clock face. It was nearly four. That would give him a little over an hour and a half to do some more exploring.

It was nearly four.

Something about that struck a chord with him. He had an idea. He ran back into the bedroom, picked up his notebook from where he'd set it on the desk and returned to the clock. He opened the book to where he'd translated the poem that was written above the bar and reread the passage again.

"A good man's sacred stone left four him to die… Four and twenty blackbirds baked in a pie…"

The phrase "left *four* him to die" seemed quite odd. Jack looked up at the clock and back at the unusual passage. The realization hit him like a slap to the face. He finally understood. This was no clock and this certainly was no poem. It was a puzzle and the poem was the key: specific instructions on what figures to move and when to move them.

"A good man's sacred stone left for him to die," Jack said again. He looked up at the woodwork. There it was in the upper left. Beside the figure of the man's head was a carving of a windswept tree with a tombstone beneath it: a good man's sacred stone. Left *four* him to die must have meant that he had to turn this figure at four o'clock. He had six minutes to go.

The figure of the tombstone was quite high up: nearly twelve feet from the floor. If he was going to be able to reach it, he'd have to find something to stand on, and quick. At first he thought of grabbing the chair from the desk in the bedroom, but realized at once that this wouldn't be tall enough. He was fairly certain that there weren't any ladders in the house. There was probably one in the carriage house out back, but he knew that he wouldn't have enough time to go looking for it. Just then, he remembered the old steamer trunk in the trunk space.

He tossed his notebook onto the floor, raced into the back bedroom and threw open the trapdoor. Without even bothering with his flashlight, he made his way down the passage until he reached the end. Feeling around in the darkness, he grasped what must have been a leather handle on the steamer trunk and gave it a tug. It disintegrated in his hands. This was no good. He had to hurry. He managed to get an arm behind the trunk and gave it a shove. Surprisingly, it was fairly light. Jack wondered if maybe it was empty.

He pushed it down the passage until he returned to the trapdoor. He climbed out and, reaching back down, extracted the trunk with ease. As he carried it into the ballroom, he could hear a few items moving around inside. It wasn't empty after all.

It was one minute to four. There wasn't a second to lose. He ran across the ballroom, set the trunk down and stood it on end. He quickly climbed on top and reached for the carved image of the tombstone, then looked to his right and stared at the clock face. The ceaseless ticking echoed across the otherwise silent room. Then the minute hand advanced. It was four o'clock.

As he'd heard before, there was a sudden whirring sound from the mechanical space behind the façade. Jack quickly grabbed the tombstone and tried to turn it, but it wouldn't move. He tried to push it, but that didn't do anything either. He was really kicking himself for not figuring out how it moved prior to this. He tried to slide it around, but again, nothing. He then gave it a pull and it suddenly lurched forward.

There was an immediate ratcheting sound emanating from the mechanical space. This was followed by a loud thud. Jack jumped down from the steamer trunk and stared at the clock. The whirring sound stopped. Nothing happened.

He didn't get it. It seemed like this odd little poem was the answer to the mystery of the clock. It made perfect sense that this was how everything would fit together. He paced around waiting for something to happen, but after a minute, all was still the same.

Then it dawned on him. A minute had passed and the figure of the tombstone hadn't reset itself. He was right after all. There just had to be more to it. Jack ran over to his notebook and picked it up. He read the rest of the passage.

"Four and twenty blackbirds baked in a pie…"

He looked at the clock and distinctly saw the two crows. Fortunately, he already knew in what manner they moved. He'd have to push them when the time came. The question was, what time exactly was that? Four and Twenty, the poem stated. Jack already knew that in *Sing a Song of Sixpence* this meant twenty-four. Perhaps it was referring to midnight. When he'd sailed on the freighters, he'd used military time, but the day always ended with 23:59. The next minute would reset back to zero hundred hours. There was no twenty-fourth hour.

For a moment, Jack found himself thinking on the nightmare he'd had the night before. He'd never had anxiety dreams like that while sailing on the freighters. Those had started shortly after he'd quit the job. Maybe, he thought, he would seriously consider seeing a specialist on the matter.

Jack began to pace about the ballroom. He was getting too easily distracted. He needed to figure this out. Twenty-four,

four and twenty; it didn't make any sense to him. He started to think about the dream again and what had happened in it. The boat was sinking and the life rafts had already been launched. What then? Nothing. He'd woken up and checked the time. It was four-twenty in the morning.

Four-twenty! That was it! That was the answer. Just then, he remembered hearing the soft whirring sound coming from the ballroom. He'd thought, in his half-slumber, that the ghosts of Waldemere were messing with him again, but that wasn't the case at all. It was just the clock. That same sound had just occurred at four: the very moment that he had to pull down on the figure of the tombstone.

He looked at the time. It was ten past four. If his theory was correct, he had another ten minutes. He thought it best that he should put the steamer trunk back in the trunk space. Besides, the crows were only about three feet above the floor and he could reach them easily. As far as he knew, neither Emily nor Henry Engelhardt seemed to know of the trunk's existence. For some odd reason, Jack thought it best not to mention it: not for the time being at least.

After returning the trunk to its original hiding spot, Jack walked back into the ballroom and looked at the time. It was four-eighteen: a little less than two minutes to go. He walked over to the figure of the crow on the left and placed his hand upon it, ready to give it a push. The minute hand moved again. One minute to go. He wondered for a moment if it mattered which crow he pushed. It probably did. He recited the second part of the passage again in his head.

"Four and twenty blackbirds baked in a pie…"

There was no image of a pie anywhere on the clock. He was certain of this. It did say "blackbirds" though. That must have meant that he'd have to press them both. The minute hand advanced. It was four-twenty and the whirring sound began.

Jack firmly pressed on the figure of the crow and it sank into the façade. There were three loud clicks followed by a thud. Quickly, he walked over to the other crow and pressed it as well. It mimicked its mate. Again, he could hear it click three times. This was followed by a winding noise. Behind the woodwork face, Jack could hear what sounded like a crank being turned. Then, from behind him, he heard an abrupt banging sound. He turned to see that one of the wainscot panels along the wall and across the ballroom had opened up, leaving a gap four feet high and six feet wide. Jack walked over to investigate.

The space behind the wall was dark, considerably darker than the trunk space had been. There was no doubt. He would need his flashlight again. He walked back into the bedroom, picked it up from the desk, and started back for the ballroom. Just then, he thought to retrieve his digital camera from the inside pocket of his leather jacket. After all, he might discover something worth photographing. He returned to the open wainscot panel, clicked on his flashlight and crawled into the space.

Immediately after entering, he realized that there was more than enough headroom for him to stand. He shined the light down this newly discovered corridor and saw that it went back quite a distance. The floor was covered in close to a half an inch of dust. Cautiously, he proceeded.

Near the end of this hall, Jack could see that it opened up into another room. He turned on his camera and began to take pictures.

The room wasn't all that big: ten feet by ten feet at most. With the exception of an old safe, it was quite empty. He shined the flashlight around the room to see if there was anything else in here, but there wasn't. Realizing this, he walked over to the safe and investigated.

The safe sat open and completely devoid of any contents that it might have held. Jack knew at once that this room must have been a security vault. While he had been investigating Maul Manor a few years earlier, he'd come across one of these, though it wasn't quite as articulately hidden as this one was. Heinrich Engelhardt must have emptied the contents of the room and safe when he and his wife had moved from Waldemere to Engelwood. Jack took a few more pictures of the room. He felt a little disappointed that there was nothing else in here. It was true that the room was quite a find, but it would have been nice to discover something of real value: something that he could pass along to Henry Engelhardt.

Jack took one last look at the room. He'd lingered long enough. He turned back for the corridor but as he did so, stopped dead in his tracks. Just above the doorway, he could barely make out what seemed to be a few letters. He walked over and ran his left hand along them. Dust fell in his face, causing his eyes to tear up and his nose to itch. He wiped his face on the sleeve of his shirt and when his eyes had cleared from watering, he looked up at the letters again. It was another poem.

> Todesfälle sting auf der elften stunde...
> Unsere steine allein am zwölf...

He smiled and began to take pictures of this new find. As was the case before, it was written in German. He'd have more translating to do. He double-checked his digital display to make certain that he'd clearly photographed the entire passage, left the room and made his way back down the corridor.

After crawling back out into the ballroom, Jack turned and investigated the wainscot panel that had opened to allow him access to the secret hallway. It was mounted on a track of some sort. He gave it a slight pull and slid it closed. As it snapped into place, he heard a clicking sound from over by the clock. The figures of the tombstone and the two crows had reset themselves into their original positions. It would be nearly twelve hours before he could go back into this room, though he couldn't see why he would need to. He'd already discovered his next clue.

Jack picked up his notebook from the floor and walked back into the bedroom where he booted up his laptop and signed onto the net. He brought up the online translator page again and entered the words from the passage he'd discovered in the security vault. He selected German to English, pressed the enter key and read the new translation.

> *Deaths sting on the eleventh hour...*
> *Our stones alone at twelve...*

Jack thought about it for a moment and almost at once knew what the passage meant. He would have to turn and pull the figures of the hornets at eleven o'clock and pull down on the tombstones at midnight. He looked over at the clock on the fireplace mantle. It was almost a quarter to five. He didn't feel like digging the steamer trunk out again and thought to check the carriage house for a ladder. Emily would be back soon and he didn't want to attract too much attention. He quickly jotted down the translation in his notebook and shut down his laptop.

Jack stood in the doorway of the sandstone carriage house that sat at the back of the property. One hundred years ago, this building had housed Heinrich Engelhardt's horse and buggy. His coachman, Herman Schilling, and Herman's wife Viola, the head servant, had occupied the second floor. Today the building housed a bunch of junk. Jack peered into the dim light of the main room on the first floor. It was hard to pick out anything from among the clutter. Boxes and old furniture seemed to take up most of the space. Then, at last, Jack could see what he was looking for. Across the room sat an old and beat-up aluminum stepladder. He made his way through the obstacle course of boxes, chairs and tables until he reached the back of the room. The ladder seemed a little rickety and was covered in dried paint spatters, but it would have to do. He picked it up and carefully carried it back through the clutter and out of the carriage house.

He returned to the fourth floor and thought to himself where best to stash it until that night. He didn't want to leave it in the ballroom. If Emily or Mr. Engelhardt were to come up, they might see it and start asking questions about what he was up to. He planned to tell them about all of this eventually, but wanted to wait until he saw where the next clue would take him. In the end, Jack decided to hide the stepladder in the trunk space. It would be well concealed and out of the way.

As he closed the trapdoor, he heard a car pull up the driveway. Emily had returned from the market.

Chapter 16

Dinner that evening passed in relative silence and was quite uneventful. Jack never so much as hinted at what he had found upstairs that afternoon. He did mention, however, that he'd located Heinrich's death certificate. Mr. Engelhardt had never known that his great grandfather's first name was actually Hermanus and that Heinrich was a middle name. Jack also informed him about the country estate that he and his wife had retired to in Bay Village. Mr. Engelhardt was familiar with this, but had no idea that it was called Engelwood. He was saddened to hear that it had been torn down some years back. Still, he hoped that maybe Jack would be able to locate a photograph of it. Jack promised that he would do what he could.

After dessert, Jack returned to the fourth floor bedroom and spent much of the evening checking his email. One that had come in was from an architectural historian in San Francisco. Two months earlier, Jack had emailed him a layout of one of the properties that Bob Woodring had drawn. It was one of the only clues that Bob had left behind, saying where he had hidden the bodies of the girls that he had raped and murdered. Jack was still working Shelby's case and would continue to do so until he'd successfully located every last victim.

According to the email, the architectural historian was unfamiliar with a property layout fitting anything even closely resembling that description. San Francisco, as he pointed out, was too hilly for such a set-up. He might have better luck trying a location where the land was flatter. It wasn't entirely a dead end. Jack had simply managed to eliminate a possibility. Bearing this reply in mind, he would send the historian another drawing in the future: one that would better fit a hilly terrain.

Jack looked up at the antique clock above the fireplace and saw that it was close to nine. He had a notion that he would be up late figuring out the next puzzle on the clock. It would be a good idea, he thought, to take a nap. He set the alarm on his cell phone for ten forty-five, kicked off his shoes and stretched out on the bed. Within a few minutes, he was fast asleep.

The alarm pulled Jack from a deep sleep. He sat up, reached over and with his eyes still closed, deactivated the alarm. He opened his eyes to find the room quiet and calm. Soft light from the Tiffany shaded wall sconce illuminated the bedchamber. Jack rolled out of bed, put his shoes back on and looked out into the ballroom. Save for the ceaseless ticking of the large clock on the southern wall, the room was quiet and devoid of life. He turned back into the bedroom, opened the trapdoor in the floor and pulled out the old aluminum stepladder. He carried it into the ballroom, unfolded it and set it down in front of the figure of the tombstone on the left side. He gave it a little shake and thought that maybe he ought to test it out before he actually needed it. Very carefully, he started up the ladder, step by cautious step. He stopped one rung short of the top and dared not go any higher. This would be far enough anyway. He could reach the figure of the tombstone with no problem.

He climbed back down and walked over to the other tombstone on the opposite side of the clock. It was set at the same height as the first. Again, there would be no issue in reaching it. There were still five minutes to go. He walked back into the bedroom and opened his notebook. He wanted to make sure that he'd gotten the passage right. He reread it once again.

"Deaths sting on the eleventh hour... Our stones alone at twelve..."

There was no doubt in his mind. He'd have to turn and pull the figures of the hornets at eleven. As with the crows, there we're two hornets. It was a hasty assumption, but Jack concluded that he'd have to turn both of them. He'd start with the one on the left, followed by the one on the right.

He returned to the ballroom, flashlight in hand and stationed himself before the left-hand hornet. It was still another minute before eleven. The anticipation was killing him. He could only hope that operating the figures on the clock wouldn't make too much noise. The last thing he wanted to do was disturb anyone in the house at that hour. A thought crossed his mind just then. He'd pulled out the ladder, but didn't need it until midnight. If operating the clock did make a noise, someone might come up to investigate. They'd surely discover the ladder.

It was too late for him to go and hide it now. It was just a few seconds before eleven. He'd have to take the chance.

The minute hand advanced and the whirring sound began. He had fifteen seconds to complete the function. Jack immediately turned the first figure of the hornet to the right and gave it a tug. This was followed by a winding sound and a sudden thump. The noise reverberated across the otherwise quiet ballroom. Someone surely heard that but there wasn't a moment to lose. He walked over to the other hornet and likewise turned it and pulled out. Again he heard the winding sound and thump. As expected, nothing happened.

He stepped back and listened for the sound of approaching footsteps but could hear none. Perhaps, he thought, Mr. Engelhardt was a heavy sleeper. Either that or he had simply attributed the sound as another fourth floor disturbance. Emily, Jack remembered, tried not to venture up to the fourth floor at night if she could help it.

After realizing that no one was coming, he figured himself safe. The minute hand advanced and the two hornets remained in the position that Jack had moved them to. He had another hour until the next step had to be completed. He clicked off the flashlight and returned to the back bedroom.

Jack sat on the bed and tried his best to keep himself awake. He thought that maybe he would attempt to read his father's book on pipe organ repair, but at once realized that this would put him to sleep faster than anything else he could imagine. He walked over to the desk and booted up his laptop, got online and busied himself by trying to locate some information on Engelwood in Bay Village. An initial search turned up nothing. He then thought to do a property trace and went to the county recorder's website. In no time at all, he'd compiled a short list of owners that followed. He began to type these names into the search engine and after trying the third, that name being Morris Costin, he located an image of a half-timbered mansion on the Cleveland Memory Project website.

From what he could tell, it was quite a sprawling estate that sat on a wooded piece of land near the lake. The name Engelwood was appropriate to say the least. It was a shame though, Jack thought, that the house no longer existed. He'd have liked to have seen it in person.

By eleven-thirty, small drops of rain began to pelt the window. Its soft droning started to hypnotize Jack and he found it harder and harder to keep himself awake. At one point, he caught himself starting to nod off. Quickly, he jumped up, lightly slapped himself in the face and started to pace about the room. This wasn't working. It was only making him more tired.

He walked into the bathroom, turned on the cold-water at the sink and splashed some on his face. That did the trick. He dried off, walked back into the bedroom and checked the time. It was still five minutes until midnight. Realizing that staying in the bedroom might make him want to fall asleep again, he picked up his flashlight and returned to the ballroom.

The ticking from the clock continued, but seemed a little louder than he remembered. With that, he noticed a sudden drop in the air temperature. Something was happening and he didn't like it. He was ready to perform the next step in the instructions and the last thing he wanted was to be interrupted by another paranormal disturbance. Just then, he remembered the recorder crystal that Amy had given him earlier that day. He ran back into the bedroom and retrieved the small box from a side pocket of his jacket. As he stepped back into the ballroom, he could distinctly hear the whispering voice from over by the clock. Again, he thought he heard the word "thevshi" uttered. He opened the box and withdrew the crystal. It was quite warm to the touch. Realizing that he would be working over by the clock, he wanted to keep whatever was happening in that ballroom as far away from him as possible. He set the crystal down just outside the bedroom door and walked over to the clock. As he approached, he heard the whirring noise begin. He'd completely lost track of time and his cueing sound had started.

Quickly, he ascended the ladder and reached for the first tombstone. He pulled it forward and could hear the same ratcheting sound he'd heard earlier that day. It was followed by a thud. He jumped down, dragged the ladder to the other side of the clock, climbed up and pulled down on the other tombstone. As he did, he felt himself begin to lose his balance. He jumped clear of the ladder and landed hard on his side. At first, he thought that he'd missed his window, but after a second, heard another slow ratcheting sound and a thud.

At first, nothing happened, but after a moment, he heard a slamming sound from somewhere downstairs. That had done it. He'd certainly woken someone in the house.

Jack pulled himself back to his feet and thought to hide, but remembered at once the stepladder. He quickly folded it up and carried it into the bedroom. Disappointment crossed his mind. Nothing had happened. Perhaps he'd pulled down on the tombstones in the wrong order. Regardless, he couldn't stick around to see if they were going to stay in their new positions for longer than a minute or reset themselves.

After stashing the ladder back in the trunk space, he closed the trapdoor lid and could distinctly hear footsteps ascending the stairs. He then remembered the recorder crystal outside the door. With soft steps, he crossed the room, crouched down outside of the door and scooped it up. As he stood, he turned and came face to face with a young woman with a red ponytail, dressed in a long nightgown and a pair of fuzzy slippers.

"Jack?" she announced, surprised to see him up and about at this hour.

"Hi, Emily. What brings you up here?"

Emily looked scared out of her wits.

"I didn't wish to awaken Mr. Engelhardt and 'ad no one else to turn to. I 'ope I'm not disturbin' ya."

"Not at all. What's wrong?"

"Well, I was lyin' in me bed reading to meself, when I suddenly 'eard a loud bangin' noise from across the room. I looked over and saw a part o' the wall open up. I thought that the disturbances and all that was limited to the fourth floor."

"I'm pretty sure that it still is."

"'Ow do ya mean?"

"Can you keep a secret?"

Emily cocked her head and gave Jack a funny look.

"I don't really like to keep secrets from Mr. Engelhardt."

"Just for the time being. I'll tell him about it soon enough."

Emily considered it.

"Foine. What is it?"

"Follow me." Jack led her over to the clock. "It's this thing."

"The clock?"

"Well, it's more than a clock. I translated that poem above the bar and found out that it's actually instructions on how to open different hidden doors in the house."

"I don't think I get ya."

"Okay. You see these figures on the front of the clock?"

"Yeah."

"I found out that they're actually a series of levers and draw knobs. If you move certain ones at a certain time, they operate a mechanical system inside of the clock that opens up different secret passages. I had just finished operating it when that wall in your bedroom opened. At first, I thought that I'd messed something up, but after hearing what you just said, I guess I didn't." Emily stared at him with a dumbfounded expression on her face. "Isn't that great?" he said in conclusion.

"Great?" she shouted. "Ya damn near scared me to death!"

"Quiet," Jack whispered. "You want to wake up the whole house?"

"Why not? Ya just about 'ave." Emily considered it for a moment. "So where does that 'ole in me bedroom wall go?"

"I have no idea. Want to find out?"

"Ya must be out o' your bleedin' moind!"

"Shh."

"Do ya actually think I'm goin' to go walkin' around in some secret passage in this 'ouse? I'm loikely to get lost; or worse."

"Well, would you at least show me the opening so that *I* can check it out?"

Emily thought about it for a moment and could see no harm.

"Roight, then. Let's go."

Jack momentarily slipped into the bedroom where he picked up his flashlight, notebook and digital camera. He quietly followed Emily down the stairs and onto the first floor. Immediately at the bottom of the stairs, they turned to the right and entered her bedroom. Jack could at once see the large opening in the wall. He cautiously stepped over and investigated it.

As was the case with the wainscot panel in the ballroom, this section of the wall was also on a track. Jack clicked on his flashlight, stuck his head inside and inspected the area around the hidden door. He could see a series of pulleys and rods running to what appeared to be a latching system; all of which, he figured, ran through the walls and upstairs to the clock. He entered the space, pulled out his camera and began to take pictures.

Looking down at his feet, Jack noticed that he was no longer standing on a hardwood floor, but rather was treading on stone. Shining the flashlight to his right, he could tell that the passage descended downward. He snapped another photograph.

"What do ya see?" Emily asked from back in the bedroom.

"Stairs. They go down."

Jack began to move deeper into the hidden corridor.

"Wait! You're not actually goin' down there, are ya?"

"Sure."

Jack stepped out of sight, leaving Emily standing in her bedroom by herself. She stared at the hollow opening before her and had a sudden thought of some unearthly being emerging from the darkness. If Jack was going down, she figured that she'd at least be safe with him.

"Jack." She whispered. "Jack, wait."

There was no reply. With as much courage as she could muster, she slowly stepped over to the opening and poked her head inside. Terror shined in her eyes as she found herself less than an inch away from another face. She went to let out a scream, but Jack covered her mouth as she opened it.

"I heard you perfectly well and was coming back up," he told her. "Now, I'm going to take my hand from your mouth. Can you promise me that you won't scream?"

Emily nodded and Jack slowly pulled his hand away.

"God damn it!" she shouted. "Don't ya dare ever do somethin' loike that again!"

"Well, how was I supposed to know that you were coming in? I thought you said you were staying?"

"Let's just get this over with."

"Fine. Stay close," Jack instructed.

"No problem there."

Jack walked down the stone stairwell with Emily's hand resting firmly between his shoulder blades. Though he had his flashlight on, it was still quite hard for him to make out anything in the darkness ahead of him: only the next three or four steps. He took a few more pictures; not because there was anything of interest worth capturing, but more for the light that the flash offered. He'd hoped that it might give him a better idea of what was ahead, but it didn't. The strobe was actually a little blinding. He began to realize that taking these pictures was becoming more of a hindrance. As he went to turn the camera off, he looked at the digital display. Many orbs filled the screen. All in all, the stairwell passage was quite dusty.

Finally, they came to the end of the stairwell and the corridor continued on through a brick-lined, arched hallway. Moisture had seeped in through the brickwork and Jack's flashlight reflected off small puddles of water that had collected on the floor.

"Careful," he told Emily. "It's a little slippery up ahead."

Emily nodded and patted Jack twice on the back to acknowledge that she'd heard him and understood. They pressed on through the humid darkness until they came to another short run of stairs that carried them deeper underground.

"'Ow far down does this go?" Emily asked. Jack raised his flashlight and aimed it ahead.

"Only about five or six steps by the looks of it. Come on."

Jack could tell that Emily was now holding on tightly to the back of his shirt. She was definitely afraid.

They descended the last set of stairs and found themselves in a wide, circular room with a low vaulted ceiling. Emily looked up at this ceiling and was immediately drawn to the detail that it carried.

"We must be somewhere under the old carriage 'ouse," she pointed out. "I wonder why anyone would build a room loike this?"

"Um, that's why."

Emily finally pulled her gaze away from the detailed ceiling and noticed what Jack had been staring at the entire time. In the center of the room sat two stone sarcophaguses.

"Roight. I'm leaving now."

Emily tried to vacate the room as quickly as possible but Jack turned and grabbed her by the back of her nightgown, much as she had done with his shirt when following him down deeper into the crypt.

"Come on. Stop," he said as he shined the flashlight at her. "There's nothing down here that can hurt you."

Emily nervously peered over Jack's shoulder and glimpsed the two burial vaults in the center of the room.

"What about those?"

"What, you're afraid that a stone coffin is going to get you?"

"No, but maybe what's insoide will."

"Well I'm pretty certain that Count Chocula isn't sleeping in the basement of Waldemere. Besides, I think I know what this is. Wait here."

Jack made to walk down into the room, but Emily firmly grasped his hand.

"What are ya doin'?" she exclaimed.

"It's okay. I just have to check something out."

Emily let go of him and nervously wrung her hands as Jack approached the vaults. He shined his light on one and then the other.

"Yeah, that's what I thought," he said at last. "It's okay, Emily. You can come down."

"That's alroight. I can wait roight 'ere." She vigorously shook her head in disapproval.

"No. Really. It'll be alright," he assured her.

Seeing that there was no way around it, Emily carefully stepped down into the crypt. She stopped about five feet from where Jack stood between the two vaults.

"Do I 'ave to come any closer?"

"No. I guess you can see it from there. Look."

Jack flashed his light onto the vault that was set to Emily's left. At first, she could see nothing, but after a moment, she noticed a series of letters and numbers inscribed upon the lid.

Vater
H. C. H. Engelhardt
Geb.
7 Okt. 1828
Gest.

At first, Emily couldn't make sense of the characters, but after a moment, a sinking realization sank in.

"Is that what I think it is?" she asked as she took a slight step backwards. Jack nodded.

"Now look at this one," he instructed as he shone the light onto the other vault.

"I'd rather not."

Emily looked as though she were ready to leave again.

"Oh, come on. It's safe."

Emily anxiously read the next inscription.

Mutter
Sophia
Gattin von
H. C. H. Engelhardt
Geb.
14 Dez. 1832
Gest.

"I really 'ave to leave now." Emily turned again to walk out of the crypt, but Jack called after her.

"It's okay. They're empty."

Emily stopped and turned.

"What do ya mean, they're empty?"

"Just that. Take another look at these inscriptions. What's missing?"

Emily slowly peered back over.

"I don't know. Their death dates?"

"Exactly. This word here 'Gest' means 'Died' in German."

"So maybe no one ever got round to puttin' their death dates on them."

"No. It's nothing like that. They're buried over at Monroe Street Cemetery with their son Ludwig. I've read up on the legend of this house and it said that Heinrich Engelhardt had built a burial crypt somewhere in Waldemere, but that no one has ever been able to locate it. Obviously, no one has ever managed to figure out how to properly work the clock."

"Are ya sure those are empty?"

"I'm positive. The Engelhardts sold this house about six years before they died."

"What if after they died, they buried them 'ere anyway?"

"Like the next owner would actually let someone be buried in his basement? Come on. I'll show you."

Jack firmly grasped the lid to Heinrich Engelhardt's vault and began to slide it over. The grinding sound of stone on stone echoed throughout the chamber.

"What are ya doin'?" Emily yelled as she turned her head and cowered.

Jack finished sliding it open about a foot and shined his flashlight inside.

"You see? Nobody's home."

The vault was empty. Emily slowly turned her head and caught a glimpse of the vacant sarcophagus. She let out a sigh.

"Ya weren't certain though," she scolded.

"Of course I was. See?" Jack turned and began to slide open the lid of Sophia's vault. Again, the grinding sound filled the crypt. He shined the flashlight inside and smiled at Emily. "See? It's empty."

Emily let out the most blood-curdling scream that Jack had ever heard in his life. His eyes widened as he saw the expression of terror on her face. Slowly he turned his head and glanced into the vault. Grinning back up at him were three bony faces with long flowing hair; their skin like a powdery brown leather, their eyes little more than sunken in slits. Jack dropped the flashlight and fell over with horrified shock.

This vault was occupied.

Chapter 17

Henry Engelhardt had been awakened by Emily's screams. He quickly threw a robe about himself, pulled on a pair of slippers and walked down the stairs to her bedroom. He found her door wide open and Emily missing. After a moment though, he noticed the large opening in the wall. A male's voice was coming from somewhere down in the darkness and was approaching fast. Uncertain of what was transpiring, Mr. Engelhardt looked around the room, located an umbrella by the door and armed himself with it.

Jack stepped out through the opening and received a hearty whack to the forehead. He fell backwards and into the dark corridor where Emily caught him. Seeing her aiding him, Mr. Engelhardt lowered the umbrella with confusion.

"What's going on here?" he demanded to know. "Emily, I heard you scream. What's happened?"

"Jack's managed to locate a crypt in the basement," she informed him.

"Jack?"

"I'm sorry. Mr. Sullivan," Emily corrected herself.

Mr. Engelhardt looked over at Jack.

"Jack, I must apologize for striking you, but I heard Emily's scream and feared the worst. What are you doing down here at this hour?"

"I was going to tell you about this in the morning, but I don't think we can wait for that now. Earlier, I managed to figure out that by moving around some of the figures on that clock upstairs at certain times, secret doorways open up throughout the house. I located one this afternoon and this one tonight."

Mr. Engelhardt looked past Jack and Emily and stared into the dark opening in the wall.

"And this, you say, leads to a crypt?"

"Henry," Jack continued. "We need to call the police."

"Why?"

"Because we found human remains down there."

Mr. Engelhardt looked a little perplexed.

"Well, it's a crypt. Aren't there supposed to be dead people in it?"

"Um, not like this. One vault is empty and the other holds what looks to be the remains of three women. I don't think anyone would bury three women in one vault. It just seems a little unorthodox."

Henry Engelhardt thought about it for a moment. Jack could see and understand the conflict that he was going through. It made perfect sense to report the find but then, in the same respect, it would bring down unwanted attention upon him. At last, Henry Engelhardt spoke.

"Very well, I'll make the call. You two get cleaned up. Both of you are a sight. I expect that we'll be entertaining guests very soon."

With that, he left the room and slowly walked back up the stairs. Jack looked over at Emily and saw that he was right. She was completely covered in thick, light-brown dust. Jack looked down at his hands and saw that they too were indeed quite filthy.

"Well, I'm going up to change," he told her. "Whatever you do, don't close that panel. It'll be another half-day before I can reopen it if you do."

"'Old on! You're not leavin' me down 'ere with that thing opened."

"So don't stay down here."

Emily looked about the room.

"Just wait until I can gather some clean clothes."

Jack did as she asked. She pulled some fresh garments from a dresser and picked up a pair of shoes. Next, she walked into her bathroom at the end of the hall and collected her soap, towel and shampoo.

"Ready?" Jack asked. Emily nodded.

They climbed the stairs to the second floor where Emily put her things down in one of the spare bedrooms.

"I suspect I'll be movin' into 'ere tonoight," she said. "There's no way in 'ell that I'll ever sleep down in *that* bedroom again."

Jack finished taking a shower and donned his plaid terrycloth bathrobe. He walked back into the fourth floor bedroom and pulled out a change of clothes from the dresser across the room. As he laid them out on the bed, there was a knock at the door.

"Yes?" he called out. The door opened and Emily entered.

"Jack, I..."

She noticed at once that he wasn't dressed and averted her eyes.

"It's okay," Jack assured her. "I'm wearing a robe. What is it?"

"The bobbies, um... the um... police are 'ere and they'd loike to speak with ya."

"Alright. I'll be down in a moment. Thanks."

Emily left the room with her hand still shading her eyes.

After dressing, Jack went down to the second floor where Emily informed him that the police were waiting for him in the parlor. He could see beyond her, two officers standing by the side door. There were a few voices coming up from what he assumed was her former bedroom. Emily didn't seem to mind and Jack seriously doubted that she'd ever go in there again, except to remove the rest of her possessions.

Jack turned, walked down the hall, and knocked on one of the large pocket doors.

"Enter," Henry Engelhardt instructed.

Jack walked into the front parlor and saw two Cleveland police officers standing at one end of the room. Mr. Engelhardt was seated in a chair by the fireplace, which he'd apparently had Emily light before the police arrived.

"Is this him?" one of the officers asked.

"This is Jack Sullivan," Mr. Engelhardt announced.

"Mr. Sullivan," the officer continued, "please take a seat."

Jack did as he was told.

"I was just telling the officers here," Mr. Engelhardt continued, "that you're the one who managed to figure out what that clock upstairs does."

"Mr. Sullivan," the officer interrupted, "we understand that you're the one who located the hidden room as well as the human remains."

"That's correct."

"Would you please describe for us the events that lead up to your discovery this morning." It wasn't so much a question as it was a command. The officer pulled out a notepad and a pen and stood ready to take down Jack's statement.

Jack proceeded to tell the officers about how he'd figured out how to operate the clock and his discovery of the security vault on the fourth floor earlier that day. He told them how Emily had come upstairs after the passageway had opened in her bedroom and about how they went down together and explored it.

"And why would you open a coffin in the first place, Mr. Sullivan?" the officer continued.

"Because I believed it to be empty."

"Why would you suspect that a coffin is empty?"

"Well, the people whose names appear on it are actually buried at Monroe Street Cemetery. I didn't think that there could possibly be anyone else inside. Do you know who they are?"

"We have no idea," replied the officer. "A forensics team is carefully extracting the remains as we speak. Currently, we're treating this as a crime scene. You may all have to find other accommodations for the remainder of the night."

Mr. Engelhardt cast Jack a glance that showed that he was less than pleased with this news. Jack tried to think of how to fix this and ultimately came up with a solution.

"You know," he began, "if you close that access panel, it can't be opened again until around noon."

"Regardless of that," the officer went on, "we don't want to take any chances of the crime scene being contaminated."

Just then, a heavyset man in a white Kevlar suit entered the parlor with a clipboard and turned to the officer that hadn't been interviewing Jack.

"Well," he started, "I think we can say that any evidence of a crime was wiped away a long time ago."

"How so?" the other officer asked.

"Those dead girls down in that room, they've been dead for many years now."

"How many years?"

"I dunno. A hundred, maybe more."

The officer that had been interviewing Jack closed his notepad and tucked his pen back into his shirt pocket.

"I think we have all we need here," he said as he turned to his partner.

"Do we still have to find other accommodations for the remainder of the night?" Mr. Engelhardt asked.

"Not unless you want to." The officer turned to the forensics investigator. "Are you guys just about done down there?"

"Oh yeah. We removed the bodies and have all the pictures we need."

"Good." The officer turned back to Mr. Engelhardt. "We're going to look into this and will let you know what we find. In the meantime, I would avoid going back down there. The ceiling in that hallway didn't look very safe. I'd be worried about a cave in or something."

"I understand."

"All right then. You have a good evening, Mr. Engelhardt."

"Thank you. I'll show you out."

Henry Engelhardt escorted the officers and the forensics investigator out of the parlor. Jack remained and considered carefully what he had just heard. The remains found in the crypt were over a hundred years old. He had an idea what this meant. A moment later, Emily ducked her head around the corner.

"What 'appened?" she asked.

"Nothing really. They just asked me a few questions. Turns out those girls have been dead for a long time."

"I know. I overheard someone mentionin' that. Are ya goin' to be okay, Jack?"

"Me? Oh yeah. I'm fine. How are you holding up?"

"Still a little shaken, I think. I just can't get passed the thought that I've been sleeping in that room for the last month and 'ad no idea that there were three dead people on the other soide o' me wall."

"I'm sure you'll get over it."

Just then, Henry Engelhardt entered the parlor through the pocket doors coming from the dining room.

"Well, everyone, I think we've had enough excitement for one night. I strongly suggest that we all return to our bedrooms, except for you Emily. You'll be staying here on the second floor from now on. We should all try to get some sleep and enjoy what's left of the evening. Anything that has to be said can be discussed in the morning. Now, goodnight everyone."

Mr. Engelhardt crossed the room, exited through the pocket doors that led into the main hall and climbed the front stairs. Jack took this as his cue to return to his room as well. Emily extinguished the fire that had been burning in the grate. She would find it quite hard to sleep after an evening like this.

Chapter 18

Jack awoke that Friday morning to overcast skies and a light drizzle that left its traces on the windowpane. Looking over at the clock on the mantle, he could see that it was well after ten. Emily hadn't come up to call him for breakfast and it was likely that, considering the events that had unfolded during the night, everyone was having something of a lie-in. Although it was becoming quite late, Jack didn't feel like getting out of bed just yet. The room seemed cold to him and he found it to be more comfortable under the covers. He rolled over and tried to get back to sleep, but found that he couldn't. There was no fighting it. He was up.

After shaving and brushing his teeth, Jack finally heard the familiar dainty knock on the bedroom door.

"Yes?"

Remembering how she had walked in on Jack the previous night while he was still in his bathrobe, Emily opened the door an inch, but didn't look in.

"Are ya dressed, Mr. Sullivan?"

"One second." Jack stepped from the bathroom and tossed on a tee shirt with a silk-screened image of a ship bearing the words "Cleveland Steamer" printed across it. It had been a gift from his friend Geoff and was something of an inside joke between the two of them. "Okay. You can come in."

Emily opened the door, but didn't enter.

"Seein' as it's quite late in the mornin', we've decided on brunch instead o' breakfast. It should be ready in about twenty minutes."

"Thank you, Emily. I'll be down in a few."

Emily nodded and closed the door. To Jack, she seemed a little distant. It was back to calling him "Mr. Sullivan". Perhaps, he thought, Henry Engelhardt had reprimanded her for her informal slip-up the night before. He only hoped that she hadn't received too much of an earful.

After Jack had finished dressing, he came downstairs and found Mr. Engelhardt already at the dining room table, reading the morning papers. He looked up and smiled coyly.

"Good morning, Jack. How did you sleep?"

Jack took a seat at the table beside Mr. Engelhardt.

"Probably about as well as you did," he replied.

"Well," Henry Engelhardt continued nonchalantly, "I'd say that was really something of an interesting night. You really do know how to have a good time. We must do that more often."

There was something odd about his demeanor that was throwing Jack for a loop. Jack squirmed uncomfortably in his seat.

"I don't know if I'd go as far as to call it a good time."

"Oh, come on, Jack. Secret passages, skeletons, police, the coroner's office: we don't get that kind of excitement here at Waldemere every day."

"Coffee, Mr. Sullivan?" Emily asked as she entered the dining room with a carafe in her right hand.

"Yes. Thank you, Emily."

She poured him a cup and quietly left the room.

"Now Jack, I know that you might think that I'd be a little upset with you about keeping secrets from me, but I did say that it was alright for you to explore the house as you saw fit. I hired you to investigate this house and to clear my great grandfather's name at all costs. If that entails you withholding information from me for a time, then so be it. But I do want you to know that you can tell me about anything that you might find. After all, you may be surprised at what I may already know."

Jack was a little surprised by this statement.

"And did you know anything about the clock or the crypt?"

"Some, yes. I had heard a rumor about there being a crypt located somewhere in the house and suspected that the entrance must be located on the first floor. I actually thought that it was somewhere in the utility room and never would have suspected that it was actually in Emily's bedroom."

"I see."

"And as far as the clock goes, I knew that it must have had something to do with opening the door to the crypt. I just had no idea how to get it to work. Remember, I'd just fixed that clock last week and knew that there were spare parts. I just couldn't figure it out, but you did. You see? Your research is already paying off."

"I'm sure it's not what you were expecting though. I would have…"

Jack was interrupted by the sound of a bell echoing through the house.

"Don't answer that!" Mr. Engelhardt called out, presumably to Emily: his voice slightly agitated and severe. Jack was confused.

"What's going on?"

Mr. Engelhardt relaxed his expression.

"Reporters. Apparently, news travels faster in this town than I would have first thought. They started showing up around nine, but I haven't talked to any of them as of yet."

"Do you think you will?"

"I'm not sure. I figure that they'll eventually go away. Still, this is bigger news that I imagined it would be."

"Well, a lot of people are familiar with this house and the legends behind it. Folks are curious about what happens here. Truth be told, the place is something of a Cleveland icon."

"Be that as it may, I'd just prefer to have a little privacy on this."

"Well, apparently people already know about it. Would you prefer that I go and talk to the media? I can be very discreet."

"That's okay. If they wish to hear about what happened here last night, it's probably best that they hear it from me."

Jack nodded in agreement. There was a moment of silence between them. As he took a sip from his coffee, Jack considered how best to approach the next topic. Delicately, he decided.

"Which brings me to what I've been wanting to discuss with you," Jack began. "Last night, that man from forensics had mentioned that those corpses were about a hundred years old; give or take. There happened to be three of them, female by the looks of it, and they were stuffed inside of a vault that was originally supposed to contain the remains of your great grandmother. That vault was located in a room that, I'm assuming, no one but your ancestors knew about."

Mr. Engelhardt could see where he was going with this.

"Okay, Jack. Go ahead and say it."

"I'm sorry to have to tell you that it looks more and more like the stories about your great grandfather may be true."

Henry Engelhardt let him continue.

"Everything seems to fit," Jack explained. "Three girls that worked for the Engelhardt family go missing during the late eighteen hundreds; your great grandfather is accused of murdering them..."

"And was cleared."

"Because there were no bodies found."

"Now I heard that one actually *was* found."

Jack thought about this for a moment.

"Yes, the remains of a girl were discovered floating in the water near Whiskey Island, but she was never actually proven or positively identified as Katherine Fitzgerald. All that the record stated was that she closely resembled her. In truth, it could have been anyone."

"My great grandfather was a kind and generous man. He donated often to charitable organizations. My father even described him as being a kind and loving gentleman. I can't see how someone like this could be capable of murder."

"Well, those girls had to end up in that vault somehow. I'm sorry, Henry, but all the evidence points to Heinrich Engelhardt. I don't know what else I can do."

"Jack, I've worked with historical researchers in the past and can safely say that so far, you're the best that I've come across. That being said, I also think that you're wrong on this. Even if those skeletons do turn out to be the missing girls that my great grandfather was accused of murdering, there would have to be someone else responsible for their deaths. I'm telling you. The man wouldn't have hurt a fly."

Jack carefully considered Mr. Engelhardt's words.

"I just feel like I've reached an impasse. I've read the court records and there isn't all that much in there: accusations and a few testimonies at best. It's not like I can go back and re-interview those witnesses. All in all, it's going to be pretty hard for me to retry and clear a man who's been dead for over a hundred years."

"But if anyone can do it, I'm sure that you can."

"Thanks for your vote of confidence," Jack snorted.

"I *am* confident, Jack; so to the point that I'm willing to stake a larger claim on it. I'm raising your salary by another hundred dollars per day."

Jack shot him a look of astonishment.

"That's really not necessary."

"I know, but I really want you to see this through. I'm telling you that Heinrich Engelhardt was no murderer. There has to be someone else. You need to find out who that person was, no matter what it takes."

"No matter what it takes?"

"You heard me."

Jack was resolved.

"Okay. I'll stay on, but I should tell you right now, that things might get a little bumpy. I'll have to dig a lot deeper into your family's history than I would normally care to go. I may find a few things that you won't want me to find, or care to know about yourself. My methods at this point can be a little unorthodox. Also, I'll need unlimited access to the house. There may be more secret passages that will reveal further clues."

"I wouldn't expect anything less. Are we agreed to the new terms of your employment then?"

He extended his right hand to Jack.

"We are."

Jack shook his hand and nodded. Just then, the doorbell cried out once more. Mr. Engelhardt looked up and saw his next course of action.

"Okay then, Jack. I guess it's time we broke our silence."

He stood up from the table and walked through the parlor and into the main hall. Jack was curious and followed. As he entered the hall, he could see Mr. Engelhardt walking down the short run of steps at the foyer. He looked to his right and noticed that Emily was watching them intently. Henry Engelhardt opened the front door and greeted a reporter that held a microphone in her hand. Behind her stood a tall and broad-shouldered cameraman.

"Good morning, sir," the reported began, "My name is Christine McGovern and I'm with Channel 7 News."

"Good morning," Mr. Engelhardt replied with a broad smile. "How can I help you?"

"Are you the current owner of Waldemere?"

"I am."

"And your name, sir?"

"Henry Engelhardt, Miss McGovern."

"Oh, it's *Mrs*. McGovern," she giggled as she held up her left hand to show him the wedding ring that graced it. She straightened her expression and continued with the interview. "Mr. Engelhardt. We've received word this morning of a grim discovery in your home. Would you be willing to tell us exactly what that discovery was?"

"Certainly. During the early morning hours, an associate and guest in my house had managed to locate a hidden room on the lowest level of the house. Secreted away in this room were the remains of three people."

"And do you have any idea who these people might have been?"

"We don't have the slightest idea, but police are investigating the matter and have promised to stay in touch with me on their findings."

"Now, it's no secret that many people in Cleveland have heard rumors that Waldemere was once the site of a series of brutal murders. Is it possible that the discovery of these human remains may be linked in some way with that story?"

"I think that's just speculation. After all, it was my great grandfather that was accused of those murders."

"Oh." Mrs. McGovern hadn't expected to hear this.

"It was... Mr. Jack Sullivan here who made the discovery last night." Henry Engelhardt turned and waved Jack over to the door. Seeing no harm in this, Jack shrugged his shoulders and approached.

"Mr. Sullivan," Christine McGovern said as the camera and her attention were suddenly turned on him. "What was your impression when you first made the discovery last night?"

Without thinking, Jack placed his hands on the side of his face, bulged out his eyes and silently mimicked a horrified scream. The videographer lowered the camera and almost died laughing. Mrs. McGovern was not amused. She turned to the cameraman and backhanded him across the shoulder. He straightened himself out and resumed recording.

"Let me rephrase that," she continued. "What was the first thing that crossed your mind when you made the discovery?"

"Well," Jack began, "I was a little startled at first, to say the least. I mean, who expects to find a body hidden in a house, let alone three?"

"Who indeed? And what happened immediately afterward?"

"Oh. Well, we went to get Mr. Engelhardt here and tell him of what we found."

"We?"

"Yeah. Emily, Mr. Engelhardt's assistant was with me." Jack didn't feel comfortable referring to her as a servant.

"And what was Mr. Engelhardt's reaction to this news?"

Christine McGovern gave Jack a very serious look. She could tell that he was about to repeat the expression that he had just demonstrated. Sensing that she was wise, he thought better of it.

"Well, he decided that we should call the cops." This wasn't exactly how it had transpired, but Jack didn't feel like mentioning that Henry Engelhardt had struck him across the head with an umbrella. The reporter turned back to Mr. Engelhardt.

"So you were the one that made the call and notified the authorities?"

"That's correct. They arrived shortly afterward and took statements from myself, Emily and Jack. Oh, they also removed the bodies."

"I should certainly hope so."

"Is there anything else that you would like to know?" Mr. Engelhardt asked.

"No, I think we have everything. Thank you, Mr. Engelhardt." She turned to the cameraman and made a slashing motion across her throat, indicating that he could stop recording.

"A good day to you then, Mrs. McGovern."

As he went to close the front door, Christine McGovern turned and posed one more question to Jack.

"I'm sorry, Mr. Sullivan, but have we met before?"

"It's possible," he said. "Where did you grow up?"

"Virginia. No, I don't think that's it."

"I don't know, then."

Jack realized as her eyes lit up that he had been found out.

"Wait a minute. You're the same guy that helped solve the Rebecca Lowe case back in the fall. Aren't you?"

She motioned for the cameraman to start rolling again.

"Uh… yeah. That was me. But I don't want to talk about that. The case has been solved and I only played a small part in it."

"No, I'd say you played a pretty big part. You figured out who the kidnapper was and lead the FBI to him. You saved that little girl's life."

"And witnessed a man blowing his brains out all over the place. Like I said, I don't want to talk about it."

Jack closed the door and left Christine McGovern and her cameraman standing on the front step. He turned and made his way up into the main hall where he came face to face with Mr. Engelhardt and Emily standing motionless and staring at him.

"What was that last part all about, Jack?" asked Mr. Engelhardt.

Jack had hoped that they hadn't heard any of it, but judging by their expressions, they'd caught every word.

"It's nothing. I worked a missing person's case last October and kind of got caught up in a media frenzy shortly afterward. I've been trying to put it out of my mind since."

"Maxine never mentioned any of this to me."

"Yeah, I didn't think that she would. She's aware that I'm trying to forget about it and probably didn't wish to impart any of it to a prospective employer. Besides, it's not something that I like to bring up."

"It was pretty bad, then?"

"Well, it wasn't good."

"But I 'eard 'er say that ya saved some girl's loife," Emily interjected. "That must count for somethin'."

Jack nodded.

"Still, I'd like to forget about some aspects of that case." Jack decided to change the subject. "You know? If I'm going to continue with this one, I better get moving. I'll have a lot of running around to do today if I'm ever going to get anywhere."

"But what about brunch?" Emily added.

"Ah. No time. Thanks for the coffee though. If you'll excuse me."

Jack turned and walked up the front main stairwell to the third floor. With Henry Engelhardt and Emily still downstairs, Jack saw this as the perfect opportunity to result to one of his more unconventional approaches to research. He quietly ducked into Mr. Engelhardt's bathroom and glanced down into the wastebasket. He rooted past a few used facial tissues and an empty tube of toothpaste until he reached the bottom of the can. He felt around until he finally found and retrieved what he was looking for. He walked over to a tissue dispenser on the back of the toilet, pulled one out of the box and wrapped it around his prize.

Silent as a thief, he slipped out of the bathroom and caught the back stairwell that took him up to the fourth. He put on his jacket and cap and collected his notebook. He had a very important stop to make that day and although the company where he was going was really quite friendly, the place itself gave him the creeps.

Chapter 19

When Jack had pulled out of the driveway at Waldemere, he noticed that the reporter and cameraman were still on the scene. They were apparently recording the part of the news story where the reporter leads in or gives the conclusion. Jack paid very little attention to this. He only hoped that he wouldn't be stopped and asked further questions regarding his connection to the Rebecca Lowe case. As far as he was concerned, he'd had enough of it.

Two weeks after she'd been rescued, Rebecca Lowe had personally requested to meet Jack face to face. After much consideration, he'd finally agreed to do so. At first, he thought that it was just going to be him stopping into her hospital room and meeting with her and her parents. He was quite surprised to find a camera crew and reporter waiting for him. He was about to turn and leave when Special Agent Andrew Spurlock approached and convinced him to just go through with it. Jack did. He pasted a smile across his face, met with Rebecca and her family and even sat for a brief interview with the media. Afterward, he stepped out of that hospital room and the public limelight with hopes of never being considered famous for something like that ever again.

It was true that Jack was still on the case: to a certain point. He'd agreed to continue to help the FBI with their investigation into the other possible victims of Bob Woodring, but it had been slow-going these last few months. Furthermore, he had a promise to keep to Shelby. To him, that mattered most.

It was just after one-thirty in the afternoon when Jack arrived at the Cuyahoga County Morgue. If there was anyone who could help him to shed light on the identities of the three corpses found in the crypt at Waldemere, it was his cousin Pam.

He stepped out of his car under a blustery gray sky, approached the heavy steel door and pressed the buzzer.

"Can I help you?" The man's voice sounded deep and guttural as it came through the speaker box.

"Yes. I'm here to see Pamela Martin."

"One moment please."

There was silence as Jack waited for Pam. He briefly thought on the only other time he had visited the county morgue. It was then that he had first met Bob Woodring. At the time, he still had no idea that this was the man he had been hired to find or that the man had already killed nearly forty girls. The truth was that nobody knew. After all, Bob seemed like a pleasant enough individual and not capable of committing such atrocities. It was this that placed doubts in Jack's mind when it came to judging whether or not a seemingly nice person was capable of murder. When it really came down to it, Henry Engelhardt could tell Jack until he was blue in the face that his great grandfather was an innocent man. Jack needed the proof.

"Jack, is that you?" Pam's voice called from the speaker box.

"Yeah. How'd you guess?"

"I saw the case file for the three sets of remains that came in this morning and your name was listed as the finder. Figured you be down at some point. Here, let me ring you in."

The lock buzzed and Jack opened the door. The last time he was here, the hallway ahead of him was completely dark, but that had been on a weekend. Today it was quite well lit and full of activity. Looking down the hall, he could see Pam approaching.

"Hi, Jack. It's good to see you."

"Thanks. It's good to be seen. How's Trish doing?"

"Pretty good. They've had a surprisingly busy winter at Killington Hill. You should call her when you get a chance."

"I should. It's been close to two months since I've heard from her."

"Well, I know she'd love to hear from you. I talked to her this morning and told her about your find. What were you doing at Waldemere in the middle of the night?"

"Oh. I've been staying there for the past few days. It's part of a research project that I'm working on."

"Really? How much longer are you going to be there?"

"Only until about Sunday."

"Well, like I said. Trish would love to hear from you; especially with all of this going on."

"I'll give her a shout at some point. So I was wondering if…"

"The remains that you found this morning?" Pam interrupted. "We've already started on them."

"And have you learned anything yet?"

"A little. Come on and I'll show you."

She led Jack down the hallway and into the large room at the end. There were a couple of people gathered around three tables that had been set up in the middle of the room. Their attire reminded him of something that a surgeon might wear.

"What are they doing?" he asked.

"Right now, we're taking samples: hair, skin and fingernails for the most part."

"And what will that be able to tell you?"

"Age of the corpses. Not how old they were at the time of death, we've already determined that, but how long they've been deceased. We're just doing this as an added measure. We've pretty much concluded that they've been dead for about a hundred and twenty five to a hundred and thirty years."

"And how old were they at the time of death?"

"That depends on which corpse you're referring to. Here. Let me show you. We have them laid out by height and numbered as Jane Does One, Two and Three. Let's start with Jane Doe One." Pam headed to the first table, but Jack held back. "Oh, come on, Jack. You can't still be nervous about being around a set of human remains. After all, you're the one who found them in the first place."

Jack could see the sense in this and continued to follow her over to the first table. Still, he stayed about five feet back.

"So what are we looking at here?" he asked.

"Jane Doe One. She was approximately fifty-nine inches tall, was in her mid to late teens and had dark hair: possibly black."

"Possibly black?"

"Well, it can be pretty hard to tell after this many years have gone by. Pigmentation fades, but there are usually some clues left to tell us what her original hair color was. I won't get into it right now, but trust me. The clues are there."

"Were there any identifying marks on her?"

"Aside from her injuries? None that we were able to find."

"What injuries?"

"Look here." Pam pulled on a set of surgical gloves, approached the corpse and rolled its loose head slowly to the left. This was accompanied by a slight cracking noise that made Jack's skin crawl. "There are three depressions on the skull where it appears that she was repeatedly struck with a blunt object."

"Do you have any idea what that object might have been?"

"Actually, we do." Pam turned and walked over to a table that was set off to the side. There were a few items placed about it. "The impressions seem to match up perfectly with one of these."

She held up an antique silver candlestick holder.

"Where did you find that?"

"It was in the vault with the three sets of remains. Everything on this table was." As she said this, Pam realized that he was unaware that there were further items discovered that night. "You didn't notice any of this when you opened the vault?"

"No. Nor did anyone mention it to us after the fact." Jack scanned the table. It contained another candlestick holder along with a few assorted pieces of jewelry, necklaces for the most part, and some silver flatware. Jack turned back to the table that contained the remains of Jane Doe One.

"And did she have anything on her person?"

"No. In fact, she was barely even clothed. All that she had on were some bloomers and a pair of striped stockings."

"Topless, huh?"

"We haven't yet ruled out sexual assault."

"I see. What about the next one?" Jack asked as he strolled over to the second table. He didn't get too close, as a woman was currently working on the remains, apparently removing a patch of hair at the roots.

"This is Jane Doe Two or 'The Pretty One' as some of us have taken to calling her."

"Yeah? Why do you call her that?"

"Obviously because she was a redhead."

Jack smirked. Pam was quite proud of her curly red hair; a Martin family trait that Jack's mother had also inherited, but had skipped Jack entirely.

"So what have you learned about her?"

"Well, let's see. She was somewhere in her mid-teens when she died, was approximately sixty-two inches tall and had this beautiful head of long red hair."

Jack stepped in to get a closer look.

"Hmm. How did she die?"

"Preliminary results show that she was asphyxiated, most likely due to strangulation, possibly with a rope."

"Strangulation? That's horrible."

"That's not the worst of it."

"I don't know what's worse than that."

"Jack, she was pregnant."

Jack felt his heart sink. He had the utmost sympathy for this girl.

"You're right. That *is* worse. How far along was she?"

"About three months, which means she probably knew that she was expecting."

Jack could only imagine her pleading for the life of her unborn child as she was having the breath choked out of her. The person who had done this truly was a monster. Jack quickly wanted to change the subject and scratch this thought from his mind.

"And what was she wearing?" he asked.

"Fairly plain clothes. A white shirt, simple black dress, stockings, black boots and appropriate undergarments fitting a woman living in the late eighteen hundreds. Oh, you know what, though? This one did have something on her when she died."

Pam walked over to another table that contained a pile of woman's clothes that Jack assumed belonged to Jane Doe Two. She reached down to the side and held up a small metal chain with a couple of items dangling from the end.

"What's that?"

Pam walked back over and handed it to Jack.

"It's a chain containing two keys," she informed him. Jack looked down and examined it closely. There were in fact two keys, both quite old, hanging from the end of the chain. The larger of the two, a cast iron one, reminded Jack of the keys that Henry Engelhardt had on his key ring the first day that he'd arrived at Waldemere. The other was considerably smaller but also cast iron. "Since they were found at Waldemere," Pam continued, "I'm thinking that you may have some luck in figuring out what they go to. You're there until Sunday, you said?"

"That's right."

"Well, hopefully you can find out what doors they unlock."

"Thanks," Jack said as he placed the keys in his pocket. "So who was the last one?"

"Jane Doe Three? She's the tall one."

"How tall?"

"Seventy inches; that's five foot, ten."

"Yeah, that's pretty tall."

"Especially for a woman living in the Nineteenth Century, Jack. People were considerably shorter back then."

"And how did she die?"

"Asphyxiation."

"Strangled?"

"We don't think so. There weren't any marks around her neck. We're guessing that she was suffocated."

"So other than being tall, what else do you know about her?"

"Let's see. She was in her late teens or early twenties, had dark brown hair and might have come from a rich family."

"How would you know something like that?"

"Well, Jack. She has very good teeth. Back then; many people couldn't afford to see a dentist. The fact that she still had good teeth this late in life indicates that her family was better off than most."

"How was she dressed?"

"Ah, now that's our other clue. She was wearing a very fine dress with a lot of lace and frills. Also, she had this on her."

Pam walked over to another table and, just as she had picked up the key, lifted what looked to be a silver locket.

"May I see that?" he asked.

"Of course."

Pam handed it to Jack. The small silver locket was oval in shape, about two inches in height and had the letter "S" stylistically engraved upon the face. He carefully pried it open. Inside were two tiny photographs. The one on the left was that of a girl, possibly in her early teens. The one on the right was of a man with a large mustache and a woman with her hair fashionably pulled up. Jack had an idea as to who this girl might have been.

"Just off hand," he said as he closed the locket and passed it back to Pam, "do you have any idea what these girls might have looked like?"

"Well, sort of. Do you see that man seated at that desk over there? He's doing facial reconstructions based on the bone structures of the remains."

Jack followed Pam's gaze and saw a man seated at a desk working on a computer with two images on the screen. The image on the left was of a decomposed face while the one on the right belonged to that of a healthy young woman. He was currently working at reconstructing a mouth.

"Well here," Jack said as he reached into the inside pocket of his leather jacket. "I have a picture that might be able to help him."

He pulled out his digital camera and handed it to Pam, who looked very confused.

"I don't get it."

"Oh. I'm sorry."

Jack took the camera back from her, turned it on and set it to the playback function. He scrolled through the images until he came to the one of Waldemere and the Engelhardt family posing before it with their servants.

"What am I looking at here?"

"It's a picture of your possible victims."

Pam took the camera from him and stared at the digital display screen on the back.

"Is there any way that you can zoom in on any of these people?"

"Not on here there isn't. Hold on." Jack turned the camera off, flipped open the bottom and ejected the memory card. "Here. Load this into your computer."

Pam took the memory card from him, walked over to her desk and inserted the small black cartridge. After opening a few windows, the image popped up on her screen with crystal clear detail.

"So what is this?" she asked again.

"It's Waldemere in 1879. You see this tall, proud looking girl here on the right?"

"Yes."

"That's Anna Stadler. She's the daughter of Heinrich Engelhardt's cousin."

"And who's Heinrich Engelhardt?"

"He's the man seated here in the center. He built Waldemere."

"Oh, okay."

"Well, Anna was twenty years old when she went missing, shortly after this photograph was taken. I'm willing to bet that she's your Jane Doe Three. Take a look at her face and look at the picture inside of that locket."

Pam opened the locket and compared the two images.

"Yeah, I see a resemblance. It could be the same person."

"Okay. Or I was thinking that it might be a younger sister, but yeah. The same person works for me too."

"You said *victims*. Where are the other two?"

"Over here," Jack said as he pointed at the screen to the two girls standing on the far left-hand side. Pam took a closer look. The shorter of the two had black hair, the taller girl's was lighter and could possibly have been red.

"So who were they?"

"Servants. One is Katherine Fitzgerald and the other is Harriett Fischer. Harriett vanished in 1881 and Katherine, the following year."

"And how old were they when they went missing?"

"Harriett was seventeen and Katherine was sixteen."

"Hmm. That doesn't help us much. The ages are too close. Although the attire found on Jane Doe Two does seem to fit with what they're wearing in this picture. Hey Tom," Pam called over to the man that had been working on the facial reconstructions, "Come here and take a look at this."

The man stood up and strolled over to them.

"What is it?" he asked.

"I want you to take a look at this photo and tell me what you see."

The man closely studied the faces of the people on the screen for a moment before his expression widened with obvious excitement.

"Son of a gun!" he declared. "That woman on the right looks just like Jane Doe Three."

Pam and Jack looked at each other.

"It's Anna Stadler," Jack said at last. "Oh, here," he said as he reached into his pocket and withdrew a wad of tissue.

"Oh, the trash is over there," Trish told him.

"No. Open it."

"Do I want to?"

"Yeah. You'll want to compare the DNA in that with Jane Doe Three. I guarantee it'll be a pretty close match."

Pam opened the wad of tissue and examined its contents.

"It's a fingernail clipping," she pointed out. "I'm guessing it's not actually hers though."

"No, it came from one of Anna Stadler's relatives. I nicked it from his wastebasket earlier this morning."

"So he doesn't know that you've obtained his DNA?"

"Well, after I told him earlier this morning that I'd be using some less than orthodox methods, he still gave me the go-ahead to continue my research."

"That sounds like consent to me. I'll have it tested, but it may take a couple of weeks."

"Pam, I only have a couple more days left on this project. Can you do any better than that?"

She thought about it for a moment.

"Well, I can try to fast-track it, which means we'll have the results back in a few days' time. No guarantees though."

"That's fine. Whatever you can do."

"Excuse me," broke in the man who had been working on the facial reconstructions, "but would I be able to save this photograph to my computer? I have a feeling that it's going to be a big help."

"I have no problem with that."

"I'll put it in an email and send it over to you in a minute, Tom," Pam told him. "Jack, I have a feeling that all of this is really going to help us out a lot."

"My pleasure."

"Pardon me, Dr. Martin." Jack and Pam looked up to see a woman in her early forties standing just on the other side of Pam's computer screen.

"Yes, Famin?" Pam asked.

"I was just running a toxicology screen on the remains and came up with an interesting result for 'The Pretty One.'"

"Jane Doe Two? What is it?"

"Well, I was initially looking for opiates to determine if any of them had been drugged prior to death, none of them were, but Jane Doe Two had heightened traces of mercury in her hair follicles."

"Mercury?" Pam exclaimed. "What on Earth could that be doing there?"

Jack thought about it for a moment. Something sounded familiar about all of this. Then it dawned on him.

"Calomel," he announced.

"What?" Both Pam and Famin seemed to ask him that at the same moment.

"It's calomel; a mercury derivative used during the Nineteenth Century to treat a wide variety of ailments, including depression."

"How did you know that?" Pam asked.

Jack looked at the picture of the redheaded maid on the left-hand side of Pam's computer screen and over at the tables that contained the three sets of human remains. He stood up and walked over to the middle table. Pam and Famin followed. He looked down at what was left of this once bright and shining individual and then back up at his cousin.

"Pam, I'd like to introduce you to Katherine Fitzgerald."

Chapter 20

Jack walked into McNamara's Public House on Lake Avenue just before six that evening. Happy hour was in full swing and the place was packed to the gills. Still, he managed to find an opening in the crowd near the end of the bar. He squeezed in and ordered up a pint of Guinness from Lucy, the tall blonde who was bartending that evening.

"Hi, Jack," she greeted with a broad and beautiful smile. "What have you been up to?"

"Not much, really."

"My ass. I hear that you've been staying at Waldemere these last few days. Is that true?"

"Sure is," Jack said as he nodded. "I've been doing some research there for the new owner."

"That's great. Have you found anything interesting?"

Jack realized that she hadn't heard about the three corpses that were discovered the night before and was pretty relieved about this. He'd regretted speaking with the reporter earlier that day, as he didn't like the idea of the entire greater Cleveland area knowing his business, but now the damage was done. He looked around the barroom. No one seemed to give him a second glance. Perhaps, he thought, that the story was never aired.

"Nothing too interesting," he said as he turned back to Lucy. "Same old same old: building dates and the like."

"Yeah, I guess that's not very interesting at all. Any ghosts?"

Jack pondered this for a moment. The less she knew the better.

"Come on. There's no such thing as ghosts," he lied.

Lucy finished pouring his beer and handed it to him.

"So how much longer will you be there?"

"Another couple of days. Oh, I'm getting my findings published in The Argus next week."

"I'll be sure to pick up a copy."

She walked down to the other end of the bar and took another drink order.

"Jack," called a voice from across the room. "What are

you doing standing there by yourself? Come on over and join us."

Jack turned to see Jerry, Brion and Ed hovering around a table in the corner. It was Jerry who had called him over. Jack waved, picked up his settling glass of Guinness and crossed the room.

"What are you guys up to?" he inquired.

"Happy hour," Jerry replied. "We saw that you were pretty busy this morning."

As Jerry said this, Jack knew that the story had aired after all.

"You saw the news?"

"Yeah. That's really something," continued Jerry. "Have they found out anything else?"

Jack could see no harm in telling them about the events that had transpired that afternoon.

"We know a little more now than we did this morning. I just came from the county morgue where I was helping my cousin to identify the remains."

"Any luck?" Brion asked.

"Some. We were able to make comparisons to a photograph that I had come across a few days ago."

"So who were they?"

Before Jack could answer Jerry's question, the front door of the bar flew open and in walked Joe and Geoff, two of Jack's oldest friends. Geoff walked over to the table where Jack was standing with Jerry, Brion and Ed. Joe approached the bar and flagged down Lucy.

"Can you turn down the jukebox," Joe asked. Lucy was a little confused as to why, but obliged him nonetheless. A wave of disappointment washed over the crowd as the Flogging Molly song that had been playing suddenly ceased.

"Hey! I just played that!" someone shouted from the bar.

Joe picked up the TV remote and turned it to channel five. The news was just beginning.

"Oh for cryin' out loud!" Jack exclaimed as he turned to Geoff. "Can you get him to turn that off?"

"Why didn't you tell us you were going to be on the news?" asked Geoff.

"Didn't think it was important. How'd you find out, anyway?"

"My mom called and said that it was the lead story at five o'clock."

"Oh." This was getting so much more attention than Jack had hoped for. Still, maybe it would drum up interest in the article that he was writing for The Argus. He could only hope that some good would come from it.

"Our boy Jack has made it to the headlines again," Joe announced. Everyone in the bar turned and stared. Jack could feel every eye upon him. He simply raised his hand and gave a single, shy wave.

"Is this really necessary?" he asked turning to Geoff.

"I think so. Guys?" He looked over at Jerry, Brion and Ed who all nodded in agreement.

"Hey," Joe shouted, "it's starting." He turned up the volume and everyone's attention was directed at the television that hung on the wall above the beer taps. The news anchor began to speak.

"We begin this evening with a story that we first broke at mid-day on Cleveland's Near West Side: the gruesome discovery of three sets of human remains located in a Victorian mansion along Ohio City's historic Franklin Boulevard. Our own Christine McGovern has obtained an exclusive interview with the owner of the home and picks up the story there."

The image on the screen flashed to a shot of Christine McGovern strolling up the sidewalk, along the wrought iron fence, just outside of the house: likely the shot that was being taped while Jack was pulling out of the driveway. She began her story.

"Long has it been said that the Heinrich Engelhardt House, more famously known as Waldemere, has been the scene of an ongoing haunting that has resulted in its ownership changing hands every few years. Within the last month, it has changed ownership again. This time, it has fallen into the possession of Mr. Henry Engelhardt, great grandson of the original owner. It has also been said that Waldemere holds many secrets. One of those secrets was given up early this morning."

Henry Engelhardt's face filled the screen.

"During the early morning hours, an associate and guest in my house had managed to locate a hidden room on the lowest level of the house. Secreted away in this room were the remains of three people."

"Three people whose identities have yet to be revealed," Mrs. McGovern continued. "Cuyahoga County Coroner Mark Kimble has had his team on the case since the bodies first came in early this morning."

An elderly man, who Jack had caught sight of at the morgue earlier that day, now spoke.

"Currently, we're running forensic analysis tests to determine things such as age, ethnicity and cause of death."

"And do you have any idea how long these remains have been in that house?" the reported asked.

"Well, preliminary findings indicate that they may have been down there for well over a hundred years, but we're still running our tests to determine that."

"Well over a hundred years," the reporter continued. "All of this seems to perfectly fit with the stories of three murders that allegedly happened at Waldemere during the early 1880's."

"I think that's just speculation," Henry Engelhardt explained. "After all, it was my great grandfather that was accused of those murders."

"Accused and acquitted," Christine McGovern added. "Which leaves a new mystery hovering over the house. Interestingly enough, it was a local historian who has been staying at the house that made the grim discovery during those early morning hours."

Jack's face filled the screen: his name and title appearing at the bottom. Everyone in the bar perked up at the sight of him.

"What was the first thing that crossed your mind when you made the discovery?" the reporter asked.

"Well, I was a little startled at first, to say the least. I mean, who expects to find a body hidden in a house, let alone three?"

"Who indeed?"

The screen now flashed to an image of Christine McGovern standing in front of the closed gate and the end of the driveway, the massive edifice of Waldemere looming behind her.

"Mr. Sullivan, as some of you may remember, was the man who led federal investigators to a house in Parkington last October where 12-year-old Rebecca Lowe was rescued from her abductor, ending a two-week search for the girl. But for the three people whose remains were found in Waldemere this morning, it seems that his services may have come about a hundred years too late.

"Reporting from Ohio City, Christine McGovern, Channel 7 News."

"Thank you, Christine," the anchor concluded from back in the studio. "An update from the Cuyahoga County Coroner's Office indicates that possible identifications may have been made late this afternoon, but officials are withholding those names pending DNA test results."

Jack had sincerely wished that the reporter hadn't brought up the Rebecca Lowe case. He'd mentioned to her earlier that he didn't want to talk about it. Apparently, she felt it her duty to do so in his stead.

"Shots!" Geoff demanded.

"Too early," Jack explained.

"Come on. Shots. Let's go."

Geoff threw an arm around Jack and guided him up to the bar where Joe was waiting for them.

"Two Jameson's and a SoCo," Joe ordered.

Lucy pulled down the bottles and poured the appropriate shots.

"Hello Luce," Geoff greeted with a poorly impersonated British accent. "Had a busy night? We've been busy ourselves." He picked up his shot of Jameson's just as she'd finished pouring it. "Pardon me, Luce."

Geoff had long been a fan of the movie *A Clockwork Orange* and that had been one of his favorite lines from the film. He recited this line to Lucy every chance he had. In her opinion, it was getting old.

Jack lifted up his Jameson's and Joe his tumbler of Southern Comfort. The three clinked their glasses together, tapped them down on the wooden bar and downed the alcohol in one gulp.

"Seconds!" Joe instructed.

"Really, no," Jack insisted. "It's way too early to get into that."

It was too late. Lucy was already pouring.

"To the celebrity," Joe said as he raised his glass again.

"To whoever's paying for all of this," Jack added with a smile.

Again, the three touched glasses, tapped them on the wooden bar-top and drank. As Joe set his glass down, he turned to Jack.

"So what time are we starting on Saint Patrick's Day?"

Jack had almost entirely forgotten that their band was scheduled to play that Monday up at McNamara's. He reached into his memory and suddenly remembered the time.

"Five-thirty," he said. "We should try and meet up here at a quarter to five though to set up and run through a sound check."

"I should be done with work early enough that day," replied Joe. "Are you coming up?" he asked as he turned to Geoff.

"I won't be here at five-thirty, but should be up shortly afterwards."

"Cool." He turned back to Jack. "We're not going to have any time to practice between now and then. Are we?"

"I seriously doubt it," Jack told him. "Not with everything that's going on. And not like you need it either."

Joe knew that he was right. Their band, Whuppity Scoorie, had been diligently practicing for the last three months. It felt good to take a week or two off prior to the gig.

"Jack," Jerry said as he approached from behind with a tall, black draught in his left hand. "You left your Guinness at the table."

"Oh, I knew something was missing here," he said as he accepted the glass from Jerry. "I was going to come back in a minute anyway. Guys?"

He turned to Geoff and Joe and tilted his head to the right, indicating that they should join them at the table.

"Sure," Joe said as he picked up his bottle of Rolling Rock and started over to where Brion and Ed were still standing. Geoff followed.

As soon as Jack began to cross the room, he caught sight of a familiar face sitting among the crowd at the end of the bar. Though many people surrounded him, the man was talking to no one. He certainly wasn't a regular at McNamara's and Jack had a pretty good idea as to why he was there. He turned to Joe and Geoff.

"You two go on ahead. I'll be over in a few minutes."

They proceeded to the table and Jack walked over to the man near the end of the bar.

"Hello Drew," he said as he approached.

"Jack. I thought that you might be up here. Saw your car outside and figured that I'd stop in."

"It's better than sitting outside and waiting to follow me."

Jack had met Special Agent Andrew Spurlock the previous fall when he'd been working the Rebecca Lowe case. Agent Spurlock had been staking out McNamara's and had followed Jack for a few days before finally introducing himself. Afterward, Jack had assisted him in tracking down Bob Woodring and in locating Rebecca Lowe. He was currently helping him to find the other missing girls that Bob Woodring had abducted, but it was an arduous task and Jack had hardly made any headway on it.

"So I see that you're back in the public spotlight once again," Agent Spurlock continued. "I thought that you were done with all of that."

"So did I. I really wish that they hadn't brought up the Lowe case in that news report."

"I know. You've had a pretty hard time of it."

"Can I buy you a drink?" Jack asked.

"Sure. I'm off for the night."

"Great. What'll you have?"

Drew Spurlock looked up at the row of taps along the wall. He noticed one that stood out from the rest.

"You're kidding me. They have Yeungling up here?"

"Sure do."

"I haven't had that since I was working out of the Pittsburgh Bureau four years ago."

"Lucy," Jack said as he raised his hand into the air. "Can I get a Yeungling for my friend here?"

"Sure." Lucy grabbed a clean glass from the stack behind the bar and poured the agent a beer. He gladly accepted it and took a long, deep pull.

"Damn, that's good," he said as he set the glass down. "Sure brings back memories."

"Well, I'm guessing that you're not here for the Yeungling. What brings you into McNamara's?"

"You do, Jack. Any time that a report is filed regarding the discovery of human remains, the FBI is always contacted. It's standard protocol. Someone in our office read over the report and brought to my attention that you were the one who had made the discovery. I swear, the shit you get yourself into sometimes."

"I know. It was the last thing that I expected to come across last night."

"So how did it happen?"

"Well, I've been staying at Waldemere the last few evenings and have been doing research on the house for Henry Engelhardt."

"And that's the new owner?"

"Yeah. I've also been trying to help clear up the mystery surrounding the allegations that his great grandfather murdered three people."

"It looks like you're going to have an even harder time of trying to do that now."

"Tell me about it."

"So what do you think, Jack? Do you think he did it?"

"It might look that way, but Henry swears up and down that his great grandpa wasn't capable of such a thing."

"Everyone's capable of murder, if they're pushed far enough."

"I know. Still, I've promised to stay on the case and see what I can turn up, but so far, it doesn't look good. I stopped and paid a visit to my cousin Pam at the county morgue this afternoon and I think we may have been able to identify the remains."

"Really. Who do you think they are?"

"Well, they seem to match perfectly with the three girls that Mr. Engelhardt was accused of murdering back in 1883."

"So the outlook doesn't look too good for him."

"I wouldn't go that far. I mean. Anyone could have killed them."

"But it was most likely him?"

"That's a possibility that I can't shake. Still, I've promised to look into it further."

"Well, if there's anything that the bureau can do to help, just let me know. We owe you a few favors as it is."

"Thanks. I'll keep that in mind."

Just then, Joe came over and got Jack's attention.

"Hey, we're starting up a game of darts," he said as he approached. "You in?"

"Yeah, I'll be over in a few."

"Who's your friend?"

Jack looked at Drew Spurlock to see if it was okay to give up his identity. Drew nodded.

"Joe, this is Special Agent Andrew Spurlock of the FBI. Drew, this is my friend, Joe."

Agent Spurlock shook Joe's hand.

"Joe, it's nice to meet you."

"Thanks. And you. We'll be warming up," he said as he turned back to Jack. "Just come over as soon as you're done here."

"Will do."

Joe turned and walked back to the others who were tossing darts at the board. Jack could tell that he was mouthing something to them, likely the identity of his friend.

"Well Jack," Agent Spurlock said after taking another sip from his beer. "I should probably let you get to your game. I can't stay long anyway."

"So be it. Hey, you should try and come up here on Saint Patrick's Day. My band is playing at five-thirty."

"I'll see what I can do. I'll talk to you soon, Jack. Take care."

"Thanks. You too."

Jack turned and started over to his friends by the dartboard. As he approached, Joe chimed out the four notes that used to introduce the old television show *Dragnet*.

"Very funny," said Jack as he set his Guinness down on

the table. "But Sergeant Joe Friday was a narcotics officer with the Los Angeles Police Department and not an FBI agent."

"Only you would care to know something like that," Joe pointed out.

Chapter 21

Almost every single window was dark when Jack returned to Waldemere that night. The exception was a light that blazed from the third floor turret room and a window beside it. Henry Engelhardt, he assumed, was still awake. As Jack pulled into the driveway and parked in the back, he noticed a light coming from a bedroom on the second floor as well. Walking down the driveway, he heard the side door open and saw Emily stick her head out.

"'Eard ya pullin' in and thought I'd get to the door before ya rang the bell," she told him. "It's a little late and I didn't want ya disturbin' Mr. Engelhardt. 'E's only just now gone up to bed."

"Thanks. Sorry I missed dinner."

"Oh, that's alright," she told him. "I made ya up a plate."

"You didn't have to do that."

"It's no problem. I 'ave it down in the kitchen. Come on."

Jack followed her slowly down the stairs and past her former bedroom. As she passed the bedroom door, her pace quickened slightly. They entered the kitchen and she turned on the light.

"I'm guessing that you're still a little nervous about coming down here," Jack pointed out.

"Is it that obvious?"

"Slightly."

"It's bad enough that I 'ave to be down 'ere by meself whenever I 'ave to do the cookin' or cleanin'."

"You shouldn't have anything else to worry about," Jack told her. "They've removed the bodies from the crypt and I seriously doubt that they're going to find any more."

"I know. It's just the thought that somethin' loike that was down 'ere this 'ole toime and I had no idea."

Emily pulled a plate of baked salmon, wild-grain rice and asparagus from the refrigerator. She removed the plastic wrap that had been covering it and placed it in the microwave oven.

"Looks delicious."

"Mr. Engelhardt recalled Ms. Rybarczyk tellin' 'im that you're a Catholic. 'E remembered that it's Lent and that ya can't eat meat on Froidays."

"That was very nice of him, but he didn't need to accommodate me like that."

"Oh, it was no problem. Besoides, I think it turned out rather well."

"Now I *really* feel bad about having missed dinner."

"But ya didn't miss it. It'll be ready in three... two... one."

The timer on the microwave oven beeped and Emily removed the piping hot plate. She carefully handed it to Jack, pulled out a matching set of flatware from a nearby drawer and snagged a dark green cloth napkin from a stack under the cupboard.

"Smells great," he noted.

"Wait until ya try it. Oh, can I get ya somethin' to drink?"

"A pop would be great." Jack had had more than enough beer.

"Sure thing." Emily reached into the refrigerator and pulled out a can of cola. "Ice and a glass?"

"No thanks. The can's just fine."

"Roight, then. Let's go upstairs; and quickly if ya please."

Jack nodded. Again, Emily rushed past her old bedroom and seemed quite relieved when they had made it back upstairs and into the main dining room. Jack found a seat at the table and set down his plate. Emily laid out the napkin, arranged the silverware upon it and handed Jack the can of cola.

"Are you going to hang out for a bit?" Jack asked.

"No, I think that I'll retire for the evenin'. I'm still a little weary from last noight."

"Okay."

"When you're finished, ya can just leave everythin' there. I'll come and clean it up in the mornin'. Goodnoight, Jack."

"Goodnight, Emily."

She turned and exited the room, closing the large wooden pocket doors behind her. Jack felt funny sitting in this room with all of the doors closed. It reminded him of being placed in a box. Still, he was glad to see that Emily was calling him by his first name again.

After Jack had finished his late dinner of salmon, rice and asparagus, he made his way back upstairs and into the fourth floor bedroom. He hung his jacket and hat in the closet and kicked off his shoes. His feet and his head were both screaming at this point and he looked forward to getting a good night's sleep. Still, there was just one thing that he needed to check before turning in.

He pulled out the keys that Pam had given him earlier that afternoon and closely examined them. They did seem quite old and that they could possibly unlock a couple of doors in the house, but Jack had another idea as to what they might fit.

He crossed the room, rolled back the area rug and lifted open the hatch of the trapdoor. He extracted the stepladder and leaned it against the wall. Again, without grabbing his flashlight, he jumped down into the trunk space and crawled towards the small area in the back. Feeling around in the darkness, he located the steamer trunk and found a leather handle to pull it by. Just as had happened the first time he'd tried this, the handle disintegrated in his hand. He slid the trunk over, got behind it and pushed it back to the entrance of the passage. He jumped out and lifted the steamer trunk with ease.

Jack looked at his right hand. It was now covered with a powdery orange residue; most likely what was left of the leather handle. He walked into the bathroom and washed his hands. After drying them, he returned to the bedroom and sized up the trunk. He'd never actually had a chance to look at it under proper light. With the exception of a few wooden strips that ran across it, the trunk was wrapped in a dark tin covering. Most likely, it was constructed of wood. Nearly every one that he'd come across was. The hinges, latches and lock all seemed to be made from black cast iron: very durable.

Jack picked up the keys and approached. As he knelt down, he closely inspected the lock on the front of the trunk. The keyhole certainly seemed like it might be a match for the larger of the two. He inserted the key; so far, so good. He turned it and the lock jumped open. Just as he'd guessed, the trunk had belonged to Katherine Fitzgerald.

He popped the two latches on either side of the front, carefully raised the lid and peered inside. The first thing that he saw was a frilly woman's dress. It was dark green, made of satin, had many small bows and was trimmed in lace. Being as careful as he could, he gently removed it and set it on the bed. There was another dress, equally as elegant, just below it. This one was of a ruby red color and was trimmed in dark blue velvet. Again being as careful as possible, he pulled it out and set it next to the first.

Next, he located a pair of black satin gloves. The hands were dainty but the sleeves were quite long. He turned and set these down beside the dresses. Under the gloves was a tall pair of black leather boots with dark wooden heels. Shoelaces had once run up the front, but all that was left was a dry-rotted cording. The feet that wore these had to have been quite small, Jack thought. He removed the boots and set them down on the floor beside him.

Next to the boots, Jack found a pair of ladies' slippers. These were made of suede and were as green as the first dress he'd discovered. Most likely, they were part of a matching outfit. As he set them next to the boots, he noticed some pieces of paper that had been stuffed inside of one of the slippers. Jack reached in and pulled out a wad of cash. At first he'd thought it counterfeit, as the bills were quite large, but then remembered that currency back in that period was considerably larger than it was today. He counted the money and saw that it came to sixty-two dollars. This he carefully placed back inside of the slipper.

Looking back into the trunk, he saw what appeared to be an old glass perfume bottle. Attached to the top of it was a sprayer with a length of tubing and a squeeze ball at the end. The bottle itself was empty. Its, contents, Jack figured, must have completely evaporated many years earlier. Regardless, he unscrewed the top and took a whiff. There were still traces of the fragrance in the bottle. To Jack, it smelled familiar; something like rosewater. He replaced the top and set it down on the floor.

There were still a few items left inside the trunk. He next

pulled out a porcelain doll, which he at once assumed to be very valuable. As carefully as he could, he placed it on the bed a good distance away from the dresses and gloves. The last thing he wanted to do was accidentally knock it off the bed when placing the dresses back in the trunk. The next thing he found was a brilliantly jeweled necklace. Again, this seemed to be very valuable. He placed it beside the porcelain doll. Looking back into the trunk, he located a small silver cup; heavily tarnished to the point where it had turned almost completely black. Upon closer inspection, he could make out what looked to be tiny fingerprints set into the tarnish.

Jack had an idea. He crossed the room and pulled the digital camera from his jacket pocket and turned it on. He set himself to the task of documenting every single article that had been found thus far in the trunk. When he came to the silver cup, he turned the camera to the macro setting and focused in on the small fingerprints. He began to take pictures. With some luck, these fingerprints could be used to positively identify one of the corpses as Katherine. As he slowly turned the cup, he noticed another feature that had been hidden under the tarnish. Very faintly, he could make out a scrolled engraving with the letters "KBF" embossed upon it. Jack lifted his head and thought about it for a moment.

"Katherine Bridget Fitzgerald," he said as the girl's full name came back to him. He took a few more photos of the silver cup and set it down inside of the trunk. There were two items left.

The first one that he lifted was a small book. Carefully, he opened it and examined the contents. It was a photo album. There were many pictures of people that he didn't recognize at all. In some cases, he didn't need to. Katherine had identified the people in there by writing their names below their images. One picture of a man with a mustache and a plug hat was labeled as "Papa": obviously her father. Another photograph that she had marked as being "Mama" showed an image of a woman with light hair in plain attire. Jack began to take pictures of these. He made his way through the pages that followed and continued to take snapshots, but none of the names here seemed familiar to him. Near the end, he came to a photograph of three children.

These, Katherine had indicated as being "Mary, Michael and I": likely a portrait of her with her brother and sister. Jack turned the page and found himself looking into the face of a girl with black hair and soft dark eyes. The name written below simply said "Harriett". Jack knew that it had to be Harriet Fischer. On the next page, he found another print of the image that Belinda Hyde had in her collection: the one of Waldemere. Although he already had it, he took another picture for good measure. This time, he set the camera to macro and got close ups of all of the faces.

That was it. That was the last photo in the album. Jack closed the book and placed it back inside of the trunk. He reached over and pulled out the final item: a leather-bound book, roughly measuring six inches by eight inches. He went to open it, but at once realized that it was locked. Quickly, he withdrew the key from the front of the trunk and selected the smaller key on the chain. He inserted it into the lock on the side of the book, turned it and the lock opened. There were no pictures in this book, only words that were written in an elegant hand. He began to read.

The Journal

of

Katherine Bridget Fitzgerald

Castlebridge, County Wexford, Ireland

26th May 1878

I have just departed from Westport in County Mayo with my brother

Michael and sister Mary on the Steamer Hibernia. Mama and Papa tell us that there will be a better life waiting for us in America. When we get there we are to stay at my Uncle Malachi's. Mama and Papa are to join us in a few years. Papa has given me this journal that he paid a half-pound for to write down all of my adventures in. When he and Mama arrive we can all read it together.

I have never met Uncle Malachi but Papa says that he is a good-natured man and that I don't have to be afraid of him. I'm more worried that he will not like us and will send us back to Ireland. Mama always says that I am a handful and will someday be the death of her. I hope not to be the death of anyone. How could I live with myself?

5th June 1878

We have been on the sea for two weeks and have just arrived in New York. Michael says that we are to meet someone named Mr. Landry, a friend of Papa's, who will take us to a station. There we will step on board a railroad train that will take us to a place called Ohio, where Uncle Malachi lives. I can't wait to ride on a train. I never have before. Michael says that they move faster than the fastest horse could run. I can't think of it.

7th June 1878

Mary, Michael and I are now

in a city called Cleveland. That's in Ohio which is a state. They have counties here but it's not like in Ireland. Each state has many counties and there is no counting them there are so many. Cleveland is not as big as New York but is just as smoky. Uncle Malachi lives in a place in Cleveland called The Angle. A train goes passed his house twice a day and we have to close the windows when it does or the house will fill up with smoke.

His house is on Washington Street which was named after the first president of America. A president is like a king but only rules for a short time. Uncle Malachi tells me that the church at the top of the street is named after him. I *didn't know that he was a saint. I asked him if I should call him that, but he told me that I can call him "His Holiness."*

Jack chuckled softly as he read this passage. He was quite familiar with Saint Malachi's Church and was pretty certain that it hadn't been named for a man that lived on The Angle. Still, he liked the sense of humor that this man seemed to have. Jack browsed over the next few pages and could tell that it was more of the same; general observances of Cleveland in the late 1870's as seen through the eyes of a twelve-year-old Irish immigrant. Thirty-two pages in, Jack came across a passage that caught his attention.

21st January 1879

I have just come to work for a very nice family on Franklin Street named the Engelhardts. They are very nice people and have promised to pay me quite well for my cleaning services in their home, where I am to remain during the term of my employment. They have two sons and a daughter that are a few years older than I am, but all are very nice and don't tease me

Also living here is another girl named Harriett. She is two years older than I am and is very kind. She cooks the food here along with Mrs. Schilling. She's the one in charge of all the cooking and cleaning. Mrs. Schilling and her husband, Mr. Schilling, live in the carriage house behind the big house, which is called Waldemere. That's where I live with Harriett and the Engelhardts.

Also living here is Miss Anna. She's a cousin of the Engelhardts and is to give me and Harriett our lessons. Miss Anna is going to be a teacher and has promised to practice her teaching with us. His Holiness says that this will be a great opportunity to learn how to better read and write. He says that I am already *good, but can always be better. I can also make some money and will be able to save up for pretty dresses and other fineries.*

I wish that Mama, Mary and Michael were here to see me and see how far I've come. I pray for them every night, but know that they are safe with God in Heaven now. I hope that Papa will come to Cleveland soon. I write to him often but haven't heard from him since word came of Mama's death. How I miss her so.

Jack stopped reading for a moment. Somewhere over the course of the last thirty-two pages, Katherine must have lost her mother back in Ireland and her brother and sister. With the exception of "His Holiness", she must have felt so alone. He was curious to know the circumstances surrounding this, but decided that he would read on. He could always go back later and find out what had happened.

He skipped ahead a number of pages, past little dealing of Cleveland and everyday life of a young girl growing up in the Nineteenth Century, to an entry that he thought might contain a clue that was relevant to his research. He wasn't let down.

27th August 1879

Miss Anna has left us. Harriett and I waited for her all day yesterday but she never came back. Mr Engelhardt has said that he last saw her two nights ago at Reservoir Park in the company of a man. When Mrs Engelhardt heard this she got furious. She was mad because Mr Engelhardt didn't go over and bring her home. Now Mrs Engelhardt fears that she could be anywhere. Mr Engelhardt believes that she may have left town.

This doesn't sound like Miss Anna. She left her clothes and many of her pretty things. She also never said good-bye to me and Harriett. I will *keep praying that she comes back. Harriett is a Lutheran and doesn't pray as much as I do. She thinks it funny of me to do so. Still, I will keep it up. Prayers never hurt no one.*

Jack thought this passage interesting. It seemed to coincide with what Heinrich Engelhardt had testified to at his deposition, but Jack now knew that she hadn't left town in the company of a stranger. His discovery in the crypt the night before had proven otherwise. He scanned the next series of pages, nearly a year and a half of them, and read more of the same. Initially, it was about hopes that "Miss Anna" would return but the later parts were small tidbits of daily life at Waldemere. It wasn't until he reached early 1881 that he found something of relevance written again.

26th February 1881

Harriett has me worried. I know that she goes to him in the middle of the night. She thinks that I am asleep and sneaks out of the room. After an hour she comes back in and gets back into bed. I can hear that she's breathing heavy and must have had an exciting time. I think to ask her about it but am afraid of what she would say or do if I told her that I knew.

I'm worried that she'll get caught. She would have to leave Waldemere and I'd be all alone. Perhaps I'll talk to her tomorrow and maybe convince her to stop.

27th February 1881

I've spoken with Harriett and she's glad that I know. Now she feels like she won't have to sneak out of the room anymore. She's asked that I keep it a secret though. I tried to talk her out of going to him but she wouldn't hear any of it. I tried to explain to her that if she got caught that she'd be dismissed. She told me that it was worth it.

1st March 1881

  I found a necklace this morning in our room while I was cleaning. I know that it belongs to Mrs. Engelhardt as I've seen her wear it before. He must have taken it and given it to her. I told her that she should return it. She got angry with me and told me that I had no business going through her things. She called me a dirty little Catholic girl and I cried.

  I am so afraid for her.

2nd March 1881

  Harriett has apologized for what she called me yesterday and we are friends again. She tells me that everything is going to be fine, but won't tell me anything else. All that she'll say is that she'll tell me all about it tomorrow. I'm praying for her.

3rd March 1881

Harriett is gone... as are a few items in the house. Last night I heard her getting out of bed and she never came back. The only conclusion that any of us can come to is that she got frightened and decided to leave the house. She left all of her belongings here, but judging by the value of what she stole she should have no trouble buying new clothes. I wish that she would have told me that she was leaving. I might have tried to talk her out of it or may even have come with her. I have hidden the necklace in my trunk. I'd return it, but don't want to be blamed for taking it.

Jack looked over at the necklace that he had just pulled out of the trunk and set on the bed. He figured it likely that this was the same necklace that Katherine had hidden in this trunk more than a hundred and twenty-five years earlier.

The police came to the house and Mr. Engelhardt told them about what had happened last night. They asked me if I knew anything, but I lied. I said nothing about the necklace or about Harriett sneaking out of bed during the night. I feel horrible. I shall certainly have to make penance for lying. I do hope that dear Harriett is all right.

5th March 1881

I keep hoping that Harriett will return in the night and take me away with her. Though she has stolen and therefore sinned, I think that I could forgive her

I would insist that she go to penance for what she has done, but I don't think she would. Harriett never comes for me.

Miss Bertha, our neighbor, has funny ideas about Harriett and Miss Anna. I think she might be mad. That being said, I refuse to write down any of her ideas in this journal.

For about the next year's worth of entries, it was more of the same: work at Waldemere and small pieces of daily life. In late 1881, Jack read that "His Holiness" had been killed in a bar fight in the Angle. This left Katherine on her own. She continued to write to her father, but hardly ever heard back. Somewhere around mid-May of 1882, Jack came across another entry of interest.

19th May 1882

Mr. and Mrs. Engelhardt have decided to throw me a coming-out party tonight. It is such a surprise and they are so wonderful to work for. They have bought me the most beautiful green dress and slippers to match it. Seeing also that I am now turning sixteen, they have offered to move my living quarters upstairs to the fourth floor into Miss Anna's former bedroom. Mr. and Mrs. Schilling will be moving into the bedroom that Harriett and I once shared on the first floor. Mr. Schilling suffers from terrible spells of rheumatism and being in the big house might be better for him.

As of tonight, the gentlemen will no longer call me Miss Katherine. It will be Miss Fitzgerald from here on. I am so excited that I can hardly breathe. My only wish is that Papa was here to see me. I will write to him and tell him all about it though. I am told that the guests will be arriving at seven and I must get myself ready. I cannot wait to try on the pretty green dress.

20th May 1882

Last night was absolutely the best night of my life. Mr Engelhardt had hired a band to play for the party which was held in the ballroom outside of my new bedroom on the fourth floor. I met many of Mr and Mrs Engelhardt's friends and their friends' families. Such wonderful people. I danced with a few young men, including Mr and Mrs Engelhardt's sons Konrad and Ludwig. Both were quite charming and gentlemanly. I was rather enchanted by one Mr Oliver Dell, a clerk in Mr Engelhardt's bank. He has such a beautiful face, stands up *straight and smiles at me often. Mrs. Engelhardt tells me that if I keep dancing the way I did last night that I should be married off in no time.*

I can see the lake and the island from my new bedroom window. I can't imagine why Miss Anna would ever have wanted to leave a place that had such a wonderful view, unless her beau was anything like Mr. Dell.

Jack continued to read, skimming through pages that didn't seem to carry much value to his case. Still, he thought, this was an excellent glimpse into what life was like among Cleveland's upper crust during the Nineteenth Century. Many a historical society would be happy to have this. He immediately thought of Orin Drury and his archive. If Jack had a chance, he would photocopy the journal and hand its contents over to him. It would be a great addition to his collection.

In mid-June, Jack came upon an entry that he found quite alarming.

13th June 1882

For the past few days, I've noticed

him watching me while I work. I wouldn't have written anything about it except for the fact that I find it exciting and worth writing about. We talk every now and again and it feels good to have someone that I can share with. My life has felt so empty since Harriett left and His Holiness died. Sometimes I wish that Miss Anna would return but she's been gone for so long now that I'm certain that she won't.

I know why he's looking at me and am sure that it's not because he wants to be my friend. Still, I enjoy his company and am glad for it.

Jack skipped ahead a few entries.

19th June 1882

He came to me last night. It

first I was afraid that we might get caught but he assured me that we wouldn't. He took me to a special place where nobody would find us. I had never been touched like that before and at first didn't want him to. After a time though, it felt so good and I didn't want him to stop. He told me that it would be our secret and as long as I never told anyone, it would be like it never had happened. He asked me if I could keep a secret like that and I told him that I could. He then took me.

Afterward, I began to see why Harriett would go to him in the night. Maybe it was their secret as well.

Jack could see the connection here, but was getting frustrated that Katherine hadn't given a name to her and Harriett's secret lover. He read through the next few entries, but for about a week's worth, there was no mention of the affair. Finally he came across another, but again, it didn't give a name.

The secret rendezvous seemed to go on for nearly two months before Katherine wrote something that really struck Jack as having any bearing on his research.

2nd September 1882

I am with child. I have no doubts about it anymore. My regular womanly functions have ceased. At first I was worried that I might be ill, but after this much time has passed, I am certain that it must be a baby that grows within me. I am terrified to tell him as he may have me remove it. I could never take the life of one of God's creatures, born or unborn, and have decided that I should run away before it ever came to that. I have sixty-two dollars saved and if I need it will use it. In the meantime, I have decided to keep my condition hidden and will continue to do so for as long as I can.

7th September 1882

Have been ill these past five days. Could not attend to my regular duties, but am back to work now. Still feeling sick but am managing.

He continues to watch me and I'm aware that he wants to get me alone so that he can have his way with me again. I have no desire to be with him. Not until my health has recovered.

21st September 1882

I am in bed again. I have no urge to eat or move. I don't even wish to write.

25th September 1882

Doctor Matthews visited me this day. He asked me many questions concerning my condition and I lied to him. It was all I could do to keep the true nature of my ailment a secret. As I was told, if I never said anything about it to anyone it never happened. The doctor believes me to have an illness of the brain. It's just as well. Mrs. Engelhardt came in this evening and had me take a spoonful of bitter medicine. She tells me that I will have to take it two times a day until the bottle is empty.

28th September 1882

I'm still in bed. The medicine is putrid and I have no urge to go on. I can't imagine how other women manage to do this.

2nd October 1882

Resolved, I will tell him of my condition. I've been in this bed long enough and have decided that the time has come for me to face what I have feared most. If he tells me to get rid of the child, I will leave. He won't be able to stop me.

That was the last entry. The pages that followed were blank. Jack looked at the date of the last entry, compared it to his notebook and knew at once why this was. Katherine Fitzgerald had vanished the following afternoon. Apparently she had told her secret lover and he was able to stop her after all.

It was tragic, Jack thought. All that remained of this girl, aside from her corpse, was a steamer trunk and the few items that it contained. He gathered the dresses, gloves, boots, slippers, necklace and porcelain doll and placed them back in the trunk.

Now knowing that the contents were quite valuable and fragile, he gently lowered the trunk through the hatch and slid it back to where he had found it. He'd certainly never stand on it again as he had a few nights earlier in the ballroom. Once he had placed it where it should be, Jack turned and crawled out of the trunk space. He set the stepladder back inside, closed the trapdoor hatch and replaced the area rug.

The journal he held on to. He wanted to make copies of its contents and give them to Orin Drury. He'd have just given him the journal itself, but it didn't belong to either of them. In truth, it belonged to no one anymore: no one but a girl whose life had been tragically cut short at the hands of some monster whose identity still remained a mystery.

Chapter 22

A loud calamitous bang rang out across the entire fourth floor of Waldemere. Jack sat up with a sudden shudder. The sound echoed for a moment; then all was quiet.

He jumped out of bed and fumbled around in the darkness until he found his robe. Carefully, he crossed the room and turned on the Tiffany light by the door. The sound had come from somewhere out in the ballroom. For a moment, he thought that the clock had crashed to pieces. Upon opening the door and looking through the dim light that was cast across the floor from his room, Jack could see that all was still intact. He heard a hushed voice.

"Thevshi," it whispered.

A chill ran up his spine. Someone must have been treading upon his grave. He heard it again.

"Thevshi." The voice was a little louder this time.

Jack slammed the door with his heart racing. He had no appetite for flirtations with the Other World, but saw that there was no escaping it. Something was going to happen that night whether he wanted it to or not. He thought back on what Katherine Fitzgerald had written in the final entry of her journal.

"Have decided that the time has come for me to face what I have feared most."

Suddenly, he remembered the recorder crystal that Amy had given him the day before. He crossed the room to the desk, picked up the small box and opened it. The crystal was still warm. Clutching it with a closed fist, he walked back over to the door, opened it and tossed the crystal into the ballroom. He heard it skip across the floor and come to rest somewhere near the clock. The room went silent.

Jack had hoped that the disturbances would cease following the discovery of the three bodies in the crypt. It was his guess that these events were directly related to the fact that these girls had never received a proper burial.

An ephemeral light flashed across the far end of the ballroom. It lasted for one fleeting moment and was gone. Apparently, he'd been wrong in his line of thinking. The haunting continued.

There was a soft scratching sound now coming from over by the clock. It was as if something small was being scraped across the floor. Jack closed the door half way, crossed the bedroom to the desk and picked up his flashlight. He returned to the door, clicked on the flashlight and looked out across the ballroom.

Nothing.

Cautiously, he stepped across the threshold and into the darkness. The air had turned quite cold and Jack could almost see his breath. He moved closer and closer to the clock. He had no doubt that all of the sounds he'd just heard had originated from that area. Every ounce of his being was screaming at him to retreat back into the bedroom, but his curiosity was getting the better of him.

Jack was about ten feet from the clock when his foot slightly slipped on something. He aimed the flashlight at the floor and saw at once that it was the smoky recorder crystal that Amy had given him. He crouched down and picked it up. Any warmth that it once held was now gone. If this crystal was to effectively do its job, Jack knew that he must put as much distance between it and himself as possible. He cast the stone again across the room, this time in the direction of the turret. He heard it tumble a few times and come to rest along the eastern wall.

"Thevshi," the disembodied voice whispered again. It was much closer now and seemed to be coming from just behind the front of the clock. Jack warily approached with his flashlight casting its soft glow about the wooden façade. The hand-carved figures were all set in their regular positions, but the faces of the man and woman seemed to be staring down at him. This was absurd. Jack looked closer and realized that it was all a trick of the light. Perhaps Heinrich Engelhardt had meant for it to be so.

As Jack scanned his flashlight along the frontispiece, he thought for a moment that he heard what sounded like a pin being plucked at. It softly resonated and just like that, had ceased. He placed his right ear against the wood. There were soft mumbles reverberating from within the mechanical space, but what they were saying, he could not tell. He then heard the pin plucking again. This time, it was gently ringing out a series of notes that brought to mind the sound a music box might make.

Jack took a few steps backwards and apprehensively stopped six feet from the clock. None of this made any sense. When he had investigated the inner workings, he saw no indication of any such device that would make this sound. He began to wonder if the tones were actually coming from a room on a lower level of the house and were being carried up through one of the shafts in the back. Just then, he heard a stentorious cranking sound from within the clock. A set of doors that he'd somehow overlooked flew open, revealing a large brass disk. The disk began to turn and the ballroom was suddenly filled with a melodic song. Jack recognized it at once as *The Aquarium* from Camille Saint-Saëns' *Carnival of the Animals*.

This was it. This, he realized, was how the clock chimed. He'd often wondered what a beautiful clock such as this might sound like and now that he finally heard its voice, he was both mesmerized and terrified. As the brass disk continued to turn, Jack noticed that the wooden figures scattered about the clock were now moving of their own accord. The crows bobbed in and out. The hornets wiggled back and forth. The crossed swords swung to and fro while the heads of the man and woman slowly turned from left to right. Jack could see the tombstones reverently bowing in time with the music. The two sunflowers, set at the opposite lower corners of the clock, slowly turned at the same pace as the brass disk. All of this seemed to form one carefully orchestrated macabre dance and Jack, entranced to behold the spectacle, knew not what to make of it.

The whispering began once again, but was covered for the most part by the music coming from the clock. Still, Jack managed to hear a gentle feminine voice that seemed to be speaking through sobs.

"Lost. Is all lost," the voice whimpered.

Jack had no doubts that it was the same voice he'd been hearing all along, as the Irish accent was very distinct. The crying seemed to be getting louder with every passing moment and it soon reached the point where it had exceeded the decibels being put out by the clock. It was right in his ear now and he swore for a moment that he could feel a cold breath on his neck. A chill ran up his spine but he was too terrified to move. The voice then screamed.

"I have no urge to go on!"

Jack instantly snapped out of the clock's trance and turned to run for the bedroom. In his haste, he lost his footing, slipped and fell to the floor: his flashlight landing some distance away from him. The crying was unbearable. He wanted to get away, but at the same time wished to ease the suffering that this soul was enduring.

As he pulled himself to his feet, Jack heard again the sound of something small clattering across the floor. Suddenly, the air was rent by the sound of two loud stomps over by the turret. With that, the clock ceased its music and the doors closed again, leaving the entire ballroom in utter silence.

Jack was certain that the event had ended. As he dusted himself off, he looked around the room and saw that all was calm. The figures on the clock were no longer animated and had returned to their original positions.

The flashlight sat about fifteen feet from where he stood. He crossed the room and as he crouched down to pick it up, heard the stomping again. An icy wind seemed to blow up from out of nowhere that cut straight down to Jack's very soul. He could hear the small clattering sound once more and as he shone the flashlight in the general direction of the source, saw something small flying right at his face. There was no time to avoid it. All that he could see was a red flash as the recorder crystal struck him squarely between the eyes.

Jack grabbed at the bridge of his nose in pain and turned for the bedroom door. He'd had enough. As he staggered across the ballroom, small pebbles began to rain down on him. They seemed to be materializing out of thin air. With every step he took, the pebbles got larger and larger. By the time he had reached the doorway to the bedchamber, they had turned into stones of a significant size. He entered the bedroom and slammed the door. After a moment, he heard the shower of rocks on the other side cease. It took everything he had in him to fight off the temptation to reopen the door and look back into the ballroom.

After throwing the lock on the bedroom door, Jack crossed the room and removed his robe, setting it across the back of the chair by the desk. He hurried into bed and climbed under the covers. There he lay for several minutes before finally being able to calm himself down enough to fall asleep. In his last moments of consciousness, Jack realized that the recorder crystal had actually done its job. The spirits had focused most of their energies upon it instead of him and it was the crystal that had gotten thrown across the room this time. Unfortunately, he just happened to be in its path.

Bad luck for him.

Chapter 23

When Jack awoke the following morning, he seriously considered quitting the case and vacating Waldemere as fast as he could. He'd resigned himself to do so if another disturbance had occurred and now that one had, he found himself torn. There were serious doubts in his mind that he could endure another night such as that, but he'd come so far in his research and could see the end in sight. Furthermore, he only had one more night to contend with. As he sat in bed, he milled the situation over a few times in his head before ultimately coming to the conclusion that one more night at Waldemere wouldn't kill him. He'd tough it out and see this case through to the end.

While brushing his teeth, Jack heard a knock at the bedroom door. He quickly rinsed the foamy toothpaste from the brush, tapped it on the edge of the sink to knock the excess water off and tossed it into his travel case. He donned his robe, unlocked the bedroom door and opened it.

"Good mornin', Jack," Emily greeted with a warm smile. "Sleep well?"

Jack was a little perplexed. He looked past her and into the ballroom where he expected to see the floor covered in pebbles and stones. Much to his astonishment though, the room was perfectly clean.

"Um, yeah," he answered with bewilderment. "Just fine."

"Is everythin' alright?"

"Yeah. I just…"

Jack scratched the back of his head. He was at a total loss. For a moment, he thought that Emily had come up earlier and cleaned up the mess, but she showed no sign that she was wise to what had happened the night before. After a moment, her expression changed and he could see that she was catching on to the fact that there had been another disturbance.

"Oh me goodness," she said with realization. "Somethin' 'appened up 'ere again last noight. Didn't it?"

"You didn't hear anything?"

"Not a sound. What 'appened?"

"Well, there was some stomping, some screaming, I had a crystal thrown at my head, the clock finally chimed…"

"The clock did *what*?"

"Yeah. It was quite pretty, too. Here. Check it out."

Jack walked out into the ballroom and approached the clock. He located the doors on the front and carefully eased them open revealing the large brass disk.

"What's that?"

"It's called a Reginaphone. It was made by the Regina Music Box Company and was all the rage during the late eighteen hundreds. You see, this disk here spins, much like a record, and these impressions on it strike the pins. It works on the same principle that a music box does."

"And it went off just like that?"

"Pretty much. What has me baffled is the song that it played."

"What song was that?"

"It was a movement from *Carnival of the Animals*."

"What's so strange about that?"

"Well, Saint-Saëns didn't compose it until 1886 and even at that, the music wasn't published until the early 1920's."

"So?"

"So it's not the original song that was on here. This disk must have been changed by a later owner. Oh, the figures on the clock also moved to the music."

Emily gazed up at the figures and tried to picture them moving about. The thought made her shudder.

"I think they're creepy enough as they are roight now. I can't imagine what they'd look loike in motion and to be 'onest, don't want to."

"Oh," Jack said as he remembered the rest of the event. "Rocks also fell from the ceiling."

Emily looked up and tried to locate broken plaster.

"It's an old 'ouse. Little bits o' the ceilin' are bound to crack and fall."

"No. I'm not talking about little bits of the ceiling. I'm talking about a hailstorm of pebbles that appeared out of nowhere."

"In what part of the room did this 'appen?" Emily asked,

still scanning the ceiling for damage.

"The whole room."

"Um," Emily began as she looked around with doubts. "Okay, so where are these rocks now?"

"Don't know. At first, I thought that you had cleaned them up, but almost at once could tell that you had no idea that anything had happened up here last night."

"Will ya be leavin' us, then?"

"I thought about it, but have decided to stay. After all, what's one more night?"

"Mr. Engelhardt will be pleased to 'ear this."

"Is he about this morning?"

"I'm afraid that 'e 'ad an early appointment and will be tied up in meetin's throughout the afternoon. 'E shouldn't be back until closer to dinnertoime."

"It's just as well, I guess. I have some running around to do this morning, anyway."

"Breakfast will be ready in about ten minutes," Emily informed him.

"I'm going to have to pass as I really should get started."

"Very well. What toime should we expect ya back?"

"That depends on how much I can dig up."

"Well, good luck then and I'll be seein' ya later."

Emily turned and started back down the stairs. As she did, it seemed to Jack that she was taking another glance about the ballroom; possibly trying to imagine pebbles and stones strewn about the floor.

By eleven o'clock, Jack was driving east on Franklin Boulevard under a cold and cloudy sky. He usually spent his Saturday mornings watching cartoons or listening to NPR, but had no time to do either. He'd have tuned into his regular radio programs, but there was no point in it. He would only be in the car for a few minutes. The last thing he needed right now was to get wrapped up in listening to the What Do You Know Quiz.

As Jack drove past Franklin Circle, he suddenly remembered that it was March 15th. This was just another day to most: one month until taxes were due. To others it was the Ides of March, but to Clevelanders, it was Buzzard Day. Every year on this day, the turkey vultures would make their annual return to the rookery on the outskirts of Hinckley. Sometimes they'd arrive a few days early, but these birds, the fair people of Hinckley would dismiss as some odd species of crow that was just passing through. Crow or buzzard, Jack didn't care. It meant that spring was just around the corner.

    The black Mazda Protegé 5 pulled up outside of Carter's Closet on West 25th Street. As Jack stepped from his car, he made certain to pick up his backpack. He slammed the door, locked the car with his fob, and walked into the store. The aroma of Captain Black and the familiar sound of hammered dulcimer music greeted him as he entered. Standing behind the counter was a bespectacled Orin Drury, dressed in his usual Nineteenth Century attire, and puffing away at a pipe. Spread out on the counter before him was that morning's issue of The Plain Dealer.

    "Had a busy week now, haven't we, Jack?" Orin declared without even giving his guest a glance.

    "I guess so," Jack replied as he approached the counter.

    "Haunted houses, corpses and hundred year old mysteries galore. That much I could deal with." Orin pulled his glasses up to the top of his head and looked at Jack. "But TV reporters and newspaper articles… I think I can pass on those."

    "Newspaper articles?"

    "Yeah. You've made the celebrated pages of The Plain Dealer. You weren't aware of this?"

    "No."

    "Well, it's a pretty good article, but it doesn't say much more than what was on the news last night."

    "Hmm." Jack considered this for a moment then remembered his backpack. "Oh. Speaking of last night, I found something that you may be interested in."

    He reached into the bag, withdrew Katherine Fitzgerald's journal, and handed it to Orin, whose eyes seemed to light up slightly.

    "Let's see," Orin began. "Personal journal, Eighteen Seventies, leather bound." He flipped through a few of the pages. "This belonged to a woman," he added as he noticed the delicate penmanship. He held the book up to his nose and took a whiff. "European, if I'm not mistaking."

He handed the book back to Jack.

"I know all of that already."

"Oh, I thought you wanted me to authenticate it or something."

"Not exactly. I just thought that you might be interested in the contents."

"Contents?"

"Yeah, here."

Jack opened the book to the first page and held it out. Orin pulled his glasses back down and read the title page.

"The Journal of Katherine Bridget Fitzgerald," he carefully recited. "Castlebridge, County Wexford, Ireland." Orin ran this through his mind a couple of times. He'd just recently come across that name. After a few moments, he remembered where. He glanced at the newspaper and back at the journal. His eyes were on fire now. "Where did you find this?"

"It was in an old steamer trunk, stashed away in a crawlspace at Waldemere. Found the trunk a few days ago, but only recently acquired the key that opens it."

"And where'd you find this key?"

"Around the neck of a dead girl."

"One of the skeletons at the morgue?"

"Uh huh."

"Fascinating," Orin said as he took the journal from Jack.

"Yeah. I thought you might be interested in it. Gives a good description of what life was like back then for an Irish immigrant working in a big house like Waldemere."

Orin began to slowly flip through the pages.

"Have you read it yet?"

"The important parts."

"Jack, every part of this book is important."

"Well, I'm sure it is, but I just scanned through most of it and took note of the entries that had to do with my case."

"And did you find anything of use?"

"Some. Katherine Fitzgerald talks about the first victim, Anna Stadler, leaving them. There's more to do with the second victim, Harriett Fischer. They were apparently quite close and shared the same bedroom on the first floor."

"Is this the same room that the crypt was located off of?"

"Yeah. Whoever killed Anna Stadler must've hidden her body somewhere, waited until everyone was out of the house, and moved her body down to the crypt when the coast was clear. She also mentions that Harriett Fischer was romantically involved with someone, but she never gives a name."

"No name, huh?"

"I thought that weird too. Perhaps she was afraid that her journal might be discovered and didn't want to incriminate anyone. What's more, Katherine ended up having an affair with the same person that Harriett did."

"She never put two and two together. Never thought that there might be a link between the person Harriett was involved with and her sudden disappearance."

"Apparently not. The only conclusion that I can come to is that it must have been someone she trusted deeply."

"I can see that," Orin agreed.

"Anyway, Katherine ends up pregnant and decides to confront her beau on the matter. That's the last entry. I guess it didn't go over as well as she'd hoped it would."

"Thanks Jack. You just ruined the ending for me."

"Okay, here's another spoiler. You know that movie *Titanic*? The boat sinks."

Orin closed the book and ran his right index finger along the spine.

"Can I keep this?" he asked.

"I would say yes, as it'd make a great addition to the archive, but I'm inclined to say no, as it's not mine to give. The truth is, it's not anyone's."

"Spoken like a true archivist."

"I don't see any problem with making photocopies though."

"Gotta love modern technology. Come on down," Orin said. "I've got a copier in the archives room."

Jack stepped behind the counter and followed Orin down the heavily worn wooden stairs that led to the basement. They walked past rows of bookshelves and filing cabinets until they came to a photocopier tucked neatly into a corner of the room. Orin plugged it in and gave it a few moments to warm up.

"Don't use it very often, do you?" Jack asked.

"Not really. The fact is that rarely anybody but me comes down here. I don't get a lot of regular visitors for this feature of my business, and even when I do, I usually don't let them make photocopies."

"Why not?"

"Well, repeated exposure to light like this can damage some of the older documents. I prefer that people make handwritten copies, and even at that, I'd like them to use a pencil."

"A pencil?"

"Yeah. Pens have a tendency to explode. If that happens, it could easily ruin a priceless document."

"Makes sense."

Orin opened the journal to the first page and placed it on the glass. He pressed a green button on the copier and after a few moments, a grainy version of the page appeared in a slot below.

"This might take a while, Jack. I figured that you might be back at some point before you finished your research at Waldemere, so I pulled down the files on the house. They're in a box beside that desk over there." Orin pointed across the room to a small cardboard box that sat upon the floor next to the desk with the Oriental Express lamp. "All I ask is that you read only one folder at a time and that you don't re-file anything. Just leave the closed folders on the desk when you're finished with them. Oh and…"

"No pens," Jack said.

"Very good. You'll find some pencils in a jar on the desk."

"Thanks."

Jack walked over to the desk, pulled out his notebook, and drew a pencil from the jar. He removed the lid from the top of the cardboard box and examined its contents. There were many files here. Each was contained in a tan folder with a tab at the top. Upon these tabs were written the specific subjects to which they pertained. *Purchasing Orders, Land Transfers, Ledgers, Surry and Middleton, Aesthetic Influences*, Jack read to himself. He then came to a title that jumped out at him:

Lawsuits. He pulled the file, placed it on the desk and opened it.

From what he could gather, there were quite a number of cases set against Heinrich Engelhardt. All had come from former builders of the home. It seemed that after just a few short months of working on the house, he would unceremoniously fire them and bring in a completely different crew. Jack counted them. There were nine lawsuits in all. Among them was one filed by a familiar name: Tom Jenkins. That was the name that Jack had discovered carved into the wall of the trunk space along with the date *17th October 1876*.

"Find anything interesting?" Orin called from across the room.

"Possibly. Nine different builders filed wrongful termination suits against Heinrich Engelhardt."

"Yeah. I saw that too."

"The guy must have been some kind of a perfectionist or something."

"Of course he was. Just look at the house. But I think there was more to it than that."

"How do you mean?"

Orin walked over, closed the file folder that Jack was reading, and set it to the side. He reached into the box and pulled out another file that was marked: *Plans*.

"Okay, but this is the only help that I'm going to give you."

Jack opened the file and began to leaf through the pages within. They seemed to be crudely drawn floor plan designs. Everything seemed to be where it was today with the exception of a few items.

"There's no crypt listed on here," Jack pointed out.

"That's right. You can understand my surprise when you found that the other night. As near as I can decide, it was added after these drawing were made. But look here."

Orin flipped ahead a few pages until he came to a layout of the fourth floor.

"Ah," Jack said with astonishment, "it's the security vault."

"Yeah. It must have been part of the original design."

Just then, Jack noticed a feature that he hadn't yet come

across in the house. It appeared to be a corridor of some sort that ran along the eastern wall of the fourth floor bedroom: the same bedroom that he now occupied.

"What's this?" he asked. "It looks like a hallway."

"No, Jack. That's no hallway. That's a stairwell."

Jack looked closely at the drawing. He now noticed lines running across the space, perpendicular to the walls.

"A stairwell to what?"

Orin Drury smiled as he turned the page. Drawn here were three rooms that Jack couldn't place as anything he'd yet come across at Waldemere

"It's a stairwell… to the fifth floor."

"But Waldemere doesn't have a fifth floor. Not unless you count the crypt as being the first."

"The crypt isn't on here. Remember?"

"Yeah, but I haven't seen any of this in the house."

"Have you looked for it?"

"Well, no."

"There you go then, Jack. How do you know that it's not there if you haven't even looked?"

"That's a good point," Jack said as he nodded in agreement.

"You're in a rare position; one that I've never been in. I don't think that anyone knows about this floor's existence but me. Anyone else who might have known about it, Heinrich Engelhardt or the builders, are long dead. You can search for it. Tell me if it does in fact exist."

"That's not a bad idea at all," Jack said with a smile.

"Besides, look what you've been able to unearth in that house so far. No pun intended."

"But made nonetheless."

"Here's another thought, Jack. You wondered about the wrongful termination lawsuits filed against Heinrich Engelhardt. I have a theory."

"And what's that?"

"Well, I think he was hiring these guys to work on certain parts of the house and decided to change his plans from time to time. Maybe he didn't want anyone to see the whole house as it would stand completed."

"How do you mean?"

"Think of it. He'd gotten an idea to build a room but didn't want anyone to know about it. Let's use the crypt as an example. He hires one guy to build the crypt chamber then fires him. He then hires another guy to build the passageway and when that's completed, fires him. Afterwards, he hires someone else to wall off the passageway then gives him the axe. Finally, he hires someone to build a doorway that leads to what *appears* to be an alcove, but it's actually the walled off passage to the crypt. After the work is done, he goes in himself and knocks down the wall that's been erected, thus making the doorway, passage and crypt chamber fully accessible and no one is any wiser of its existence. Oh sure, there are rumors of there being a crypt in the house, but no solid proof."

"You think this is why he fired these people?"

"It's as good a theory as any."

Jack looked at the drawing and for the first time noticed a name scribbled in the lower right-hand corner: *T Jenkins*.

"Hey, I know this guy," Jack pointed out.

"Know who?"

"This Jenkins. His name in carved into the wall inside the trunk space where I found that journal."

"Trunk space, huh? Thomas Jenkins was one of the last people to work on Waldemere. Certainly one of the last to file a lawsuit."

"These are his drawings?"

"Must be. His name's on them."

Jack thought about it for a moment.

"I know what you said about photocopying older documents, but…"

"I think I can make an exception, Jack, but just this once. I didn't really expect you to sit here and draw out all of these pages."

"And I wasn't looking forward to drawing them either."

"Besides, you might miss something detrimental."

Jack headed west on Franklin with his backpack sitting on the seat beside him. It contained two very important items. One was the journal of Katherine Fitzgerald, which Orin was now quite pleased to have a copy of. The other was a set of photocopies of what Waldemere had looked like near the end of its building phase. Perhaps this stairwell was still there and perhaps it wasn't. Jack knew how he'd be spending much of that evening.

Chapter 24

"You're back sooner that I thought," Emily mentioned as she let Jack in through the side door.

"Yeah. It didn't take me nearly as long as I thought it would to find what I was looking for."

"And what was that?" she asked; her curiosity piqued.

"Do you have a few minutes?"

"To be 'onest, I 'ave all afternoon. Dinner doesn't need to be started until foive and the laundry was finished an hour ago. What is it?"

"Come on upstairs. I'll show you."

Emily followed Jack up the stairs to the fourth floor bedroom where he took off his coat and hung it up in the closet. After doing so, he opened his backpack, removed a couple of items, and set them on the desk.

"What this?" Emily asked as she picked up the small leather-bound book.

"Open it and find out."

Emily did so, but was slightly confused as she read the name in the front.

"Who's Katherine Bridget Fitzgerald?"

Jack realized that Emily really didn't know much about the legends behind Waldemere or any of the research that he had done thus far on the house. He would need to shed light on the matter.

"Maybe I should start from the beginning. Henry's great grandfather, Heinrich Engelhardt, was accused of murdering three girls in this house back in the late 1870's and early 1880's."

Emily seemed to grow slightly tense.

"Three girls? Loike the ones we found the other noight?"

"Precisely."

"Oh my God." Her heart sank at this.

"Anyway, there was a hearing and Heinrich Engelhardt was cleared of all charges against him."

"But we found…"

"Doesn't necessarily mean that he did it. In truth, it could have been anyone. As to who these girls were; one was the daughter of a cousin. Her name was Anna Stadler. She was the first to go missing. Almost two years later, another girl, a servant named Harriett Fischer, had vanished from the house. The following autumn, the other servant disappeared. And *her* name was…"

"Katherine Bridget Fitzgerald?"

"That's right."

Emily began to slowly flip through the pages of the journal.

"So what was she loike?"

Jack thought about it for a moment.

"To be honest, she wasn't that different from you. She was a servant here in this house, was an immigrant from British controlled Ireland, and conducted herself in a very ladylike fashion. Oh, she too was a redhead."

Emily's heart sank even further. It troubled her to hear that someone so like her could wind up dead and forgotten in a crypt below the house for so many years without anyone even knowing that she was there. She closed the book and inspected the leather cover.

"Where did ya foind this, anyway?"

Jack had considered not mentioning his discovery in the trunk space, as he had wanted it to remain a secret, but realized that it would be best to share what he had found with Emily.

"It was in a steamer trunk that I came across in the back of that trunk space beneath the floor," he explained.

"Ya mean there's really a trunk in there?"

"Yeah. Actually I'm a little surprised that you didn't know about it."

"To be 'onest, I never went in. Between the two o' us, I 'ave a sloight fear of the dark."

"Your secret's safe with me," Jack assured her, though he already knew that she was. He could tell it from the moment that they had entered the passage to the crypt the other night.

"So what else was in this trunk?"

"Quite a few things. It was mostly clothes and shoes…"

"Shoes?"

"Well, yeah. I mean, a pair of slippers and an old pair of boots."

"Can I see?"

Jack considered it for a moment.

"I don't really feel like going in there and digging it all out right now, but yes. You can see it."

He pulled out his digital camera, turned it on, set it to the playback mode and handed it to Emily.

"What's this?"

"It's a camera. You use it to…"

"I know what it is. Why did ya pass it to me?"

"Because I photographed everything that was in that trunk. Here. Just hit this button and it'll advance to the next picture."

Emily began to scroll through the images and soon came to the ones containing the beautiful dresses.

"These are absolutely amazin'."

"Yeah. I thought so too."

"And all o' this is still down there?"

"Sure is."

"What are ya goin' to do with it?"

"Me? Nothing. None of it's mine. I guess I was eventually going to tell Henry about it. Seeing as it's in his house, I would naturally assume that it should now belong to him."

"What's 'e goin' to do with a bunch o' old dresses?"

"I don't know. Sell them, perhaps. Some of those items I'm sure are quite valuable, like that porcelain doll and the perfume bottle. The necklace once belonged to his great grandmother, so I'm certain that he'll want it back, it being a family heirloom and all."

"I guess so." Emily looked a little put out. Jack could tell that she really had her eye on the dresses, but he had an idea.

"I'll tell you what. When I mention it to Henry later on, I'll ask him about the dresses and shoes. I don't see why he'd have a problem with giving them to you."

"Ya mean it?"

"Sure. After all, they had once belonged to a servant girl in the house and I think they should again. Besides, after reading that journal, I believe that Katherine Fitzgerald would have wanted them to go to someone like you."

"Jack, you're absolutely amazin'!" Emily declared as she tossed the camera on the bed and threw her arms about him. Jack was quite surprised by this sudden burst of emotion, but found her embrace warm and comfortable. Emily found it pleasing as well. After a moment though, she realized what she was doing and felt that she may have crossed a line. Slowly, she pulled herself away but found her eyes locked with Jack's. Her breathing had gone short and for a very brief instant she thought that they might actually kiss, but Jack took a step back and turned his head away. Emily followed suit.

"As far as the journal itself goes," Jack continued as if nothing had happened, "I'm pretty sure that Henry will want to keep it, though I think it should go to an archive or the Special Collections Department of the Cleveland Public Library."

"Yeah," Emily said, still slightly breathless. "An archoive." Quickly she composed herself and turned back towards Jack. She would push the matter of what had just transpired between them, but would do so delicately and with tact. She wanted to see where this could go. "So ya brought me up 'ere to show me this journal then? Or was there more that ya wanted me to see?"

"Now that you mention it, there is," Jack said with a smile. As he slowly walked towards her, Emily found it hard to breathe again. The tension in the air was thick and her heart was pounding. Jack stopped two feet from her and paused. She could feel the blood racing through her veins and her face and chest begin to flush. Just then, Jack held up a stack of papers.

"I came across these building notes and drawings while doing some research earlier this morning," he explained.

Emily looked down at the papers that he held in his hand and back up at his face, which looked as relaxed and easygoing as possible; a stark contrast to what she was feeling. Either they had different things on their minds or Jack was avoiding the issue. Emily let out a sigh and took the papers from Jack. She quickly flipped through the pages, which didn't seem to make much sense to her anyway, and handed them back. In truth, she didn't really even look at them. She tossed her head to the side, flipping a few auburn locks of hair over her face and asked Jack again in a somewhat sultry voice.

"And this is *all* ya wanted to show me?"

Jack briefly stared at her, but didn't know what she was getting at.

"Well, look at it," he said. "Those drawings show a hidden stairwell on the other side of this wall over here that leads to a fifth floor."

Emily gave up. Jack was completely oblivious to her intentions.

"A fifth floor," she said shortly. "Waldemere doesn't 'ave a fifth floor."

"According to this it does."

Emily snatched the papers from Jack's hand and looked at them once more. She studied the drawings and now saw what he meant.

"None o' this is supposed to be 'ere."

"The crypt wasn't supposed to be there either," Jack pointed out, "but there it was."

"No, I mean that this drawin' shows a door out in the ballroom that leads to a stairwell. I can tell ya roight now that there's no door there."

"Well let's take a look."

"Okay, but you're wastin' your toime."

They walked out into the ballroom, started towards the stairs that led to the lower floors but stopped short and turned to the left to face a blank wall.

"According to the drawings, it should be right here," Jack said.

He ran his right hand along the wall but could find no access way.

"And I'm tellin' ya, there's no door."

"Maybe there's some trick to it, like the security vault and the crypt."

He continued to feel the wall for a seam, but there was none to be found.

"Ya can't open what isn't there," Emily pointed out.

Jack crouched down and tried to locate a gap where the wall met the floor, but again, nothing. He placed both hands on the wall as he slowly felt his way up. Emily thought that he looked a bit ridiculous, but wondered what it would feel like to be that wall, with Jack's hands carefully running all over her. She briefly entertained the idea of making a pass at him again, but felt that the moment had come and gone. Just as it was beginning to look as though Jack were giving up, he balled his right hand into a fist and firmly knocked upon the wall with a fierce slam. Almost instantly, the knock was answered by a slightly delayed bang. The phantom echo seemed to come from deep on the other side of the wall. Emily and Jack looked at each other with astonishment.

"So there *is* something back there," Jack said with amazement.

Emily smiled. Jack was indeed quite clever, but the question remained as to how one might gain access to this hidden passageway.

"Good," she said, "but there's no door. 'Ow do we get in?"

"Your guess is as good as mine."

"Well, I'm off then. I've spent enough toime up 'ere dillydallying about."

Emily was quite upset that Jack hadn't read the signs that she was giving him and could see that there was nothing else for it. As far as the passage went, it would take further research on Jack's part to figure out how to get in. Just then, Jack turned around and looked at the clock.

"That's it!" he declared.

"That's what?" Emily, who had been descending the stairs, stopped and turned.

"Time. It all has to do with the right time. The security vault and the crypt had to be opened by operating the clock at a certain time."

"Okay. So what do we do, and when?"

Putting her frustration with Jack aside, Emily found her curiosity piqued.

"I don't know, but the message to get into the crypt was located in the security vault."

"So?"

"So I'm guessing that the next message is located back in the crypt."

"Oh no," Emily protested. "There's no way in 'ell that

I'm goin' back down there again."

"Come on, Emily. The police have removed the bodies. I can assure you that it's perfectly safe."

"Safe me arse! The bobbies told ya that tunnel could collapse at any given moment."

"Doesn't matter anyway; not right now at least. I can't get back down there until midnight at the earliest."

"And I'm tellin' ya that you're out o' your bleedin' moind!"

"Look. That's got to be where the next clue's located. If you don't want to go, that's fine. You don't have to. *I* can go down."

Emily's mind skipped ahead to a dirty thought, but she scratched it at once from her imagination.

"Well, good luck then. You'll need it. Be sure and let me know in the mornin' 'ow it all goes."

"Will do."

Emily thought she'd give it one more go, but would try to be a little more obvious.

"I'm goin' downstairs to 'ave meself a nap. Ya interested?"

"Yeah. A nap sounds like a great idea," Jack said with a nod. "Make sure you wake me up before dinner."

With that, he turned and walked into the bedroom, closing the door behind him. Emily had it figured. Jack must have been some kind of an idiot.

As promised, Jack had mentioned the steamer trunk to Henry Engelhardt over drinks by the fireside in the parlor after dinner. Henry had no problem at all in imparting the wardrobe to Emily, but was quite interested in the other items, especially his great grandmother's necklace. Though he was extremely curious about the contents of the trunk, he felt that there was no need to be going through them at that late hour. He decided that he would do so in the next day or two. He'd have planned to do so that following morning, but would be out of the house again for much of the day, as he had further appointments. This struck Jack as odd. Tomorrow would be a Sunday and hardly anybody but real estate agents worked on Sundays.

At nine thirty, Mr. Engelhardt excused himself to retire for bed. It was a half an hour past his normal turn-in time but he invited Jack to remain in the parlor for as long as he wished. Jack gladly accepted this offer and decided that he would stay for another drink or two. They shook hands and parted company for the evening. As Jack heard him slowly lumber up the front stairwell, he saw the pocket door that led to the dining room inch open. At first, he thought that the ghostly disturbances had finally come down from the fourth floor, but a moment later saw Emily peeking her head in.

"So what did 'e say?" she asked with anticipation.

"He said that I can stay down here for a while if I so chose."

"Not that. About the trunk."

"He looks forward to seeing it in the next day or two."

"The contents, Jack. What did 'e say about the contents?"

"Looks forward to seeing those too."

Emily could tell that he was toying with her.

"Jack..."

"Okay. The clothes and shoes are yours."

"Yes!" Emily whispered as she pumped a fist into the air.

"I expect that he'll tell you so at some point tomorrow. Care for a drink?"

"Oh, Jack. I probably shouldn't even be in 'ere."

"Nonsense. What's your poison?"

Emily looked nervous. She could hear Mr. Engelhardt moving around upstairs but realized that he was in for the night. She slowly crept into the parlor and approached Jack.

"Bombay Sapphire on the rocks," she said with a hushed voice.

Jack pulled a glass from the shelf, tossed in a few cubes of ice, and poured her a generous portion. He handed it to her and raised his glass.

"To health," he announced. "Sláinte."

"To 'ealth."

They clinked their glasses together, took sips from their drinks, and smiled.

"So do you know what kind of appointment Mr.

Engelhardt has tomorrow morning?" Jack asked.

"Can't say I do."

"Hmm. It's just funny to make an appointment on a Sunday morning is all."

"I guess so. Never really thought about it to be 'onest." Emily took another sip from her glass. "So what are your plans for the evenin'?"

"Me? I'm probably going to stay in. Still want to check out the crypt later on tonight. See if I can find the next clue. Why?"

"Well, I was thinkin' we moight visit that pub ya were tellin' me about the other day. The one that plays punk on the jukebox."

"Oh. The Spitfire. We'll have to do that another time."

"But it's Saturday noight. Who stays in on a Saturday noight?"

"Someone with a lot of research to do."

"Suit yourself then, Jack."

Emily finished her gin in one big swallow and Jack did the same with his scotch.

"Another?" he asked.

"Only if you're joinin' me."

"Sure."

Jack poured out two more glasses and took a seat in one of the armchairs by the fire. Emily chose the one across from him. They sat in silence for a while and simply enjoyed the quiet of the evening. After about ten minutes, Emily spoke up.

"So what do ya think is up on that fifth floor… if it does exist?"

"Oh, I don't know," Jack replied. "Could be anything. Could be nothing at all. I do know this. It's likely to have been hidden and kept a secret for well over a hundred years. Imagine it, Emily; walking into a room that no one has been in since the late 1800's. It must be like some kind of time capsule: left perfectly untouched and preserved since the last person walked out of there."

"I already know what that's loike."

"Huh?"

"The crypt… two noights ago."

"Oh, yeah. But this is different. This is a living space, not a burial chamber."

"Ya don't know that for sure."

"Yeah. I guess I'm speculating."

"And 'ow do ya know it 'asn't been touched in over a 'undred years?"

"Well, I have a friend that's something of a historian. Knows a fair amount about Waldemere. He's the one that clued me in to the drawings of the house and the fifth floor. Said that no one but him knows about it possibly being there. I can't wait to see if he's right."

"Loikely to be a real mess up there. Ya foind another floor in this 'ouse and it'll just be one more floor that I'll 'ave to clean."

"Sorry to saddle you with more work. Might be worth it though if it means making a great discovery."

"Speak for yourself. You're not the one who 'as to do all the sweepin' and dustin'. What's more, if it's anythin' loike the discovery in the crypt, ya can keep it."

Jack downed the last of his Irish whiskey and looked at the clock on the wall. It was nearly ten.

"Well, I'd better be going up," he announced. "Want to rest up a little before going down into the crypt to start my search."

He stood up and stretched. Emily quickly shot the last of her drink and set the empty glass on the table by the wall.

"I'll walk ya up," she offered. "Nothin' better to do on a Saturday noight, I guess."

"You should go check out The Spitfire."

"What, by meself?"

"Sure. You don't need me to come with you."

"But I won't know anyone up there."

"That's fine. I don't know too many people up there either but I'm sure you'll have no problem making friends."

"Pass. Better to do it in familiar company."

"So be it."

They walked up the stairs in relative silence. When they had reached the top of the stairs at the fourth floor, Jack paused and gave the blank wall another look.

"Jack, there's still nothin' there."

"I know," he said. "I'm just trying to figure out where the door would be, if not here."

Emily watched as Jack ran his right hand along the wall once more. Again she wondered how that hand would feel against her bare skin. She decided to give it one last try. Maybe he'd be more at ease after a few drinks.

"Ya know, there are better things up 'ere to touch than some dingy ole' wall."

"Yeah, I know. The clock's much more fascinating."

"Colder."

"Huh?"

"You're gettin' colder."

Jack decided to play along.

"The bar?"

"Okay. A little warmer."

"The newel post here at the top of the stairs?"

"Warmer still."

Jack could now see where she was going with this. He hesitated before continuing.

"Um, you?"

Emily smiled.

"On foire, love."

With that, she placed her hands on the sides of Jack's face and moved in to kiss him.

"Hold on a sec," he said as he stepped out of the path of her lips. Emily was quite surprised at his sudden resistance.

"What's wrong?"

"Nothing's wrong," he assured her.

"Am I not pretty or somethin'?"

"No, Emily. You're absolutely gorgeous. It's just..."

"Just what? You're not a poof are ya?"

"A *what*?"

"A twink. You know, a queer?"

"Oh," Jack laughed, "it's nothing like that."

Jack was nervously trying to decide on how best to say it. Finally, he decided that vagueness was the best route to go.

"It's just that I'm seeing someone right now and if I were to be with you tonight, it would do her a great dishonor."

"Oh," Emily said and paused for a moment as she looked at the floor. "I'm sorry. I should've asked ya if there was anyone in your loife."

"There's no reason to apologize or feel embarrassed. If I weren't with… who I'm with right now… I'd be very happy to be with you."

"I need to go to bed."

"I'm sorry, Emily."

"Don't ya apologoize either," she said as she turned and walked down the stairs. "I'll see ya in the mornin', Jack."

Emily felt quite foolish. She knew that he wasn't an idiot and that there must have been a perfectly good reason for him ignoring her advances earlier that day. She never would have guessed that he had a girlfriend of any sort. He'd never mentioned it, but then, she'd never asked. When she reached her bedroom on the second floor, she closed the door and threw the bolt. The day hadn't gone anything like she'd hoped; neither had the night for that matter. All that she wanted at this point was to put the events of the evening behind her. Sleep was the best cure for that.

Jack shook his head, walked into the fourth floor bedroom, and closed the door behind him. The first thing he noticed was that the Tiffany shaded wall sconce by the door was burning bright. The second was the distinct aroma of patchouli.

"That was quite brilliant, Jack."

Shelby was sitting Indian-style on the bed watching him as he entered the room. Jack's heart skipped a beat at her sudden appearance, but instantly, he was overcome with joy at seeing her.

"Shelby? How did you…"

"Get here? That was easy. I just thought really hard about you and bam. The next thing I know, I'm sitting here in this bedroom."

Jack ran over, jumped on the bed beside her, and gave her a huge embrace.

"God it's good to see you."

"Thanks, Jack," Shelby said with a smile. "It's good to be seen." She looked about herself at the amazingly beautiful room that she was now in. "So this is Waldemere"

"Yeah, part of it anyway. You should see the rest of the place."

"Is it anything like this?"

"Even better. So what was quite brilliant?"

"How's that?"

"When I came into the room, you said 'that was quite brilliant.' What did you mean?"

"Oh. The way you handled yourself outside the door there."

"You saw that?"

"I did. And thank you for saying what you said and *not* doing what I was afraid you were going to do. Who was that anyway?"

"Her name's Emily. She's Mr. Engelhardt's servant."

"Pretty girl."

"Yeah, well." Jack wanted to change the subject. "So why did you come all this way to see me?"

"Just that; to see you. You haven't stopped by your place in Lakewood for three days now and after what you told me had happened the night before, I got a little worried. Are you alright?"

"I'm fine. There was another disturbance last night though."

"And yet you're still here. I thought you were going to leave if anything else happened."

"So did I, but it wasn't as bad as what had happened the one night. Amy gave me a crystal that would draw most of the negative energy away from me."

"And it worked?"

"For the most part, yeah."

"Well that's a relief."

"Oh, there's something else that she suggested and I want to try it out while you're still here."

"Um, Jack. I'm here for the whole night; if you haven't figured that out yet."

"You are?"

"Of course. I'm not going to let some other ghosts get their hands on you. You're mine."

"My hero," Jack jested.

"So what were you going to try out?"

"Wait here for a second."

Jack jumped off the bed and removed his shoes and socks. Reaching into the left pocket of his pants, he retrieved a small handful of coins, which he sorted through until he had separated the pennies.

"What on Earth are you doing?" Shelby asked.

"One more second."

Jack placed the pennies, seven in all, on the floor in a tight area. He stepped onto them and looked up at Shelby.

"What?" she asked.

"Okay. Come here."

Shelby climbed off the bed and walked over to him.

"Now what?"

"I want you to kiss me."

"What?" She was slightly taken back by this request.

"Kiss me like you've never kissed me before."

"Shouldn't you lie down or something?"

"Not if this works." He looked intently into her bright blue eyes. "Just kiss me."

"Okay," she said with a curious smile. "Here goes." Shelby closed her eyes and pressed her lips tightly against Jack's. At first he felt completely fine, quite giddy actually, but after a moment the room began to swim. A second later, everything went dark.

Jack awoke on the bed a few minutes later, somewhat confused as to what had gone wrong.

"What happened?" he asked.

"What do you think happened? The same thing that always happens when we're together physically. You became overwhelmed and passed out."

"That wasn't supposed to happen."

"And why not?"

"Because Amy gave me a solution that might keep that from happening in the future."

"You told Amy about me?" Shelby seemed overjoyed at the thought. "What did she say? Does she want to meet me?"

"Hold on. I didn't tell her about you. Not directly."

"Oh. So what *did* you tell her?"

"I just asked her how to go about keeping one's self from being overwhelmed when having physical contact with a disembodied spirit."

"You *what*?"

Jack shrugged his shoulders.

"Well what else was I supposed to say?"

"Why don't you just try telling her the truth? She seems like one of the few friends you have that would actually believe you and understand all of this."

"I know. I should probably tell her. I think she's figured out some of it anyway."

"Please tell her, Jack. It's not good to keep your friends in the dark."

"I'll think about it." Just then, Jack remembered that he had a mission to accomplish that night. "Oh. What time is it?"

"I don't know. Somewhere around eleven, I think."

"Crap!"

Jack sprang up from the bed and ran over to the clock on the fireplace mantle. It was just before eleven.

"What is it?" Shelby asked.

"No time to explain. Come on."

Jack threw open the bedroom door and ran out into the ballroom. As he approached the clock, he could hear the whirring noise beginning. There wasn't a second to lose. He turned the first figure of the hornet to the right and pulled out on it. He heard the familiar winding sound and thump, and raced over to the other hornet. He repeated the maneuver and again heard the telltale sounds that told him he had successfully achieved the first steps to opening the crypt.

"What the hell was that all about?" Shelby asked.

"Oh. I had to do that at exactly eleven o'clock or else I wouldn't be able to get into the crypt."

"Get into the… What are you talking about?"

"The crypt." Jack then realized that he hadn't yet mentioned any of this to Shelby. "Okay. Hold on. Let me go back a couple of nights. I discovered that the clock was actually some sort of a machine and that these figures are like draw knobs on an organ."

"So that's what you needed your dad's book for?"

"Exactly."

"I remember you telling me about this clock, but I had no idea it was anything like this."

"Really quite remarkable. So anyway, I figured out how to work it and learned along the way that I had to move certain figures at precise times on the clock. One set of functions took me into a security vault located over there across the room."

Jack pointed to an area of the ballroom where the hidden panel now sat closed.

"But I don't see anything."

"Trust me. It's there. So once I was inside, I found another set of instructions and followed them. I had to turn these two hornets at eleven o'clock and pull down on those two tombstones up there at twelve."

He pointed at the carved figures of the tombstones that flanked the front of the clock.

"Weird. What happened when you did that?"

"It opened a door off of Emily's bedroom that led to the crypt."

"And what was in this crypt?"

"Um." Jack hesitated.

"Jack. What was in the crypt?"

"Three human skeletons," he mumbled.

"Three *what*?"

"Emily and I found the remains of three girls who had been murdered in this house during the late Nineteenth Century. Pam and I identified them late yesterday afternoon. It was all over the news last night and in the paper this morning."

"What's with you having this knack for finding human remains?"

"I've been wondering that myself."

Shelby was now a little perplexed.

"So you're trying to open this crypt again? Why?"

"Earlier today, I went to my friend Orin's and he showed me some pretty compelling evidence that there's another floor above us. I'm guessing that the only way to gain entry is by using this clock again."

"What does any of this have to do with a crypt?"

"Well, I found the instructions for opening the crypt in the security vault. I'm guessing that the next set of instructions is somewhere down in that crypt."

"And you don't think Emily will mind us traipsing down into her bedroom at this hour, especially after you just shot her down?"

"She's moved into another bedroom since then. And what's this 'us' business?"

"Come on, Jack. Do you really think that I'm going to let you go unaccompanied down into a crypt in a notorious haunted house at midnight?"

"Well when you put it like that…"

"I'm not leaving your side for a moment." Shelby looked back up at the immense clock. "So we have until midnight?"

"Yeah. That's when I have to pull down on the tombstones."

"That gives us almost an hour. Let's lay down for a while. I can think of no better way to pass the time."

Chapter 25

Shelby woke Jack up at five minutes before midnight. Every ounce of him wanted to remain in bed with her, but he knew that he had to complete the functions on the clock. Reluctantly, he rolled out of bed and put on his plaid robe. The crypt would be quite chilly and he would need all the warmth he could get. As he opened the bedroom door, he remembered that he would need the stepladder to reach the tombstones. He turned around and walked back towards the trunk space.

"Where are you going, Jack," Shelby asked. "The ballroom's that way."

"I know, but the tombstones are too high for me to reach."

"So?"

"So I need to get something."

He rolled the area rug back, exposing the trapdoor.

"What's that?"

"It's a trunk space. They used to store steamer trunks and the like in these back during the eighteen hundreds."

"So you're getting a trunk?" Shelby asked as Jack lifted up on the trapdoor.

"Even better," he replied and withdrew the stepladder.

"Oh, of course. How stupid of me. Everybody keeps a ladder in their trunk space these days."

Jack gave her a coy smile.

"I stashed it here a few nights ago."

"Whatever."

He carried the stepladder across the room and opened the door. The ballroom outside was awash in darkness. Realizing that he would do better if he were able to see, he set the ladder down, walked over to the desk, and picked up the flashlight.

"Helps if I can see," Jack pointed out.

"What's that?"

Jack flashed the light at Shelby a couple of times and tucked it into the pocket of his robe. He picked up the ladder once again and entered the ballroom with Shelby close behind him. They stopped a few feet away from the left-hand side of the clock, where Jack opened up the ladder and positioned it below the first tombstone. He pulled out the flashlight and shined it on the clock.

"Still about a minute to go," he noted.

"Why don't you just turn on the lights or something?"

"What? You got a problem with my flashlight?" he joked. "The lights are all burned out. Keeps happening every couple of weeks, I guess."

Shelby had a good idea why but didn't feel like bringing it up. She thought it better to change the subject.

"Jack, are you sure you want to go through with this tonight?"

"Absolutely. I mean, I could wait until tomorrow and do it at noon, I suppose."

"So why don't you?"

"Determination," he said as he climbed the ladder.

"More like stubbornness. We talked about this. Remember?"

"I'm all set to go," he added. Just then, the whirring noise began. He quickly pulled down on the tombstone. As he did, he could hear a ratcheting sound that was followed by a thud. He quickly scampered down the ladder, dragged it over to the other side of the clock, climbed back up, and pulled down on the first tombstone's mate. Again there was a ratcheting and thud.

"Now what?"

No sooner had she said this, than there came a slamming sound from somewhere downstairs. Shelby gave a start and looked about herself with surprise. Jack thought it slightly amusing to see a ghost that was startled. Typically, when it came to ghosts, the shoe would have been on the other foot.

"It's okay," he assured her with a chuckle. "It's just the door to the crypt sliding open."

Shelby screwed up her face and belted Jack in the shoulder as he stepped from the bottom of the ladder.

"You could've warned me or something."

"Yeah, I could've. But where's the fun in that?"

Shelby looked around at the dark and empty ballroom.

"So where to now?"

"The crypt," Jack told her. "It's this way."

He led her back across the ballroom, but quickly darted into the bedroom and picked up his digital camera. They continued down the stairs and as they came to each level, Shelby would stop to have a brief look around. Jack was glad to see that she was fascinated by the house, but knew that they needed to press on. Within a couple of minutes, they were down on the lowest level of the home, standing just outside of Emily's former bedroom.

"Are we there?"

"Yeah. The entrance to the crypt is just off this bedroom. You really don't have to come with me if you don't want to."

"And why wouldn't I want to come with you?"

"I don't know. I guess it's just that Emily had such a hard time going down in the first place. When I had mentioned that I'd be coming back down again, she wouldn't have anything to do with it."

"Well, I'm not Emily."

"Obviously."

"And I promised you that I'm not leaving your side."

Jack considered it for a moment.

"Okay then. We go together."

With that, Jack opened the bedroom door and was greeted by a cool draft of stale air coming up from the crypt. They cut through the bedroom and stood at the entrance to the crypt passage.

"So this is it?" Shelby asked as she inspected the void before them.

"It's a little slippery towards the bottom of the stairs, so be careful."

"Jack?"

"Yeah?"

"Ghost."

"Where?" Jack's eyes darted about apprehensively.

"No, Jack. Me. Ghost. Me no slippy slippy on floory floory."

"Oh." Jack suddenly realized that warning a ghost about there being a wet floor ahead was indeed quite idiotic. "Come on."

"After you," Shelby said with a smirk. It was now her turn to have something of a laugh.

They descended the flagstone stairs until they came to the brick-lined arched passageway. The dust was no better than it was the night that Jack and Emily had gone down. To Jack, it seemed to have gotten worse. As they made their way through the passage, Jack briefly flashed his light at the wall. He could now see what the police had been talking about when they'd mentioned that the whole place could collapse at any time. The mortar that had once held these bricks in place was now more to the consistency of wet sand. Jack quickened his pace slightly.

They soon came to the short run of steps that brought them down into the crypt room. There before them sat the two stone sarcophaguses. Jack shined the light around the room in hopes of locating some words engraved somewhere, but could see none. As he stepped down into the center of the room, he thought that he heard Shelby starting to cry.

"What's wrong?" he asked.

"Nothing, Jack. It's not me."

He cast the light slowly around the room, but could see that they were in fact alone. As he slowly turned back towards the stairs, Shelby stopped him.

"Jack, wait! Go back a little."

Jack panned the light back until it was shining on the end of the room just opposite the stairs.

"Hold it there," she told him. Jack did as instructed and shined the light on the blank wall before him.

"What is it?" he whispered.

Shelby walked down the short run of steps and entered the crypt room. She slowly approached the area where Jack was shining the light.

"What do you mean 'what is it?' It's your friend, Emily."

"What?"

"Jack, she's right there, crying."

"No, she isn't."

"Quit playing around and ask her what's wrong."

"I'm not playing around, Shelby. There's no one there."

"Of course there is. I'm looking right at her!"

"How do you know that it's Emily?"

Shelby was getting frustrated with him.

"Come on, Jack. Bright red hair like that…"

Jack thought about it for a moment and suddenly everything made sense.

"Katherine," he said with amazement.

"Who?"

"It's Katherine Fitzgerald."

"Who's Katherine Fitzgerald?"

"She used to be a servant here."

"What happened? They give her the axe or something?"

"No. The rope."

"The *what*?"

"She was strangled to death… a little over a hundred and twenty-five years ago."

Shelby was speechless for a moment as she gazed upon the girl, who was facing the wall, crying with her head in her hands.

"What should we do?" Shelby asked at length.

"I don't know. Maybe you should try to talk to her."

"Right." Shelby cautiously walked over to Katherine, but looked back at Jack, who gave her a nod of reassurance. Mustering up the courage to do so, Shelby addressed the girl. "Are you okay?" she asked with an elevated volume of her voice. She jumped back in surprise.

"What'd she say?" asked Jack.

"She told me not to yell at her."

"Okay, so don't yell at her. Try again."

Shelby nodded.

"Are you Katherine?"

Jack could here whispers coming from the blank area along the wall. Shelby turned and looked at Jack again.

"Well?"

"Yeah," Shelby said. "Her name's Katherine."

"Ask her if she's the one who's been whispering at me up on the fourth floor."

Shelby did so. When she got her reply, she turned and faced Jack with a slight touch of horror in her bright blue eyes.

"She says that she hasn't been whispering at you. She's been screaming at you."

"Screaming. Why?"

"She's been trying to get you to run away."

"Run away from what?"

"From... *him*!"

Jack could see the panic in Shelby's eyes and although she didn't say it, he could tell that she wanted him to leave Waldemere at once.

"Ask her what she's talking about. Who does she want me to run away from?"

"Does it matter, Jack?"

"Of course it matter's"

"Fine, I'll ask." Shelby turned back towards the wall. "Who should Jack run away from?"

There was a long pause.

"What's she saying?"

"Hold on." Shelby seemed to be nodding with what Katherine was telling her, but looked considerably confused. Finally, she turned to Jack and gave him an answer. "She won't give any names. Says that he swore her to secrecy. She says that she's seen him watching you. You've come closer than anyone else has come before. Even closer than the Youngs. Who are the Youngs?"

"They used to own this house. I've come closer to what?"

"Finding out the truth. This house has been holding its secrets for many years now. She says that Mrs. Young almost found out everything, but was driven to madness before she could get close enough."

"Ask her if she's seen any kind of poem or phrase written anywhere in this room."

"Katherine, have you seen any words in this room? A message or a poem?"

Shelby looked slightly taken back by Katherine's reply.

"What is it?"

"She's shaking her head and crying. I don't think she wants to talk anymore."

"Katherine!" Jack shouted, talking directly to the girl that he couldn't see. "I need to know if there's anything written in this room."

"That's not going to do you any good, Jack. She can't hear you." As Shelby told him this, her eyes widened with surprise.

"What is it?"

"Jack, say her name again."

"Why?"

"Just do it."

"Katherine!" Jack obliged.

"Oh my God…"

"What is it?"

"She's looking right at you. I think she can hear you."

"Katherine," Jack said again. "Is there anything in this room?"

Jack heard Katherine's reply as plain as day.

"Thevshi," she whispered.

"Thevshi? What's that mean?" Shelby asked.

"It means 'ghost' in Irish," Jack informed her.

"Irish, huh? That explains the odd accent."

"Katherine, I know there's another ghost here, but Shelby won't hurt you."

"No, Jack. I don't think that's what she means."

Jack seemed perplexed.

"Okay, so what then?"

"She thinks that *you're* the ghost."

Jack was at a total loss. None of this made any sense.

"How can she think that I'm a ghost if she's the one who's dead?"

"I don't think she knows that, Jack," Shelby whispered to him. "Either that or she hasn't accepted it yet." She could see the intention in Jack's eyes, but stopped him short of his next question. "Don't do it, Jack."

"Do what?"

"I know what you're going to ask her. You're going to ask her who murdered her, aren't you?"

"It would solve so much if I could."

"Well, you can't," Shelby explained still talking in a whisper. "A shock like that could traumatize her for a long time to come."

"Fine. Katherine, I won't hurt you. I just need to know if

there is anything written anywhere in this room. If you tell me, I'll leave you alone."

Shelby's ears perked up and Jack could tell that Katherine was giving an answer. As she turned towards Jack, her eyes darted across the room and in the direction of the stairs.

"She's gone," Shelby sighed.

"What did she say?"

"Something about how they would read it to each other every night, but that only Harriett and Anna knew what it meant."

"Read it to each other every night?"

"Something in German. Does that mean anything to you?"

"Tons. The clues that I've been finding are written in German. Was there anything else?

"That's all she said. After that, she ran out of the room. Jack, is everything alright?"

Jack grew quiet. He started to pace about the crypt, biting at his fingernails in deep concentration, his footfalls tapping softly against the cold flagstone floor. What could Katherine have meant by that, he wondered. Perhaps Anna Stadler would read to the girls every night, but why would she read them something that was in German: something Katherine couldn't understand? Maybe Anna and Harriett were trying to teach Katherine how to read German. That didn't make much sense either. He was going in the wrong direction with this and knew it. This was going to take a while to figure out. He turned and hopped up on Sophia Engelhardt's unused sarcophagus and sat himself down to ponder the concept further.

"What are you doing?" Shelby asked. "Show a little respect."

"No, it's okay. Mrs. Engelhardt is buried over at Monroe Street Cemetery beside her husband and son. The vault's empty.

Jack's words hung in his mind for a moment. This vault wasn't always empty. Until just a few nights earlier, it had contained the remains of three girls. Three girls, stuffed into one grave for just over a hundred and twenty five years. He looked down at the inscription on the lid.

Mutter
Sophia
Gattin von
H. C. H. Engelhardt
Geb.
14 Dez. 1832
Gest.

That was in German, but Katherine had said that they'd read it every night. He knew that they were *inside* the stone coffin and wouldn't have been able to see this from where they were lying. There was only one other solution. He jumped down from the sarcophagus, took a firm grasp of the lid, and began to slide it open.

"Hey!" Shelby shouted. "Don't open that!"

"But I have an idea."

"I don't care what you have. Put it back!"

"Emily and I opened it the other night. This is where we found the remains of the three girls."

"So why are you opening it now?"

"Call it a hunch." Jack turned the lid so that it now sat perpendicular with the vault. He crouched down on the floor and shined his flashlight up at the underside. "Ah ha!"

"What is it?"

"Come have a look."

Shelby crossed the room and crouched down beside Jack. She too looked up at the underside of the lid, but found herself quite confused.

"What's that say?"

"I don't know. I don't speak German."

"Ein mann eine Frau," Shelby tried to pronounce. "So is that what you were looking for?"

"Sure is. Katherine told you that they would read it every night. They were stuffed into this vault for so many nights that there would be no counting them. I figured that it had to be down here somewhere."

Jack pulled out his digital camera and took a picture of the inscription. He played the image back on the digital display and compared it to the original. It was perfect. He had everything he needed to translate the next set of instructions for operating the clock.

Ten minutes later, Jack and Shelby were back up in the fourth floor bedroom with Jack sitting at the desk, his laptop opened before him. He typed in the phrase as it appeared on his camera and hit the *enter* key. A moment later, a translation appeared on the screen.

"So what's it say?" Shelby asked from where she sat on the edge of the bed.

"One Man, one Woman."

"That's it?"

"Yeah, that's it."

"Not much of a clue, is it?"

Jack thought about this for a moment. He looked up at the clock on the fireplace mantle. It was just about one in the morning. These instructions were becoming quite obvious. He would have to turn the heads of the man and the woman at one o'clock. Both of these figures were placed rather high up on the clock, even higher than the tombstones were. He was glad that he'd left the stepladder in the ballroom. He'd certainly need it again.

Jack and Shelby walked back into the ballroom and Jack positioned the ladder beneath the figure of the man.

"This should only take a moment," he told Shelby as he started up.

"What do you think will happen?"

"I don't know. Hopefully it'll open up a door that leads to the fifth floor."

"Wish I could just walk through walls like ghosts do in the movies. I'd be able to tell you what's up there."

"Yeah, I know. What kind of a ghost are you anyway?"

"One that's still restricted to physical boundaries; and tied to you. I can only go where you go, or have been."

265

Jack would've liked to have continued the conversation a little more, but the low whirring noise had just started. He reached up and turned the head of the man to the left. It clicked as he advanced it until it would go no further. Immediately, there was a ticking sound that reminded Jack of the cliché sound that a time bomb makes. He climbed down the ladder, dragged it to the other side of the clock, and did the same with the head of the woman. Again, this was followed by a clicking sound.

Jack descended the ladder and stepped a few feet back, watching and waiting with anticipation for what would happen next. He felt Shelby take his hand and could tell that she too was interested in what was about to happen. After a few more minutes, the whirring sound stopped and there was a clicking sound. The two heads returned to their original positions leaving jack quite confounded.

"So what now?" Shelby asked.

"Now, nothing. It didn't work."

"What do you mean it didn't work? I heard it click."

"Yeah, it does that when you get the instructions wrong. See the figures of the man and woman? They're back in their original positions. That means that I screwed something up."

"Maybe you should have turned the lady's head first."

"I don't think so, Shelby. The instructions clearly state *one man, one woman*."

"Perhaps there was more to it, then."

"Most likely. Well, I can't get back into the crypt and go searching again until noon tomorrow."

"Jack, it's late. We should get to bed."

Jack nodded. It was indeed quite late. Furthermore, it had also been an interesting night. Not only had he made contact with Katherine Fitzgerald, but also Shelby had surprisingly joined him on that evening's adventures: quite an unexpected surprise. Falling asleep in her arms sounded like the perfect way to end the night.

They walked back into the bedroom and Jack closed and locked the door behind him. He dropped his robe, turned out the light by the door, and crawled into bed beside Shelby. Wrapped in her warm embrace, Jack fell asleep almost immediately.

Chapter 26

Jack awoke the next morning to the sound of someone knocking on the bedroom door. He rolled over and discovered that Shelby was no longer with him. She'd told him that she would stay the entire night and must have left around sunrise, he figured. The sun was shining brightly and it was just after ten. Again he heard the knocking. He climbed out of bed, tossed on his robe, and answered the door.

"Good mornin', Jack," Emily said as she was putting on a jacket. "Mr. Engelhardt 'as already left this mornin' and I'm off meself to do a bit o' runnin' around."

"I see."

"Just wanted to inform ya that breakfast is on the table and that I won't be back for a few hours. Oh, 'ow did it go last noight? Did ya find what ya were lookin' for?"

"Yes and no. I got back into the crypt and found an inscription, but when I tried to operate the clock, it didn't work."

"Really? Do ya think ya moight've mistranslated it or somethin'?"

"I don't think so. More than likely, there was more to it that I missed. I'm going to have to go back down and have another look."

"Well, suit yourself."

"I know that this has to open a door to the fifth floor."

"Okay, just don't go poundin' any 'oles in the walls or anythin'."

"I'm sure it won't come to that."

Emily zipped up her jacket and pulled her long red ponytail out from the back of her collar.

"Will we be seein' ya at dinner then?"

"I'm not sure yet. My week's up and this is my last day here. I'll probably be packed and ready to leave by this evening."

"Well, Mr. Engelhardt should be back later this afternoon and I'm sure that 'e'll want to see ya before ya leave."

"Oh, without a doubt. I won't leave until he gets back."

"Roight. I'm off then. Good luck."

"Thank you, Emily. You take care."

"I will."

Emily turned and headed back down the stairs. Jack closed the door and decided that he'd slept in long enough. It was time to get moving. There was still so much to do that day and if it was to be his last one there, he knew that he'd have to make the most of it. As it was, there would be no time that morning to listen to the Irish radio program. He would have to pull it up later that week from the online archives.

At five minutes past twelve, Jack was cautiously making his way back down the passage that led to the crypt. He'd turned the figures of the hornets at eleven and had pulled down on the tombstones at noon, opening the hidden door in Emily's former bedroom. He knew that there had to be more to the inscription somewhere in the crypt, but he still had no idea where that might be. As near as he knew, there was nothing else written on the underside of Sophia Engelhardt's vault lid, but then, it was quite dark and he may have overlooked something.

As Jack descended the short run of steps that carried him down into the low-ceilinged crypt room, he shined his flashlight about the walls and could see that he was very much alone. Furthermore, he could hear no whispering or sobbing. Had Katherine been there again, she might have been able to direct him further. Communication with her, for his part, was quite limited. On a couple of occasions though, he'd managed to pick up a few words here and there. He could certainly use the help. He waited for a moment and realized that he would have to do this on his own. He began his search of the room.

There was nothing written above the doorway, as there had been in the security vault. He cast his light about the ceiling and inspected the details. Perhaps, he thought, there might have been something written up there, but the more he looked, the less he saw. He then decided that there was nothing else for it. He walked back over to Sophia Engelhardt's vault and slid it open. Crouching down, he could see the passage that he had discovered the night before, but nothing else. He walked around to the other side of the vault and saw that this part of the lid was blank. He then stuck his head inside and flashed the light on the underside of the lid there. Again there was nothing.

This was certainly getting him nowhere. The only other words that appeared in that crypt were the epitaphs that were engraved on the outside of Sophia and Heinrich Engelhardt's vaults. Just then, Jack had an idea and wondered how he could have been so absent minded not to have thought of it before now.

He strolled over to Heinrich Engelhardts vault and took a firm grasp of the lid. He slid it open so that it too was now perpendicular to the rest of the vault. Crouching down, he aimed the flashlight at the underside and saw what he'd expected to find. There, engraved into the stone, was another passage written in German. Jack smiled as he pulled out his digital camera and snapped a shot of the newly discovered phrase. The image was clear and he'd have no trouble translating this final piece of the puzzle.

Just to be certain that he'd gotten the entire message this time, Jack walked around to the other side of Heinrich's vault and looked at the underside. It was blank, as was the section in the middle. There was nothing else on the lid. Satisfied that his work there was concluded, he closed both vault lids and walked back up the stairs and out of the crypt.

Jack sat at the desk again with his laptop open before him and carefully typed in the phrase he'd just discovered under Heinrich Engelhardt's vault lid. The translation came back and he quickly jotted down the words.

"One heart; my place of secret keeping," he recited to himself. The next step was quite obvious. Also, at one o'clock, he would have to do something with the carved image of the heart that was placed directly below the clock face.

Jack looked up at the clock that sat on the fireplace mantle in the bedroom. It was nearly one and he had very little time to waste. He walked out into the ballroom and climbed the ladder that was placed before the figure of the man's head. For the first time, he realized that this figure bore a striking resemblance to the image of Heinrich Engelhardt in the group photograph of Waldemere. Looking across the room, he noticed that the figure of the woman was a good likeness of Sophia. He glanced down towards the floor and saw the image of the heart just below the clock face. Perhaps, he thought, he should have figured out how to move it before he actually needed to. There was no time now. The minute hand advanced and the low whirring sound began.

Firmly grasping the figure of Heinrich Engelhardt's head, and he was now certain of this character's identity, he turned it until it would go no further. As it started to make the ticking sound again, Jack quickly came down from the ladder, dragged it to the other side of the room, climbed back up, and turned the figure of Sophia. It too began to click. Without wasting any time, Jack descended the ladder and walked over to the image of the heart. As he had done with the images of the crows, he pushed on the heart and watched as it slowly sank into the surface of the facade

Almost at once, Jack heard a banging sound from right behind him. He turned to see that another wainscot panel had opened up in the ballroom just opposite from the one that led into the security vault. That must have been it, he figured. That must be the way into the fifth floor. Still, he was troubled by the fact that this panel that had just opened was nowhere near the stairwell that was indicated on Mr. Tom Jenkins' drawings or the hollow space on the other side of the wall near the main staircase that led to the lower floors. In fact, it was on the wrong side of the house altogether. Jack realized that the only way to learn where this led was to go in and check it out. He walked into the bedroom, grabbed his flashlight and camera, and walked back into the ballroom and over to the open panel. He clicked on the flashlight, crouched down, and entered.

Much to his surprise, this corridor was quite low, and Jack found that he would have to crawl the entire way through. It wasn't long before he realized that the passage was blocked up ahead. It was a dead end. He wrapped his knuckles on the closed off section, but the wall was quite solid. There was nothing beyond it.

As he turned to leave the passage, he noticed a considerable amount of dust now coated the back of his hand where he had knocked upon the wall. Thinking that there might be more to this corridor, he aimed his light back up at the blocking wall. There was, in fact, something carved upon it.

Jack held his breath and closed his eyes as he wiped the surface clean. After a moment, the dust had settled and Jack opened his eyes once again. There he could see, engraved into the woodwork, another phrase written in German.

"Eine und eine halbe Sonnes. Ich bin alleine," Jack attempted to pronounce. He pulled out his camera and snapped a picture.

Satisfied that he'd captured the image in full detail, he crawled back out of the passage and slid the panel shut behind him. As he did so, the figures of Heinrich and Sophia Engelhardt up on the clock turned their heads and the engraved heart popped back out. The clock was now ready to receive its next set of instructions.

Jack walked back into the bedroom and sat down at the computer. He cleared the last phrase that he'd just translated and typed in the new one. After double-checking to make sure that everything was properly entered word for word, he tapped the *enter* key and read aloud the newly translated phrase.

"One and a half suns. I am alone."

Jack reflected on this and wondered what it might mean. One and a half was obvious. That meant one-thirty. He was stumped on the part that mentioned the suns. As near as he knew, there weren't any suns anywhere on the clock. It would require taking another look. He got up from the desk and returned to the ballroom.

Standing before the massive clock, Jack could see that he had to make haste in figuring out this part of the puzzle. It was nearly one-thirty and his golden moment would soon be lost. He scanned the clock as quickly as possible but again he could find nothing that even remotely resembled the sun. He gazed up at the images of the windswept trees that hovered over the tombstones in hopes of locating a sun somewhere up there, but there was none to be found. He next thought that he'd search out images that were round, possibly with radiant beams. There were only two and those were a couple of flowers that sat at the bottom left and right corners of the facade. In a way, they kind of looked a little like stars. Jack then finally understood what the riddle had meant. These were in fact sunflowers.

"One and a half suns," he said again and as he did, the

whirring sound started. Jack walked over to the sunflower at the bottom left hand side of the clock and remembered that it was slowly rotating when the clock had chimed. He crouched down and dialed it clockwise until it stopped. The room was suddenly filled with the sound of a loud thud and for a moment, Jack had thought that the spirit of whatever had thrown him across the room had returned. Realizing that it was just the clock, he stood up and raced over to the other sunflower. This too he turned clockwise until it stopped. Again, there was a thudding sound.

Jack stood up, took a couple of steps back, and faced the clock. The whirring sound ceased and nothing happened, but the two sunflowers remained in the positions that Jack had just set them to. For a moment, he wondered if there was more that he had to do. Perhaps he'd overlooked an essential part of the instructions. He thought about the rest of the passage and recited it.

"I am alone," he said. "What's that even mean?"

As soon as he said this, he heard a winding sound coming from the clock. At first, the sound was rather quiet and barely even audible, but as the seconds ticked away, the noise grew louder and louder. Something was definitely happening, but one thing was clear. No door had opened.

The winding sound continued to grow in volume for another thirty seconds, then as suddenly as it started, it ceased. Jack was at a loss. As near as he knew, there was nothing else to the phrase that he'd just translated. That was it. He'd obviously messed something up and his opportunity to find this hidden fifth floor had come and gone. He would be leaving Waldemere that evening with no answers.

Feeling extremely downhearted, he made his way to the bedroom. There was still some packing to do before he would be ready to leave. As he reached out to open the bedroom door, the entire ballroom burst to life in a commotion of music and activity. Jack turned to find the panel below the clock face wide open and the brass disk slowly rotating, playing *The Aquarium* once again. The figures about the front of the clock were moving around of their own accord. The clock was now chiming with life in its own unusual way.

Jack approached the clock and watched with amusement

as it performed for him. He figured that, if anything else, he was getting a free show. Either that or the clock was mocking him. Perhaps it had done this to Mary Young as well, he thought. If it had, he could see why she would lose her mind and try to destroy it.

After a couple of minutes, the music stopped and the figures returned to their usual lifeless state. Jack shrugged his shoulders at this and turned for the bedchamber once more. As he drew closer though, he could swear that he heard music, and thought that perhaps the source was somewhere in the bedroom. He continued on at a quickened pace and as he opened the door, realized that he was in fact correct. The music was indeed much louder in the bedroom. He wandered about the room aimlessly and noticed that the sound was more distinct closer to the window, though it seemed to be coming from below him. He thought about it. There were more bedrooms beneath him and perhaps this was the source of the music, but he also had another idea: one that made better sense. Also beneath him was the trunk space. In that trunk space, he'd located a name, one that read Tom Jenkins. Mr. Jenkins had made the drawings of the fifth floor and must have left a clue. The entrance to the hidden level of Waldemere was right below his feet.

Jack quickly rolled back the area rug and threw open the trapdoor. As he did so, a surge of melodious music burst forth from the passageway. He jumped down into the dark crawlspace and clicked on his flashlight. The source of the music was just up ahead. As he made his way past Mr. Jenkins' name and neared the wider area at the end of the passage, he could see another brass disk slowly spinning on its axis. The Reginaphone was set into the wall and until now had been cleverly hidden by a sliding panel. It was playing Beethoven's *Moonlight Sonata.*

Casting his light about the wide area at the end of the trunk space, Jack could see Katherine Fitzgerald's trunk sitting just as he'd left it the other night, but there was something slightly different now. He could have sworn that he'd shoved it back up against a wall. There was now a space behind it. He slid the trunk over and at once noticed that the wall behind it was in fact opened and the passage now continued on.

Jack made his way down the extended tunnel until he

reached a point where the ceiling was much higher. He stood up and found a narrow set of stairs before him. This was it. This was the secret stairwell that he'd been looking for. Just behind him, he figured, was the section of wall that he had been rapping on the day before: the place where the door was originally supposed to be. Upon close examination, he could see that at one time there may have been a door here. It was certainly framed in like a doorway, but the plans must have been changed before one could be installed. Jack turned and faced the stairs once more. There was nothing left for him to do but to make his way up and see where they would take him.

Chapter 27

At the top of the stairs, Jack came to a landing and a narrow door. He located a small brass doorknob, turned it, and stepped across the threshold.

He found himself now standing in a broad room with a ceiling about eight feet high. This was considerably lower than the other four levels of the house: almost twice as low. Light was streaming in from a small bank of windows above. These were set near the center of the room and at once, Jack could see why this floor had gone unnoticed for so many years. The houses on either side of Waldemere would have obstructed any view of the windows. Had any one of these houses been torn down, the windows would be exposed and the secret of the fifth floor's existence would have been surrendered.

Lining the walls in this room were mahogany bookshelves that contained many volumes. He caught sight of the titles and realized that they were all written in German. The areas of the walls that the bookshelves didn't cover were painted in a dark hunter green. To his right sat a large oak desk with a matching chair placed before it. Jack had just entered Heinrich Engelhardt's private library.

To his left, the fifth floor continued on. A low and wide archway led into a second room. Jack cautiously proceeded and discovered a bar, barstools, a liquor shelf and a billiard table. All were covered in over a hundred years worth of dust and the walls were detailed with soot-yellow colored wallpaper that bore a cabbage rose pattern. The room very much reminded Jack of a saloon that might be found in an old western movie. Again, a bank of windows near the center of the ceiling illuminated the room. Peering ahead, he could see yet another, final room, bathed in darkness where no windows existed. This was located at, what he figured to be, the front of the house. He turned his flashlight back on and walked through another low, broad archway.

Jack cast the beam of his flashlight about this room and at once noticed a very large bed placed up against the farthest wall. It was set close to the floor, had large posts at every corner, was draped in silk swags and heavy velvet curtains, and was finished in thick gold braided cords and tassels. Piles of pillows were arranged along the headboard. The walls of this room were drenched in a deep burgundy color and the décor appeared to be very Middle-Eastern in appearance. Across the room sat a daybed and two comfortable-looking armchairs. This must have been some secret bedchamber that Heinrich Engelhardt used when he wanted to get away from the rest of his family.

Jack suddenly remembered the rest of the passage that was included in the last set of instructions for operating the clock.

"I am alone," he said to himself.

Remembering the digital camera in his pocket, Jack pulled it out and started to photograph the rooms one by one. He started with the bedchamber and took care to account for every little detail: especially the grand, oversized bed. He next moved back into the bar and billiards room. Again, he documented everything. Much to his surprise, there was still a fair amount of liquor in the bottles behind the bar. Seeing no real harm in it, Jack pulled out a glass and poured a small shot of what he assumed to be hundred-some-year-old whiskey. As soon as the drink crossed his lips, his mouth burned with fury. He certainly wasn't going to help himself to a second.

He walked back into the library and started by photographing the stairwell, landing and door. After he had done so, he moved on to the books. Perhaps in the future, he guessed, he might attempt to translate the titles. He took two pictures of the bank of windows that ran along the ceiling and finally turned his attention towards the oaken desk. As he approached, he noticed a small, leather-bound book placed in the center. He picked it up, opened it, and read the title page; which to his relief was written in English.

H. Engelhardt
of
Waldemere

Jack knew it almost at once that he'd successfully located Heinrich Engelhardt's personal journal. All of his questions were about to be answered. He took a seat in the heavy oak chair, turned the page, and began to read.

> My house is complete and I have just moved in. It is so much more than I could ever have hoped to imagine. The walls are sturdy and my family is in agreement with me. It shall make a fine home.
>
> The neighbors glare at me with contempt. They are so envious of my new dwelling as it rivals any that has yet to be seen here in our fair little city.
>
> My cousin's daughter has come to stay with us for the time being. Sophia and I do hope that she enjoys her time with us. Ludwig is ill again.

Jack continued to read, but it was more of the same: brief entries on daily life at Waldemere. This journal, aside from its historical context, really wasn't all that interesting. Jack browsed the pages that followed. There was some mention of business deals and banking, none of which he found intriguing. About three-quarters of the way through the book though, Jack came across an entry that really jumped out at him.

> Ludwig has gone mad. Sophia and I keep him confined to his room most days. Were any word of his condition to escape, our family would be in utter ruin. It's a terrible thing to have to keep my own son under lock and key, but then it's for everyone's safety. I'm aware of his conduct with the servants and highly disapprove. I fear that one day he may actually do them harm.

The pages that followed again contained talk of life at Waldemere. Perhaps, in the future, he would compare the entries in this journal with those in Katherine's, just to get a clearer idea of what was going on. Right now, he wanted to read more about Ludwig Engelhardt. He hoped that there might be some talk of his suicide that would clear up the matter once and for all. He read an entry that talked of Harriett Fischer's supposed burglary of the house, but the passage was brief and again, seemed to be quite uninteresting. It stated no more that what was found in the court report. Furthermore, there were no clues of suspicion or foul play mentioned concerning her demise.

Near the end of the book, Jack found the entry that he had been searching for: more important than Ludwig Engelhardt's death.

Ludwig has finally murdered. A servant in our house has gone missing and I found my son pacing about his room in a state of complete madness. I now suspect that he may have been responsible for the sudden and unexplained disappearances of the other two girls. I also now realize that he may have been bringing them up to my personal quarters and seducing them one by one. This is a terrible thought and I find it most grievous to bear. He will not say what he has done with the body and I now fear the worst. I can never let him out of this house ever again. Enough damage has been done.

    Jack flipped the page and saw that the rest of the book was blank. Heinrich Engelhardt must have decided at that point that it was best not to write any more. Jack sat back in the chair and tried to take it all in. It was now obvious that Ludwig Engelhardt had been the murderer, as well as Harriett and Katherine's secret lover. Jack could only imagine what Heinrich Engelhardt was feeling that day in court. There he sat, accused of three murders that he didn't commit, while his son was locked up at home and kept hidden away like a dirty little family secret.
    As far as Ludwig's own death went, Jack could only see

two possibilities. Either Heinrich had ended his son's life and disposed of the wretched creature with his own hands or Ludwig had felt guilty about what he'd done and finally decided to end his own miserable life. It really didn't matter. The man was dead and with him the opportunity to kill again.

Jack now had his answers. He could leave Waldemere with the satisfaction that he'd solved this case and successfully cleared Heinrich Engelhardt's name. He looked up at the bank of windows above. The sun was no longer streaming in and had moved substantially into the western sky. It was getting late in the day and both Henry and Emily would be back soon. He picked up Heinrich Engelhardt's journal and gave the fifth floor one final look. This was the culmination of one week's worth of research. Everything that he'd done had led him here. He snapped one last picture of the room for good measure, tucked the camera back into his pocket, turned and reentered the hidden stairwell, closing the door tightly behind him.

"So there you have it," Jack said as he reached for his distressed leather jacket.

Henry Engelhardt stood with a look of complete surprise on his face. The journal that Jack had just handed him was all the proof that he needed to back up this amazing story. The two men were standing in the front parlor ready to say their goodbyes.

"So it was Ludwig all along? I was so worried that it actually *was* my great grandfather that had perpetrated these crimes."

"Heinrich Engelhardt talks about many things in that little book. You may find much of it quite interesting. It's a good glimpse into what life was like when this house was new. That, along with Katherine Fitzgerald's diary, should paint a complete picture of things."

"Incredible," Henry said as he inspected the leather-bound journal.

"I'll be publishing all of this in that article for The Argus, if you'll still allow me, that is. I'd set out to clear your great grandfather's name and have done so. Unfortunately, it comes at the expense of your grandfather's brother."

"Jack, you go ahead and write the article. Do what must be done. A murderous great uncle is something of an embarrassment, but it's not half as bad as it being a direct forebearer."

"Very well."

"Would you like me to cut you that check now?"

"No, Henry. That's okay. I should have my report completed in a couple of days. I'll run it over on Tuesday. You can pay me then."

"As you wish. Are you sure you won't stay for dinner, Jack?"

"I'm sure, but thanks for the offer. I have to get home. There are a couple of cats that are probably missing me immensely right now. That and I have an article to write."

"Well, it's been a real pleasure having you here with us; an adventure too. It's not every day that you learn about secret passages and hidden crypts in your house. I must make it a point to see this fifth floor for myself."

"Just remember, at one thirty you turn both of the sunflowers clockwise. It'll open a hidden door in the trunk space. You won't be sorry."

"Thanks again, Jack, for everything. Emily will see you to the door."

Emily entered the parlor through the pocket doors that led to the main hall. Apparently, she'd been standing out there the entire time awaiting her cue.

"Are ya ready to go then, Mr. Sullivan?"

"I am," Jack said as he picked up his suitcase.

"Roight. If you'll come with me."

Jack followed Emily into the main hall, down the corridor, and to the side door.

"Emily, thank you again for the hospitality," he said as she reached for the doorknob.

"Now don't ya be a stranger or anythin', Jack. I 'ope to see ya again soon."

"I'll be back on Tuesday. Hopefully, we can catch up then."

"Tuesday it is. Be safe now."

"Thanks. You too."

With that, Jack walked out to his car and tossed his suitcase on the passenger seat. He backed out of the driveway and took one more glance at the house. Waldemere truly was a wonder to behold.

Chapter 28

Jack set his suitcase down at the top of the stairs in the living room of his apartment and scooped up Fionn, his adoring yellow cat, who affectionately pressed his face against Jack's chin.

"What's up, Stinky? You miss me or something?"

The cat closed his eyes and seemed to smile as Jack rubbed his left ear. Jack looked across the room and could see Aislinn sitting on the windowsill staring out the window and chattering at a few starlings that had congregated at the top of the neighbor's chimney. She could really care less that Jack was home. Perhaps she'd bother him later that night by lying across his shins.

Jack looked about the apartment, but there was no sign of Shelby. This, he thought to be quite odd. She now spent most of her time there. Jack briefly sniffed at the air, but the scent of patchouli was absent. Shelby was definitely gone, but where she was, he couldn't even guess.

With a chance to be alone for a while, Jack unpacked his suitcase and washed a load of laundry. He fed and watered the cats, ran the vacuum, changed the litter in the cat boxes, and took out the trash. After he finished with his cleaning, he pulled out his notes from Waldemere and set them on his desk. He booted up the computer and without even thinking, began to type out his article for The Argus.

The words came to him a lot easier than he imagined they would. While driving home from Waldemere, he'd contemplated a few times how he would begin. Each idea seemed more boring or dry than the last. Now that it came down to it, the story was streaming like gold from his fingertips. Before long, he was finished. He went back and proofread the article once more, made the necessary changes, and inserted a few photos that he thought would add to the story's character. Below these, he added captions. Once he was satisfied that all was as it should be, he copied the story and pictures, pasted them into an email addressed to Timothy Moon at The Ohio City Argus, and sent it off.

As he saved the document to his computer and backed it up on a disc for good measure, he heard the door at the bottom of the stairs open and close, followed by the sound of light, feminine footsteps accompanied by a hint of patchouli.

"For the life of me, Shelby," he began, "I can never figure out why you still use the door. I mean; you're a ghost. You can pass right through it."

"Force of habit, I guess. Besides, it's a little creepy to walk through things."

"How do you mean?"

"Well," she thought about it for a moment as she sat down on the armrest of the loveseat by his desk. "It's kind of like putting your face in a sink full of ice-cold water."

"You mean it stings?"

Shelby searched for the best way to describe it.

"No, it doesn't sting. In fact, it doesn't feel like anything. It's just that you don't want to do it because it doesn't seem natural. You do it if you have to, or if you really want to. But then, you'd *really* have to want to do it, I guess."

"Hmm." Jack considered this and started to get something of an idea of what she was talking about.

"Welcome home, by the way," Shelby added as she leaned over and gave Jack an enormous hug and a soft kiss on the side of his lips. "So how was your last day at Waldemere?"

"Productive," he replied, feeling quite charged by Shelby's embrace. "I finally managed to locate the fifth floor."

"You did? How'd you do that?"

"Turns out that there were more words written inside of the other vault. It contained the next set of instructions."

"And that opened a way to the fifth floor?"

"Not exactly. It opened a hidden panel in the ballroom that contained another riddle. After I found that and translated it, I managed to open a passageway to the fifth floor. The funny thing is that it was quite literally under my nose the entire time."

"How do you mean?"

"It was in that trunk space below the bedroom that I was staying in. At the very end of the space, there was another panel that had slid open. I crawled along until I found myself in a stairwell that took me up."

"And?"

"And what? It took me up to the fifth floor."

"So what was up there?"

Jack could tell that she was intrigued by all of this.

"Well," he said with a smile, "there were three rooms. The first was a library, the second was a barroom, and the third was a bedroom. They were Heinrich Engelhardt's private quarters. Quite elegant too, I might add, but I'd recommend staying away from the whiskey."

"That's amazing, Jack."

"Oh, here," he continued as he pulled out his camera. "I got some pictures." He turned it on, set it to the playback mode and started to scroll through the photos one by one. "See here? This is the bedroom that I was just telling you about."

Shelby looked closely at the screen with her mouth slightly agape.

"That is truly amazing," she declared.

"It gets better." Jack advanced to the pictures of the barroom. "Check it out. Here's the bar, and on this side of the room is a billiard table."

"Wow!"

Jack clicked the button a few times and brought up the next images.

"Here's the library, some books on the shelves, a desk…"

"What's that?" Shelby asked as she noticed the small, leather-bound book on the desk.

"That," he said with a smile, "is what solved this whole mystery. It's Heinrich Engelhardt's personal journal. It tells about Waldemere and his life with his family in that house. It also says who killed Katherine Fitzgerald."

"And?"

Shelby's face was alive with anticipation.

"Oh, I don't know. Maybe I shouldn't tell you. I hate to give away the ending of a story."

He loved to toy with her.

"Jack!"

"Okay, fine. It was Heinrich's son, Ludwig. Turns out that he was quite insane."

"Really?"

"Yeah. They kept him locked up most times. I'd read that there were suspicions about him and why neighbors rarely saw him. I suppose that this was the reason why."

"Wasn't he the one that you'd said had killed himself in that bedroom you were staying in?"

"Yeah. That's him."

"Couldn't live with the guilt?"

"I've thought about that too. Have a couple of other theories though, but I guess they're not that important. It was a long time ago and is irrelevant to what I was hired to find out. Besides, if he hadn't killed himself when he did, he'd still be long dead by now."

Shelby chuckled slightly at this.

"I'd imagine so."

Jack shut down the computer and clicked off the monitor.

"Finished my story for The Argus," he added.

"How'd it turn out?"

"Not bad, I think. I'll let you read it when it comes out on Tuesday."

"Awe, come on. Can't I just take a small peek?"

"No. You'll have to wait like everyone else. Besides, I never let anyone read any of my stuff before it gets printed."

"Rats."

Jack wanted to change the subject and there had been something eating at him that he was curious about.

"So anyway," he started, "I was a little surprised not to see you here when I got back."

"Yeah, I've been going out every once and a while: the beach, mostly. You know, trying to clear my head a little and get some perspective on a few things."

"Such as?"

"Oh, nothing really in particular, I guess. It's mostly small things, like why I'm here or why I'm attached to you. That sort of stuff."

"I thought it was love?" Jack chuckled.

"Well, yeah. There's that. Duh. But it didn't start out that way. Remember? It was business. Somehow I'd managed to cross from one reality I'd been living in, back into this one. Why did that happen, and how?"

"I don't know, Shelby." Jack's face was now quite serious. "I don't think either of us will ever know. Trish couldn't explain it, and she's an expert on the subject. I think we'll just have to accept it for what it is and see where it takes us."

Shelby stared at the floor while Jack said this. As he concluded his thoughts on the matter, she began to nod her head in agreement. There really was nothing to be done about it. After a moment of silence passed between them, she lifted her head and smiled at Jack.

"Well," she said, "truth be told, there's no place I'd rather be than here with you right now." She leaned in and gave Jack a warm snuggle. "I'm glad you're home."

Jack could feel nothing but love passing between them. He was glad to be home too.

Chapter 29

Jack awoke early that following morning with Shelby's warm body pressed against his; the top of her head tucked perfectly under his chin. He looked down at her bare arms and softly traced his right index finger across the back of her left hand. He still couldn't figure out how it was possible that a ghost could be so tangible to him. There was definitely some kind of magic or divine intervention at work here.

After a moment, Shelby stirred and looked up at him through her amazingly bright blue eyes.

"Good morning, my beloved," she whispered.

"Good morning," Jack replied. "I'm sorry. I didn't want to wake you."

"No, it's okay. I wanted to get up anyway. I was having a pretty weird dream as it was."

"Really? About what?"

"Nah, it's dumb and you'll probably laugh."

"No I won't. Go on. What is it?"

Shelby considered it for a moment, lightly bit her lip, and puffed out a gentle sigh.

"Okay. You were in it, and you were standing by something like a long and narrow lake, maybe a very slow moving river. On the far side, about five hundred to a thousand feet across the water from you, was a sandy beach with something that reminded me of a small amusement park. The side that you were on had a bar and a boardwalk that went out a little over the water. It was nighttime and you had a glass of Guinness in your hand. I think you must have bought it inside the bar and had taken it out with you.

"Anyway, you're standing there by yourself and you keep looking at the water for some reason; kind of like you expect to see something in there. Whatever you're looking for, you can't see it and it's almost like you're not supposed to be able to."

"And where are you throughout all of this?" Jack asked.

"Not with you, which is odd. I don't know how I can see all of this, but it's like I'm kind of looking down at you."

"You're right. That is a weird dream."

"No, that's not the weird part. After a few minutes of debating something, you drink the last of your Guinness, set down your glass, and jump into the water, but you never come back up."

"Oh. Did I drown or something?"

"No, you didn't drown. You just... vanished."

Jack thought about it for a moment.

"Yeah," he said at last. "That's an odd one. But hey, it was only a dream. I'm still here and I'm not planning on leaving you anytime soon. Don't think I could anyway, even if I wanted to."

"But Jack..."

"No. Let's just spend the whole day in bed: just you and I."

"Jack, you *do* have to leave though."

He looked at her with bewilderment.

"What are you talking about?" he asked.

"Come on. Have you already forgotten what today is?"

"Not at all. It's Monday and I'm spending it with you. No haunted houses. No hidden rooms and secret passageways. No writing and no research."

"What about playing?"

Jack cracked a coy smile.

"Ooh, I like the way you think," he said as he rolled on top of her.

"Not what I meant, you loon," Shelby laughed. "It's Saint Patrick's Day, isn't it?"

"Saint Pat's?" Jack had completely forgotten. His eyes lit up like a child's on Christmas morning.

"And you have a show to play with the guys," Shelby reminded him. "And a couple of other shows to attend. And some serious drinking to do, according to what you've told me."

"My God!"

"No 'my God' right now. Get up!"

Jack rolled off of Shelby and jumped out of bed. He tossed his robe around himself and ran for the bathroom.

"Damn!" Jack cursed from behind the door. There was too much to do and not nearly enough time to do it all. He'd certainly be late for breakfast at McNamara's.

"I'll um..." Shelby stammered. "I'll um... just um... wait... here, I guess."

Jack walked back out of the bathroom with a foamy toothbrush clutched in his hand.

"Like hell you will. You think I'm going to leave you behind on a day like this? It's Saint Patrick's Day for cryin' out loud and we're spending every moment of it together."

Shelby jumped up and, ignoring all modesty, threw her arms around him; pressing her nude body against his. Jack dropped his toothbrush.

Eleven-thirty found Jack and Shelby pulling up outside of McNamara's Public House on Lake Avenue. They were lucky to find a spot right in front of the pub that morning, as most of the street was full. The bar would be packed as well. Jack stepped out into the bright morning sunshine and felt the warming rays beat against his face. He smiled with the satisfaction that spring was right around the corner. Shelby, not wanting to attract attention, decided to walk through the passenger-side door of the car. It would be quite awkward for Jack to have to explain to the bar patrons how his passenger door opened and closed of its own accord.

They walked into McNamara's and were immediately welcomed by the melodious droning sound of bagpipe music. Gary, the bar's proprietor, was also a Cleveland fireman. Each year, he'd bring in a friend or two from the firefighter's pipe and drum band. This year was no different. With *The Rising of the Moon* playing triumphantly from the piper in the corner, Jack made his way through the crowd and up to the bar where he ordered a Guinness. Any other day, drinking this early would have been unheard of, unless he was trying to kill a hangover. This was St. Patrick's Day though: a special occasion.

Working behind the bar that morning were Megan and Amanda. Gary had doubled up on bartenders for the day and, with the crowds that were expected, he would have needed to. This all would have been far too much for just one person to deal with. It was Amanda that served Jack his Guinness.

"What's the good word, Jack?" she asked as she handed him the glass of thick, frothy stout.

"Oh, nothing new. Happy Saint Pat's."

"Thanks. Are you guys playing up here later?"

"We are indeed. Oh," Jack remembered, "I was actually hoping to run into you up here earlier this week. I've been doing some research and came across a phrase written in German. I was hoping that you would have been able to make heads or tails of it."

Amanda read and spoke perfect German. If anyone could've made sense of the passage written above the bar at Waldemere, she certainly could've.

"Sure. What's the phrase?" she asked.

"Well, I've already translated it and figured out what it meant."

"Okay, so what did it mean?"

"Oddly enough, it was a set of instructions. I'd thought that it was a poem or something at first, but was wrong on that."

"You could've just called."

"Thought about it, but didn't want to bother you."

"Oh, it'd have been no bother."

"Thanks. I'll remember that next time."

"Sully!" The familiar and joyous voices that called out to Jack came from near the other end of the bar, rather close to the bagpiper. Jack looked down and saw Jerry, Ed and Brion cheerfully waving, beckoning him to join them. He and Shelby gladly obliged.

"Jack, Lad," Jerry greeted with a handshake as he approached. "A very happy Saint Pat's to ya!"

"And to you." Jack returned with a broad grin.

"We'd offer you a seat," Brion began, "but…"

Jack could see that there were no more seats to be had. Every barstool was taken and likely had been for about the last hour or two.

"Shouldn't you be playing a show right now?" Jack asked Ed in an elevated voice, trying to be heard over the bagpiper a few feet away.

"I'm in between gigs," Ed explained. "We played downtown this morning at six and don't have to be at The Old Angle until two."

"You're going to miss the parade again this year."

"Yeah, but for what they're paying us, it's worth it."

"I can imagine so."

"Oh, my brother Joe's around here somewhere."

"Turn around, Ed," Joe said from behind him.

"Oh, there you are," Ed laughed.

"Good to see you, Jack," Joe said as he extended his hand.

"You too, Joe," Jack replied as he shook it. "Busy day, then?"

"Always. We have two more gigs today and are probably hitting up The Harp later on. You going?"

"Of course."

Out of the corner of his eye, Jack caught Shelby smiling. He could tell that she was excited about the day ahead of them.

"You'll stop in at The Old Angle after the parade too, won't you?" Ed asked. "Wouldn't be the same if you didn't come up and do a song with us."

"Yeah, we'll be there," Jack said with a grin. "We don't have to be back here until a quarter to five for sound check."

"We?" Jerry asked.

Jack was referring to Shelby and himself, but quickly covered it up.

"Oh. Yeah. You know. Me and the rest of the band."

"Thought they were all working."

"Well, yeah. They are. But in case anyone gets out early, we're going to meet up at The Old Angle for a drink before coming up here."

"Hey, guys," Gary, the owner of McNamara's, broke in from behind the bar. "There's plenty of food on the table over there. Go get some breakfast."

The guys all looked at each other and nodded in agreement. Breakfast was just what they needed. They crossed the room, grabbed paper plates and plastic flatware, and helped themselves to generous helpings of a full Irish breakfast of bacon, eggs, biscuits with Kerrygold Irish butter, blood sausage and boxty potatoes. They returned to the bar and dug in. Not a word was said between them until every last morsel was gone. Jerry was the first to speak up.

"So Jack, have you finished up at Waldemere?"

"I have," Jack said as he lifted his Guinness. He took a swig and washed down the last of the boxty. "Just got home last night. Wrote the article for the paper and sent it off to the editor. It should be out tomorrow morning."

"That's great. I look forward to reading it."

"Thanks."

"So what did you find out?" Ed asked as his picked up his empty plate and tossed it in the wastebasket.

"Quite a lot, but you'll have to wait until tomorrow to find out exactly what. I will tell you this; you won't be disappointed."

"Nice," Brion chimed in. "How long is it?"

"A couple thousand words or so, plus pictures and captions. It'll take up a page or two, I think."

As he said this, a long bus pulled up outside of the bar. The sudden hissing of the air brakes drew everyone's attention to its presence. After a moment, the doors opened and a middle-aged man in a chauffeur's uniform stepped out. The bagpiper ceased playing and Gary spoke up.

"It's okay, everyone. He's early. We still have about fifteen minutes until we leave for the parade. There's plenty of food left, so help yourselves. I don't feel like taking anything home."

"Jack, are we taking the bus to the parade too?" Shelby asked.

Jack smiled and slowly nodded.

"Well, guys," Jerry put in. "I think we have time for one more." He flagged down Megan and ordered another round for the boys. They drank their brews in haste and within fifteen minutes, Jack and Shelby found themselves riding on the bus with Jerry, Brion and most of the other McNamara's patrons, heading for the annual Saint Patrick's Day Parade downtown.

The bus let the McNamara's crew off on the corner of East 9th Street and Lakeside Avenue. It was a few blocks to the parade route, but they covered the distance in no time at all. By one o'clock, they could hear the pipes echoing from up Superior Avenue. Everyone leaned forward and cast their gazes east. In the distance, they could see the approaching police motorcycles, followed by a pipe band and six fire engines with their flashers and sirens blaring. A few moments later, the parade strode past.

The crowd waved and cheered as the firefighters and police bands made their way down the street. It was one of the few days of the year where the public could come out in droves and acknowledge their gratitude for the fine job that Cleveland's finest and bravest were doing. With bagpipe music heavy in the air, Brion pulled out a flask of whiskey from his jacket pocket, raised it to the marchers, and took a deep pull.

"What are you doing?" Jack asked. "You're a lawyer. You know you can't have that down here."

"Oh, I'm sorry," Brion said as he passed the whiskey to Jack. Jack looked at the metallic flask and shrugged his shoulders.

"Eh, why the hell not?"

He put the flask to his lips and took a swig. At seeing this behavior, Shelby jabbed him in the side of the gut. Jack lurched forward.

"Really hits ya," Brion said with pride.

"Sure does," Jack said, handing the flask on to Jerry. He gave Shelby a short, indignant glance.

The parade continued on with marching bands, east and west side Irish-American clubs, local television news personalities and publicly elected officials. Antique cars slowly rolled down the street, followed by Shriners in midget go-carts and the Irish Wolfhound Society.

Near the end of the parade, Jack saw his favorite late-night horror movie host, The Ghoul, riding by in a white 63' Ford Galaxy convertible. The man, dressed in his button covered lab coat, broken sunglasses, fright wig and fake goatee, waved gloriously from the back of the car. Even though he'd been off the air for a few years now, he was still regarded in Cleveland as something of a living legend. The annual Saint Patrick's Day Parade wouldn't be the same without him.

Finally, the Mounted Cleveland Police Officers made their way past, followed by men with push brooms and garbage cans on wheels. One of the last horses to cantor by dropped a pile of road-apples in the middle of Superior Avenue and the crowd cheered wildly. A man with a broom and can was there

Johnny-on-the-spot to clean up the mess.

That was it. The annual dumping of the horse signified that another Saint Patrick's Day parade was in the bag. The crowd slowly dispersed. Some headed back towards the Terminal Tower to catch the rapid home while others ducked into Irish pubs and sports bars alike. Most of the McNamara's crew headed back up East 9th to the pick up point where the chartered bus would be waiting for them. Jack, Shelby, Brion and Jerry however decided that it was a pleasant enough day to walk back to the West Side. Besides, they were only going as far as The Old Angle on West 25th Street.

The hike took just over a half an hour to make and soon they were standing in the doorway of The Old Angle. On stage was Ed and Joe's band, The Whiskey Island Ramblers. They were about halfway through a tune called *Seamus O'Reilly* that Ed had written about a con artist that had happened into his great grandfather's pub some years earlier. The man had posed as the son of a shipping tycoon from Belfast, but was actually from New Brunswick, Canada. Before finally being found out, he had taken a lawyer and a judge for quite a few thousand dollars each. The story made all the papers back in the day and Ed thought it a good subject to write a song about. The fact was that the idea was better than good. It was great. The tune had already been played many times on The Irish Show and was now recognized as the band's signature song.

Jerry made his way through the crowd and up to the bar where he ordered three beers. As the song was ending, he returned and passed the other two drinks to Brion and Jack. Noticing that his friends had arrived, Ed called Brion to the stage, where he crooned out an amazing rendition of *Van Dieman's Land* by U2.

"He really is quite good," Shelby mentioned as she leaned in to Jack's ear.

"Yeah, I know," Jack replied.

"You know *what?*" Jerry asked. Jack had completely forgotten about Shelby's condition.

"Oh, sorry. Thought you said something," Jack covered.

"I didn't say anything," Jerry replied. "What did you think I said?"

"Thought you said he was quite good."

"No. Must have been somebody else. I agree with them though."

Jack turned to Shelby and smiled. That had been a close one.

When Brion had finished, the audience let out a wild cheer. Brion bowed and stepped down. Ed turned to Jack. It was now his turn. Jack took the stage and was handed the microphone. He took a large gulp from his Guinness, set it on the railing, and turned to the band.

"Hey Jack, why don't you sing that song you wrote for your friend Gerard and that Irish pub you used to hang out at in Avon Lake?" Ed asked.

"*Sláinte*. Do you guys know it?"

"Key of C, right? I tried it out at home last night, just in case you were up for doing it today."

"Sláinte it is." Jack turned to the audience and addressed them. "This one's for Gerard."

With that, Ed and the boys began the intro and Jack soon jumped in:

I went down to Sláinte for a pint or two
and to meet with some of my friends
They're the kind that you could tell anything to
the kind that only God sends
We whittled away at our Guinness's Stout
until the hour grew bleak
Then Gerard came down to the end of the bar
and thus he began to speak

He'd tell us about what it was like
to grow up back home in Ireland
The life that he'd led and the friends that he'd had
and all that was left behind
And tales of the leaders of 1916
how they met with their cruel fate
And the heroic Pike-men of Wexford Town
in 1798

*Well he's a good man, one of the best
and as honest as the day is long
Locks up the bar and turns up the stools
and closes the night with a song
For The Patriot Game or The Green Fields Of France
And The Band Played Waltzin' Matilda
Sings us the stories of Willie McBride
and the fallen heroes of Sulva*

*Then maybe in passin' he'll happen to mention
his beloved family
His mother he tells us is just like an angel
his brothers, he's proud of all three
But then he get's quiet, reflects on the silence
doesn't show it but we know that he's sad
And in a hushed tone he smiles at us
says I wish you could've met my dad*

*For he was a good man, one of the best
and as honest as the day is long
Ask anyone that he ever knew
he never would do you no wrong
Oh he'd tell ya a story and still keep ya laughin'
long after you'd part company
I'm tellin' ya boys I wish you'd have met him
I'm certain that you would agree*

*The cards life dealt him weren't always the best
but he made the best with what he had
Do him this honor and raise up your glass
let's all drink a toast to my dad
And in the rapt silence that followed the toast
a thought had entered my mind
A realization that I could still know him
through the noble son he left behind*

*So raise up your glasses and drink ye a toast
to fathers everywhere
Cherish the memories and times that you've spent
you'll never know how long he's here
Or how proud you make him and fill him with joy
or how deep his love for you runs...
May all of our fathers live on forever
through the actions and deeds of their sons*

Again, the crowd erupted into cheers and applause. Jack stepped from the stage and rejoined Jerry, Brion and Shelby. The boys continued to drink to the lively tunes of The Whiskey Island Ramblers until a little past four. Looking at the clock, Jack realized that he needed to get back to McNamara's to set up for the gig that his own band, Whuppity Scoorie, was about to play.

He said his goodbyes, gave a brief wave to the band, and exited The Old Angle with Shelby right beside him. He could tell by the little smile on her face that she was having a good time. After a few moments of standing on the corner, Jack managed to flag down a taxi. He and Shelby got in and headed up to McNamara's.

Chapter 30

By a quarter to five, Jack had already set up the P.A. system and was two more pints of Guinness in. He was now sitting up at the bar and was deep in conversation with Positive Bill about the Philadelphia punk scene. Shelby, meanwhile, was standing across the room, reading a map that illustrated the origins of the heraldic families of Ireland. She'd often wonder if she was Irish or not, but had never mentioned this to Jack. Had she, he could have looked up her lineage for her. Tomlinson might have been an Irish surname, but most likely was Scottish or British.

After a few moments, Paul the fiddler walked through the door with his friend, John. They pulled up a couple of stools beside Jack and ordered up some drinks.

"Hey Paul," Jack said with a slightly intoxicated grin. "What's new?"

"Oh, nothing much."

"John, a pleasure as always," he said as he shook John's hand. It really was a pleasure to see John, a fellow genealogist. The two would often talk shop and today would be no exception.

"Fabulous to see you too, Jack," John said. "We saw you on the news this week. I had no idea that you were working on Waldemere. You should have called me. I'd have been more than happy to help."

Jack thought about it. Calling John should have been one of his first steps on the Waldemere project. He certainly did know quite a good deal about local German families as well as the legends that seemed to follow them. The idea had simply slipped Jack's mind.

"You're right," Jack said, "I should have called. I just got so wrapped up in it that I didn't think to do so."

"Well, did you find anything interesting, aside from three bodies?"

"I found a great deal, actually. It'll all be out in The Argus tomorrow morning."

"You're kidding," Paul declared. "You're getting your research published?"

"Sure am. I submitted the story last night."

"I'm looking forward to reading it," John continued. "I'll be sure to pick up a copy on my way to work."

At this, the door flew open and Joe walked into the bar carrying a snare drum and a stand. Following behind him was Matt, the band's bass player, who was lugging an amplifier.

"Happy Green Beer Day, boys," Joe announced as he set the drum in the corner. "Can you guys give me a hand with this stuff?"

"Sure," Jack said as he set his draught on the bar.

He, Paul and John walked out into the cool evening air and over to Joe's car. They loaded up on drums and stands, and carried them back into McNamara's. Joe and Matt set up their gear and Paul tuned his fiddle. After a brief sound check, they regrouped at the bar, ordered another round of beers and a shot of whiskey each: liquid courage, as Jack liked to call it. Nothing settled his nerves before a show better than a shot of Jameson's. They tilted them back and, after a few seconds, felt right with the world. It was now five-thirty and the crowd had arrived right on cue.

The first set lasted about forty-five minutes and they ended it with their high-energy version of *The Wreck of the Edmund Fitzgerald*. About halfway through the break, Jerry and Brion walked in with Ed and his brother, Joe. Jack walked over and gave them welcoming pats on the back.

"So how'd the rest of the show go?" Jack asked Ed.

"Went really well. Thanks again for coming up and doing *Sláinte*."

"Hey, it was a pleasure."

"So what'd we miss?" Brion asked as he ordered a beer.

"A bunch of lighter stuff. Family oriented tunes like *The Unicorn Song*. Things like that."

"Did you play *The Fitz* yet?"

"You just missed it."

"Damn."

"Come on, Brion. You've heard it like a million times before and are sure to again. Oh, are any of you going to come up and do a song with us?"

The guys looked at each other and nodded.

"Good," Jack said. "We should be starting up again in a few minutes. Joe and Matt are outside finishing their smokes. I'm going to go and hurry them up a bit. I'll see you guys in a few."

The second set was a little better received than the first. The songs were slightly more off-color and with the addition of tunes sung by Ed, Jerry, Brion and Ed's brother Joe, it seemed more diverse. By seven-thirty, the guys were on their second break and a large crowd had somehow managed to cram itself into McNamara's Public House. There was hardly room to move around inside the place and despite the chill in the air; the patio was packed to capacity as well.

As Jack stood out on the patio with his friends and the rest of the band, Shelby came up and tugged at his sleeve.

"Ring, ring," she said. Jack knew at once that she wanted to talk to him.

"Excuse me, guys," he said as he started to step away. "I just remembered that I need to make a phone call."

He pulled out his cell phone and pretended to dial a number.

"Hey, what's going on?" he said into the phone, but made certain to look directly at Shelby.

"Not much. I just wanted to say thank you for taking me out with you today. I'm having a great time."

"I'm glad to hear it. How do you like the music?"

"Better than I thought. You guys really sound good together."

"Thanks."

"I think you should play out more."

"I'd like to, but everyone's so busy with work and that."

"Oh. So are we going somewhere after this?"

"Yeah. There's a band that I want to see up at The Harp. They usually don't start until around ten or so, but we should be done playing by then. Kick back and enjoy the rest of the show. I'll talk to you again when we're done."

"Jack, there was something else that I wanted to ask you."

"What's that?"

"Um, that girl over there, that's your friend Amy, right?"

Jack looked over at his group of friends. Amy was among them, laughing and carrying on.

"Yeah, that's her. Why?"

"Uh, she keeps looking at me."

"Really?"

"She can't see me. Can she?"

"I don't think so. She would have said something if she could."

"Are you sure? I swear she keeps looking right at me. I'm not talking about small glances either. I mean full eye contact."

"I'll check it out, but I don't think that she can."

Jack put his phone back into his pocket and rejoined his friends who were in the middle of talking about disaster movies. After a few moments, Jack turned to Amy.

"Hey, can I talk to you for a second?" he asked.

"Sure."

She followed him across the patio to where he was certain that they would be out of earshot of the others.

"What's up?" she asked.

"Nothing really. I just kind of noticed that you're staring off into space every once in a while. Is everything okay?"

"Oh, everything's fine."

"So what is it then?"

"Nothing. I'm alright."

"And aren't you a horrible liar. Come on. Out with it."

Amy debated for a few seconds if she should say anything or not. Finally, she made up her mind.

"Okay, it's like this. I have a strange feeling that I'm being watched by somebody."

"How so?"

"I don't know. I can't really explain it, but it's sort of like there's an extra set of eyes upon me that shouldn't be."

"What, like someone's looking at you through the fence?"

"No. Closer than that."

"How close?"

"Like a few feet away; and she's been looking right at me all night."

"She?"

"Yeah. I'm pretty sure that it's a female."

"But you can't see her."

"No."

"Has she said anything to you?"

"Not that I'm aware of."

"Good."

"Good how?"

"Oh, I don't know. Do you feel threatened in any way?"

"No. Why? Do you know anything about this?"

Jack felt like he'd already asked too much.

"No," he lied. "I wouldn't worry about it though, not if you don't feel threatened."

"Jack, come on. What do you know?"

"I know nothing."

"And he'll deny me three times before the cock crows," Shelby whispered in his ear. Jack stifled his laughter.

"It's not funny, Jack," Amy insisted. "It's eerie as all hell. Now if you know something, you'd better say it."

"I need to get back inside. We'll talk about this another time."

He turned to the guys, nodded, and walked back into the bar, leaving Amy standing by herself, completely bewildered at the conversation she and Jack had just had.

The last set was usually the one that Jack would save the most off-color songs for. Many times in the past, he'd play shows that were more family oriented, but by the end of the night, most families would be gone. It was on occasions like this that he'd bust out the more raunchy tunes. It got so to the point that this type of a third set was expected. He didn't disappoint the crowd. The band started off with a song called *Seven Drunken Nights*. Most bands only played the verses for Monday through Friday: clean verses. Much to the audience's delight, Jack pulled out Saturday and Sunday: the rare, dirty verses.

He followed the rest of the set with songs like *I'm A Drunk, Punch The Clown, Nookie Greene, Go On Home British Soldiers Go On Home, The Foggy Dew* and an original tune that had become something of a signature song for Whuppity Scoorie called *My Last Ride On The S. S. Filthy Whore*. They finished the show, as they always did, with *The Parting Glass*. By nine-thirty, they were taking down their equipment and loading it into their cars. After settling his bar tab and imbibing one more pint of Guinness, Jack and Shelby were on their way to their next destination to meet up with the rest of the crowd.

The Harp was a much larger pub than McNamara's, but it too was packed to capacity. Jack waited at the bar for nearly five minutes before he was finally able to get service. Not wanting to wait that long again, he decided to order two drinks for good measure. He'd be double-fisting it for the remainder of the evening.

In no time at all, he located the rest of the crew out on the patio, which was now covered in a giant tent. At the far end, a stage had been erected and a Pogues cover band was now filling the place with familiar Irish tunes. Conversations bounced in all directions that evening and nearly every topic was discussed from favorite beers to plans for the coming summer. Jack was looking forward to spending as much time as he could out at his parents' place on Catawba Island. Perhaps he'd even spend some time boating with friends or island hopping.

About halfway through the band's first set break, a familiar figure approached Jack, dressed in his usual Nineteenth Century attire.

"Orin," Jack said upon recognizing his friend. "I'm surprised to see ya here."

"What, are you kidding me?" Orin replied. "It's Saint Pat's. I look forward to this day all year."

"What a coincidence," Jack managed to pronounce. "So do I."

"Figured as much. I can also see that you're well into your cups."

"Can ya blame a fella?"

"Guess not. So how did things ultimately go at Waldemere?"

"Oh, that's right. I was gonna to tell ya. I finally fifth the found floor. I mean. I fifthly found the fine… Ya know what I mean."

"Yeah, I get it. So what was it like?"

"Ya wouldn't believe it. I got pictures and I found out who killed those girls."

"Really?"

"Yeppers."

"And how did you discover the identity of this killer?"

"I found Heinrich Engelhardt's journal."

"Is that a fact?"

"It is."

Orin grew silent for a moment before continuing.

"And?"

"And the killer's not who we thought it was."

"Okay, Jack. So who was it?"

"That, you'll have to wait until tomorrow morning to discover."

"Why? What happens tomorrow morning?"

"The article that I wrote on the matter will be *buplished* in The Argus."

"You're kidding."

Jack's face broke into a broad and drunken grin.

"You're not kidding."

"Nope," Jack said with satisfaction.

"Jack, I really wish that you would've held off on doing something like that until after you had double-checked all of the facts. Publishing this soon sounds a little hasty."

"Ah, hasty shmasty."

"Well, you sound pretty sure of yourself."

"Why wouldn't I be?"

Before Orin could answer, Jerry, Brion and Ed came over with drinks in their hands. There was an extra Guinness for Jack.

"Looks like someone's running low," Brion announced as he passed the beer to Jack.

"Thanks, Lad." he said as he accepted the glass. He raised it into the air and proposed a toast. "To all the kisses I've ever snatched… and vice versa."

The guys raised their glasses as well and downed hearty gulps.

"So who's your friend?" Ed asked as he noticed Orin.

"Oh, I'm sorry, guys. This is Orin Drury."

After shaking hands, Orin posed a general question about Jack.

"Um, he's not driving himself home, is he?"

"Not a chance," Jerry replied. "One of us will take him."

"Okay. I'm just checking." He turned his attention to Jack. "I enjoy reading about you, but don't want to see that you've taken out a family of four."

"Not happening," Jack assured him.

"Good. Well, you enjoy the rest of your night. I have a couple of friends that I'm supposed to meet up with." He turned back to Jerry, Brion and Ed. "And it was nice meeting you guys, as well."

Jack watched as Orin disappeared back into the crowd. There was something definitely odd about the conversation they'd just had.

Around one in the morning, Jack and Shelby were heading west down Clifton Boulevard in Jerry's white pick-up truck. Jack had been out of it for quite some time by now and it took some serious convincing that he wouldn't vomit in order to get a ride. Jack was true to his word. Though everything was spinning, he managed to keep his head straight enough.

It wasn't until after they had crossed West 117th Street that Jack finally said more than two words.

"I really love ya. You know that?"

Jerry was a little surprised to hear this, but just chalked it up as another one of Jack's drunken ramblings.

"Alright, man."

"No, not you," Jack laughed.

"Oh, who then?"

"I was talkin' to *Shebly*."

"Who's Shebly?"

"I mean Shelby."

Jerry was still a little baffled.

"Okay, who's *Shelby*?" he asked.

"This is Shelby," Jack said as he pointed to the back seat. "She's sitting right behind ya. Say hi, Shelby."

"Jack. This might not be the appropriate time for this,"

she pointed out.

"Sure it is."

"It's what?" Jerry asked.

"A good time for ya to meet Shelby. She's been hanging out with us all day."

"Really? And she's sitting behind me?"

"Yeah."

Jerry glanced into the rear-view mirror and smiled.

"Oh, there she is," he said, trying to humor Jack. "Hi, Shelby." He was pretty certain that Jack wouldn't remember any of this in the morning.

Jack shook his head.

"Ah, ya can't see her."

"Now how do you know that?"

"Duh. She's a ghost."

"Jack," Shelby interrupted. "Really. You should stop. Why don't you close your eyes for a few minutes? We're almost home anyway."

"Yeah. You're right."

"I'm right?" Jerry asked.

"No," Jack responded in a whisper. "Quiet time now. Shh, shh, shh, shh."

Jerry smiled as he pulled onto Hathaway Avenue.

"Yeah. Quiet time."

A moment later, the white truck stopped outside of Jack's place and Jerry helped his friend out.

"Do you need a hand getting inside?" Jerry asked.

"Nah," Jack assured him. "I have Shelby."

"Okay," Jerry laughed. "I'll leave you to it then. Maybe I'll see you at McNamara's tomorrow evening."

"Maybe."

With that, Jack stumbled up the steps and to the front door. Jerry watched for a moment just to be certain that Jack got in okay. For a moment, he thought that he saw the front door open on its own, but realized that this was ludicrous. As he drove away, he wondered if he too might have had just a bit too much to drink.

Chapter 31

Jack's head was swimming. Although he couldn't remember it, he was pretty certain that he'd thrown up after he'd gotten home. The bitter taste of stomach bile clung like a film to the inside of his mouth and his throat carried the distinct burn of acid. He fumbled around with a bottle of ibuprofen until he'd successfully managed to remove the lid. He shook two tablets out, popped them into his mouth, and chased them down with a gulp of water. Placing the bottle back inside the medicine cabinet, Jack turned out the bathroom light and returned to bed.

Three hours later, he was standing in the shower, washing away the remnants of his hangover. The hot water that beat against his head was invigorating and he slowly felt the life returning to his extremities. He dried himself off and dressed. Walking into the living room, he found Shelby sitting on the couch watching the morning news with Aislinn curled up beside her.

"Good morning!" she shouted. "How do you feel?"

"Do you really have to do that?"

"Do what?"

"Talk that loud."

Shelby thought about it for a moment.

"Yes! Yes I do!"

Jack slumped down on the couch beside her. Though his body felt more alert than it had earlier, his head was still screaming.

"No. No you don't," he mumbled.

"What? You think you can drink like that and get away with it?"

"I'd like to."

"Not going to happen."

Jack jumped slightly at the sound of a horn from out in the driveway. He got up and walked to the window. Down below was parked a maroon van with the words *Westlake Cab* printed on the side. The taxi he'd called for nearly an hour earlier had finally arrived. He didn't hold it against the taxi company. He was pretty sure that they had their hands full.

"Well, cab's here," he informed Shelby. "Are you coming with?"

"Of course. Just give me a few minutes to powder my nose."

"Shelby…"

"Okay," she chuckled. "Let's go."

The taxi dropped them off at The Harp, where Jack's black Mazda Protegé 5 had been safely parked for the night. He glanced through the back window and was happy to see that his guitar and sound system were undisturbed. With that, they got into the car and made their way east.

"Um, Jack?" Shelby began.

"Yeah?"

"Home's the other way."

"I know. I want to stop by the grocery store and pick up a copy of The Argus. I'm curious to see how the article came out."

Jack pulled onto Bridge Avenue and a moment later, entered the supermarket parking lot. He pulled up in front and put the vehicle into park but left the engine running. As he started to get out, Shelby stopped him

"You're just going to leave your car here?" She asked.

"I'll only be a second."

"What if someone tries to steal it?"

Jack had suddenly remembered that no one could see Shelby.

"I don't know. Yell 'BOO' and shove them out."

As quickly as he could, Jack darted into the store and a moment later returned with a short stack of newspapers.

"*A copy* of The Argus usually denotes *one copy*," Shelby pointed out.

"I know. Thought I'd grab a few spares. You want to read it?"

"Sure."

Jack pulled the car into a parking spot and turned off the engine. He opened the top copy of the paper, found where his story began on the center page, and began to read.

THE MADMAN OF WALDEMERE
Nineteenth Century Murder Mystery Solved
By
J. M. Sullivan

As we move through this amazing thing called life, we find ourselves wanting many things. Some of us seek wealth, others piece of mind. When it really boils down to it though, the one thing that we all find ourselves desiring most near the end of our time here is an unblemished legacy. Mark Twain once said that you should live your life so well that even the undertaker will cry at your funeral. I agree with Mr. Twain. I'm certain that many of us do.

It's a safe bet that about a hundred years ago, there was another man from our fair city who stood by this belief as well. His name was Heinrich Engelhardt.

Sadly, Mr. Engelhardt's name has received nothing but tarnish these past few years. Allegations have been made, again, that he murdered three girls in his home: famously known as Waldemere. In 1883, these charges were first put against him, but he was cleared on all three counts. Each disappearance was easily explained and simply put; there were no grounds for accusations. Or were there?

But did these murders actually occur?
Yes.

Did Mr. Engelhardt know who the murderer was?
Yes.

Was he himself the murderer?
Not at all.

Upon invitation of Waldemere's new owner, I was brought in to research the legends behind the house and to find the truth regarding the strange case of Heinrich Engelhardt. At first, I must confess, I didn't believe there really was anything to be learned. I couldn't have been more wrong. Heinrich Engelhardt, in all actuality, was something of a colorful character and he did in fact lead a very interesting life. That life went something like this.

Hermanus Conrad Heinrich Engelhardt was born on October 7th 1828 in the City of Nuremberg, Bavaria to parents Johann and Maria Stadler-Engelhardt. At a young age, he came to these shores with his family and settled here in Cleveland. His brothers took jobs in the construction field while young Heinrich found employment as a cabinet maker with a firm called Darrow and Associates: a prominent area clock manufacturer.

During the 1850's he would meet and marry a German-born woman named Sophia Lutz. Born to Heinrich and Sophia would be five children: Conrad, Ludwig and Tillie. The other two children, Heinrich and Maria, would die in infancy.

Over the course of the next few years, Heinrich Engelhardt would make some very wise investments that would later pay off. By the 1870's, he had amassed such a fortune in these investments that he was wealthy enough to become a financier. Thus he entered the banking industry.

It was around this time that he found himself with more than enough means to erect a fine home for his family on Franklin Street. So it came to pass that in 1876, construction was completed on a grand manor house that he named Waldemere: a true monument to his own success.

It was no secret that Mr. Engelhardt liked, on occasion, to have his privacy, even from his family. In building Waldemere, he made certain that he could have this luxury while at home. Cleverly hidden in the house is a fifth floor that contains Mr. Engelhardt's private chambers. Further secrets include a security vault and a burial crypt beneath the house. Access to these hidden rooms can only be gained by operating a giant clock in the fourth floor ballroom: likely built by Heinrich Engelhardt himself.

Shortly after moving into Waldemere, the Engelhardt family was joined by Miss Anna Stadler, a daughter of Heinrich's cousin. The 20-year-old was the first to vanish. This occurred in the summer of 1879. There was some question regarding her disappearance, but it was suspected that she had run off with a young man.

The next to go missing was a 17-year-old servant in the home named Harriett Fischer. It was believed that she had robbed the house in the night and her sudden absence was explained away without question.

Finally, in October of 1882, another servant named Katherine Bridget Fitzgerald went missing. One week later, a body was recovered near Whiskey Island that closely resembled her. The death was believed to have been a suicide.

One year later found Heinrich Engelhardt in court facing charges for the deaths of these three young women. There was a formal hearing and he was cleared on all counts. No trial was ever held.

Tragedy would strike the family again in 1891 with the untimely death of Heinrich and Sophia Engelhardt's youngest son, Ludwig: likely from a suicide. Shortly afterwards, The

Engelhardts erected a house in Dover Township, now Bay Village, that they called Engelwood. Mr. and Mrs. Engelhardt would reside here until their deaths in 1906. They are buried together beside their son Ludwig at Monroe Street Cemetery on Cleveland's West Side. The rumored vaults beneath Waldemere, if they did in fact exist, would be empty... or so it was believed.

Again, when I first came to Waldemere, I didn't think there was much more that could be learned. True, I found the house to be quite odd, but nothing more than that. Two things really jumped out at me though. One was the immense wooden clock built into the fourth floor ballroom. The other was an unusual phrase engraved into the woodwork above the bar in that same room. The phrase was written in German and even after I had translated it, it still remained something of a mystery. The passage made absolutely no sense whatsoever.

Upon closer inspection of the clock, I discovered that there was more to it that one might first think. Many of the hand-carved figures that graced the facade could be turned or moved. Also, on occasion, there would be a strange sound emanating from within the clock. Eventually, I put two and two together and solved the riddle. I had to move certain figures at certain times: the clues to this having been left in the passage written above the bar.

I soon found a hidden room that contained another set of instructions. After applying these, and much to the shock of an employee in the house, it opened a hidden door in a bedroom on the first floor. Through this door was a corridor that led down into the fabled crypt. The corridor was in pretty bad shape and was in danger of collapsing at any moment.

Located in this crypt were two vaults. Knowing that the Engelhardts were interred at Monroe Street Cemetery, I opened one. Of course, it was empty. Upon opening the other, I was quite surprised to make the discovery of three sets of human remains. The authorities were summoned and the skeletons were taken to the county coroner's office for further examination.

The next day, I made it a point to stop by there in the hopes that I could help to identify the remains. Based on a photograph that was discovered of Waldemere and its earliest occupants, we were able to determine that the remains had in fact belonged to Anna Stadler, Harriett Fischer and Katherine Fitzgerald.

Anna Stadler apparently had been suffocated and stuffed into the vault. Harriett Fischer, on the other hand, had been bludgeoned repeatedly by what seems to be a candlestick holder: one of the items she'd been accused of stealing. She too was stuffed into this vault, along with a number of other valuable items: the rest of her supposed larder.

Katherine Fitzgerald had been strangled to death. What's more, she was pregnant at the time of her murder. Located on her person was a chain containing two small keys. I had an idea what at least one of them would open.

I returned to Waldemere and pulled out an old steamer trunk that I had discovered a few days earlier. As suspected, one of these keys opened this trunk. The other key opened a diary that was stashed away inside.

In this diary, Miss Fitzgerald gives a good look at what Waldemere was like in those early days. She also speaks at length about the disappearances of Anna Stadler and Harriett Fischer. Furthermore, she mentions an affair with a man in the house, but never gives his name.

I was still in the dark on whom this murderer could be. What was certain was that it was the same man that she had been involved with, just as Harriett Fischer had been. This involvement ultimately led to her death.

I knew that the answer had to reside within the mystery of the clock. Upon researching the house further, it was brought to my attention that aside from a crypt, there might be a fifth floor. I began my search. The clue had to be somewhere in the house: somewhere I had already been. I soon found myself back in the crypt and it was there that I ultimately located the next riddle. After translating it, I soon found myself making my way up a set of stairs and into Heinrich Engelhardt's personal living quarters on the fabled fifth floor.

These quarters consisted of three rooms. The first was a library. After that, it led into a barroom with a billiards table. Beyond this was a bedroom. While investigating these rooms, I managed to locate a book sitting on a desk in the library. Upon opening it, I was filled with delight to learn that it was Heinrich Engelhardt's personal journal.

As I read the words written upon the pages, I found myself, as had been the case with Katherine Fitzgerald's diary, getting a good look into life at Waldemere in those early years of its being. There was much talk about business deals and the like, but eventually I found passages that made reference to the sudden disappearances of the girls in the house. It wasn't until Katherine Fitzgerald had vanished that the truth was finally revealed.

Widely among the neighbors of Waldemere was it whispered that Heinrich and Sophia Engelhardt's son Ludwig was quite disturbed. Long periods of time would pass without him being seen out of doors. Mr. Engelhardt often attributed this to his son frequently being ill.

In fact, Ludwig Engelhardt was mentally unstable. Heinrich had suspected that his son had been involved with at least one of the servants and had genuine fears that he might someday harm one of them. Little did he know that Ludwig would murder three times: one, a cousin and the other two, servants. Heinrich Engelhardt's final journal entry talks of his discovery of Ludwig's murderous habits. No further entries are made. It can only be guessed that he had written too much as it was.

It is not known who is currently lying in the grave that was given to Katherine Bridget Fitzgerald, but the name and epitaph will undoubtedly need to be changed.

In 1883, Heinrich Engelhardt had to face a judge and serious accusations of murdering three young women in his house. One can only imagine how torn he was to have to face these charges knowing that it was his own son that had committed the heinous crimes. When all allegations of wrong doing were dropped, Mr. Engelhardt must have breathed a sigh of relief and could only have hoped that no one would look closer at the possibility of these acts having been committed by Ludwig.

Eight years later, Ludwig would be dead and with him the opportunity to murder again. Was it guilt that drove him to end his own life? Possibly. A true answer to that question may never be learned.

The only question that can be answered here is this. Did Heinrich Engelhardt murder three girls in his home between 1879 and 1882? The answer is a resounding no.

Let it be known from here on out that a

man once dwelled within the Ohio City neighborhood of Cleveland's near west side and that he was as decent a man as the next. Let also be put to rest, these horrible accusations of murder. It's a very safe bet that Hermanus Conrad Heinrich Engelhardt really did try to live his life so well that even the undertaker would have cried at his funeral.

"So what do you think?" Jack asked Shelby as he closed the paper.

"I think it's brilliant."

"Thanks."

Jack started the engine and put the car in gear.

"So where are we going now?" Shelby asked.

"Back to Waldemere."

"Really? Why's that?"

"I still have to get paid for all of this. Do you mind coming with?"

"Not at all. It'll be nice to finally see the rest of the house, and in daylight too."

As Jack pulled onto Franklin Boulevard, large drops of rain began to slam against his windshield. He turned on his headlights and wipers and continued west.

Chapter 32

Within a few minutes, Jack was standing at the front gates of Waldemere: an umbrella in his right hand. While exiting his car, he managed to remember the chuckhole that he'd stepped in the first time he arrived at the house. He certainly didn't feel like walking around the rest of the day with a soaked foot. After standing in the pouring rain for a couple of minutes, the front door opened and Emily stepped through, opening an umbrella of her own as she did.

"Hey, it's your girlfriend," Shelby teased.

"Knock it off," replied Jack out of the corner of his mouth.

Emily approached the gates and pulled out a large and archaic looking key.

"Ello, Mr. Sullivan," she greeted in her familiar Cockney accent. "Looks loike were 'avin us a bit o' rain today."

"It does at that. How've you been, Emily?"

"Oh, can't complain. Thing's 'ave been pretty quiet around 'ere since ya left us."

"You mean, quiet as in…"

Jack pointed up at the upper floors of the house.

"Well, yeah. That too," she said as she opened the gate. "But there 'aven't been any bodies found or secret passages openin' up in the middle o' the noight either."

"Which I'm pretty sure you're quite glad of."

"Stop flirting, Jack," Shelby whispered into his ear.

Jack shot her a brief look, but almost immediately turned his attention back towards Emily.

"Mr. Engelhardt is expectin' ya. Actually, we thought ya moight be by a little earlier than this."

"Would've been, but yesterday was Saint Patrick's Day."

"I see. Say no more. Come on then, Jack. Let's get ya out of this rain."

Jack and Shelby followed Emily through the front door of Waldemere and into the foyer. Shelby looked down and noticed at once the beautifully tiled mosaic floor.

"That's quite beautiful," she pointed out. Jack slowly

nodded once to acknowledge that he'd heard her and agreed.

"If you'll wait up 'ere in the 'all, I'll go and fetch Mr. Engelhardt for ya."

Jack followed her instruction and walked up the short run of steps and through the double glass doors that led into the main hall. Shelby lingered a moment in the foyer and continued to admire the floor. Once Emily was around the corner and out of sight, as well as earshot, Jack turned back to Shelby.

"Come on. It's just a floor."

"I know, but it looks so pretty."

Finding it hard to pull herself away, Shelby finally joined Jack at his side in the main hall. A moment later, they could hear heavier footsteps than Emily's approaching.

"I'm glad you came by, Jack," Henry Engelhardt said with a smile as he rounded the corner. "Please, won't you join me in the parlor?"

Jack nodded and followed him in with Shelby close behind. A fire was burning in the grate and the room seemed more warm and inviting than it ever had before. Mr. Engelhardt motioned for Jack to have a seat in one of the two armchairs that were drawn close to the fire. Jack gladly accepted it and sat down. As he did, Mr. Engelhardt slid closed the pocket doors that led back into the main hall.

"Can I offer you a drink, Jack?"

"Oh, no thank you," Jack declined. "A drink is probably the last thing I need."

"Ah. Emily told me about your festivities last night. Actually, I've found no better cure for that than the hair of the dog itself. A scotch might help to clear your head."

Jack considered it for a moment and, not wanting to seem rude, accepted his offer. Mr. Engelhardt poured out two glasses of scotch and handed one to Jack.

"Well, Jack. Here's to your head."

"And to yours."

They raised their glasses and each took a sip. As Jack set his drink on the nearest table, he turned to Mr. Engelhardt, who was just sitting down in the other armchair by the fire.

"So have you had a chance to read The Argus this morning?"

"I did, Jack."

"And your opinion?"

There was a moment of silence between them before Mr. Engelhardt gave his reply.

"Jack," he said at last, "I loved every minute of it."

Jack breathed a sigh of relief. He was genuinely worried when Henry Engelhardt had paused like that. Usually this was a precursor to someone trying to find the best way to give a negative criticism without sounding too harsh. Mr. Engelhardt had simply done it for dramatic effect.

"The way you so accurately chronicled the life of my great grandfather," he continued, "was absolutely perfect. And how you put yourself in his shoes like that, the part with the hearing and how he must have felt so torn: amazing."

"I'm glad that you enjoyed it," Jack said with a sense of pride.

"Enjoyed it? No. I loved every word. Actually, I read it twice."

"Twice? Really?"

"Really. In fact, I'm going to make certain that I frame a copy of it and hang it right here in the parlor: a place of honor within the walls of Waldemere."

"Thank you. That's an honor for me."

Henry Engelhardt smiled as he took a sip from his glass.

"But enough about all of this talk of honors and glory, Jack," he said as he set his glass back down. "You didn't come all this way just for a critique on your article. I owe you a check now. Don't I?"

"Oh, there's no rush."

"Nonsense. I'm sure that you'll be wanting to get back to bed. I've had my share of hangovers and can tell you that after a dram of scotch, there's nothing like a good, long nap. I'm just going to go up and fetch my checkbook. I'll be right back."

With that, Henry Engelhardt exited the parlor through the pocket doors that led to the dining room. Seeing that he'd be back in a moment, he saw no need to close them.

"So what do you think?" Jack quietly asked as he turned to Shelby, who had been standing in the corner turret, looking out a window.

"I think that I would make for a good Lady in Black," she replied.

"A lady in *what*?"

"You know, the Lady in Black. She's the ghost who looks out of old Victorian mansion windows in all the old Gothic ghost stories."

"And don't you look just the part," Jack jested. At this, Shelby finally turned her gaze away from Franklin Boulevard below. What she saw standing behind Jack at the pocket doors across the room scared her out of her wits.

"Um..." was all she could utter.

Jack was terrified. Whatever could have had that affect on her must truly be horrifying. Jack mustered up what courage he could and slowly turned around. The doorway was empty.

"What is it?" he whispered. "What do you see?"

"Jack, they're all here."

"Who's all here?"

"You know who I mean."

"The girls? Katherine, Harriett and Anna?"

"There's also a man with them."

"A man? Heinrich Engelhardt?"

"I don't think so."

Again, Jack nervously turned and faced the doorway, but could still see no one there.

"What does he look like?"

"He's not old; about your age, maybe. He has sharp features and dark brown hair that's slicked back. He's dressed funny."

"Funny how?"

"Old clothes, I guess."

"Ludwig."

"Jack, he's nodding. That must be his name."

At this, Henry Engelhardt walked right through the area where the four ghostly apparitions were standing: a big smile on his face and a checkbook in his hand.

"I heard you talking to someone," Mr. Engelhardt said as he pulled out a pen.

"Oh, I was just thinking out loud. Sorry. I do that from time to time. It helps me to remember things."

"Ah, fair enough. So who do I make this out to?"

"John M. Sullivan is fine."

"Very well." He began to scribble in the checkbook. "Let's see, your original rate was two hundred per day and I said I'd double it. That makes four hundred, but then I told you I'd tack on an extra hundred per day to see this job through, which you did. That makes five hundred, times seven days, is three thousand, five hundred dollars. John Hancock and here you are."

He pulled the check from the book and handed it to Jack. Jack accepted the note and examined it. In no less than a second, Jack could see his folly in all of this. Everything came crashing in on him as though the world were falling apart. His heart sank as the gravity of what he'd done slowly hit him.

"My God," Jack muttered, "How could I have been so stupid?"

"What's wrong? Is the amount okay?"

"The amount on the check is just fine. It's the exact amount that we agreed to."

"So what is it then?"

"It's the phrases written throughout the house. It's the court depositions. It's the titles of the books in your great grandfather's library. It's... the handwriting."

"And what's wrong with the handwriting, Jack?"

"There's nothing wrong with it. You have good penmanship."

"What about the other stuff? What's wrong with all of that?"

"Nothing wrong with that either. It's all written in perfect German; and for a very good reason."

"What reason is that, Jack?"

"Your great grandfather couldn't read a single word of English, let alone write it." Jack held up the check. "Not only am I something of an expert on geographical vernaculars, but I also used to study calligraphy in college. It's the same handwriting that was in the journal that I found on the fifth floor."

Henry Engelhardt took a step back and smiled.

"You really are the best historical researcher that I've ever come across. I guess I overlooked a few things."

"I guess so. I'm just surprised that I didn't see it right away. The clues were all around me."

"You'll have that."

"So you knew about the fifth floor all along then?"

"Of course I knew. It's my house. That and I have a great memory."

"How do you mean?" Jack was perplexed.

"I was quite young when my grandfather Conrad passed away, but I clearly remember his delirious ramblings near the end. 'One-thirty sunflowers,' he would say. 'That's where he killed them.' I just thought him mad. It wasn't until I started to read about the allegations against my great grandfather that I started to understand what my Grandpa Conrad might have been talking about. He knew something and he'd managed to keep it a secret for all of those years. Now that he was on his deathbed, he felt the need to tell someone. As it turned out, that someone was me: his ten-year-old grandson. When I first saw the clock on the fourth floor and the two sunflowers in the corners, I knew at once what my grandfather was talking about. I started by fixing the clock. That crazy lady had done some pretty significant damage, but I had it up and running in no time at all. Once I was sure that it was back in working order, I waited until one thirty, turned the sunflowers, followed the music that was coming from the trunk space and soon found myself on the fifth floor."

"What about the crypt?"

"That, I didn't know about. Had I known that there were three bodies stashed away in the cellar of this house, I might never have started any of this."

"So why did you?"

"I already told you that. I wanted to clear my great grandfather's name."

"What does that matter? As far as anyone was concerned, it was just an urban legend."

"An urban legend with historical facts to back it up."

"So why go through all of that trouble to hire me on and plant a bogus journal. You could have just come forward and openly dispelled all of these myths about your great grandfather yourself."

"No. Someone would have come along and looked into

it. Eventually they would have found the truth. I needed someone who was well respected in the historical research community to put their name beside a testimonial that cleared Heinrich Engelhardt's name once and for all. You seemed to come highly recommended."

"But I still don't understand why this is such a big deal for you. Are you really that proud that you can't stand to have a possible murderer in your lineage? I have one in mine; a Seventeenth Century pirate named Bloodybones Lunsford. Get over yourself."

"Can't do that. Not in my field anyway. A name synonymous with serial killings can ruin a business opportunity in this town."

"A business opportunity?"

"For my son Fred and I. We're expanding our firm to include Cleveland. I've been viewing offices downtown these last few weeks. We're hoping to have our branch open by June. We needed damage control on this one. I'd say thirty-five hundred dollars is a good price to pay for it."

"Viewing offices downtown? That explains the absences from the house; even on Sunday."

"Very good, Jack."

"But how do you even know that it *was* your great grandfather that killed those girls? It could have been your great uncle, just as you suggested in that forged journal."

"There was something else that my grandfather Conrad had said to me. I thought he was just making up a funny rhyme. 'Lew said he knew... so he threw Lew... and so Lew flew.' I must have recited that to myself at least a hundred times. It wasn't until I read up on the history of this place that I finally understood what it meant. My grandpa said '*he threw Lew.*' If he had been referring to himself, he'd have said '*I threw Lew*' but he didn't."

"Lew?"

"That's a nickname for Lewis, or *Ludwig*."

"Oh."

"That only leaves one other culprit: Heinrich Engelhardt. My great uncle Ludwig knew what his father had done. Maybe he was going to say something. Whatever the case may have been, my great grandfather needed to dispose of him, and so he did."

"He threw him from the upstairs bedroom window?"

"That's right. My grandfather was the smart one. He knew well enough to keep his mouth shut."

"Something you expect me to do."

"Naturally. You've already released your findings on this matter. How would it look if you suddenly retracted that article? Your reputation as a historical researcher in this town would be in ruin, especially if the one item that brought you to your conclusion was a poorly forged journal. That'd be quite an embarrassment. Wouldn't you say?"

"It was a set-up from the start: the article in The Argus."

"Of course it was. Mr. Moon certainly wasn't aware of it, but when I explained to him that it would make for a great story, he seemed very enthusiastic. The only stipulation was that he not let you know that I'd clued him in to this story, otherwise the whole deal would be off."

"Jack!" Shelby shouted. "We need to get out of here!"

"What?"

"Trust me, Jack," Mr. Engelhardt continued. "You really don't want to go changing your story now. Not after all of this."

"Jack! They're telling us that we should leave while we still can."

Jack's eyes darted about the room and a chill ran up his spine. The temperature in the air fell drastically and he could swear that he could now see his breath.

"The haunting," he whispered.

"Oh yeah, that. It's the only thing that I didn't fake."

Booming footsteps could be heard descending the back stairs. The hardwood floor of the parlor seemed to creak and moan with each approaching footfall.

"Shelby?" Jack whispered.

"Jack! Now! We have to go! Oh my God!"

Henry Engelhardt smiled again.

"I suggest you take that check and spend it in good health, Jack. You have yourself a good day now and, oh, don't be a stranger."

Shelby grabbed Jack's arm and dragged him to the front

door. Before he knew it, they were standing outside of the house in the pouring rain. Waiting for them by the front gate, her red ponytail soaked through, was Emily.

"You," Jack shouted. "You knew about all of this!"

"I'm sorry, Jack," she said with tears in her eyes. "I was sworn not to say a word."

"So you let him play me like that from the start?"

"If I'd 'ave said anything about it, I'd 'ave lost me job."

"So *you* played me too. Get out of my way."

Jack pushed past her and through the iron gate.

"I'm sorry!"

"My ass!" he shouted from half-way across Franklin.

"No, Jack! You need to get me out of 'ere."

"*Get you out of here?*" He'd reached his car but was standing in the rain facing her. "Why would you want to leave a place like this? Nice secure job and all."

"The ghosts," she whispered. "They're everywhere."

Jack could see the panic in her eyes and, for a brief moment, felt sorry for her. Then again, she'd brought this on herself and it seemed only right to him that she should do something about it herself. He gave her one last, cold look.

"Get *yourself* out of here."

Jack got into his car and started the engine. He cast one final glance back at the Flemish gables and formidable turret of Waldemere. The sandstone cherubs that flanked the main entryway seemed to be looking down at him with mocking smiles. If he never saw the place again, it would be too soon.

Chapter 33

Jack sat in silence up at the bar at McNamara's Public House on Lake Avenue, a cold and frothy Guinness before him. He'd been there for nearly forty-five minutes now, stewing over and over again in his head what had just happened. As it was, he hadn't said more than two words to anyone since arriving. It was obvious that he was in a foul mood and didn't want to be bothered.

"Jack, you can't get yourself too worked up over this," Shelby told him. Jack simply gave her a short glance. "So, you screwed up. It happens to everyone at some point. We can't be right all the time."

"I was so certain," Jack seemed to mumble to himself.

"I know, but you're going to have to get over it. And look on the bright side..."

"Bright side?"

"Yeah. You did get paid for your services, and quite well I might add."

"Thirty pieces of silver to sell out my trade."

"Well, I can tell that nothing I say or do is going to make you feel any better about this. I'm going to go outside for a while and leave you to your thoughts."

"Don't do that. It's raining."

"Again, Jack. Ghost. Remember?"

"Oh yeah."

Shelby stood up and walked through the closed door that led to the back patio. Jack looked down at his untouched Guinness. Shelby was right. He'd simply have to get past this and move on. He picked up the glass and finally took a sip. As he set it down, he heard the front door open, accompanied by a cold draft. Usually Jack would have turned to see who had entered, but at this point, he really didn't care. As it was, the newcomer pulled up the stool beside him and ordered a hard cider.

"Well, Jack, all things considered, it was a good article."

"I don't want to talk about it."

"Come on. It might make you feel better."

"Orin, did you come all this way just to cheer me up?"

"No. I came for a drink. Okay, and I guessed that you would have figured out the truth by now so, yes. I thought you could use a friend."

"Thanks. That means a lot."

"I also came to show you this." Orin handed Jack a beat-up calfskin book, about four inches wide by six inches high.

"What is it?"

"Open it up and find out."

Jack flipped the book to the first page and found that he was unable read the script inside. He could, however, just barely make out the name *Engelhardt* scribbled on the first line. Jack began to chuckle to himself.

"You had it all along?"

"That's the real McCoy," Orin declared.

"Heinrich Engelhardt's journal."

"Yeah, but it's more like a record of business deals; some of which seem pretty shady. There's nothing interesting in it though. Nothing about murders anyway. I seriously doubt that he'd write about something like that."

Jack nodded as he handed the book back to Orin.

"Thanks. Wish I'd have known about it sooner."

"You didn't ask."

"Well, I'll make sure to in the future."

Orin could see that he was getting frustrated.

"Jack, I can't just come out and give you the answers. I'm actually sworn as the archivist not to. I really shouldn't even have shown you that. I'm only allowed to make available those documents that I'm asked about. It's a non-interference clause in my job description; observe and record, but don't get involved."

Jack heard the front door open again and saw his friend Amy enter the bar. Gazing just beyond her, he could also see that it had stopped raining. She walked past, smiled and seated herself at the far end, where she ordered a glass of Yuengling. Jack was about to flag her down to join them when his phone rang. He looked at the caller I.D. and saw that it was his cousin Pam.

"Excuse me for a second, Orin. I need to take this."

"Of course."

Jack stood up, walked a few feet away, and answered his phone.

"Hello?"

"Hi, Jack. It's Pam."

"Hi, Pam. How are you doing?"

"I'm good. Thanks. The reason I'm calling is to let you know that I got the results back from that DNA test that you asked me to run."

Jack had completely forgotten that he'd had Henry Engelhardt's DNA tested against the corpse he believed to be Anna Stadler.

"So what did you find?"

"Well, you were right. It was a match with Jane Doe Three."

"I figured as much."

"There's more. I wanted to compare it to the other three sets of remains."

"Three sets? I thought there were only two other victims."

"No, there were two more Jane Does, but one of them was pregnant. Remember?"

"Yeah, that's right. I didn't think about that. This must be my day for missing the obvious."

"What do you mean?"

"Forget about it."

"Alright. So anyway, when I got the results back, I found that the DNA sample you gave me was an even closer match to the fetus in Jane Doe Two than it was to Jane Doe Three."

Jack shook his head.

"I'm not surprised. Thanks for calling, Pam. I'll give you a shout later on."

"Okay, Jack. You take care."

"Will do. You too."

Jack hung up the phone and reclaimed his seat beside Orin Drury.

"Is everything okay?" Orin asked.

"Yeah. Just fine. Katherine Fitzgerald's unborn child was a closer genetic match to Henry Engelhardt than Anna Stadler was. It makes sense. The child would have been one of

Henry's great aunts or uncles, had it been born."

"I see."

Jack took another swig of his beer.

"I just hate this whole thing," he said, still dwelling on the case.

"You act like you've never failed before."

"I never have, not when it comes to something like this"

"Well, there's a first time for everything: first kiss, first car wreck, first big failure as a historian. You know, you can also look at it this way. All those stories that have been told about Waldemere over the years have built up quite an amazing legend. You've just played a role in yet another chapter of that house's sordid history. You've added to the mystery and legend behind it. You're now a part of that story."

"And all I can hope is that someday, someone else will come along and set that story right once and for all; even if it comes at the expense of my reputation."

"I'm sure that someone will. I just hope that you can accept it when it happens."

Jack suddenly remembered Amy sitting by herself at the far end of the bar. He glanced down and waved her over.

"You know, Orin, one of my friends just got here and I really need to talk to her about something. Would you excuse me for a few minutes?"

"Certainly. You take your time. I'm not going anywhere any time soon."

"Thanks."

Amy came down and was about to join them when Jack motioned for her to join him out on the back patio. As she passed Orin, she cast him a funny smile.

"I read your article this morning," she told Jack as he opened the back door. "Very intriguing."

"Thanks."

She could tell that he wasn't satisfied with it, but decided not to bring it up.

"So who's your friend?"

"Inside? That's Orin Drury."

"*That's* Orin? The guy with the big gun?"

Amy turned as though she were about to walk back into

the pub, but Jack stopped her short of the door.

"Hey, I'll introduce you in a bit. There's something else I wanted to talk to you about."

"And what's that?"

"Well, do you remember that odd question I asked you last week about how to keep myself from being overcome while having physical contact with a spirit?"

"Yeah, and I have the strangest feeling that this all has to do with what I experienced up here last night."

"Anyway, the copper didn't work."

"That's funny. It should have."

"Do I need to use a lot of it?"

"Not really. It just needs to be fairly pure."

Jack quietly laughed to himself.

"What is it?"

"Pennies."

"Yeah, Jack. Pennies are like, hardly even copper."

"I know. I'll try something else."

Amy was growing more and more confused.

"Are you going to tell me what this is all about?" she finally asked.

Jack considered it for a moment. He looked over at Shelby who was standing in the corner with a huge grin on her face. Jack nodded once and smiled. He'd start off with a simple question.

"Do you scare easily?"